# DOUBLE JEOPARDY

## OF GOLD & BLOOD
## BOOK THREE

### Jenny Wheeler

Published by Happy Families Ltd



ISBN 978-1-99-117252-5 (Large Print)
ISBN 978-0-473-44818-9 (Paperback)
ISBN 978-0-473-44819-6 (E-Pub)
ISBN 978-0-473-44820-2 (Kindle)
ISBN 978-0-473-44821-9 (Apple Books)



Print Edition First published October 2018

# OF GOLD & BLOOD SERIES

Poisoned Legacy Book One

Brother Betrayed Book Two

Double Jeopardy Book Three

Tangled Destiny Book Four (Christmas novella and Prequel)

Unbridled Vengeance Book Five

Of Gold & Blood Boxed Set/Book Bundle Books 1 - 3

"For the time is coming when everything that is covered will be revealed, and all that is secret will be made known to all." - *Matthew 10:26 - New Living Translation.*

**If you enjoy Double Jeopardy, get a FREE PREVIEW of Tangled Destiny, a Christmas Novella and Book Four in the Of Gold & Blood series.**

Tangled Destiny details can be found at the end of Double Jeopardy

# One

*Sacramento Theater, August 1869*

Sebastian Russell tugged at his unfamiliar starched collar and cast a quick sidelong glance at the woman seated next to him in the velvet-curtained balcony box. Huldah Wilmington's big-boned frame rose out of a tidal wave of frothy skirt, her blunt, short-necked face emerging from a frilly neckline in dazzling turquoise, a house sparrow in parrot's plumage. Despite his discomfort, Seb's blood pressure spiked with secret amusement as he turned away from Huldah to peer down at her daughter Isabella, who was commanding center stage in a Parisian melodrama that had taken London and New York by storm and was now enjoying a star turn in California's capital city.

The contrast in demeanor between the widowed older mother and her charismatic daughter couldn't be more pronounced, and Huldah clearly shifted between contradictory responses, alternately glowing with pride at Isabella's obvious talent and worrying about the propriety of the girl's determined dream to make her name on the stage. *The Corsican Brothers*, adapted from an Alexandre Dumas tale, was Isabella's first big break, and Sebastian had been pressured into evening dress to accompany Huldah and family friends Alycia and Basil Stockton to see it.

Before the curtain rose on the first

act, Huldah had eagerly told Seb that "Queen Victoria saw it four times when it was on at London's Princess Theater," as if the monarch's approval of the show when it was first staged a decade ago made it perfectly respectable for her precious Isabella now.

He sighed, and the enveloping dark warmth of the full house pressed down on him. If only he could quietly and unobtrusively melt into the darkness with its lingering chocolate aroma from half-time treats. Disappear off the face of the earth, never to again have to start awake with midnight terrors or to drag his leaden feet from bed to floor every morning. He glanced at Huldah once more, anxious that she might read his thoughts, but he needn't have worried. Her muddy eyes were fixed on Isabella's graceful form, her protruding lower lip dropped open in rapt attention; like most of the audience, she was captivated by the action on stage.

The story unfolding was of twin brothers with a psychic link and a carbine-touting mother; a tale of death, murderous duels and chivalrous revenge, and Sebastian could hardly bear to sit still and watch it. Four years of brutal Civil War fighting had convinced him nothing honorable came from the barrel of a gun; and the one brother's claim that if his twin was dead he'd know it because his ghost would visit made him itch as though he had fallen in poison ivy. He thought of Robert, the one and only friend he made when he first arrived in Boston from Hong Kong as a twelve-year-old orphan. If anyone would communicate from beyond the dead it would have been Robert, and no, he hadn't heard a peep. It was all nonsense. For the thousandth time he asked himself, as he had every day since General Robert E Lee surrendered, how can a man keep going when all hope that life — or God — is good has gone?

He kept up a brave face with his brothers, rebuffed any attempt they made to talk about the war because if you hadn't been there you couldn't understand — and tried to act as if everything was going just fine. Peace had been made, and he had survived with both arms and legs intact. For that miracle he was eternally grateful. But he had imagined when the barbarity of war was over that his life would return to some kind of 'normal', and it was taking him a long time to understand there was no going back. The innocent 22-year-old who had joined up with best buddy and fellow engineer Robert Kingsley seven years ago had fled the field and would never return.

Sebastian looked across the narrow aisle to where the ferociously successful merchant Basil Stockton sat, his chunky work-calloused hand affectionately entwined in his wife Alycia's long, elegant fingers. Basil's broad shoulders and square frame stretched his evening suit in all the wrong places; his tanned skin and the dark brown hair that frizzed around his ears proclaimed him a man who preferred moleskins to formal suits. His wife, slightly leaning into her husband's protective bulk, was immaculate in a beautifully tailored cream suit marked with a thin red stripe, her white-gold chignon tucked low on her neck, her drawn-back hair framing her perfectly calculated beauty. As a couple, they personified the old adage that opposites attract. Seb knew that behind Alycia's cool, assessing exterior lay a compassionate, generous heart. And as unlikely as their union might seem to outsiders, he had sensed in the few months that he'd been working for Basil that they were bound by a deep love that enabled them to face trouble head on.

Basil was resolute, wily, unaffected by how much money he or others had, and he seemed more than willing — insistent, even — that Sebastian take over scoping for new business opportunities for him when the couple returned to their main operation on the East Coast in a few days' time. His training as an engineer — completed just before he'd joined up — gave him perfect credentials for assessing the coming industrial boom and advising Basil on the myriad of big projects — whether it be irrigation, mines or railways — that were under way in the Golden State.

His reverie was interrupted by Basil coughing, and he came back to the present with a jolt. The mood in the gallery had subtly changed while he'd been wool-gathering. An intense silence had invaded the house; the crowd had been attentive before, but now Basil and Alycia were hanging on the edge of their seats, gazing down in fixed anticipation. They must be coming up to the scene which accounted for the play's remarkable popularity — the one when the ghost appears and begs his brother to avenge his death. He knew it was only a stage play, but bilious acid rose in his throat, and he was vaguely aware he was gripping the arms of his chair.

The engineer in him knew all about

the 'glide trap', the clever bit of stage machinery which gave such a convincing, eerie impression, but even he was surprised at the apparition's dramatic effect. As the audience strained forward, a ghostly male head appeared, gradually rising to full body height, increasing in stature as he neared his shocked twin.

Seb felt a slight current of air behind him and glanced back to see the door to the box open and a dark-suited man slide into the row behind them. His movements were calm and studied, and for a moment Seb wondered if he was one of the theater attendants preparing to show them out after the performance. On stage the bereaved brother was howling with rage, and an involuntary gasp — was it shock, or sympathy? — rose in one rolling wave from the stalls and echoed around the circle.

There was a sharp movement to Sebastian's left, the loud report of a pistol discharging, and Alycia slumped forward.

An iciness invaded his core at the percussion. Acrid, sour smoke hit his nostrils, and he reared up in his seat. His legs, which moments before had felt like jelly, propelled him out of his seat. A red, bloody hole had torn open Alycia's immaculate cream stripes. Beside him, Huldah emitted a keening shrill of terror; across the aisle Basil reached forward to catch his wife's slumping body.

He was upright, turning as if in slow motion, towards the shadowy form that stood transfixed, pistol still raised, observing his handiwork. The iron smell of blood and cordite, his ringing ears, the nervous sickness in his gut — he was back there on the battlefield, hopelessly trying to stanch Robert's wound as the peculiar sizzling sound of musket Minié balls fizzed overhead.

He could barely see. His eyes were streaming, and the box was dark, but his intention was deadly. This time the killer would not escape. He lunged forward and wrenched the man's arm so forcefully he shrieked and the gun clattered to the floor. Then pandemonium erupted in the auditorium as the gaslights came up and people began making a panicked dash for the exits. Others stood craning their heads, trying to see what was happening.

Underneath the uproar Seb was aware of Basil's deep base voice. "Alycia, Alycia! Don't die on me, my sweet lady. Not now. Don't die on me now." The big man was very gently rocking his wife in his arms. Her head was tilted back, her profile like marble, and he was peppering her forehead with tender kisses as she bled into his encircling embrace.

# Two

Alycia's hair fell across her porcelain cheek, and the sight of it flowing free was almost as shocking to Isabella as the rusty stain that leaked across her expensive silk dress, the blood matching the striped fabric. It seemed indecent for the woman who had in recent months been such a loving presence in her life — like the grandmother she'd never had — to be exposed like this, even if she was never going to know it. Like seeing her caught naked.

*The first dead person I've ever seen. But why did it have to be Alycia?*

Her heart pitched wildly in her chest, and she clutched at her ribs at the stabbing pain. *Dead. Alycia is dead*.

Kind, wise Alycia.

*Why on earth would anyone want to kill her?*

A numbing, frozen claw grabbed her heart, and she no longer felt the knife between her ribs. She put her hands over her ears to shut out the sibilant, hateful chorus that whispered in her head.

*Alycia is dead.*

The medics who had attended her placed her on a stretcher at the box entry, while they worked fervently to stanch the bleeding. When they'd acknowledged there was nothing more they could do for her, they'd stood quietly aside, giving up the space to Basil, who stood guard over her, like a faithful watchdog in shock, not ready yet to allow anyone to move her. For that, Isabella was selfishly grateful.

When she heard the shot ring out she was backstage, about to make her next entrance, and at first she thought it was one of the actors messing about with a dueling pistol loaded with blanks for the final dramatic showdown when Lucien challenges the man who has killed his brother. Then she heard the swelling audience uproar and knew it was something much more serious than an actor's jape, but she still did not imagine it could be anything that would destroy part of her family.

She'd immediately wanted to go to the box where her mother and her other guests were seated, to rush straight there to check they were all fine, but the theater security men would not let her leave until they were certain they had got the shooter arrested and he had no accomplices.

It had felt like an eternity before they escorted her to her mother and the others. And when she finally got here she'd had to confront one of the worst things that could have ever happened to her.

She squeezed her eyes tightly shut. There would be a time for tears, but it wasn't now. The theater was a dark vacuum, the air empty with that sense of the show being over, the box where they gathered, the last area to remain lighted. Huldah was sitting staring vacantly into nothingness, the lines that ran down her cheeks darkened, wet furrows. Basil was crouching beside Alycia, stroking her face and whispering to her, a gray-faced automaton seemingly unaware of anything else around him.

Only yesterday they'd been laughing together about what they'd get up to when her season in *The Corsican Brothers* was over. Working on their next strategy to find her brother, Alejandro. That was how he'd been baptized, but he could have died years ago, he could be called something else entirely, he could have long gone from California, could be a 'farm slave' in the Midwest ...

Ever since she'd discovered last year that she was adopted, Alycia had been her mainstay, even though they weren't related by blood. Huldah had fought to stay open-minded, but she struggled to not act threatened when Isabella wanted to do all she could to find Alejandro. It was so much easier to talk about it all with Alycia than with Huldah. Alycia had encouraged her, had paid a private detective to dig into their history.

Now that she was gone, who could Isabella turn to? She looked down at her surrogate grandmother's pale, serene face. She almost felt her presence hovering. What did they say — it took three days for the spirit to truly leave the body? At that moment she believed it with all her heart.

What would Alycia say to her? *Be strong and courageous, Izzy. You've got it in you.*

She slipped into a back-row seat, on the edge of dizziness and fearful of fainting, and rested, gathering her strength, breathing slowly. The icy panic that had seized her melted, and a liquid peace flowed up from inside her. What was that verse Alycia sometimes read to her when she was feeling discouraged? Somewhere in *Joshua*. That's right, she was to "be not afraid, neither be dismayed, for the Lord is with you wherever you go." She steeled her weak legs and stood and moved to Basil's shoulder. She stroked his back and whispered quietly, "Are you OK there, dear friend? Is there anything I can do to help?"

His face was a blank mask as he looked up. "No, dear Izzy. There's nothing. Nothing any of us can do." He gave a huge sigh. "Nothing at all."

She moved to the front of the box to gather up Huldah, take her home, get her to bed. The curtain was down on the Sacramento's stage, the scene of her triumph in what felt like another lifetime, and she wasn't the same girl who'd basked in the limelight an hour before.

*Be strong and courageous, Izzy. You've got it in you.*

She was going to keep pursuing her hopes of making a career on the stage. And she was going to jolly well keep looking for Alejandro. Alycia would insist on it. She just hoped her dear grand-mère was right.

# Three

Alycia's killer was a wretched scrap of humanity. Seb looked at the gaunt, empty face staring up from the heavy-plank floored cell and recognized the glazed-eyed vacuum of a man who has been asked to endure more than he can bear. He'd seen it at Gettysburg, where his regiment had suffered the heaviest losses of the war.

Polk sat in a collapsed squat, long arms dangling over knees on a rawboned and scraggy frame, as though he no longer had any use for them. A lock of lank blond hair fell over a face hollowed out by starvation. Apart from the incongruous well-cut dark suit, he was like so many of the veterans dawdling on street corners throughout the land.

*I could have been one of them.*

So far the police captain had got very little information from him: a single name, "Polk", and rank, "Private, 1st Confederate Regiment, Army of Tennessee." It was four years since the war ended, but Polk didn't seem to register it. He'd become agitated when questioned, his eyes doing a frenetic jig around him as if he was expecting a bombardment, mouth opening and closing like a fish, with no words bubbling out.

The Sacramento County Prison was located in the basement of the Sacramento City Water Works building on I Street, very close to the river. Murky, stagnant-water smells permeated the air, but there was no hint of daylight in the massive gloomy underground cell, shut off from all hopes of escape.

Faint train noises filtered through the thick brick walls — the Central Pacific Railroad was next door — but inside, life stopped.

Seb felt that strange dislocation he'd known before. The disruption of death. A choking outrage closed his throat, disbelief that the sun was rising on a normal day when life could never be normal again.

He shivered, suddenly cold although his armpits were sticky. Basil stood beside him, hunched over and gray with fatigue, both of them still in evening suits that smelt stale from being worn too long. It had been a very long night.

Once he'd restrained Polk, the man had lapsed into a vacant acquiescence, making no further attempt to escape.

Seb handed him over after giving the sergeant a brief statement and returned to the box to coax Basil into releasing Alycia into the care of one of the city's undertakers, called in by the police.

Mabel and Joseph Reeves — a mother and son team who'd carried on the business after Joseph senior, the county coroner, had died — had handled the situation with quiet understanding, but Basil still insisted on accompanying his wife to their premises in J Street. He'd left reluctantly only after Mabel had reassured him of her tender touch and satisfied him that Alycia would be well looked after.

"What's going on, Reb?" As a temporarily sworn deputy in a neighboring district, Seb had some standing with the local cops, and the police captain had agreed to him and

Basil being given access to the prisoner.

The prisoner's head jerked up, and a glimmer of intelligence flared in his brown eyes. "Reb? You'd be one of those Yankee blues, I wager." He glared at Seb for a few seconds then his eyes skittered away.

Seb stepped closer to him. "I was one of those Yankee blues. You're right there. But the war's been over for years. You know that, don't you?"

Soft brown eyes engaged Seb's. "Some people's, maybe. Not mine."

Seb sighed. "That lady you shot tonight. She had nothing to do with the war. You know that, don't you?"

Polk's head dropped to his chest, and tears trickled down the haggard trenches in his lined face.

"Do you even know who she is?"

Silence. Then Polk shook his head

slowly from side to side. "It doesn't matter. She was a spy. They're all spies. But it doesn't matter. It's all over now."

Seb shot a hopeless glance at Basil, who'd covered his mouth and turned away, as if recognizing conversation was pointless.

"No, Polk. You're wrong. She wasn't a spy. But you're right about one thing. It *is* all over now."

He stepped towards Basil, casting his arm lightly around the older man's shoulders. "Don't think we're going to learn anything useful here, my friend. I think we need to get you home to rest."

Ten minutes later Basil stumbled wearily into his hotel room, Seb's arm still protectively across his shoulders. A fur stole hung over the back of an armchair, and Alycia's familiar lily of the valley fragrance hung in the air. Basil turned and gripped his hand. "Seb, you've done a great job, you really have. And I don't feel it's fair to ask you for more." He gestured to one of two armchairs set up in the sitting room that opened into the bedroom. "I don't want to do it, but I've got no choice."

He collapsed into one of the chairs and glanced around him, as if looking for answers. "That man Polk. He's just a crazy. A madman, the poor devil. Still fighting the war. It doesn't make sense that he came after Alycia. Just no sense."

Seb sank slowly into the chair beside him and nodded. "I agree. It doesn't make sense."

Basil tapped his fist lightly against his closed lips, and his gaze clouded for a few seconds before snapping back. "And

I can't live with that Sebastian. I have to understand what's happened here. It will be hard enough living without her ..." He trailed off and swallowed rapidly several times. "Hard enough. But I have to know why. That man. The suit. The gun. He looks like he's barely able to put food on his table."

Seb nodded again.

"And the police — they're competent enough. But I want my own man on it, Sebastian. I want you."

"Me?" Seb raised his eyebrows.

"Yes, Sebastian, you. I need to know who's behind this. Who organized it. And why. It doesn't feel like a random act. It was planned. And that man in the cell has no rhyme or reason to be doing it."

He let out a long sigh. "Spies." The word was a drawn-out, sibilant sigh. "It's nonsense."

Seb slumped forward in his chair, elbows on knees, chin resting in his hands, overcome by a feeling of light-headedness. Deal with Johnny Reb and his craziness? He'd seen the last of Johnny Reb in 1865 and he'd been trying to forget him, in sickness and in health, day and night, ever since.

He'd been twelve when he was sent back to his Boston uncle — his mother had died at his birth — after the death of his father in Hong Kong. He'd grown from a callow teen to a seasoned soldier on American soil — become a Yankee — but he barely lasted a month in Boston after his return from the front, his uncle and so many of his old friends dead. He didn't want to stay and be reminded of all the loss.

He'd drifted aimlessly West, gradually healing during solitary days in the saddle in the emptiness of big open spaces, until one day it dawned on him to seek out his first family. Reuniting with his two half-brothers, John and Nathan, last year was the best thing he'd done since the peace was signed. He'd enjoyed the feeling of being with people who genuinely cared for him, and the work Basil offered was just what he'd been craving to get himself established again.

And now Basil was asking him to willingly return to the snake pit of his fears, the dread that he would be forever pursued by death and loss, never able to make a good life with a good woman. Even the smell of the cordite in that confined space of the theater box, the reek in the prison ... He'd felt his world closing in around him again, like a tomb. He didn't want to have anything more to do with conflict and death. He was trying to find his way back into the light.

"Seb, are you okay? You're not sick?"

Basil sat erect in his chair and regarded him with a grave expression.

Sebastian took a deep breath and straightened up. "Sorry. I'm fine. Just a little tired. We both need to try and sleep." He looked full into Basil's weary face and smiled, willing himself to be strong. "I quite understand your case, Basil. Anyone would. And, of course, I will do my utmost to find who killed Alycia. It's the most natural wish in the world, to see she gets justice."

His mind flashed back to Polk, a madman bound for execution who seemed to have no comprehension of what he'd done. *God help me if I ever slip that far. Am I already just a little bit crazy?*

"I'll get onto it first thing in the morning."

Basil gave him a hard look. "Yup. I suppose like it or not, there will be one. For us, at any rate."

# Four

"You can't mean that!"

Isabella Wilmington stood, arms folded, chin thrust forward, hips angled in a fighting stance, and glared at Sebastian.

"It's self-evident," he said in a strong, deep voice. "I can't see how you could think anything else."

She felt her face flush with annoyance. Sure, this man was a lot older than her — what was he, thirty or something? And she was nineteen, well, nearly twenty, but that didn't excuse him dismissing her so lightly.

"Just how can you be so sure that Alycia's death had nothing to do with our search for my brother? She was pouring a lot of time and money into finding him. Maybe someone took exception."

"What? And hired some clapped-out, crazy rebel to assassinate her?" His laugh had a derisive edge. "You're confused. She wasn't Abraham Lincoln."

She moved her hands to her hips and her voice rose a register.

"Maybe the 'clapped-out rebel' wasn't as crazy as he led you to believe. He got the job done, didn't he?"

They were standing either side of the dining table in Basil Stockton's hotel suite, several hours after Alycia's funeral. The mourners had all departed, her mother had retired to her room, and Basil had collapsed into exhausted sleep. It had seemed like the best possible time to get Sebastian Russell to one side and explain why it was important to keep up the search that Alycia had so strongly supported.

Except the conversation was not going how she had planned. Sebastian was being difficult. She stood back and coolly regarded him. Lightly freckled face, framed by short, copper-colored hair and matching trimmed mustache and beard, deep brown eyes and thick, reddish-brown eyebrows.

Sebastian Russell was what her mother called a "fine figure of a man". Tall and strong-shouldered, with a confidence that didn't need to draw attention to itself. Quiet and deep, this one. Pity he was so dogmatic. And staring back at her as though she was some spoiled brat who needed to be brought into line.

"Maybe he's a lot smarter than you give him credit for. Tell me if I'm wrong, but you don't know a thing more about him now than you did two minutes after he fired that pistol at Alycia. Would I be right in that?"

She didn't much like the triumphant note her voice had taken, but heck, he deserved it.

He sighed. "Polk. We know his name. It's Polk." He flashed her a brief, self-deprecating grin. "That's if he's telling us the truth, mind you. Maybe he's got us all outfoxed."

He gestured to one of the dining table chairs. "Look, let's sit down, Isabella. I don't want to fight about this. Let's try and sort out a plan that suits us both."

She dropped into the chair on her side of the table, and he sank into the one on the opposite side.

"So tell me." Her voice was crisp and businesslike. "How do you see things progressing from here?"

He cleared his throat and spoke more softly. "I have promised Basil I will do all I can to find out what led this man to carry out this act. I agree with you it all seems more than strange. Basil isn't convinced it was the random act of a crazy man, and I tend to agree. Too much doesn't add up."

She nodded and took a deep breath before she spoke. When she did, she struggled to sound conciliatory. "I don't have a problem with that. I want Alycia's killer to be fully identified as much as you and Basil do. Well, there's no doubt who pulled the trigger. We just don't have a clue what led him to do it."

Seb nodded. "But I can't see how it's got anything to do with your brother. I mean, he's been missing for seventeen years. We've no clue if he's even alive.

My apologies for speaking plainly, but what possible connection could there be?"

Isabella felt her temper rising again. Heat flushed through her, and it took all her self-control to speak slowly and moderately. "I'm not saying there is a connection. Or that there isn't. I am saying that Alycia and Basil were generous enough to pay for a private investigator to search for any clues to him — and that now Alycia is gone, Basil is still willing for that to continue. I would simply appreciate that you, as Basil's man here in California, give your support to that and don't undermine it."

Sebastian frowned. "Isabella, you're a smart girl. You know that in the last decade, hundreds of thousands of young men — many your brother's age, and some younger — died. Some in battle, many more from disease. It just seems like a fool's errand to spend money on trying to find someone who — if he did live, and we've got no reason to believe he did — probably ended up marching off to war with the rest of his generation, to die unnoticed in the mud of some equally unknown field. It's what's happened to thousands of families. I'm sorry, but that's how life goes. Maybe being out here in California it wasn't so obvious as it was back East."

Her head jerked up and she held herself tight as tears threatened to flood her. She would not let this curmudgeon see he'd upset her. Her throat blocked, teeth gritted, solar plexus locked down, as the wave of intense grief passed and she held fast. She was not going to let him kill her hope, slim as it may be. A long silence ensued as she deflected her gaze to the floor and took some deep breaths. When she felt ready, she raised her eyes and leveled her gaze back to his implacable brown eyes. Ready, aim, fire.

"Sebastian, I can't pretend to understand what you experienced as a Union man. I know that, so please don't take offense. What you've seen and done — it's beyond my ken. I get that. But the war is over. We're into the next act. And this is where things do get better — families are reconciled, the lost are found. Maybe you've lost sight of that. God forbid that you're not just as mired in the past as Johnny Reb Polk in the county prison."

She saw his eyes flicker in surprise. They sat, both looking at the table top rather than each other, for what seemed like a long time.

Sebastian coughed. "I stand

rebuked." He flashed her another wry smile. "I deserved that. I'm letting my disenchantment show. You probably consider it insufferable cynicism. It's not something I'm proud of."

His tone put a full stop on the conversation, and neither of them seemed to be capable of starting the next sentence. They were sitting in painful silence when they were startled by an urgent rapping on the door. They turned as one, and Seb half-rose, calling permission for the visitor to enter as he stood.

The police sergeant who had been in the theater box when Alycia was killed stepped into the room. "Mr Russell—" He stopped in his tracks at the sight of Isabella.

Seb cleared his throat. "Continue, Sergeant. Miss Wilmington is aware of all the circumstances here."

"I see, sir. I just thought you should know … I mean to say, I have something I need to tell you." Again he looked uncertainly towards Isabella, and then to Sebastian.

"Go ahead, Sergeant, please. You obviously consider it important."

"The thing is, sir, the prisoner Polk, well, he's died by his own hand. Hanged himself in his cell, he has. Just a couple of hours ago."

Sebastian's tanned face drained to chalky white. He sank back down in the chair he had just risen from. The iciness Isabella had felt when Alycia died gripped her core, and she guessed her own face was also fading to a sickly pallor.

"Hanged himself?" Sebastian's query was a faint echo of the sergeant's announcement. "How? There wasn't anything in that cell he could use when I was there."

The sergeant tapped his foot and reddened. "We don't know, sir. Someone must have supplied him with a rope. We just don't know who or how."

# Five

The recently elected Senator Hector de Vile paused at the bottom of the stairs leading to the photographer's studio and gestured to the advertising stand announcing Charles Durant's offer. "Ugly people's pictures taken at half-price." He smiled at his twenty-year-old son, taking in the lean symmetry of his face, the sparkling gray eyes under the shock of wavy dark hair. "Guess we'll be paying full price."

Alexander's face flashed with good humor and he started up the stairs. De Vile once again thanked his lucky stars for the luminous young man who bounded ahead, two steps at a time, with effortless grace. The summer recess from Washington's 41st Congress was giving him a chance to coach Alex in their extensive business interests before he returned to Capitol Hill at Christmas, and he was relishing the time he and his boy were spending together.

Charles Durant's Pine Street studio sat above the United States Bakery in Nevada City, and the yeasty smell of warm bread permeated the stairs. They were on a mission to get some cartes de visite, the calling cards that had become popular during the Civil War, when soldiers had sent them home as poignant mementos. Hector needed some taken for his senatorial work, but he also planned to get a father-and-son sitting done together. It was time Alex started assuming a more prominent role in the business, and about time he had his own card anyway.

They stepped into the airy studio, and de Vile saw that Durant's newspaper advertising was well justified. "Special attention in the construction of light, which enables the operator to take likenesses of the children in one, and of grown persons in two to four seconds," it claimed, and the set up did not disappoint. One corner of the room was boxed off — he guessed that was for the dark room — but light flooded in from several overhead skylights onto the rest, comfortably set up with armchairs, a sofa and an occasional table. In the center of the room stood a finely polished, mahogany-cased camera on a tripod.

A bespectacled man emerged from the dark room wiping his hands on a small towel in jerky abrupt gestures that mirrored the harassed frown on his pale, lined face. He checked his movement as he recognized de Vile. "Ah, Senator. A very good day to you." He looked from de Vile to Alex and back. "Tell me, how can I be of assistance this fine morning?"

"You advertise good prices and fine-quality reproduction on cartes? I believe your ads claim 'No two-dollar work done in this establishment' and 'Cartes de visite at San Francisco prices?' My son and I wish to take advantage of your offer."

Durant beamed and dropped the towel onto a cupboard by the darkroom door.

"Delighted to help. Do take a seat."

It was magic. There was no other word for it. Alex shivered with the thrill of seeing the image appear before his eyes in the photographer's solution, a cloudy mass swiftly resolving into the sculpted lines of their two faces, his father's stern and authoritative, and his — well, he had an inner glow that was directly related to his fascination with the whole process.

From the first moment Charles Durant had begun to explain what was involved in taking their pictures, he'd been enthralled. It all happened so fast. Within fifteen minutes Durant had his father posed, pictured, and was ready to move on to the next study. The secret of the wet-plate process he was using — the one everyone used these days — was speed. You had to move fast or it dried too soon and the image failed to take. With an experienced flick of the wrist the photographer poured the collodion solution onto the glass plate for the next image, a steady elegant stream first pooling in the center, then adeptly tipped to each side in turn, until the plate was evenly covered. Flowing the plate, he called it. The chemicals had a sickly-sweet smell, and Alex didn't think he had ever seen anything as remarkable, ever. He had to get one of these cameras and start taking pictures himself.

"Your turn now, Mr de Vile, and then we'll take one of you both together, if that's what you wish."

Charles Durant stood waiting for him to assume the seat before the lens.

"Mr Durant, do you ever take pupils? I mean, give instruction? I admit I am fascinated. I would love to learn more."

Charles Durant glanced nervously to his father. "I'm not sure …"

"Alexander, you've got plenty to learn without taking on photography, surely." His father frowned. "Leave that to the technicians. I've got a brilliant future planned for you in business."

"Yes, of course, Father. The business

is extremely important. But surely, no harm in taking up a hobby? I find the whole thing completely mesmerizing." He laughed self-consciously. "You're crazy about your horses and racing. I guess it's just that photography does it for me."

Charles Durant cleared his throat noisily. "Gentlemen. Conversation to be resumed. Now Mr de Vile, settle down and concentrate. Portrait number two is under way."

"Can I watch you pour the solution on?"

Durant looked doubtful. "I usually prefer my clients to get themselves settled—"

"I'll sit immediately. I promise. I just love the way you do it."

Durant nodded reluctantly, and a fluttery, empty feeling gripped his innards as Alex followed him into the darkroom to watch the process begin all over again.

# Six

Senator Hector de Vile had been home from the photographic sitting for several hours, but he could not settle to anything. The memory of Alex's excitement when gazing into the alchemy of the developing tray clawed at his guts. Was nearly twenty years of father-and-son harmony to be destroyed by one chance meeting? Damn his idea of having their portraits taken, even if he did need more cartes for the Senate election scheduled for next month. He was very secure in the seat he'd been appointed to last year when the elected man died in office, and he confidently expected to be returned with a bigger majority than the previous incumbent. But he didn't need anything happening to draw negative comment.

For the first time in his life he wished his first wife was still alive — and what a turn-up that was, for she'd truly been a piece of baggage. No one had mourned her violent death last year. But at least if Bertha was here he could go over the story again — her story of how she came to have a toddler in her care when they'd first met.

She didn't have a maternal bone in her body, and she'd told him so many different versions of who he was — she called him Alejandro — and how she'd come by him. It changed depending on what day it was, on her mood and whim, but he hadn't been particular on knowing the details anyway. It served his own purposes to present a wife and son to his dictatorial father back East, so he didn't ask. He'd taken woman and child to meet his father — his "evidence" to satisfy his father's demands before he would hand over his inheritance — and when she'd flitted off a year later with a high-rolling gambler who offered a lot more money and excitement he hadn't been too bothered.

He sipped his mid-afternoon brandy and sighed. From his perch high on Nabob Hill he looked down the valley to Nevada City's Broad Street, where townsfolk would be bustling about their daily business. He'd made his fortune several times over in the last fifteen years, and he was intent on ensuring it was protected and passed on to Alex. To be able to pass on a substantial fortune ... Well, it made him feel it had all been worth it. He paid the price a dozen times over in the tough calls he'd been forced to make, and he wanted to leave it all to someone he'd raised up when he was dead and gone.

He pulled out his gold fob watch from his waistcoat pocket to check on the time, just as his housekeeper tapped on the drawing-room door. "A Mr Hiram Williams here to see you, sir. Shall I show him in?"

He was right on time. Hector de Vile felt the acid reflux subside, and he let out a breath he didn't know he'd been holding. He nodded towards the stocky, white-haired woman who stood at the door. Mrs Galveston was a Cornish widow who'd been with him for fifteen years, her upright resilience providing backbone to his family life when he was taken away on business. Alex had called her Oma from his first days in the household.

"Yes, do please show him in."

Hector rose and faced the door as Hiram Williams limped hesitantly towards him and proffered his hand with diffidence. He was an old man, well into his fifties, with thinning blond-gray hair and tired eyes looking out of a heavily lined face. His mouth turned down at the corners as if to confirm there was little left in life to be pleased about, but when he spoke his voice was as soothing as liquid honey. "Afternoon, Senator. Day going well, I trust?"

"Not as well as it might, but I'm sure you'll be able to fix that."

Hiram Williams looked at him keenly through wrinkled caverns. "I'll do my best. What's the problem?"

"The problem is Alexander. He's got this mad idea he wants to be a photographer. I know you've been keeping a close eye on him for me, but this calls for a bit of extra action. You know a Frenchman. Charles Durant, with a studio in Pine Street?”

Hiram nodded and de Vile gestured to a seat beside him. “Sit down, make yourself comfortable. We need to persuade Mr Durant that taking any interest in Alexander would be a very bad idea for business. Do you understand?”

“Mr de Vile, you know I’m not in a fit enough state to get into that kind of thing. Normal surveillance is no problem, but I’m not strong enough these days to do any muscle work. Can barely stand upright on my two pins.”

De Vile nodded slightly impatiently. “I appreciate that, Hiram. You’ve been a boon reporting on things while I was away in Washington. But it’s very important that Alex focuses his attention on de Vile investments at this time. He can't do that if his head is turned with nonsense about cameras and chemicals. Find someone else to handle it, like you did a couple of nights ago."

Hiram Williams shifted uneasily in his chair. "Charles Durant is just a man going about his normal business. Isn't this all a bit heavy-handed?"

"There's a lot at stake here, Hiram. More than you know. You just keep your head down and don't ask questions and it'll be fine. I've got a lot riding on it."

Hiram gazed at him for a few more moments and then raised himself with difficulty from the chair. "Then I'll be off to my work, Senator. I'll send a boy with a message when the job's done. Like last time."

He turned and limped to the door, his

mouth more turned down at the corners than when he'd entered the room ten minutes before.

De Vile sat quietly, reflecting on the conversation. He knew that Williams didn't like to be drawn into rough trade, but this situation called for drastic measures.

His greatest fear was that Alexander would discover the circumstances of his birth from some other source, and turn on him. Accuse him of living a lie. He'd done plenty of things he wouldn't want shown in the light, but Alexander was the best thing in his life, and he hadn't even fought to get him, like he had for the rest of his estate. He had just got lucky.

He'd never wanted to know who Alejandro's parents were. Better if he didn't know. He could honestly play dumb if it ever became an issue. But under the biggest stone at the bottom of his deep hole of unwelcome memories was one lingering Bertha taunt — that the boy's father was a Spanish photographer.

How ironic it would be if, after all his careful protection, Alexander could chance upon the facts of his birth through the artist grapevine — because love or hate each other, those arty types stuck together, didn't they? He was very glad he had a doughty man like Hiram Williams on the case.

# Seven

Alexander stared at the image before him and shivers feathered up his spine. An enchanting family group stared out of the 1851 daguerreotype, as if making a silent, soulful appeal to not be forgotten. Two small children, a boy and a girl, probably no more than a year old, cuddled into a woman who was clearly their mother: she was hugging them close, one on either side. An older girl, perhaps four or five years old, sat cross-legged on an enormous cushion at the woman's feet, clasping to her chest a small dog with an eager lolling tongue that made him look as though he was positively smiling into the future. The woman had an ethereal beauty, the other-worldliness of the image enhanced by the filmy white dress she wore, with a silky fluid flowing skirt and filmy neckline reminiscent of a wedding veil. It was such contrast to the gnarly miner photographs in the collection of the same vintage Charles had been showing him that it was hard to believe she inhabited the same time and territory.

He had been so enthralled at the photographer's work that he stayed on for hours after his father left, watching Charles Durant print all of the shots he'd taken of them for the cartes, and then observe as he'd worked on new portraits for a pair of traveling musicians who'd arrived unannounced to command his services.

"The chemicals, silver nitrate especially, very dangerous." Charles raised his hand, fingers spread wide, and pointed to his eyes. "If you get it in your eyes, *très mal — non voyant*.' Blind. Alexander understood that the outcome would be bad, but the volatility of it all seemed to him to increase the mystique of the whole process.

He'd talked for hours with Durant about what he'd done and where he'd been.

He went home that night in a daze, amazed that this world of magic had been there right before his eyes and he hadn't known it. The next morning he was impatient to return and collect the completed prints for his father, just to have an excuse to talk more photography with Charles Durant

He'd known that photographers had been a constant and prolific part of life since the early Gold Rush, wandering from town to town with their daguerreotype studios on wheels, offering the men intent on making their fortune in gold a chance to record themselves for posterity. But as he neared the age of many of the men photographed, it struck him as never before that the pictures had deep significance — perhaps the last sight a mother or beloved had of the man in question. Many died of disease, misadventure or the cold and ended in unmarked graves, their families ignorant of their final end.

They paused for a morning coffee as Durant explained he'd been an itinerant before setting up studios, first in Marysville, then Sacramento, and finally in Nevada City.

"I like it here. Not too much other competition." He smiled. "We photographers often do go into partnership and set up shop together — I've had several partners over the years — but sometimes we clash. Even been instances of someone burning down a competitor's darkroom, but there's been no problems like that for a while now."

"Heck, sounds like life's got to be a bit more civilized. These photos you've been showing me — most of them look pretty raw. They hadn't exactly found their El Dorado, had they? The men look exhausted, and their clothes are pretty rough."

"Oh, Alexander, you've no idea. Conditions for the men working here in the early days — they were hard." He gestured to the pile of daguerreotypes that lay on the table before them. "The days when men just dug into river banks with picks and shovels and sluiced through gold pans — they're long gone. We're into big owners and industrial-level investment now. I guess you could say the romance has gone out of it. I mean, look at this one here. I bet he's had the picture taken to send to his mother or loved one back home. He's got the determined look of a young man intent on making his fortune. Look at the beard on one so young, his soulful gaze, with his pick over one shoulder, his panning dish with a few nuggets visible in it hugged to his side."

As Charles spoke he pointed at the image's different aspects and offered it to Alex, who took it and studied it further.

"Look at him. Probably only a couple of years older than I am now. All cleaned up in his plaid trousers and fresh, double-studded shirt. I wonder if he's even still alive — and if he is, whether he's still in California. So many of them died destitute, didn't they? His hat covers his head but you can see he's got short hair."

He picked up another image from the pile. "Not like this guy. Just look at those glossy ringlets that fall over his shoulders like a girl's. He looks like he's just come from the hairdressers. You don't see that kind of hair these days, do you? I'd say he'd have taken a bit of teasing from the other men. Do we know who took these pictures and where they were from?"

Charles picked up the image Alex had commented on and held it up for closer examination. "Actually this one is an early ambrotype. They were printed on glass and so were quite fragile, but they were less expensive than the daguerreotypes. You see the ruby-maroon coloring showing through around his shoulders and arms? That's because they often printed onto dark red glass that shone through where it was slightly underdeveloped. Whoever took these really knew what he was doing. Ambrotypes were very new in 1851, when I think all these were taken. They'd become much more popular than daguerreotypes by the late Fifties."

"How do you know it was 1851?"

"That's the only detailing they had marked on them — a date. Nothing else. No names of who the subject was. Or who took them. I came across them a few years ago when I was checking out a derelict studio up for rent in Sacramento. A whole lot of these old photos were just piled up, abandoned in a darkroom cupboard. The guy who'd been using the studio had died, and no one was claiming them, so I rescued them. I didn't want to see them lost."

They turned towards the door at the sound of heavy tramping up from the stairs below. Charles started picking up the images and tucking them back into the sturdy carrying case he kept them in. "Sounds like we've got visitors," he said. "If I had to take a guess as to who took these pictures, I'd bet on a Spanish photographer who was working in Sacramento in the 1850s, Rafael Castellanos. He was a very talented photographer, but not much of a businessman, as I recall—"

The door from the hall way slammed open and a big-shouldered man thundered into the room. Behind him trailed a second man who was nearly as big but hunched over and defensive, a second fiddle to the main instrument.

"So what does a man have to do to get his photo taken?" the first man barked, his face distorted with a nasty sneer. He raised his right hand in a fist and cracked his knuckles with an audible pop-pop-pop with his free hand.

Charles Durant frowned but stood his ground. "I don't believe you have an appointment, Mr ...?"

The bigger of the two lumbered across the room until he stood inches from Durant's chest. "Mr Nobody to you." He grabbed the photographer's shirt in his fist and lifted him off his feet. The cotton fabric ripped and Durant slipped back onto his tiptoes.

"Now look here—"

Alex stepped forward without a clue as to what he could do, but unable to stand by and do nothing. "You can't do that!

He's done nothing to you!" The words exploded out, and Alex recoiled as the big man let go of Charles and swung around to face him, his face dark and ugly.

"Oh, yeah? And who says so?"

Alex's stomach flipped but he held his determined stance.

"Mr Durant is going about his lawful business, so beat it or I'll call the constable."

He threw back his head and let out a mirthless gargle, before muscling up to Alex, chest to chest, knocking him backwards. "Fingers, get rid of this creep will you?"

"Sure thing, Knuckles." His offsider, who had been hanging back, sprang to Alex's side and grabbed his elbow, digging his fingers into the joint so hard an excruciating pain shot up his arm.

"You're history, buster," he snarled.

In the seconds that Charles Durant was free he whirled to a drawer and was pulling out a pistol as Knuckles turned back to him. The big man slashed viciously down across the photographer's shoulder with his fist and the gun dropped to the floor. Durant's arm hung useless at his side. The intruder slapped him across the face, smashing his glasses to the floor. "Pulling the draw on me, were you?" With one hand he grabbed him at his throat, while with the other he swept all of the articles on top of the cupboard to the floor in one violent movement. Glass bottles, the satchel containing the old photos, hats and shawls occasionally used as photographer's props, crashed or shattered on the floor, stomped under the bruiser's feet.

Then he dragged Charles across the room to where his camera sat on a tripod and in one sweeping blow lashed out, sending it smashing to the floor.

"No!" Charles yelled. The front of the older man's trousers was stained in dampness and the sharp smell of urine hit Alex in the throat. He pulled against the wrestler's hold Fingers held him in. Knuckles turned towards the darkroom, dragging Charles behind him.

"No, you can't! It's dangerous!" Alex was screaming, trying to pull away from Fingers to run after Charles and stop whatever was about to happen next.

He heard a crash and Durant screaming, before something hard and heavy thumped across his temple. As he sank to the floor he had one thought. *Dear God, get us out of this mess.*

Alex had no clue how long he had lain on the studio floor, but when he awoke the thugs had gone, leaving a mess of glass shards and the stink of chemicals behind them. He had been intrigued by the sickly-sweet smell of the silver nitrate yesterday, but as he lay with a thumping pain in his head, blood trickling down his face, the smell made him nauseous.

He rolled onto his knees and braced himself to stand up. The first couple of times he fell back to his knees, crippled by a wave of giddiness. As he sucked air into his lungs and waited for the faintness to pass, he was shaken by a violent coughing fit. He rolled onto his side and sat up. Smoke. He smelt smoke. His head jerked upwards and he saw a foul-smelling black coil rolling from the open darkroom. He dragged himself across the floor, scooping up the satchel containing the historic photos under his strongest side as he went.

At the darkroom door he paused, steeling himself for what he'd find. He dropped the satchel and hauled himself upright on the door jamb, ignoring the crushed glass in his bleeding palms. His eyes stung. The smoke was getting thicker by the second. But below the smoke level he made out the figure of Charles sprawled on his back, his arm flung across his face. An ugly red gash ran across his face; the silver nitrate tray lay upturned on the floor beside him.

Barely able to stay upright, Alex scuttled forward and grabbed Charles Durant by the ankles and began hauling him backwards. Even as he pulled him clear, he saw the first orange flames licking from under the darkroom table. Just clear of the doorway he lost his balance and fell backwards, his eyes streaming as he struggled to get back up again.

"We're getting out of here, Charles. We're doing it."

He doubted that Durant could hear him, but the statement strengthened his resolve. He was on his feet and had just taken hold of Durant's ankles a second time when someone came up from behind him, the pressure of a hard male body nudging him aside. His insides clenched with terror as he swung around, in anticipation of seeing Knuckles and his lethal accomplice returned, but an old man he hadn't seen before, with lanky gray-white speckled hair and a face much the same color moved with surprising haste around him.

"Leave him. I can take him." It was an order, barked with authority. Alex's hands went limp, and Durant's feet thumped to the floor.

In one swoop the stranger gathered

the Frenchman up in a fireman's lift, draping him over his shoulder like a child, and then pushed Alex, who was staring in disbelief. "Come on, son. Get moving. We haven't got a lot of time."

Alex swallowed hard, the smoke raw in his throat. He whirled and remembering the satchel, grabbed it off the floor before stumbling behind the Good Samaritan out of the burning studio. It was only as they cleared the studio that he noticed the rescuer was limping.

# Eight

"You what?" Hector de Vile stared at Hiram Williams, not believing what he'd just heard. The man had arrived and demanded to see him immediately, his clothes smelling of smoke, shifting from foot to foot, obviously rattled. Most irregular, especially on an uneventful Wednesday afternoon. And then he'd proceeded to tell him some preposterous story about Alexander getting caught in a burning building.

"I dragged him out of the burning studio, Senator. If I hadn't, there's a good chance your son would have gone down with him."

"Just what is going on?" Hector de

Vile jumped to his feet and took a step towards the dull-faced investigator, his hands itching to grab him around the neck and throttle him.

"I told you my son was not to be involved!" He roared his frustration, and then remembered that Alex could arrive home at any moment. He sank down into his chair and put his head in his hands, stroking the hair back off his forehead in jerky agitated slides. "What's going on here, Hiram? Can't these guys take an order?"

"It's most unfortunate how it all occurred, Senator de Vile. Big Man Knuckles got carried away, I grant you. But he wasn't to know Alexander would be there with the Frenchman today. It's Wednesday, after all. What business did he have being there? He should have been at his own work."

Hector's body stiffened and he once again felt the urge to ring someone's neck rise up within him. What was Alexander doing in the photographer's studio? He had told him to drop the idea of playing around with cameras and focus on his work. Why was he meddling where he wasn't supposed to be? Blast him!

"When I said I wanted the photographer warned off, I did not mean kill him." He was yelling again.

Hiram gazed at him uncertainly, as if worried about stirring up his wrath further. "He isn't dead, Senator. Leastwise not when I saw him last at the doctor's an hour ago. But he is very badly injured. Doc says he's likely to lose his sight, and worse maybe. Depending on how much of the chemicals got into his system. It's nasty stuff."

De Vile shrugged. "Dead, mortally injured, what difference does it make? I hope you made damn sure — *they* made damn sure — that my name is not going to be brought into this in any way. You never mentioned my name?"

"Of course not, Senator. As a matter of fact, having your son involved actually helps protect you, when you think about it. No one would think you'd put him at risk."

"You're damn right about that. That boy is the most precious thing I've got. I'd do anything to protect him."

A tense silence fell between them. De Vile glanced down and saw the veins on his hands were standing up from the backs of his hands, flushed with pumping rage. Among all his achievements, the wealth, power and position he'd attained, nothing meant as much to him as

Alexander. Being able to hand over the de Vile empire to his son made everything he'd had to do to get it worthwhile.

He thought back to the first days when Bertha had come into his life so unexpectedly with the child in tow. It was late 1852. She was a good-time girl who hung around the San Francisco fast set. Not a woman he'd given a second look at, though that wasn't too unusual: there were few he would. She seemed to always have money to party and buy pretty dresses; he guessed she'd been the kept woman for a string of wealthy older married men, but she was smart enough to conceal her waywardness under a frothy veil of sophistication. She alluded frequently to an 'inheritance' she'd received. And she was entertaining company so, as with him, the so-called society folks preferred not to ask too many questions. She moved in the right circles, and they had seen a bit of each other, but he'd always dismissed her as a lightweight until the day she mentioned a child. A boy she was caring for.

First she told him he was her nephew and that her sister had suddenly died. She talked of fostering him out. Then he'd confided about his family situation, how his old man was withholding his inheritance unless he was married and had produced a son by the time he was thirty. Hector was twenty-nine. Then her story changed. The boy was hers, and she had been tragically widowed.

She had been the perfect woman to take back East to his mean old man, playing the role of the happy little wife and mother to the hilt in return for a comfortable gratuity. One of the most satisfying plays of his life, conning his dictatorial father out of a substantial nest egg with a fake wife and son.

He sat back in his chair and gave a big sigh. "Sit down, Hiram. I didn't mean to fly off the handle."

"I'm fine, Senator." Hiram stood nervously at attention, his hands clasped behind his back. "I should be going soon anyway."

"Keep watching Alexander for me. It's important I know what he's up to. Anything at all — don't hesitate to report it to me."

"Certainly, Senator. I'll be going now. I need to get this jacket changed."

The doorbell clanged urgently, and Mrs Galveston's feet marched down the hallway. Seconds later the sound of her greeting Alexander floated into the drawing room, then Alexander burst into the room, his creamy complexion pink, his eyes blazing.

"Father, something terrible—" He saw Hiram and faltered. "Mr Williams, what are you doing here?"

Hector cut in. "Mr Williams is telling me of these latest tragic events, Alexander. What do you think?"

"But how did he … When did he—"

"Mr Williams and I are acquainted. Our paths have crossed from time to time. So naturally he thought it right to advise me of this terrible fire. But we're finished here — you were just going, weren't you, Hiram?"

"Most certainly, Senator." He nodded at Alexander. "Do hope your friend makes a full recovery."

Alexander looked from Williams to his father, a frown replacing the agitated mood of a few minutes before. Then he shook his head and sat down. "You never cease to amaze me. What a strange coincidence that he should chance along at just the same moment today." He stared at his father, unblinking. "It's not at all certain I would have been able to get Mr Durant out without help."

"Alexander, I'm perplexed that after my specific instructions about leaving the photography thing alone you were back there today. What is going on?"

"I thought I would just pass by and pick up those cartes you ordered. Mr Durant said he'd have them all ready by mid-morning. And we just got talking, so I ended up staying longer than I planned. Just as well I did maybe, though Mr Durant is very seriously hurt. His eyesight may be permanently damaged from the chemicals they threw at him." He shook his head. "The doctor can't say yet. And apparently just a random attack. I don't understand it."

"Call Mrs Galveston and ask her to bring us some tea. Let's just try and regain our composure."

As his son obediently stepped out of the room, Hector's eyes followed him.

Bertha had barely maintained the charade of happy family life until they'd got back to California. He and Alexander had been a team ever since, with support from stout-hearted Mrs Galveston. As he looked back down the tunnel of time to those early years, he acknowledged the cost. What was one French photographer in the long ledger? Another expendable. Just like Bertha. Over the years she surfaced now and then with vague threats of blackmail, and he paid for her silence. At one stage they even had a fairly satisfactory business arrangement, with him the silent partner in a bar she part-owned and successfully managed. But last year she overstepped the mark again, over-estimated her leverage, and he'd had to finally settle things once and for all.

He smiled brightly as Alexander bustled back into the drawing room, followed by Mrs Galveston with a tea tray. Yes, it had cost him his soul to come out on top. He was in no doubts where he was headed when he finally ended his run. That's why he was more determined than ever to hold onto what he'd got and not let go.

He'd never really known whether Bertha was Alexander's mother by blood or not. Then when Huldah's daughter Isabella turned out to be adopted last year, he'd wondered all over again what Bertha's involvement had been. He still didn't really know. They'd kept it all pretty quiet, and he had no proof, but he wasn't taking any chances. The one thing he knew for sure was he was not Alexander's blood father. And if he had anything to do with it, he would die the only person who knew it.

# Nine

Rosie Kelly dipped her spoon into the ice cream, scraped around the side of the dish and consumed it in tiny nibbling bites, camping up a delighted swoon. "Yuuummm!"

Isabella giggled, despite her gloomy mood. Rosie could make one syllable like "Yum" sound funny — and Irish. She had a natural gift for comedy, as Isabella had seen when they were on stage together last year with Lotta Crabtree's troupe.

"Shush!" Rosie waved the spoon in the air reprovingly. "It's just as well we're here in Basil's suite or the 'rising star' would be attracting negative attention."

Isabella's mood sobered. "I know. Isn't it terrible? Here I am in mourning for Alycia and I can still laugh with you. It's not right, is it?"

"Oh, I don't know about that. What do you think Alycia would say?" Rosie regarded her with big green eyes that shone out from under a tumult of red brown curls.

Isabella licked her lips and tasted the lingering strawberry sweetness as she considered the question. "She'd approve of us still finding things to laugh about. Yes, she'd want us to behave so as not to attract attention. She'd want us — well, me anyway — to wear mourning, and not be loud and obnoxious. That goes without saying. But she wasn't a killjoy. She'd concur with what the Good Book says: 'A merry heart doeth good like a medicine.'"

Rosie flashed her a warm, complicit smile, and Isabella's heart lifted in gratitude. Having Rosie here was such a boon. Between them sat a cedar tub lined with a porcelain dish containing the most delicious strawberry ice cream.

"She knew ice cream is the answer for everything." Isabella laughed. "I remember Graysie telling me one of the first outings she had with Alycia was to an ice-cream parlor and she just took charge."

This particular pottle of deliciousness had been delivered via a street vendor, the tinkling of sleigh bells on her cart having attracted their attention to the street below.

Being in mourning meant that Isabella was restricted in her movements, and not able to work for at least the next few weeks because although Alycia was not a blood relation, she regarded her as close family. She would have to wear black, lie low and postpone any future stage work for a little while. Just as well the *Corsican Brothers* season closed the night Alycia was shot.

It was times like this that she really missed not having the other two Russell brothers' partners — Graysie and Pania — here, but both were visiting family with their new husbands, her half-sister Graysie to Australia with Nathan, and Pania to New Zealand with Sir John. It was just so complicated. She hadn't known anything about having a half-sister, or about being adopted until last year. She might never have found out but for some villain trying to blackmail Huldah.

Over the last nine months she'd come to adore Graysie. Alycia was Graysie's aunt, so if they ever found her twin, Graysie would also be gaining a half-brother. She thought that was the main reason Alycia had been so determined to help — she liked the idea of returning Graysie's other sibling to the family.

"Wake up, acushla!" Rosie laughed as she gently tugged at her hair, which had grown back well from the drastic shearing she'd given it last year. "You're day-dreaming!"

Isabella gave her own cheek a light slap, a burlesque gesture that got them both laughing again. "Silly me! There's been so much going on, and now with Alycia gone …" Tears flooded to the back of her eyes and threatened to overflow.

What was wrong with her? Laughing one moment and crying the next. She bit her lip and wandered to the window that overlooked the main street. As she looked down on the morning crowds going about their business she glimpsed Sebastian Russell's tall, supple figure threading his way through the pedestrians thronging the footpath.

She'd not seen him since their discussion — more of a sharp disagreement, really — on the night of Alycia's funeral and felt strangely conflicted when she thought of him. He was a man of integrity, she felt sure of that, but so closed and bitter with it.

She turned to Rosie. "I think Sebastian Russell's heading this way. Do I look okay?"

Rosie raised finely arched eyebrows above eyes that sparkled with mischief. "You look perfect, you sweet girl. But why should you care about him? Didn't you say he wasn't much fun?"

Isabella's face grew warm. "Fun? No,

not exactly fun. He's complicated. I think he had a bad time in the war. Is that a stupid thing to say? Does anybody have a good time in war …? But you know what I mean. He seems to have a bit of a chip on his shoulder. Maybe I just feel sorry for him."

"Complicated and nursing a shattered heart? Now that sounds dangerous. Irresistible, even."

Isabella leapt at her friend and playfully covered Rosie's mouth with her hand to muffle her. "Stop teasing!" she squealed. "You've got it all wrong." Rosie struggled and pretend-talked through Isabella's fingers as they tussled back and forth, giggling.

If Isabella hadn't been expecting it she'd never have heard the light tap on the door that preceded Sebastian Russell's entry into the room. She let go of Rosie and stepped away quickly, smoothing the skirt of her black gown as she turned to the door.

"Mr Russell, Sebastian, hello. Nice to see you. I think you've met my friend Rosie Kelly before?"

He stood in the entry way, hand still on the door knob, as if unsure of his welcome.

Isabella prompted: "When she came to dinner in Grass Valley last year? You may not remember."

Sebastian dipped his head and his copper hair glinted. "Nice to meet you again, Miss Kelly. Very welcome, I'm sure, at this sad time."

He closed the door quietly behind him. His springy curls framed a face which still showed a ghost of a bright, boyish innocence, but on a second look the heavy fatigue lines around his eyes and mouth canceled out any youthful glow. It was like getting a glimpse of the irrepressible sprite that had long ago been banished by death and sorrow, *At moments like these he looks older than his years,* Isabella thought.

Sebastian looked from one to the other expectantly and gave a weak smile. "Everything okay? What have you been up to?"

"Um, this and that." Isabella felt her cheeks flushing to a light pink and ran her hands down the black dress again.

*Broken the rules and feasted on ice cream. Not exactly like I'm in mourning.*

Rosie cut in. "Actually we gave ourselves a little treat this afternoon." Her mischievous eyes flickered. "Shure we did." Playing Irish again. "Guess what we did?"

Sebastian looked from one to the other, and a slow smile curled up from the corners of his mouth and lit the rest of his face. "I have no idea."

Rosie stepped to the table and gestured to the cedar tub with its porcelain lid surrounded by their dirty dishes and spoons. "Voila! Ice cream! And we've saved some for you."

His eyebrows shot up, and then he accepted the proffered dish and spoon. "Well, this is a surprise. A nice one for a change. Thanks a lot."

"Hope you like strawberry. It's got real fruit in it."

Sebastian sank into a dining chair and rolled a spoonful around his mouth. "Mmm. Very good. It's a long time since I had ice cream! And strawberry! That's something else."

They watched in silence as he spooned his way through the rest of the melting pink confection.

"The ice cream's been our main excitement. We haven't been up to much apart from that. Can't really, under the circumstances. What about you?" Isabella fiddled with a black jet pendant that hung on a ribbon at her throat, on loan from Huldah to lighten the austerity of her dress.

Sebastian shook his head. "It's been very slow. No indication of who Polk might have been working with, or for, if anyone. We're still at a dead end on that one, I'm afraid." He grimaced. "Sorry, bad choice of words, but you know what I mean."

Isabella clasped her hands tightly in her lap. "So we still have no idea whether Alycia's death was a random act, or someone had a motive."

"Sums it up exactly. Although what a motive could be beats me."

"And what about Hiram Williams? Have you talked to him?"

Sebastian's head jerked back. "I don't follow. Why would I?"

Isabella's face felt hot, and she fiddled with the jet pendant, lifting its weight off her neck and then lightly dropping it again. "Just because he's out there working at street level. He's been investigating Alejandro for months now in his unobtrusive way. He probably hears all sorts of rumor and innuendo. I'd have thought it would be worth checking."

Sebastian regarded her with a steady, measured look. "I suppose ... I haven't seen him since before Alycia died. Maybe he's been away. I don't know. It's a very long shot but I could ask him, I guess."

"It's important, Sebastian. I mean if Alycia's shooting had anything to do with

Alejandro, then he may be the one who knows the most." She sounded desperate, even to her own ears.

Sebastian looked at her kindly, as you might at a small child, and her pulse quickened.

*He's doing it again. Treating me like a baby.*

"Isabella, we've been through this already haven't we? The likelihood of it having anything to do with your brother is so small as to be negligible. You've got to let it go. You're indulging in wishful thinking and setting yourself up for disappointment."

Isabella's chest tightened, and her breath came in pinching huffs. "Well, Sebastian, the way I see it, the only disappointment I'm experiencing is in you and your closed mind." The sharp words were out before she could stop them. Any hint of the cherubic sprite disappeared as she stared into his face. Dark shadows rimmed his eyes, his jaw clenched, and his mouth set in a thin, tight line.

"Isabella, don't harp on. I've got a lot more experience with this kind of thing than you do. Just drop it."

She continued to glare at him, refusing to blink. Rosie had hit the nail on the head. *Why should I care what he thinks? He certainly isn't any fun. And I doubt with all my heart that he knows better than I do when it comes to Alejandro.*

She blushed at the fleeting recognition that ten minutes ago she had imagined him to be attractive, had sought his approval. How dumb could she be? She was just going to have to find a way around him.

# Ten

Tucked in a quiet corner of the Ebner Hotel's downstairs bar, Seb huddled over an ale and tried to work out how he had managed to get things so disastrously wrong with Isabella. Basil had entrusted him with protecting their extended family — Isabella and Huldah and, of course, Rosie as their guest — as well as pursue information about both Alycia's death and Alejandro's whereabouts. That was enough to have on his plate, without having to deal with an over-sensitive child as well.

He gazed into his beer pot and sighed. He normally wouldn't seek comfort in his cups, but he'd had to escape the freezing mood he'd triggered upstairs and find somewhere to think.

The girl was fixated on finding her brother, and what chance was there of that ever happening? His throat closed up as he thought of the money Alycia had poured into the search for the missing twin. It had been seventeen years since anyone had seen the boy, for goodness sakes. And six months of fairly intensive investigation by Hiram Williams had turned up nothing: no leads, no clues, no suggestion of where to turn next. They were fast running out of possibilities, and this silly girl kept on breathing down his neck.

He looked up from his glass and glanced around the K Street saloon. Ebner's was one of Sacramento's most desirable hostelries, with 36 'superior' rooms on its two upper floors and a liquor business in the basement. Not the sort of place he would be staying at if he wasn't attached to Basil's business. At this hour, Wednesday late morning, it was thankfully quiet, with just a few salesmen and visitors frequenting nearby tables. Too early for any lunchtime traffic, or for the card sharps and gamblers who would turn up later in the evening.

He idly glanced to the bar, where a man was talking with the bartender. He was stocky and muscled and wore a well-cut coat that looked a little flashy for Sacramento, state capital though it might be. He had a newspaper open in front of him and was pointing to an article. Asking about something to do with the town, no doubt.

Seb glanced away and took another sip. Something was jangling at the back of his mind. He glanced back. The bartender had looked up from the newspaper and turned in his direction. The visitor swung on his heel to follow the barman's gaze and faced him, folding the paper and putting it under his arm.

The confident pivot was so familiar that the mouthful of beer caught in Sebastian's throat, and he collapsed into a paroxysm of violent coughing. As he struggled to regain his equilibrium, a heavy lump in the pit of his stomach confirmed what he already knew: his day had just gone from bad to a whole lot worse.

The one man he had hoped never to see again was advancing towards him, arm stretched in greeting, and four years vanished in the seconds it took for him to cover the short distance to Sebastian's chair. "Tiger, old chap! What a piece of luck! When I saw the *Daily Union* this morning I knew I had to look you up! It said you were staying at the Ebner, so it wasn't too difficult to ask upstairs and discover you were most likely down here."

Sebastian began to rise from his chair, propelled by some ingrained courteousness that bewildered him. His mouth went dry as his jaw was buried against Corporal Edmund Quincey Jnr's linen-jacketed shoulder with its faint citrusy smell of Quincey's trademark Florida Water cologne. He had grown a neat blond mustache, and the corners of his eyes had feathered into tired, cynical lines, but there was no mistaking that this was the man who had been Seb's immediate superior for two years of war service.

Failing to register Seb's reluctance, Quincey slipped the newspaper onto the table and held him at arm's length, like a close friend. "You're looking good, Tiger. After reading today's paper I wasn't sure if I should offer congratulations or condolences."

Seb stepped back out of his reach and gestured to the spare chair. "You've got me beat, Quincey. I haven't got a clue what you're talking about. I haven't seen the paper."

Quincey stared in disbelief and then laid the newsprint flat on the table before him, pointing at a prominent double column of type. The front page headline read: "Man Apprehended in Theater Shooting Commits Suicide."

Seb glanced up, his pulse racing. "What the hell?"

Quincey looked at him quizzically. "You're the hero! Enjoy it."

Seb pushed himself to his feet, hands

on the table, his half-finished drink in front of him. "I don't want to read this."

"Oh, come on, old chap. It's out there now. You may as well enjoy what they're saying about you. Tell you what, I'll get something to drink. Can I get you something a bit stronger than a beer, old man? Looks like you need it." He strode back to the bar.

With rising nausea Seb read the account of Saturday's shooting. He could see it had all the elements to tickle a journalist's fancy. The victim: "Mrs Alycia Mountfort Stockton, wife of merchant and resort owner Basil Stockton and daughter of the wealthy New York property baron William Perrin Mountfort." The setting: "Eerily reminiscent of the President's tragic shooting at Ford's Theater four years ago." The capture: "The assassin was immediately apprehended by Corporal Sebastian Russell, a veteran of the Army of the Potomac, in a fearless capture which showed no concern for his personal safety. The assailant was taken into custody by County Police within minutes of the attack."

And the final cherry: "The perpetrator died before any further information as to motive could be gained."

Quincey returned and set a whiskey before him. "I didn't realize you'd come West. I've been back East until six months ago." He hesitated. "Seriously, Tiger. Basil Stockton must be pretty happy with you right now. You're well placed to enjoy some special favor after what you did, aren't you?"

The nausea Sebastian was already feeling turned into a burning sensation in his throat.

"Look here, Quincey. Shut up, will you. I don't want to talk about it."

Memories of Quincey's notorious mendacity flooded back, and he had a nearly uncontrollable urge to get up and walk away.

Quincey barreled on, impervious to his mood. "Look, I offer commiserations, of course I do. I'm sure her family is still in shock. But don't you deserve some recognition?"

Seb shook his head and pushed the newspaper back across the table. "Drop it, will you? You and I think very differently about these things."

"I know how it feels, old man. I lost my wife a year ago. One reason I decided to hit the road and try something new."

All the pain Sebastian had been tamping down inside overflowed.

*You lost your wife? And a poor sad cow she'd be, wedding you. She's probably happier dead.*

He closed his eyes and ran his fingers over his eyelids, breathing deeply as he did to give himself time to regain control. "Oh? I'm sorry to hear that. I hadn't heard you married."

*And why would I? I was never happier to see the back of anyone in my life.*

"Yes. Married Delia Samuels. You remember old Colonel Tom. His youngest daughter. Pretty enough little thing." He paused as if he was tempted to say more, but reconsidered. "Died before she reached full term. Baby died too."

Sebastian could imagine the agonies the faithless Quincey would have put Delia Samuels through.

"You're not married?" Quincey asked casually.

"No. Not married."

"Surprising. Nothing wrong with your looks. Guess the army didn't give either of us much to set up house with, did it? The 'heroes of the Potomac' deserved better." He flashed a conspiratorial look at Seb, as if sharing a private joke, and Seb felt the bitterness rise in his throat again. "Still, I suppose nothing's changed there. It's always been every man for himself. That's why I think you should be pushing the advantage—"

"Quincey, haven't I made myself clear? Drop it. Just shut up, will you?"

Edmund Quincey Jnr stared at him and spread his hands wide, palms upwards. "No need to get on your high horse, Tiger."

The back of Seb's neck itched at the continued use of his wartime nickname, coined originally because of his excellent night vision — like that of the wild, the others said. That and his coloring. He scowled.

"What's wrong with you?" Quincey asked, with a puzzled expression.

Seb wiped his hand across his neck, massaging away the prickling sensation.

*I'm losing it. Quincey is an untrustworthy ass but I'm no better.*

"Look, Edmund, sorry. It's been a hectic time. And I don't want to be reminded of the war. I've put all that behind me."

Unbidden, an image of Sarah flooded his mind. Raven-haired, dimpled, sweet-natured Sarah, her head thrown back, laughing, a few nights before Robert died. Her face flushed pink with excitement, eyes flashing as she danced a two-step polka with Quincey.

*All behind me. If only that were true.*

*I'm no better than he is and an even bigger liar.*

"Thing is, Tiger, things haven't gone so well since Delia died. Oh, I've got some opportunities here in California, no question about it. Some big opportunities. Might even be another wifey in the wind." He shot Seb another conspiratorial 'boys will be boys' look. "Can't help it if the gals like me, can I? But I thought us being old comrades in arms and all, well, maybe we could stick together. Give one another a hand up, so to speak."

*Over my dead body.*

"Not much going on with me right now, Edmund. Sorry I can't be more help."

"Oh? And what about that cute little piece I spoke to earlier when I was looking for you? The actress. What's her name? Isabella? Got any dibs on her?"

Seb couldn't hide his shock. "Isabella? She's just a kid. For goodness sake, Edmund. Find someone your own age."

Quincey threw back his head and laughed. "Why would I want to do that? She's a pretty little heifer — just coming into peak blooming, if you ask me. You don't want to wait too long or they go to seed."

He took a slug from his whiskey, took in Sebastian's expression and guffawed. "You always were a bit of a sober-sides, weren't you? I see that hasn't changed any. Come on, loosen up and let me buy you another drink."

# Eleven

"Mr Williams, I really must emphasize how important this whole matter is to me. I'm not willing to drop it now."

Isabella's hands moved restlessly in her lap, though she'd wanted to appear as serene as she could to the old man who sat before her, his horn-handled walking cane leaning against his thigh. His gray eyes were piercing but the sharpness was mellowed by a sadness that showed in his slumped shoulders and downturned mouth.

"I understand, Miss Wilmington, I do, but it's not possible for me to go on."

Hiram Williams had been shown into the suite by the hotel manager and without any opening niceties stated his business: he wished to resign from his work as an investigator on her behalf.

Isabella's heart contracted into a tight knot as she sat very still and listened. Rosie sat motionless in an armchair across from her, watching the exchange.

"Mr Williams, I feel it is even more important than previously that we continue. With Alycia's tragic death, how can we be sure this attack wasn't somehow linked to your inquiries into Alejandro? Perhaps someone wants to stop our searching? Have you ever felt any concerns yourself?"

Hiram's mouth seemed to turn down even further, his shoulders sink lower. "Concerns, ma'am? I can't say that I understand your meaning." The lines on his face deepened in the harsh noon light.

"Well, say someone objected to Alycia

funding this search? Maybe you were getting closer to finding out what had happened than they liked, and they took action to stop it." She gazed at him, appealing to his better nature, his curiosity, his anything. "Maybe you have been a lot more successful than you give yourself credit for."

He shook his head sharply, and a stringy blond-gray lock fell over his forehead. "Fact is, Miss Wilmington, I haven't found a single piece of evidence that your twin is still alive. I am sorry to say it, but that's how it stands. And I've run out of places to look next. No, it would be best for you to save your money and give up on it."

Isabella was on her feet before she realized it, hands clenched at her side. "I am very sorry, Mr Williams, but I will *not* give up on it! I will not."

She looked at Rosie in despair. "What do you think, Rosie?"

Rosie stood up and put her arm consolingly around her friend's shoulders, drew her to a sofa and sat down alongside her, maintaining her light embrace. "Sit here, dear friend, and take it easy. As for what I think … Well, Mr Williams, can I ask you straight out, did you ever come across this man Polk in your dealings? Not necessarily in relation to Alejandro, but in any way, shape or form. Did you know him?"

Hiram Williams' face darkened and his jaw tightened. "I can't see what that's got to do with—"

"Please, Mr Williams, just answer the question."

Hiram Williams opened his mouth, but before he'd got his next word out there was a clattering at the suite door, and

Sebastian Russell stepped in, bringing with him the smell of fresh bread from the bakery down J Street.

"Oh, sorry to interrupt." He was in black riding jacket and boots and exuded fresh energy, his cheeks and eyes bright. "Just been getting in a morning ride."

Hiram levered himself to his feet, leaning heavily on his cane, eyes questioning.

Isabella gestured to him. "Mr Russell, meet Hiram Williams. Mr Williams, this is Sebastian Russell, Basil Stockton's California manager."

"Good morning, Mr Williams." Sebastian gestured to Hiram's chair. "Please don't stand on ceremony for me. I'm pleased to finally have the chance to meet. You've been working for Mrs Stockton for the last few months, I believe."

Hiram Williams sank back down with a relieved nod. "I have. With very little success, I'm afraid." He ran his hand down the cane's smooth horn handle. "As a matter of fact, I've just come to offer my resignation to Miss Wilmington. I don't see any avenues that justify continuing."

Sebastian sat in the armchair Isabella had vacated and steepled his fingers, elbows resting on his thighs. "I see."

The clock on the mantel chimed twelve noon.

The last chime rang away. Rosie shifted on the sofa and the black taffeta of her skirt whispered around her. She leaned back and regarded Sebastian, her hands in a prayer position up to her lips, as if deep in thought. "When you arrived, Mr Russell," she said, "I had just asked Mr Williams if he has ever come across the prisoner Polk at any time." She brought her hands to her sides in a quick decisive movement. "Mr Williams? I would still be interested in hearing your answer."

Hiram Williams looked at his feet and shuffled his stubbed brown boots. "I saw him around." His deep musical voice sounded a reluctant tone. He glanced over at Seb. "He was well known down the rough end of town — around China Slough and the bottom of I Street. He had bats in the belfry. Had a wife and three children he was trying to feed and he couldn't do it. His voices got in the way."

"Voices?" Rosie leaned forward. "What voices?"

"Who knows? He was barmy-brained."

"Poor man," said Seb. "But getting back to the point, it seems to me, Mr

Williams, that even if you feel you've hit a brick wall where Miss Wilmington's twin is concerned, there still may be leads you could follow on our behalf as far as Mrs Stockton's death is concerned. You know Mr Polk's acquaintances by the sound of it."

Hiram Williams tugged at the sides of his worn jacket and shook his head. "It would be a waste of time, Mr Russell. He's just a loony. I want nothing more to do with it."


Rosie stirred sugar into her tea and tapped a gay tattoo with her spoon on her china saucer. "That went well." She flashed a smile at Sebastian.

After Hiram Williams had left they'd ordered tea and biscuits and were sitting around the dining table, not saying much.

"No point in being morbid, but I got the distinct impression there was something Mr Hiram Williams wasn't telling us. Anyone else agree?" Rosie looked around the table.

Sebastian broke an oatmeal biscuit into pieces. "I don't want to agree, but I think you're right. He definitely didn't like you asking him about Polk. I picked up on that much." He put a morsel in his mouth.

"I wonder why." Isabella had been quiet and withdrawn since Williams had left. "I suppose there's only one way to find out, and that is to ask."

There was a rap at the door. "Not more visitors," groaned Isabella. "I'm a little over people paying their respects."

An apologetic Ned Castleton, the Ebner's manager, put his head into the room. "Corporal Edmund Quincey Jnr to see Mr Russell. Are you available, Mr Russell?"

Before Sebastian could answer, Quincey pushed into the room past Castleton. "Tiger—" He stopped and looked around him. "It feels like someone's died around here." He shrugged apologetically and grinned. "Sorry. Bad joke. But come along, folks! Jolly up. It can't all be bad."

Sebastian had slowly risen, the pleasure of his morning excursion draining away as he regarded Quincey.

*Can't the bastard just leave me alone?*

"Come on, old chap. Introduce me to these charming ladies. They make even mourning dresses look enchanting."

*He always had the corniest chat-up lines, and yet women seem to fall for them like bees on honey.*

Isabella's lips were pursed.

*Maybe not all of them.*

"Edmund, meet Miss Isabella Wilmington and Miss Rosie Kelly. This is Corporal Edmund Quincey Jnr. Edmund and I were at Gettysburg together."

Isabella gave him a quick nod and remained silent; Rosie acknowledged the introduction with a light "Pleased to meet you, Corporal Quincey."

"Forgive us, Edmund. Perhaps not the best time for a social call. We were just chewing the fat on a family matter. Maybe another time?"

Quincey strode to the table, pulled out a chair next to Isabella and sat down with a decisive thump. "Nonsense, Tiger. We spent years together. I practically *am* family. What's the problem?"

Isabella sat up straighter and raised one eyebrow to Sebastian, as if to say, "Friend of yours?" She reached for the teapot. "Can we offer you some tea, Corporal Quincey? We wouldn't want any friend of Mr Russell's to think us rude."

Sebastian's mild amusement turned to acid in his mouth.

"Thank you very much, Miss Wilmington. I do wish to offer my condolences." He glanced around him, his mask one of concern. "I am sure it's been a very difficult few days for you all."

Isabella offered him a biscuit with a wan smile. "It has been hard, I admit. We were all very fond of Mrs Stockton. And now the shock's fading we want answers. We want to understand why that man shot her."

"Then Pinkerton's what you need. Pinkerton's — or me."

Isabella's blue eyes widened and she tilted her head on a slight angle. "I'm not sure there are any Pinkerton's agents in Sacramento, Mr Quincey."

"Then it will have to be me, won't it?"

"In the spirit of one forthright comment deserves another, why would that be, Mr Quincey? Why would it 'have to be' you?"

"Forgive the immodesty, but I've got what it takes, Miss Wilmington. I've done work for Pinkerton's back East. I might even still be working for them if I hadn't suffered personal loss and decided to come out West and start over." He ran his hand over his smooth chin and flashed his straight white teeth in a quick smile. "I know my way around the darker corners of life, Miss Wilmington. I confess it. So entering the world of the criminal mind won't be hard for me. And I'm looking for something new, something a bit different. This sounds like it could be just the jape.”

“Good of you to offer, but we’re not in the market for any extra help right now, thanks Edmund.” Sebastian had not meant to sound quite as loud and definite as he did, and he sensed rather than saw Isabella wince as he spoke. He knew Quincey would not have missed it either. “I can handle any inquiries that need to be made on our behalf.”

Quincey frowned. “Really? I was under the distinct impression from Miss Wilmington that she was looking for help.”

Isabella looked demurely into middle space before focusing on Edmund with large, docile eyes. “Oh, we are making inquiries. It was more about who would be making those inquiries. If Mr Russell — Sebastian.” She broke off and smiled sweetly. “If Sebastian is happy to take over from Mr Williams we really have no need of any other service. He is a temporarily sworn deputy back in the Sierra Nevadas, you know."

She rose from her chair and dipped her head in a slight bow. "Now, if you gentlemen will excuse me, I think I need a little quiet time to recover. Thank you for visiting, Corporal."

She flashed a friendly smile at Sebastian and she and Rosie left.

*Checkmate. How did she do that? Got exactly what she wanted — someone to replace Hiram Williams in an active investigation — with that liquid voice that can turn positively syrupy when she wants something.*

And Quincey's offer would be hanging there like a sword on a rope. Drag his feet on the investigation and she'd ask him to take over.

"Well, there we have it, Quincey. I'd better get started. Which way are you going from here?"

Since Edmund had drawn attention to Isabella's 'blossoming' a few days ago, Seb had to accept it: on that one point he was right. Isabella had turned from an impulsive chit to an alluring woman overnight and it seemed to have happened when he wasn't looking.

He didn't relish playing Polk-investigator, but at least it meant Quincey wouldn't have any excuse to go near Isabella. It was worth taking the job on just to assure himself of that.

# Twelve

"Git out of here. She don't need your kind."

Brawny arms folded in an aggressive defensive stance, her dark eyes glittering with animosity, a solid, square-faced woman with legs like tree trunks blocked entry to the Polk family shack, but as far as Hiram Williams could tell she wasn't Mrs Polk.

He took a step back, unsteady on his feet on the unpaved ground, and prodded his cane to anchor himself. The house he'd sought out was little better than a tumbledown shed, the rough-sawn walls exposing gaps where the boards didn't meet.

Not too bad in summer, when a gentle breeze might freshen up the stuffy interior, but wet and cold in the winter. The air was ripe with the foul smell of waste from nearby slaughterhouses that backed onto the river in this poorest part of town. Hiram pinched his nose to block the smell, and waved away a couple of blowflies that buzzed in the stinking air.

When the rains came — and every year they inexorably came — the residents would be forced to scramble to higher ground, erecting tents and crude tin shelters until the waters receded, returning to face the stinking carcasses and contaminated flotsam left behind by the receding water. Inevitably the pathetic trove of household goods and modest food supply they'd scrabbled together since the last flood — anything they couldn't carry with them — would also be carried off.

This was the last part of Sacramento to stand unprotected by flood-preventing levees, and only the poorest of the poor lived here, surrounded by gutters that trickled with sewage and animal waste. As he stood and faced off to the angry woman, two grubby boys pushed past her and half-danced, half-ran to the drain out front, waving sailing boats cobbled together from sticks and bits of cloth. They were chattering excitedly, intent on the contest. "Mine'll beat yours!"

"Sam and Sol, you come here this minute!" the woman hollered like an army sergeant, and the boys took about the same amount of notice as untrained privates in the early war years.

Hiram grasped his cane firmly and started back towards the doorway.

"Madam, your assistance, please."

Distracted from the boys, she swung back to fix him with a hostile glare. "I told you, git out of here. Your kind only bring trouble." She started towards him as if ready to see him off. "You've already brought trouble. Now git!" She grabbed him by the left elbow — the one that didn't hold the cane — and began to propel him towards the pink-tinged drain where the children played.

"No! I've got money. Money for the family." Hiram was choking the words out, struggling to breathe and talk while being propelled down the street.

The woman stopped suddenly and released his arm so abruptly he staggered to stand upright. "Why would you bring money?" Her face scrunched in a suspicious scowl. "No one brings money."

Hiram was hit by a wave of dizziness,

and his head dropped down as he rested on his stick. "I need to sit down. Some water ..."

The woman stepped in close and supported him on one side as she yelled again to the boys, "Sam, go and git some water. Now! We need it now."

The boy lifted his head up from the game and cantered back into the house, emerging with a chipped cup of water which he offered the woman. "Here it is, Aunt Bet. Can I go and play now?"

She nodded and passed the cup to Hiram. "You'd better come in and sit down." Her expression was grudging but the hostility had moderated, and Hiram followed her into the shade of the shanty. It was mean and barren, but it was cooler inside than out on the street, and he plopped onto a broken-backed chair with a sigh of gratitude.

He sipped at a second cup of water as he gathered himself. The two-room shack had no windows. In the dim light he could see that one room contained bunk beds, and the one he was sitting in had a rough table and kitchen shelving. There was no running water, so the household hauled buckets, which sat against the wall in one corner.

Hiram reached inside his jacket to bring out a wadded envelope. "My name is Hiram Williams." He raised his eyebrows in a question. "But I don't know yours."

She replied with obvious reluctance, "Mrs Burton Purdy."

"I see. Is Mrs Polk here? Peter Polk's wife? I have got the right place?"

She nodded. "Yes, you have the right place but she's not well. She's away at her sister's getting her head right. Her boys are staying with me for a few days. Her husband was short of a sheet, and she ain't far behind."

"Short of a sheet? You mean crazy?"

"Yep. Have to be to do what he did, wouldn't you?"

Hiram shifted uneasily in his chair. "Well, as I said, I've got some money for the family. Mr Polk was entitled to some army pension money. Quite a goodly sum. Should see the family through for a few months, anyway."

"Pension money? My husband's a veteran and I ain't never heard of any pension money."

"Maybe he didn't serve as long as Mr Polk. "

She regarded him with implacable suspicion. "He served longer."

"Maybe he was in a different regiment."

"Same regiment. They went through a good part of the war together. And they both came home with a screw loose."

Hiram shrugged. "Well, I'm not sure of all the ins and outs, Mrs Purdy, but I'm guessing you won't refuse to take this for Mrs Polk just because you don't get the way army rules work."

"Army rules!" she scoffed. "I reckon I've seen you hanging around the place looking for Polk before." She regarded him coolly, as if waiting for her second sight to kick in. "Yeah, I seen you around here before. And I bet you Polk didn't just go and kill that old lady all by himself. He ain't got the brains for it — not nows, anyway." She refilled Hiram's cup as she pondered the situation. "Nope. I bet he had some help gitting there. And I bet this is the payoff. The one thing Polk was always straight up on was caring for his family. And he knew he wasn't doing it — couldn't do it."

She stretched out her hand. "So let's have it, then. The guilt money. Peter's final throw of the dice."

Hiram handed her the envelope. "You've got it all wrong." Even to his own ears, he didn't sound convincing.

"Yeah, yeah, I know. That's about the same time pigs fly."

She scowled at him and then opened the envelope with surprising delicacy, her thick fingers leaving grimy fingerprints on the white paper. She drew out the thick wedge of notes and flicked them through, as if she was shuffling cards.

"My, my. Well, he might have turned up his toes, but didn't he do well. I s'pose Mrs Polk has to thank you for keeping your end of the deal. You could've just left him hanging. So to speak." She flashed a lopsided grin. "And we wouldn't have been any the wiser."

Hiram stood with difficulty. "You've got it all wrong," he said.

"Oh yeah? So if Mr Burton Purdy kicks the bucket like old Polk did, I can expect the same pension payout? Lord forgive my soul, but it would almost be worth it."

He stared into her mocking face and couldn't bring himself to lie.

# Thirteen

No one would ever call Mrs Caroline Studebaker beautiful. Her eyes were two hard, round peas set too close together in a flat doughy face, her laugh reminiscent of a donkey hee-hawing through big teeth. But there were other compensations. Edmund Quincey Jnr tightened the arm he had looped around Mrs Studebaker's waist to draw her closer and smiled down at her with the high-charged charm that made women melt. She was already pink-faced and breathless from the circling exertion of the mazurka. Caught in the high beam of his charms, unused to such close attention from the catch of the dance floor, Caroline flushed to cerise and gulped out a nervous bray.

The music came to an end and Quincey led his partner from the dance floor. He had been in a Front Street bar on his first day in town when he heard about the rich widow who presided over the biggest emporium in town. It was an omen, he decided, and it hadn't been difficult to worm his way into her confidence and offer to escort her to the civic fundraiser to complete the Central Pacific Hospital, due to open before the end of the year on D and 13th streets. A vague claim to having been a past acquaintance of her husband's, the soothing balm of restorative sympathy for her recent loss, some judicious name-dropping about his dead wife's family back East, and she had welcomed him into her circle.

The four-story, six-ward Central Pacific was a source of civic pride as the first purpose- built hospital for railway employees in the world, so while most of the more than $60,000 cost was being borne by the railroad company, the town authorities was making a big effort to contribute the $4000 or $5000 it was estimated would be needed to complete the project.

Before his death Armin Studebaker had been on the hospital board, and so his widow was held in high regard by many of the surrounding dancers. Quincey, a total newcomer, was unknown, though he could count on the fact that a number of the ladies present would already be measuring him for size. He glanced around him as he steered Caroline off the floor and corrected himself. One person. He knew one person other than Caroline here. A familiar throb of sexual excitement pulsed as he spotted the young woman he'd met at Sebastian Russell's hotel earlier in the week. The charming little Irish entertainer. What was her name — Rosie someone?

She was standing in a cluster in one corner with several other young women dressed in the white dresses with the red cross armbands of Civil War nurses. On cue, as the dance floor cleared, the Master of Ceremonies stepped up and announced they would now receive entertainment from the Hospital Quartet.

The crowd clapped in enthusiastic response and the four women and one man — the so-called doctor — launched into a set of pastiches of popular songs parodying Doctor Wunsuponatyme and his right-hand woman, the Matron of

Neverminditsnamia. The audience responded with raucous good cheer and cat-calls.

Quincey stood with his arm lightly circling Mrs Studebaker's waist and devoured the sight of Rosie Kelly — that was her name, now he remembered — the prettiest of the quartet by far, with red curls that haloed her flashing green eyes. If he didn't have more engaging business at hand … and then he remembered who was hosting Miss Kelly in town.

No way did he want to stir up any more trouble with Sebastian Russell. He'd had enough problems five years ago with that stupid nonsense over the girl from Boston — Robert Kingsley's sister, as he recalled. He couldn't afford any scandal from his past to spoil his prospects here.

He shot a quick secretive smile at Mrs Studebaker, and she responded with a flutter of eyelashes. Yes, things were progressing nicely. After his last marriage disaster, he was determined that any new proposition included a woman with full ownership of her own estate, someone who wasn't beholden to a father or brother to pass over the loot, as had happened with Delia.

He gripped the widow Studebaker's waist just a little more tightly than he intended as the unpleasant confrontation with Colonel Tom rose again to mind. Delia had barely taken her last breath before he got the 'mount up and move out' message from her father, who made it abundantly clear that nothing that she was entitled to when she lived — and she was heiress to a fortune — was going to be transferred to him, her bereaved husband.

Mrs Studebaker, by all accounts a shrewd and hard-headed money manager, held very firm control of the mercantile business her late and much older husband had deeded to her. And there was no father or brother to complicate matters this time round.

The entertainment finished, supper was served, and Mrs Studebaker was taking some satisfaction in introducing "Corporal Quincey, formerly of the Massachusetts Infantry, an acquaintance of Mr Studebaker's" to her circle. The evening was winding up with a few more rounds of the dance floor, and Edmund had relinquished Mrs Studebaker's hand to Dr Fox, one of the senior physicians, when he spotted Rosie Kelly out of the corner of his eye.

"Miss Kelly. How very pleasant to meet again." He gave a mock bow in greeting. "On the job, I see. No rest for the wicked." He flashed her a smile and saw her shoulders stiffen.

*Thought she was tracking me down, the little minx, but perhaps not. Wonder if Russell's been warning her off.*

"Enjoying your night out?"

"Perfectly well, thank you." Her response was off-hand, and she maintained her distance. Not what he usually expected from a woman.

"So where's your guardian tonight?"

"My guardian? I'm not sure I follow." Her eyes slid over the dance floor and back to his face. "Do you mean my host, Mr Russell? Well, really it's Mr Stockton who's been kind enough to arrange our accommodation."

"Good old Sebastian hasn't got two pennies to rub together, so I'm not surprised he's not footing the bill!"

"Is that so? You know Mr Russell well, do you, Mr Quincey?" There was a hint of acid in her tone. "Well enough to know what he's been doing since you last saw him — four years ago, was it?"

"I might not have seen him, but I've got a pretty good idea. Let's say we were very close when we were in the unit together. Me, his best friend Robert and him. Going into battle together can do that. Makes friends of chaps who might otherwise not have much to do with one another. But I have to say …"

Rosie looked at him with raised eyebrows and fixed attention.

"Well, he was a pretty bad loser. Let's just say that."

"Really?" She drawled the word theatrically and made as if to move to the side of the dance floor. "A bad loser? At what? Cards?"

His neck pricked with irritation. Was this chit of a girl making fun of him? "It was a lot more serious than that, I'm afraid. You'd be wise to give Mr Russell a wide berth."

She stopped mid-step and stared at him, eyes wide in surprise. "I can't imagine what you are hinting at, Mr Quincey. From what I understand, Mr Russell is a man of impeccable integrity. Perhaps too much so for his own good."

"Well, I wouldn't argue there. Like a dog with a bone. He doesn't want it himself, but he makes a God almighty row when another dog takes it."

He ushered her out of the dance-floor traffic to a quiet table on the side wall, collecting a couple of glasses of fruit punch from a passing waiter's tray on the way.

"Like a dog with a bone. Not a picture

I reconcile easily with Mr Sebastian Russell."

"Ah, you've no idea, Miss Kelly. He couldn't take it, that's all. Wouldn't have made it through without me. Practically went to pieces when Robert died. And then when Robert's sister ... Well, let's just say he was unhinged over Sarah. I'd be careful around Sebastian Russell. He's a feller who wakes snakes. Always looking for trouble. And I wouldn't want to see another young lady getting hurt."

"*Another*. What do you mean?"

"I've no doubt the disgraceful way he behaved towards Sarah Kingsley resulted in her death — just a few months after that of her brother. And Sebastian Russell had a big hand to play in both events."

"Really, Mr Quincey, you shock me."

"Good. Because someone has to warn

you about the man."

Rosie Kelly's gorgeous eyes were somber as she regarded him over her drink. Her shoulders rose, as if she had come to a decision, and she half-rose from her chair. "I really had better get going."

Edmund Quincey rose with her and saw Mrs Studebaker being escorted back by her waltz partner. Her step was light, her arms swung freely at her sides, her shoulders relaxed, as she moved towards him. At least Mrs Studebaker was having a good night. Over her shoulder he saw the tall figure of Sebastian Russell making his way towards the Irish singer.

"Your ride has arrived, I see," he called after her. "Remember what I said, Miss Kelly. You've had fair warning."

She flicked an uncertain glance back at him and he watched as she walked out, trailed by Sebastian Russell.

*Nothing like mounting an offensive in anticipation of attack.*

He wheeled and braced himself to welcome back a lucent Mrs Studebaker.

*She already looks like she's fallen half in love with me.*

He ushered her back to her seat with a light proprietorial touch to her elbow as she sank down gratefully and took the drink he offered.

*I don't need Sebastian Russell queering my pitch, that's for sure. Another disaster like the Delia fiasco would sink me, plain and simple.*

# Fourteen

"I'm done for, mon cher. Done for."

Charles Durant groaned and lifted an arm to his bandaged eyes. "Even if I survive this, I will never work again. And how can a man live if he can't work?" He spoke in a raspy whisper, the words coming in laborious bursts with long pauses between each phrase.

Alex leaned into his bedside. "Don't talk, Mr Durant. You'll tire yourself out. I just wanted to come and see what you needed. How I could help."

"You've already been wonderful, son. The food you brought, paying for the doctor, arranging the nurse to feed me and change my dressings. Merci beaucoup, is all I can say."

Durant's simply furnished room in Mrs O'Donnell's boarding house was hot and stuffy at the fag end of a long, dusty day. Wisps of goose down from a tear in the bedcover danced in the rays that slanted low through a window at the back of the house. The only noise was the squeak of the tap handle as the housemaid pumped water for the kitchen from the barrel in the yard below.

The fresh bandages the nurse would apply before bedtime sat soaking in a bowl on the small bedside table. The room smelt of brandy and the syrupy fragrance of honey, which had been applied directly onto his face and arms as a natural antiseptic. Underlying the brandy and honey was the faint, familiar tang of eucalyptus, common anywhere laudanum was administered. Durant was given a top-up dose every few hours to ease the pain. The benefit of him not having had a recent dose was that he could speak and think clearly, but his pinched drawn lips told Alex that the pain levels had risen to a point where another dose — with its accompanying hallucinations — would be needed soon.

The room, just big enough for a single bed, a chair and a bedside table, was plainly used only for sleeping. The rest of Durant's life played out in his studio, in the various bars where he drank with friends and in the communal dining room downstairs where Mrs O'Donnell's household shared Irish stews and pies around an old wooden table.

"Have the police been?" Alex winced at the abruptness of the question. He didn't want to cause Durant anxiety, but he wanted to know how far the inquiry had progressed.

"A young constable came, but they won't do anything, mon cher. They can't. Those men are probably already long gone. And no one except us saw them."

"I saw them. I could give them a description."

After a long silence Durant shook his head. "It won't do any good."

"I will see your studio rent is paid, Mr Durant. It will be waiting for you when you return. Don't worry."

Another long silence. "They came for me. Deliberately. I saw it in his eyes."

"What do you mean? They were just thugs off the street."

Durant moved gingerly under the sheets, trying to ease the pressure on his bruised back and shoulder. "They were thugs all right. But they were on a mission. They'd been sent."

Alex squeezed his eyes tightly shut and shook his head to dislodge the image of the big man striking Charles and dragging him, dashing the poisonous silver nitrate in his face.

"They wanted to finish me, and they've succeeded."

"No. No! Don't say that!"

"Promise me you'll look after the daguerreotypes. Promise."

"The images? Of course."

Alex had told him of rescuing them. He didn't want Charles to think he'd stolen them.

"Those photographs are special. Try and find who took them, who those children are."

Durant gave a long low moan and gritted his jaw. As if she'd been awaiting a signal, Mrs Whitney, the stout, middle-aged nurse he'd engaged, bustled into the room after a cursory knock. She nodded at Alex. "Time to go, I'm afraid. It's time for his next laudanum, Mr de Vile. He'll be dopey for the rest of the night. You'd better say goodnight till the morning."

Alex stood slowly and reached over to gently take the hand that was closest to him. "Promise me you'll do all you can to get well again, Charles" he whispered. "And I'll take care of your photographs for you."

# Fifteen

"Thank you so much for showing me home, Mr Russell. I do appreciate it."

Rosie Kelly looked at him with her sharp green eyes that missed very little, as they halted at the main entrance to the Ebner and gave him a fleeting smile. "I'm especially grateful to be sprung from Corporal Quincey's paws." She slid a sly little glance at him from under her long black eyelashes. "He doesn't like you very much, does he?"

Sebastian shrugged as if it were neither here nor there to him what Edmund Quincey thought.

She pierced him with a shrewd stare. "Something seems to have created bad blood there, that's for sure."

Pedestrian traffic in the few blocks they'd walked from the fundraiser to the hotel had been limited to a few carousing clerks and tradesmen weaving their way home from a night's drinking to sleep before another working day tomorrow. They had fallen into a relaxed side-by-side step, savoring the fresh night air, observing the sights, neither of them feeling the need to talk. Well, not quite true, he admitted. From the moment he'd laid eyes on Edmund Quincey leering over Rosie, alarm bells had sounded. He was itching to know why Quincey felt the need to attend a local fundraising event, but he wasn't going to admit his curiosity to Miss Kelly.

She started up the stairs to Basil's suite where they were all still staying, and he followed behind, giving her plenty of space. When she reached the doorway of their suite she halted. "I'd be careful around Corporal Quincey if I were you, Mr Russell. I wouldn't like to see your reputation mauled."

He opened the door for her, and she preceded him into the open living area, where Isabella sat quietly reading by lamplight at the dining table. "Rosie!" she said. "I couldn't sleep and of course I can't really go out. Come and sit and tell me all about it before you go to bed. Sorry if you want to sleep, but you must humor me first." She gave her friend a flickering smile and patted the seat next to her. "Did you have fun?"

"Yes, it was all fine. I was very glad to see Mr Russell, though. I was quite ready to come home when he arrived to chaperone me." She gave Sebastian another quick smile, dipping her head.

"He saved me from the clutches of Corporal Quincey."

"Quincey? What was he doing there?"

"Apparently he's very thick with the widow Studebaker — she's one of town's richest women, if you didn't know. Pretty well glued to her side all night. And the only time she wasn't present — when one of the bigwigs insisted on dancing a waltz with her — Quincey made a beeline for me. Funnily enough, he seemed to want to talk more about Sebastian than me. Crushing for a girl's pride." She shot a wry smile at Isabella, who was gazing at her open-mouthed. "Just kidding."

"Sit down for a minute, Sebastian, and tell us how you've managed to upset Mr Quincey so. I thought you hadn't seen him in years." Isabella's tone was playful as she pointed to the chair opposite her on the other side of the table. "Hot chocolate before bedtime, anyone? I'll order some in." She crossed to the doorway and hauled on a bell pull to summon the night manager.

Sebastian grasped the back of the chair but didn't sit. "I'm pretty tired. All I'm good for is a long sleep." He squinted an apology as she returned to her seat.

"Nonsense! Please stay. We haven't seen you all day and I'm getting cabin fever."

After another few seconds of further resistance he sat down. "There's really not much to tell, and I'm not sure why he'd be taking after me. He came out ahead last time we wrangled." He shrugged. "I found he couldn't be trusted. He's the sort of fellow who looks after himself, first and foremost. Sounds like he's lost one heiress wife and he's looking for a replacement." He drummed his fingers on the table in a restless tattoo. "I'd think Mrs Studebaker is the one who needs the warning."

They were interrupted by the night manager, who took Isabella's order and whisked out.

"Do you mind me asking, what kind of thing did he do?" Isabella peered across the table with wide, alert eyes. "To you, I mean."

*How do I get out of this? The last thing I want to talk about.*

"Well, on the battlefield he got us into an awful mess — left us dangerously exposed on one flank and men died. Valuable men. I know it happens all the time, but I did wonder if there was something extra going on — if he was playing a deeper game than we knew."

The two young women gazed at him in enthralled silence. "Like what?" Isabella asked.

"Like him talking in places he shouldn't and tipping off the other side. Maybe even getting paid for it. Nothing you'd ever be able to prove."

The night manager returned with three steaming hot chocolates, and the smell of cinnamon and cocoa filled the air.

"And then he was less than honorable in the way he treated a young woman who came to nurse her brother when he was sick with typhoid fever. Treated her very poorly."

Rosie cleared her throat. "Strange that you should say that, Mr Russell. He seemed to hint something similar about you. And, of course, I told him he must be mistaken."

Sebastian sipped the hot liquid in silence. He'd forgotten how comforting hot chocolate could be. "As I say, things were in an awful mess at one stage. Perhaps none of us behaved at our best, and maybe we all have regrets about what happened."

He ran his fingers back through his hair, combing it off his temples, relieving some of the pent-up pressure in his head. "There were some things that happened then that I never really properly understood. They're a mystery to this day — but you can't keep looking backwards, can you?"

He glanced up from his cup and caught and held Rosie's gaze. "So what unprincipled action does Mr Quincey accuse me of?" He forced himself to sound light and jocular, but his stomach felt as though he'd swallowed lead.

Her cheeks reddened and her eyes flickered to Isabella. "Forgive me — I appreciate it's a private matter — but he hinted you'd been in competition for a young woman's attention. He accused you of being a bad loser." Her face screwed into an apologetic grimace. "I'm sorry, but you did ask."

Uninvited, the image of Sarah's stiffened body, the front of her dress soaked in blood from a self-inflicted wound, rose in his mind. The tell-tale weapon — her dead brother's pocket revolver — lay under her hand. Her sweet pale face was splattered with blood spray, but otherwise she looked as lovely, as at peace, in death as she had in life. He had never fully understood what had driven her to such a desperate act. Sheer grief, he had always supposed. But if Edmund Quincey Jnr was spreading tall tales, maybe there was more to it.

He would hate to see Caroline Studebaker end the same way.

# Sixteen

The smell of the slaughterhouse hit the back of his throat with such force it was all Sebastian could do not to gag. He was standing outside a rambling, dilapidated dwelling — it could barely be called a house — set in the midst of the railroad workshops, tanneries, opium dens, the gambling stews and brothels of Lower I Street. So this was the shore on which his old Civil War buddy Burton Purdy, one of the wiliest company quartermasters he'd ever known, had washed up.

His heart lurched as he contemplated his surroundings. The ramshackle building where he'd been told Burton lived with his family was a rabbit warren of dereliction. The eastern end sagged several feet below the western, as if its foundations were sinking into the muddy shores of China Slough, a stretch of water notorious for its foulness, which it abutted.

He couldn't imagine the cheerful efficient country boy he'd known at the start of the war ending up buried here, in the city's most noxious human waste and noisome activity. But the man he'd bidden farewell at the war's end? Burton's job required him to defend the company wagons and supplies, not engage in combat, so he had been spared some of the war's most terrifying encounters. He was one of the unit's most popular men, nicknamed 'Buffalo' for his talent for producing practically anything the men needed: food, weapons, clothing, tents and blankets for shelter. He was as versatile in what he could produce as the great beast of the plains, and with a chest and shoulders like one too.

That was before his luck ran out and he, like the rest of them, was dangled over hell. Captured by the Rebels in a freak ambush, he'd come close to starving to death as a prisoner of war, who had watched men die daily around him. When he was exchanged and returned to their unit nine months later, he was a changed man: withdrawn, distracted, given to infrequent manic outbursts where he was convinced the Confederates were coming for him again, quite unable to resume his quartermaster role. Sebastian had always hoped a return to civilian life would allow him to recover full health, but it seemed that had been a wishful fantasy. If Burton Purdy was living here, he was destitute, and more likely than not 'dying from nostalgia'. That was what the doctors called it when a man couldn't shake off his war time trauma.

Sebastian pulled a handkerchief out and blew his nose into it, trying to clear the cloying odor from his nasal passages, but as soon as he breathed in again, it was back. He hoped Burton Purdy was still living here, and that he was straight enough in the head to talk sense. His encounter with Edmund Quincey Jnr — and particularly the disquieting news that he was stalking Caroline Studebaker's fortune — had galvanized him. He had to know the facts: he couldn't let the past just lie there unexamined. He hadn't had the heart for it four years ago, he'd wanted to get as far away from the army as he could, but now it seemed imperative to dig into what had gone on in those final months.

Had Quincey been culpable in Robert's death? And why was Sarah so distraught as to take her own life? A sharp heart pain scythed his chest, so piercing he grabbed at his shirt front and hunched over to catch his breath. He felt the perspiration, cold and clammy around his collar, dripping down his back. He had avoided this topic for so long because it was so painful.

A stout woman with a milk-and-molasses complexion responded to his knock and looked him up and down suspiciously. "Don't tell me it's another Greek bearing gifts come a-knocking." She thrust her hands on her hips and scowled.

"Goodness, I hope not." Sebastian

looked behind him, as if scanning the street for another visitor. "I don't know anything about Greeks. I'm looking for Burton Purdy. Sebastian Russell is the name. I knew Buffalo in the Massachusetts Volunteers. Is he at home?"

"And why would you be asking?" She challenged him with a look he couldn't quite interpret, somewhere between distrust and curiosity.

"I just wanted to catch up with him. See how he's going. Talk about old times." He pulled at his right ear, uncertain how to continue under her withering gaze. "I know, I know. I'm not one for old times, and I'm betting Buffalo isn't either. But there's a situation that's come up. I wanted to check back with him on something very specific that happened when we were together. Ask his opinion."

"Mr Russell, I'm afraid Mr Purdy is way beyond 'talking about old times' as you put it. Has been for a long time now." She hesitated. "It's just mighty strange that you're not the first old-timer who's come a-looking for him recently. Has everyone caught the same disease?"

He shifted his feet on her doorstep, unsure how to answer. "Not the first? Oh, now I understand the 'Greeks bearing gifts'. Well, I'm afraid for better or worse, I'm not about to give you anything." He glanced around. Apart from a couple of painted women loitering outside the rundown premises opposite, the street was empty. He still had no clue if Burton was inside the house or out somewhere. "Look, could I possibly come inside for a few minutes … Mrs Purdy, is it? It won't take long, I promise."

She reluctantly stepped aside and he followed her into a room which was spic and span but, apart from a table and a couple of chairs, bare of any home comforts.

She sat on one of the chairs and gestured to him to take the other. "Mr Purdy has good days and bad days, but I'm afraid more bad than good — and today is a bad one." She flicked her eyes to the narrow stairwell. "He's resting. I don't think you'll get any sense out of him — but you've got an honest face. You're welcome to try."

Sebastian's face warmed with a pulsing sense of gratitude. "Mrs Purdy, you mentioned other visitors. Can you tell me who they were, and what they wanted?"

"One of them was a fellow with a limp and a walking stick. Old coot. Came around waving around an envelope of money for Mrs Polk. A pension payment for Polk that had been mislaid, he said. Yes, and if my aunt had been my uncle, she'd have been a man."

"Polk? Did you say Polk?" Sebastian's core had turned to ice. "The man who shot the lady at the Sacramento Theater a week ago? That Polk?"

"The same." She regarded him with wide, curious eyes. "Why?"

"Mrs Purdy you have no idea. Let me just say it's an extraordinary coincidence we've got here — and like you, I don't believe too much in coincidence. I don't want to rush you, but could I try my luck with your husband?"

Burton lay propped up on pillows in a narrow bed in a tiny room halfway up the stairs. His eyes were closed but Sebastian sensed he wasn't asleep and had probably heard every word that had been said below. Sebastian squatted on a hard wooden stool by the bedside and spoke softly. "Buffalo, it's Tiger from the 22nd. Can you talk?"

Burton's eyes flickered open. His ice blue irises looked milky and confused, and then Sebastian saw that he recognized him and terror replaced the confusion.

He looked wildly around the room, which was hardly bigger than a large wardrobe, and jerked up on the pillows. "No! No, I don't know anything. Nothing. If I say anything they'll come!"

"Who will come?" Sebastian's voice was level and soothing. He took Burton's hand and stroked it consolingly, as if settling a cat.

The fear was replaced by a flash of the old Burton's wiliness. Sebastian was certain in that moment that he might play at suffering from 'mental anxiety' — another term they gave to old veterans who acted crazy, along with 'irritable heart' — but he still had a clear understanding of what was going on around him.

"No need to be afraid. The war's been over a long time."

Burton relaxed and a brief smile washed across his face and vanished like the sun behind cloud. "Yes, Tiger. A long time. But there are still villains. Still villains ..."

The flash of awareness faded as quickly as it came, and Burton appeared to be back in his own world. His eyes were vacant and glassy.

"Burton, do you remember Corporal Quincey? Edmund Quincey? You haven't seen him lately, have you?"

Burton's hand in Seb's own stiffened, and he wrenched it away so violently he was in danger of slipping off the bed altogether.

Seb watched with narrowed eyes. "You *have* seen him. Did he come here looking for you? What did he want?"

Burton was rolling his head from one side to the other and keening, "No, no, no! No, no, no!"

Seb sensed he was frightened out of his wits. "What's wrong, Buffalo? You don't need to be afraid—"

"Noooooo!" The cry was long and anguished, and Seb recognized he wasn't going to get anything else out of Burton Purdy today.

He soothed him as best he could, backing off, stroking his forehead, whispering reassurances. "It's fine, Burton, you don't need to say anything.

It's all fine," until he settled back into his pillows again.

Sebastian backed down the stairs and met Mrs Purdy at the bottom, her face stern. "I told you he was having a bad day."

He ushered her to the front door step where Burton was not likely to overhear. "You mentioned more than one visitor had been here recently. The man with the walking stick for Polk, right? Did Polk live near here?"

Mrs Purdy nodded. "Just a couple of houses down. I look after Mrs Polk's two boys quite often — she's not particularly well herself — and now her husband's gone, even with the windfall she got she's finding it tough."

"And this windfall, Mrs Purdy. What do you make of that?"

"I don't want to talk about it." She

shrugged. "I don't want any trouble."

"Strictly for my information only. I won't repeat it to anyone."

She stared at him, her face drawn and lined. She'd been a very beautiful woman when she was younger, he could see, but the years of poverty had ground her down. Her dark hair hung dully around her face, and she was missing a tooth in her lower jaw.

She looked around nervously, checking no one could overhear, and then said in a low steady voice: "I think Polk was paid to do that job. He wasn't so wrong in the upper story that he didn't know what he was doing. He knew darn well. The one thing that sent him barmy-brained was not being able to care for his family. That upset him the most — not being able to care for them. So he found a way to do it, didn't he?

Cost him his life, but he did it."

Her voice cracked slightly, and the staunch brawny woman who had met him with her dander up had mellowed to a sad, tired matron battling to survive.

"And this man Edmund Quincey, he was our commanding officer at one time. Burton has certainly seen him recently. It was obvious from his reaction. Did you see him when he came?"

Her *café au lait* skin paled a degree and she shook her head in denial a little too vehemently.

*She's lying about that too. Both of them are frightened out of their wits.*

Sebastian's heart swelled in his chest, and a wave of sadness swept over him. Two women, two families, like many thousands of others across the land, who'd waited and prayed for their loved ones to come home from war, only to have the ashes of their lives trickle through empty hands when they did. Desperation drove a disturbed soul like Polk, but someone or something much more purposeful and sinister had plotted his path.

Edmund Quincey could wait, but the old coot with the limp had a lot of questions to answer.

# Seventeen

Isabella threw back her head and gazed at the smooth green curve of the racetrack ahead, exulting at the wind in her face and the sway of the horse under her haunches. For the first time in days she had escaped the suffocating confines of the hotel to fill her lungs with fresh air. She was gloriously alone, if you didn't count Louisiana Race Course grooms and stable hands going about their early morning duties. The stands at the Whiskey Hill track — so named because of the presence of two nearby saloons — were empty at this early hour. All she could hear was an ear-hissing breeze, carrying the clean spicy fragrance of recently planted eucalyptus trees on its dewy moistness.

Her mount, a pretty chestnut mare, seemed as keen as she was to stretch her legs, and as she bent low over the strong brown neck and urged the horse forward she could imagine she was flying. The social rituals of mourning, with their expectation that women should withdraw from all normal activity, gave her one long headache. She revered Alycia, she really did, but she couldn't fathom why it was deemed appropriate for women to seclude themselves from daily life, while men were free to continue as normal. She was just relieved she could fulfil the niceties of grief in a couple of weeks, not have to endure months of it. As she rounded the bend and headed back towards the clubhouse, she reached out and stroked the mare's neck, laughing with the sheer joy of freedom.

The Louisiana Course was one of Sacramento's most popular venues, regularly drawing visitors from as far away as San Francisco with its one-dollar entry fee to all parts of the track to see both thoroughbred racing and trotting. The manager, Mr Ellis, engaged in all sorts of harmless mischief to draw a crowd — and his 'Ladies Mornings' where women could hire a mount and enjoy the ride was one of his initiatives which disgusted critics as 'tomfoolery'. She for one was thrilled at his flair for publicity. She relished the chance to get back on a horse, and it had been simple to organize the early-morning expedition through the manager, Ned.

As she rounded the bend and came abreast the stables, the groom who had saddled her up stepped forward and raised his arm questioningly. She slowed and called, "A few more rounds, Charlie. I'm having too much fun to stop yet." She dug her heels into the mare's sides and raced on, the soothing cadence of the horse's hooves filling her with a deep sense of well-being.

*Wonder if they let men ride on Ladies Mornings.*

She surprised herself with the thought.

*Because if I had my choice I'd like to go riding with Sebastian Russell sometime …*

She was shocked with herself. What was she thinking? She'd had to sneak out of the Ebner Suite without waking Russell because she anticipated he'd object to her plans and she wanted to avoid an argument. She was sure he'd have his reasons — her safety, or social propriety or something. For a guy who came dangerously close to having a twinkle in his eye sometimes he could get all clammed up. So why on earth did she desire him as a riding companion?

She thought back to the previous night and the gossip Edmund Quincey had dished up.

If she had to choose between the two, Sebastian would win hands down in any race for the Integrity Cup. Quincey had a slick sleaziness which turned her stomach. Just looking at the man made her feel queasy. Whereas Sebastian ...

She felt the chestnut tense up, her sides quiver, and her eyes snapped up to take in the track ahead, all senses on full alert. Something had disturbed the horse, but what was it?

Her saddle lurched with the mare's

stride, suddenly not as secure as when she'd started.

*Don't tell me Charlie didn't fix the girth strap properly!*

She flicked her gaze from the course to the horse, reaching as far as she could around the animal's barrel to feel for the strap.

There it was, just out of reach. The edges of the girth strap were frayed. Maybe about to give out altogether.

She clicked her gaze forward again, pulling gently on the reins to bring the animal to a halt before the saddle strap gave way entirely. But the horse, that just a few minutes before had been docile and responsive, wasn't taking any notice. She sensed its hind end tensing and beginning to gather. It plunged on, head low, increasing speed with each stride.

Normally she'd stand on her stirrups

to regain control, but with the fragile girth strap she couldn't risk putting on the extra weight that would certainly snap it altogether. She hugged the horse with her knees as tightly as she could and slightly increased the pressure on one rein to encourage the horse to turn — one way of stopping a bolting horse.

The mare pounded on, flecks of foam whipping back from its mouth as its agitation increased. It was ignoring her commands and veering off the trail they'd previously covered into a narrowing aisle that ran from the racing track to the trotting arena. Everything around her took on an acute edge: the crystal-clear slant of the sun's rays through the picket fence that lined the alleyway, striping the ground in light and dark; the thunder of hooves in her ears and the dull taste of dust in her mouth;

the flash of something stretched across the track in front of them as the light momentarily caught it.

*The flash of something in front ...*

The mare breached the wire at the same moment as Isabella felt the girth strap finally wrench apart and she was in the air, truly flying now, towards the sharp points on the paling fence. In the split second that she was airborne she remembered that she still had the reins in one hand. She hauled herself back, tethering herself to the mare's side, waiting for the split second when it would grind to a stop in the dirt, front legs desperately clawing to gain traction as she went down.

In that moment she launched herself free and rolled clear as a thousand pounds of horseflesh came to a juddering halt. Her shoulder hit the paling with a crack that shook her every tooth. She lay in the dirt panting, shock waves of pain reverberating up her spine. The valiant mare struggled to raise her head, eyes rolling wildly. Her sides heaved with great panting breaths. Foaming lips turned back to reveal the gaping black interior of her mouth.

Then her head dropped, the heaving rib cage stilled, and the mare fell silent. Isabella shuffled forward on her behind and collapsed on the still-warm neck, burying her nose in the mane that carried that inimitable smell of horse sweat. She circled the glossy red-brown coat with her arms and the tears flooded her face. She was crying for Alycia, for mad Polk, for Sebastian, as well as for a blameless animal she'd known for less than an hour who'd died because she was unlucky enough to have Isabella on her back.

She gave way to her grief and wept. When she finally raised her head, one thought was buzzing on the edges of her brain:

*Sebastian will be furious.*

It shot through her with a rushing awareness and pushed everything else aside.

*Perhaps I don't need to tell him …*

She closed her eyes and surrendered to the dizzy emptiness that engulfed her, and felt the pain no more.

# Eighteen

Seb had to trawl a lot of bars before he found someone who could tell him where he'd be likely to find Hiram Williams, so it was late morning by the time he tracked the old snoop down to the Second Street Eureka Bathhouse, where he located him trapped in a barber's chair, a towel hung around his shoulders. The barber had just finished giving him a shave and his cheeks shone with newly washed pinkness.

"I'm in no position to talk to you, Mr Russell," Williams protested as the barber clipped away at the back of his neck. "Can't you see I'm busy?" The barber's shop was next door to the baths entry, and the perfume of toilet soaps and hair shampoo hung in the steamy warm air.

"No problem. I can wait." Seb dragged a stool from the shop waiting area and perched on it expectantly. "Having a bit of a clean-up, are you? I could do with a bath myself." He studied his fingernails and leaned back against the wall, looking for all the world as if he could sit there all day. "Might do the same myself later — after we've talked."

The sturdy Eureka building was a solid brick construction which housed public baths for men and women, as well as a dozen other rooms with private pools and other services. Barbers, ladies' hairdressers, laundry workers, and a few fortunate lodgers filled the place with a productive hum of activity. A helpful landlady had confirmed that Hiram was a guest and volunteered that he was taking advantage of the closeness of the facilities, but Hiram was far from pleased to see Seb. He shifted uneasily in the barber's chair, earning a rebuke from the barber. "Oi, keep still or I'll nip your neck."

Hiram froze momentarily, and then glanced at Sebastian. "I told you—"

"You can't talk. I know. And I told you I'm happy to wait. I figure Mrs Stockton paid you well for the months of work you did on her behalf. She deserves a full report of how you spent your time on that search, even if she isn't here to view it."

Hiram paled and his eyes darted past Sebastian's shoulder, as if looking for a way to escape.

"Can't see how there's anything sensitive about it. I mean, any information you got — whatever it was — must be at least fifteen years old, maybe older, surely."

Hiram rolled his eyes. "Easy for you to say. You wouldn't know."

"No? Well, I'm waiting for you to tell me. You won't be getting paid your final account if you don't make that report. With Mrs Stockton gone I can't even vouch that you've done the work, can I, so how can I justify paying you?"

The old man sighed in resignation. "All right. But as I told that other lass, it don't amount to a hill of beans."

Over the next ten minutes he outlined for Sebastian where his inquiries had taken him, and they were mainly to dead ends. "Miss Wilmington told me about the connection between her mother Huldah Wilmington — well, as it turns out, her adopted mother — and Mrs

Wilmington's sister, that hag who ran the hotel. Madam Ring was it? How the Madam was there the night the kid's mother was killed and all. And how she brought Isabella to her, asking for payment and claiming she was an orphan. But she's dead now too, ain't she, and Mrs Wilmington says she never breathed a word about where that girl came from. Nor did she ever mention a brother. Just told her lies. So that went nowhere.

"The coach driver that night? Well, he died in a hold-up a few months later, didn't he, and I couldn't find any of the other passengers. There weren't many, so that's not too surprising. It's plain the Madam probably took both kids, but what she did with the other one, who knows? She's gone to her grave with the secret."

The barber was finishing up. He whisked away the towel and brushed around Williams' collar with a sable-hair brush. Hiram stood up with more than his usual enthusiasm.

"I think we already knew most — all — of that information, Mr Williams."

"I know you did." Hiram paid the barber, grabbed his walking cane and turned to leave the shop.

"So I don't think I'm quite finished with my questions yet," said Seb. "How about I take you for a coffee and we continue our chat a little longer."

Hiram's steps slowed and his mouth turned down, but his shoulders had a resigned slump. "I guess I don't have much choice."

They slipped a couple of doors down the street to the popular Second Street Coffee House, slid into a window table with bench seats, and ordered coffee. After the waitress withdrew, Sebastian leaned over Hiram and fixed him with a steely eye, though his voice was deceptively quiet. "So you drew a blank on the missing boy — on Isabella Wilmington's twin." He pulled back, increasing the distance between them, but not taking his eyes off Hiram's weathered face. "But how about Mr Polk? What were your dealings with him? How did you come to be mixed up with him?"

His fresh-from-the-barber's complexion turned a ghostly white, and Hiram exploded into a coughing fit, gagging with a mouth full of hot coffee. "P-Polk? What do you mean, Polk? I–I've never heard of him." Hiram Williams was gasping and stammering and from the deathly pale of a few minutes ago, his face was flushing red.

"Come, Mr Williams, you know that's a lie. Everyone has heard of Polk. Polk who gunned down Mrs Stockton. Remember? But that isn't the only place you know Polk from, is it?"

Sebastian drew his deputy's badge from his jacket breast pocket and placed it on the table between their two cups. "You may not be aware of it, Mr Williams, but I'm a temporary sworn deputy in Nevada County — with rights recognized here in Sacramento." His voice was biting now. "If I chose to, I could arrest you right here and now."

Hiram rose up from his seat in protest, his arms braced on the table. "Arrest me? What for?" His voice was high and squeaky, his forehead shining with sweat. "I ain't done anything!"

"No? Then on whose behalf were you delivering money to Polk's widow —

large sums of money by all accounts —
just a few days ago? Virtually the day
after Mrs Stockton was shot. There's an
old lawman's saying, 'Never believe in
coincidence'."

Hiram's tongue hung out between
brown decaying teeth, and he collapsed
back down on the hard wooden seat into
another paroxysm of coughing. "I don't
know … It was just some pension …" The
words came out in barely intelligible
snatches between his explosive coughs.

Sebastian fiddled with the deputy's
star on the table between them and eyed
him coldly. "You're giving me no option
but to arrest—"

"No!" Williams had aged ten years in
the last few minutes. "No! An old codger
like me, I'd never survive jail …" He
trailed off in a plaintive wail.

"Then perhaps you'd better remember

fast. Who did that money you delivered come from, and what did Polk do to earn it?"

Hiram Williams stared at Seb across the table, his mouth moving, but no words leaving it. Then he suddenly clutched at his throat with both hands. "I … I'm … can't breathe …"

He crumpled onto the table, senseless.

# Nineteen

Sebastian had just relaxed into an armchair at the Ebner when an urgent rapping at the door interrupted his heavy-hearted musings. "Mr Russell! Mr Russell!" Hotel manager Ned Castleton's normally genial baritone had an agitated edge. "Miss Isabella's had a mishap. She's on her way back to the hotel now."

Sebastian leapt up and wrenched the door open. "Mishap? What's wrong?"

Ned's mouth screwed up in dismay. "She went riding this morning and I believe she's had a fall."

"Riding? What possessed her to—"

He was interrupted by Isabella's arrival at the top of the stairs in a wheeled bath chair held up either side by two sturdy barmen. They set her down with a light thump, and she pitched forward, restraining herself on the chair's arms as she came to rest. The front of her pale-apricot riding habit was smudged with dirt stains; one sleeve hung from the shoulder seam in shreds, exposing a raw pebble graze on her upper arm that carried on as an angry red stripe down the side of her face.

"Isabella!" He was so shocked at the state she was in he was momentarily speechless.

She went to raise her arm in greeting, winced at an obvious pain, and gave him a quick wan smile. "No need for alarm, Sebastian. Nothing broken. Just a few bumps." She began to propel herself gingerly down the hall. "I've been very lucky."

Rosie Kelly trailed behind her carrying a riding hat and gloves, her eyes downcast, unusually subdued.

Sebastian's eyes flicked to Rosie, but before he could comment Isabella said, "Rosie had nothing to do with it. I went out without her. She's been good enough to come and help get me back when I sent word about what had happened."

Sebastian thanked the men who had helped get her upstairs, ordered coffee and scones from Ned, and then took command of the chair and pushed her into the suite. He set her facing the chair he'd vacated and slumped back down into it with a huge sigh. "I'm not sure if I'm madder than an old wet hen that you went riding, or if I'm heaving a sigh of relief that you made it back alive." He wiped his forearm across his forehead, sweeping sweaty hair out of his eyes. "If

you're up to it, tell me what happened."
His voice carried a resigned tone. "And
don't miss anything out."

She gazed back at him, her stormy
eyes darkening, the light in them focused
far away, the curve of her lips set in a
pensive line. Apart from the ugly graze,
her skin was translucent, and it occurred
to him she might well be in shock, even
mildly concussed. A twig stuck out from
a tangle at the top of her head,
highlighting her feminine vulnerability.
He felt a warm surge in his chest — was
it his protective instincts coming to the
fore? — and in that instant he said a
silent thank you to a deity he wasn't at
all sure he believed in that she was still
alive.

"Take your time, Isabella. You must
still be in shock." He spoke slow and low,
hoping she would catch the gentle

reassurance he was willing her way.

She sat up and hesitantly set upon her story, prefacing some sentences with an uncertain "I can't quite remember ..." or a diffident "I think ..." and only becoming animated when recalling her joy at escaping into the fresh morning air. The arrival of the coffee and scones temporarily interrupted her account, but she resumed as soon as they were all nursing their warmed cups and picking at the hot scones decked in strawberry jam. She ended up with the finale — how the saddle girth strap came loose, rattling the mare who stumbled, throwing her against the fence. When she finished she lapsed back into the dreamy stare.

*She's showing every sign of mild shock by disassociating from her immediate surroundings.*

Seb glanced across at Rosie, who sat

next to Isabella. She hadn't uttered a peep since they'd come in. "And you, Miss Kelly. Where were you when all this was unfolding?"

"Back here, Mr Russell. Still asleep. I had no idea." She flicked a glance at Isabella, who seemed to be ignoring her. "But when Ned raised the alarm and said word had been sent from the course that Isabella had fallen off a horse, I went with two of the men from the hotel to bring her home." She glanced at Isabella, her characteristic gaiety wholly missing.

Sebastian saw an uncertain frown flash across her bright eyes, and a second later he intercepted Isabella's warning glare in response, so fleeting he would probably have missed it if it weren't for Rosie's startled eyes widening. The dreamer had suddenly switched to high alert and was warning her friend off telling him something.

He marveled at her spirit despite his irritation and felt the thudding of his heart all over again. However annoying Isabella might be, he wasn't going to ignore the danger she was in. There would not be a repeat of Alycia's tragic death.

He stood to pour himself a second coffee and grinned at Rosie. "I think we've been spending enough time together for you to drop the 'Mr Russell', Miss Kelly. Sebastian or Seb will do just fine. I don't like being reminded I'm getting a little long in the tooth. It's not all that long ago that I was your age."

She dipped her head and a smile lit up her face. "Sure thing, Sebastian. And the same applies, of course. Rosie or Rose works just fine." She pushed back in her chair and relaxed into it, releasing tiny puffs of breath as she did.

"And what is it that Isabella doesn't want you to tell me, Rosie?" He phrased the question in bland, casual tones, and she jolted in her chair and her head whipped across to Isabella, seeking desperate guidance. Isabella ignored her.

Rosie searched his eyes, shuffled in her chair and settled again, as if she'd made a decision. She again glanced nervously across to Isabella, and he sensed Isabella was not going to be pleased with what was coming next. "Isabella hasn't mentioned it yet, maybe she doesn't intend to, but she doesn't think it was an accident out there today. Someone tampered with the girth strap. It was so cut and frayed it's a wonder it lasted as long as it did — yet all the other tackle was in mint condition." She licked her lips and took another sip of now cold coffee. Sebastian saw Isabella's hands clench along the willow weave sides of her chair, her lips set in a tight closed line.

"And that's not all." Rosie's voice was growing stronger, more confident, as she gathered momentum. "Isabella is certain there was a wire stretched across the track to bring the mare down. She saw it glinting in the sunlight seconds before the horse fell. When she came round it was no longer in evidence and the track hands denied ever seeing it." She turned to her friend, appealing: "He had to know, Izzy. It's silly not to tell him everything. Who knows what's going on? It might be the same people who killed Alycia."

Isabella screwed her eyes tight and buried her face in her hands. When she looked back up she fixed her gaze on Sebastian. "I don't want to be a prisoner dragging myself around in this hotel, comfortable as it is. I don't mean to appear ungrateful, but it's getting me down. That's why I wanted to go riding. And now I suppose it will be twice as bad!" She combed her hand through her hair in choppy distracted movements. "Sorry to complain. We're incredibly lucky to have you here to support us. Goodness knows what I'd be doing if you weren't here. I just wanted to avoid more drama."

Her eyes brimmed. "I know I was the one insisting a few nights ago that Alycia's death might be linked somehow to my twin, but now that it seems more likely, I can't make head or tail of it. Why on earth would anyone want to harm me? I don't know a thing about my brother.

I'm no closer to finding him than I was six months ago!" She pinched the bridge of her nose, as if trying to bring her rising emotions under control.

Sebastian regarded her, his own heart overflowing with sadness. He would do anything to protect this young woman from attack and to help her find her brother. A few days ago he'd been consumed with one thought — his own survival. He had been living a life of 'me and no other'. Then Alycia had died, and he'd reluctantly agreed to Basil's entreaties to find the truth behind her death, still resisting the idea of pursuing the quest to find Alex. But Hiram Williams' agitated response earlier in the day was all the confirmation he needed.

*Something deep and dirty is in motion, and anyone perceived to be in its path is at risk.*

If there was any doubt that Alycia's death was planned, and not the random act of an emotionally wrecked veteran, it had been dispelled with Hiram's panicked reaction. And now the attack on Isabella — well, he still had to confirm things had happened as Rosie had indicated, but accepting the possibility and even likelihood, the need for urgency lifted to a whole new level.

"You and me both, Isabella," he said. "Don't be crestfallen. I think we might be a lot closer to discovering what's going on than someone wants. That's why you were attacked today. We just don't know yet what we know." He shrugged. "Does that make sense?"

Isabella had straightened herself in her chair and was viewing him with the stubborn, penetrating intelligence that was so much a part of her identity. She flashed him a brief smile. "I like it, Sebastian." She put an index finger in the air, and gestured, as if marking up a point on a scoreboard. "'We just don't know yet what we know.'" She enunciated each word carefully. "Let me ponder that statement until morning and see if I get a clue to what it really means."

She raised one eyebrow and gave him a dazzling grin. It had been years since he'd had anything other than perfunctory conversations with the fairer sex, and her cheeky sally brought him up short.

*Was this minx of a girl teasing him? Flirting with him, even?*

He gave her an answering smile. "Didn't your mother tell you it's rude to make fun of those older and wiser than you?" He laughed in spite of himself and was pleased to see Isabella smile in response.

"We've got to get you some rest. We can worry about what it all means tomorrow."

Rosie pushed Isabella out of the room, and when Seb was alone he let his head fall back, feeling a wave of release across his shoulder blades and down his back. He was flooded with a sense of lightness he hadn't known in months. Well, years.

He was clueless as to the origins or identity of the force that had swept him up and was buoying himself to go with it, not resist. But he knew with a certainty in his gut that what he'd learned today — about Polk, about Isabella and the racecourse attack — changed everything. He wasn't now just seeking truth. He was on the hunt for justice, and he wouldn't give up until he got it. For Alycia, certainly. But also for Isabella, for

Alex, and maybe even resolution for those troubling events from his own long-lost past.

# Twenty

Full of misgivings Alex climbed the stair to Charles Durant's room. When he reached it and knocked, he got no reply. Perhaps he was sleeping. He tried the handle to let himself in. The door wouldn't budge.

He was turning to leave when the door of the room next door flung open and Mrs Whitney, the nurse who'd been attending Charles, emerged carrying a washbasin and towel. Her mouth flew open. "Oh! It's you." She regarded him with sad, flat eyes that had seen too much suffering. "Your friend didn't make it. He died this morning." She set the full basin down on the floor with meticulous precision. "He was in a very bad way. I don't think he wanted to live the way he was, barely able to see, so maybe it's all for the best."

Alex realized that he was gaping at the nurse and blocking her entry to Durant's room. "It's locked." He had no idea why that seemed like a pertinent remark. "I mean to say …" He cast his eyes down to the threadbare runner that covered the worn floorboards. "I mean to say, can I see him?"

Her unflinching gaze seemed to be assessing his motives, and then she sighed. "You're in luck. The funeral director will be along shortly. I just locked it for safety while I went to make arrangements. But he's at peace now. No one can disturb him." She maneuvered around Alex, unlocked the door, picked up the basin again and pushed into the dim room with Alex at her heels. "He left something for you."

She set the basin down on the bedside table, and with precise, careful movements turned down the sheet which had been drawn up over Charles Durant's bandaged face, as if he was sleeping and she was trying not to disturb him.

Alex gazed down at him and felt nothing except numb surprise. He had known his life was in danger, so why was he shocked that it had come to this? And why wasn't he registering any emotion?

He flicked his attention to Mrs Whitney. "Sorry, what did you say?"

"He left something for you." She drew an envelope out of the pocket of her white pinafore. "He couldn't write because of his bandages, but he asked me to copy down his instructions. They're inside with the key."

"The key?"

Alex felt like a ventriloquist's doll, the way he was aping her speech, but the information was so unexpected he was at a loss to say anything else.

She huffed as if impatient with his dimness. "The key to the safety box. He said you were very interested in old photographs and you would find his store of old treasures there. He said no one else would value them, so he'd like you to have them."

Alex had stayed and arranged to pay Durant's funeral costs when the undertaker arrived to remove his body. According to Mrs Whitney, he had no wife or family in California and she didn't know how to contact any family he might have back in France. It seemed to Alex a poignant end to a life lived with grace and integrity. Would he end the same way, with no one except his father to speak for him? And when Hector was gone, who then?

He went to the Hotel de Paris dining room on Broad Street to absorb the note's contents over a morning coffee. It was headed "The Last Wishes of Charles Durant, photographer, of Nevada City, August 1869'.

*I, Charles Durant, being of sound mind and close to death following a murderous attack in my studio on Sunday last, hereby wish it known that any personal effects relating to my art and trade which survived the fire started in said attack should be passed to Mr Alex de Vile, who has shown me great personal kindness and expressed abiding interest in my work. Said effects to include the contents of a safety deposit box at the National Bank containing historic artefacts relating to Gold Country photographic history. Please advise my sister Mme Francois Pelletier of my death, her address to be found in the aforementioned deposit box. Requiescat in Pace.*

There was a small addendum:

*Monsieur Alex: I believe the old photographs I have collected over my lifetime have great cultural and possibly historical value, and at some later date may even prove profitable as collectibles. You seemed to have a sensitivity for these works and of all the folks I know may appreciate them the most. I pray they bring you good fortune. Till we meet again — Au revoir et à la prochaine.*

# Twenty-One

Hector de Vile sniffed appreciatively at the warmed brandy aroma that rose from an exquisite bucket-shaped runner glass he cupped in both hands. Engraved with roses, thistles and shamrocks — it came from a recognized English glassmaker — it was a sentimental memento of his most recent time in Washington. A reward for making it to the seat of government. He flicked the side of the glass with one manicured finger just to hear it sing, and his spirits reverberated with its clear ringing tone.

He had feasted on roast turkey with sage and marjoram stuffing, sweet potatoes and apples, crème caramel and this luscious brandy to finish, all enjoyed in the company of his unparalleled son, who lounged on the sofa opposite, his brandy glass resting on the dark-blue velvet ottoman that sat between them.

There was no place like home, especially when it was a Mississippi plantation-style mansion on the upper reaches of Broad Street, Nevada City — a house built by one of the town's founding fathers who had migrated on to the Comstock Lode nearly ten years ago, leaving the manor behind for de Vile to enjoy.

"Mrs Galveston outdid herself tonight," Alex said with a contented sigh. "It's a long time since I had such a fine dinner."

Hector's heart warmed again with satisfaction for all he enjoyed — the political appointment that offered unrivaled opportunities for capitalizing on his wealth, his capable son being groomed to one day take it all over as his legacy, the good fortune that had brought it all together. He grunted agreement. "That she did son. A very good meal."

They sat and sipped in companionable silence. "I guess she's the closest thing I've ever had to a mother." Alex's voice was soft with yearning.

Hector's heart thumped against his ribcage, his thighs tensed. "What an odd thing to say, Alex. What brought that on?"

Alex's glance was sharp, as if he'd been rebuked. "What do you mean? It's just an observation." He gazed out over Hector's shoulder, and the silence they had shared companionably minutes before now felt like a dividing wall. "I never knew my mother. Never known a thing about her ..."

Hector's neck itched with irritation. "I've told you many times, son, she died very soon after you were born, but she would have been very proud of you." He was talking too loud, he knew, sounded too defensive. The heat on his neck grew, and he swatted around his collar to relieve his discomfort.

"I know, Father. It's just, well, you know that photographer who did our portraits a few days ago, the one who was attacked by thugs? Charles Durant? He died today. Seems he had no family here — and it just got me thinking. You're the only family I've got. Will that be me one day? Dying alone? I don't want to be morbid but—"

"Well, don't be, then," Hector snapped before he'd got control of his temper.

"Don't be morbid, I mean," he said more slowly, more considerately. "We've got a long time to go before we have to entertain such thoughts."

"I suppose so." Alex's eyebrows furrowed in deep thought. He leaned forward, shoulders hunched, picked up his brandy glass and sipped slowly. "He left me some old photographs." He spoke in a confessional rush. "He had them in a safety deposit box. They could be worth a bit, but even if they're not, they've certainly got historical value."

"Alex! What did I tell you about wasting your time on old junk? You've got a big future ahead of you. You can't afford to fritter it away on this stuff."

"This 'old junk' is important to me, Father. I want to find out more about them — the men who took those photos and the people they pictured. It's a past era. Surely you can understand that? It's your era, come to think of it. You never know, one of them might even be of my mother."

It had been a sensitive point between them that Hector had no resemblance of his wife — no portrait, no daguerreotype — to show his son.

"Alex, I don't know what's got into you. Aren't you satisfied with the life you have? You've had more than practically anyone you can name. What's wrong with you?"

"Nothing's wrong, Father. And I'm very grateful for all I've received. I know I've been so fortunate. It's just that, well, Charles Durant really touched me. And I him, I think. Before he died he asked me to get in touch with his family in Paris—"

"What?" Hector catapulted out of his capacious armchair. "He what?"

Alex slowly rose to his feet to stare at his father across the ottoman. In a shaky, halting voice he repeated, "He's asked me to get in touch with his family. To tell them he's dead. Is there anything so wrong with that?" He shook his head, disbelieving. "For goodness sakes, Hex. Have some compassion."

Hector's head jerked and his breathing was rattling in his nostrils. He no longer saw Alex across from him. A black curtain filled his vision. "This is nonsense! Total nonsense. I won't stand for it from any son of mine. It will lead you into all sorts of harm. I forbid it. Continue with this and you aren't welcome in this house. I mean it."

A gaping silence opened between them, and Alex's stricken face swam back into view as the black curtain faded. The skin around his eyes was bunched in pain, and he clenched and unclenched his fists without seeming to be aware of his hands dangling at his side. Then he swung on his heel and stepped around the ottoman, bringing him within hugging distance. "I see no harm in honoring a promise to an old man with no family to speak for him, Father, and I'm surprised you don't share that understanding. Goodnight to you."

He stared at Hector but did not step forward to close the gap between them. Then his footsteps faded down the hall and the front door opened and closed with a click.

The day Hector had feared ever since Alex had been delivered as a cuddly rug-wrapped bundle had come — and he had no clue what he could do about it.

For a very long time after his son left, Hector slumped in his chair, finishing one brandy and starting another, going over every word of their conversation. How had they gone from a casual affection to banishment in the space of a few sentences? He shook his head in frustration at the boy's intransigence. But he also cursed his own lack of restraint. He'd been mad with rage. And why? Just to prevent his son seeing a few old photographs. Almost certainly he wouldn't be able to identify either the photographer or the subjects, so what was there to worry about?

Over the years he had known Bertha Van Werden he'd extracted painfully few morsels of information about Alex's origins, some of which had checked out, some of which hadn't. Whenever she resurfaced every couple of years pressuring him for money and hinting blackmail if he didn't comply, he'd tried to obtain additional intelligence as part of the deal. On one of those occasions she let slip that Alex's father was a Spanish photographer named Castellanos. She claimed he was long dead, and a few discreet inquiries had confirmed the existence of a photographer of that name, now deceased.

He had satisfied himself that would be the end of it. Both father and probably mother dead, and no known other relatives. No one left to appear out of nowhere and claim blood ties and obligations. Especially after he engineered Bertha's dramatic fall from grace — and final demise — last year.

He really had nothing to fear from old photographs. Even if Alex identified them as having been taken by someone called Castellanos, how would he make the missing connection and understand who the man really was?

An emptiness like none he'd ever felt before threatened to overwhelm him. Without Alex present the very air in the room felt dead, the house forsaken. His stomach fluttered uncomfortably and a nausea crept over him, closing his throat. What if the unthinkable happened and Alex somehow tracked down his family line, made contact with his twin sister. For the first time in his life he was fearful. The hot blood-rush that set his temples throbbing carried with it one panicked image: of a gray-faced old cripple with a cane. Hiram Williams.

*He must surely be the only creature alive who could connect me to that damned washed-up photographer.*

The brandy burned as it went down. His nerve-endings jangled at the jolting realization that he was exposed on two fronts. Goodness knew what Alex would do if he discovered who'd been behind the attack on the studio, but that was the least of his worries right now. He might not be able to curb his soft-hearted son — why in Hades hadn't he thought to toughen him up before this? — but he'd have no problem in silencing Hiram Williams.

# Twenty-Two

Isabella relaxed back on her elbow on her good side, the one that was the least bruised from her fall, plucked a peach from the picnic rug under her, bit into it gingerly and then sucked like mad to stop the burst of fresh, sweet juice running down her chin. The sun-warmed fruit was perfect, the red-blushed yellow skin and yellow flesh giving away with satisfying fuzzy firmness and a honey aroma as she bit into it. She smiled up at Rosie and sighed contentedly. "What a glorious day!"

Nearby, Sebastian was watering the horses they'd hired to ride the ruins at the old Sutter Fort, an open space close to town where they could enjoy exercise without attracting any attention. Horses settled, he returned and collapsed on the rug alongside them.

Isabella shifted position to catch his eye. "Seb, thanks so much for coming with us to do this. I know you're worried about safety, and we couldn't have come here without you." She looked up into his lightly tanned face, fringed with his red-gold hair, and smiled.

*If he only knew how much this means to me.*

"Don't mention it. I felt like a bit of time off and a ride too, so it's no sacrifice." He slumped down onto his back and looked up at the arching boughs of the peach trees overhead. "Strange to think this pastoral idyll — well, idyllic except for the occasional whiff from the pig pens when the breeze blows this way — was once a thriving trade center, with a hospital, casino, houses, crops and gardens."

He bit into a peach and munched contentedly. "And the peaches, the pigs, and the stables are all that remain." He lifted himself up onto his elbows and threw his peach stone into the long grass. "When gold was discovered, thousands of new arrivals overran John Sutter's estate and he got pushed off. It was death by a thousand cuts. Some blatantly squatted on land he claimed was his. Others successfully challenged his legal right to ownership. And, of course, all his workers deserted to dig for gold." He grinned and collapsed back down again. "Here endeth the lesson. Things were pretty unforgiving in those days."

"Poor chap," said Rosie. "It must have been hard."

"I'm sure it was. But he did have the satisfaction of seeing his sons do well in the new world."

"That's nice." Isabella closed her eyes in deep contentment; the sun filtering through the peaches sent flickering shadows across her eyelids. At moments like this she could almost wish a blessing on all mankind ... She sat up with a start. All mankind, that was, except the renegade who'd murdered Alycia and who'd tried to kill her on a horse.

"Seb, you're pretty well the voice of authority around here at present. There doesn't seem to be anyone else — except Mother, of course, and she's a bit distracted with her own affairs. The match-making and so forth ..." Isabella's mother ran several high-society match-making luncheons a year where eligible women and men of means paid to be introduced to a good catch. "So can I get an idea from you? When do you think I can go back to work? I mean, without causing offense."

Seb raised himself up and regarded her, his eyes steady and solemn. "I know you find this mourning caper hard, and I know you really cared about Alycia, no doubt about it. I think you've done all anyone would reasonably require." He drew his legs up into a bridge and put his elbows on his knees. "I don't think there'd be any harm in starting to make plans. It's going to take a few weeks to get things set up anyway, isn't it?"

She nodded, the singing in her heart filling her throat so she couldn't get any words out. "Oh, I'm so … I'm so grateful. I thought … Well, I thought you might not approve."

He shook his head. "I gave you a bit

of a hard time at the beginning, Isabella. I'm sorry about that. I was being a bit of an ass." He screwed up his quick expressive mouth in an apology. "What can I say? I was preoccupied by personal stuff and I didn't comprehend the full situation." He rolled his eyes dramatically. "I've seen the error of my ways."

Isabella laughed. "I don't believe it! An apologetic man! Well, let me have my dime's worth! I was acting like a bit of a brazen-faced brat as well. I was demanding, rather than explaining. So I'm sorry, too."

Rosie made a gagging sound. "Oh, for goodness sake, you two! Make me sick, why don't you. Too much sweetness and light for one day. I prefer it when you're sparring." Peals of laughter sounded from her quarter of the rug.

Isabella shot Sebastian a colluding look, her insides fizzy with anticipation. She'd thought he was a painful old stick in the mud who saw no way except his way. Excitement welled up at the thought of being able to get back to work, to return to her normal activities.

His hazel eyes twinkled. She wasn't sure if that was because of what Rosie had said, or her own remarks, but she felt trapped in their sparkling mischief. Why hadn't she noticed before how attractive he was when he relaxed? Maybe she'd never seen him relaxed? *Tether that thought.* She'd have time to consider it later. Meantime, strike while the iron was hot.

"Have you had a chance to think about what we can do about Alejandro?" she ventured. "About what else we could do to find him, I mean."

Seb's expression sobered, as if a cloud had crossed the sun. "I'll do my best, I promise, but I can't honestly say I've anything new to go on there." He looked stricken. "I'm sorry, because I know what it means to you. However, I think I have more promising lines to follow as far as Alycia is concerned. And I will go back to that Louisiana Course and talk to that manager tomorrow, see what I can dig up. I think if we can keep asking questions, we'll get there."

In the silence that followed, their eyes locked together, and Isabella had a conviction that they had exchanged some complicit message. That sense was confirmed by a warm inner glow that banished her feeling of aloneness. But if Rosie had dared to ask her what it was she and Seb had shared, she knew she couldn't for the life of her have explained it.

# Twenty-Three

Sebastian had noticed the loitering beggar woman on their way into the Sutter Fort stables, and when they returned to their horses after a couple of hours of relaxing over their picnic and wandering some of the walking paths she was still hanging around the gated entry.

She was clad in a bright orange-and-yellow Mexican skirt with a black bodice that included a hood which came up over her head, partly concealing her face. She stood defiantly close to the riding path, hooded eyes sharp in a tanned complexion, a thin nose over a wide mouth that was missing half its teeth. As Sebastian drew parallel she took a quick step closer and reached up a bony hand to grab for his mount's halter. Before her hand touched the strap on the horse's nose, he hauled the gray to an urgent stop and raised the whip stowed in his saddle in case of emergencies. The stroke hung in mid-air threateningly as he barked at her, "Step away or you'll get hurt."

She cursed under her breath and hastily stepped aside. "No harm intended. I just want food for my children."

Seb suspected that any children she had would be out picking pockets in some other part of town, but nevertheless he dug in his jacket pocket and gave her a few coins. "Now go. Vagrancy is against the law. Move on or risk ninety days in clink." She scowled and backed away, slipping the money

into a pocket in her skirt as she turned
her back on him.

An hour later, as they wandered along
the street to their hotel, he noticed the
beggar again. It was a lovely, still day,
and he could tell from his companions'
bright chatter that the couple of hours
the three of them had shared riding and
chatting at the Fort had lifted their
spirits. At Isabella's suggestion they
wandered along to the K Street market,
just a bit up the street from their hotel.
They laughingly argued over the benefits
of beef over pork before settling on pork
shanks for the hotel chef to braise with
sauerkraut for tonight's dinner. They
paused in front of a confectionery stall
loaded up with rum balls, chocolate
truffles, maple-syrup toffee and glazed
chestnuts: Sebastian had just suggested
that the ladies deserved a treat to get

them through the last days of mourning when he sensed someone watching. He maintained his relaxed stance leaning over the array of sweetmeats, but raised his head and made a quick survey of the area. He caught a flash of orange skirt disappearing behind a wagon loaded with green vegetables, and frowned. There was no rule against her walking the streets, but he would keep a wary eye out.

Isabella and Rosie agreed on glazed chestnuts for their after-dinner treat, and as the stallholder wrapped them in a twist of pretty pink paper they turned for home. "This has been so pleasant, Sebastian," said Isabella. "I want to say thank you from the bottom of my heart for this chance to escape those stuffy rooms and enjoy time in the open air. I wouldn't have felt safe without you after yesterday." She gave him a transcendent smile that hid no guile. "This is the best I've felt since Alycia's been gone."

She turned to continue to the hotel and stumbled to a halt so abruptly he was in danger of walking into her back. Hardly aware of it, he placed one hand gently on her shoulder and leaned forward slightly to see what had caused her to stop. The Mexican gypsy — if that was what she was — was blocking Isabella's path, her face dark and forbidding. By her side, hidden in the folds of her skirt, Sebastian sensed rather than saw she clasped a knife.

His hand tightened on Isabella's right shoulder as she stared into the gypsy's face. From the easy slope under his hand he sensed that she was taking the gypsy woman's appearance in her stride. Then an eye-catching, much younger woman with glossy dark hair and flashing brown eyes stepped in front of the interloper and greeted them with a casual friendliness. "Hola!" She waved a hand in greeting and flashed an encouraging smile that lit up her high cheekbones and wide mouth. "It's your lucky day. We're here to entertain you!"

She stepped aside and a band of young children — girls prettily costumed in bright circular skirts, boys in slim black trousers and embroidered bolero tops — revolved around them in a rousing, stamping, clapping dance routine, tambourines chiming and castanets clacking, circling Isabella, Seb and Rosie while two big men in black sombreros strolled in the background picking out a fast dance tune.

Isabella half-turned to Seb with a questioning look. He leaned over and half-whispered in her ear, "Just wait this out. No need to be anxious. It will work out fine." He hoped his words sounded convincing to Isabella's ears because they rang hollow in his own. He could bet that the dark-haired mandolin players were armed, and it would be sheer stupidity for him to take them on until he had a clearer idea of what he was up against.

He watched closely, anticipating the moment when the children would 'accidentally' bump into Isabella and attempt to relieve her of her purse or the ebony beads that hung over the high-necked mourning gown which doubled as her riding habit. They came very close to it several times, but always pulled back at the last second as if reading some warning in the environment. As they danced, passers-by gathered to watch and the scowling hag who had been at the Fort cycled through the crowd collecting coins. Traveling Mexicans — whether gypsy 'gitano' or not — were targeted by the anti-vagrancy laws, the so-called 'greaser law' — and were widely distrusted as thieves and ruffians. Still, people liked a bit of action.

When the dance died away the dark-haired beauty who seemed to be the lead player stepped back in front of Isabella and took her right hand firmly by the wrist. She turned the palm upwards and peered into it. Isabella gave a small cry of protest and tried to pull away, but the fortune teller chided her, "Oh, no, senorita. Don't be afraid. This is important. Very important. Lives are at stake."

Isabella stiffened, but she stopped resisting. The foreigner continued in a strangely hypnotic sing-song cadence. "Oh my goodness, I see danger up ahead for you! See here." She traced a line on Isabella's hand with one index finger. "This is your life line. And see here how it fades and divides? One line disappears and the other goes on strongly."

She lifted Isabella's hand up to face level and although Sebastian could sense reluctance in the stiffness of Isabella's stance, her eyes followed the fortune teller's finger.

The woman stared at her. "I am Preciosa, Isabella." As Isabella's involuntary start she nodded. "Yes, I know your name. I know many things about you, just by looking at your hand. I have the second sight, you see, and I have been sent to warn you. But before I tell you more, you must cross my palm with silver. Otherwise my words are cursed."

As she spoke, she was imperceptibly drawing Isabella off K Street towards a bench in a quiet courtyard. They sank onto the bench together, Preciosa holding Isabella's hand in her lap. Isabella's expression mirrored her inner turbulence, one minute resolute and skeptical, the next transparent with white-knuckle vulnerability.

Whoever had set Preciosa up for this confidence trick had briefed her well, Sebastian thought. He pulled out a five-franc coin he'd carried as a talisman, a token of memory, ever since the afternoon Robert died. As ready substitutes for the scarce American dollar, they'd been imported in large quantities during the early days of the Gold Rush. Robert had got his hands on one from an uncle who'd ventured West and had carried it as a symbol of one day finding his own Eldorado. A fat lot of good it did him … A shadow crossed Seb's soul as he recalled drawing it from Robert's pocket as he lay lifeless on the battlefield. He didn't fully understand why, but now felt like the right time to pass it on.

Preciosa barely glanced at it as she crossed it over Isabella's palm and then tucked it into a little purse at her waist.

"You are in great danger, Isabella." The gypsy's voice was barely audible above the splashing of a nearby fountain, and Seb leaned in so he didn't miss anything. "Great danger, and the choices you make today will determine your future. Whether you live or you die. Whether those you love live or die." She glanced up at Sebastian and Rosie, her face blank and far away. "And there is one very important person who is not here today who will be most affected by your actions." She paused and Isabella looked up expectantly. "You know who that is, don't you? Your brother."

Isabella had maintained a semblance of cool control as Preciosa set her trap in a sing-song cadence, but at the mention of Alejandro she took a startled intake of breath. "My brother? What do you know of him?" Her voice was higher-pitched than usual, and edged with a despair that Seb was certain Preciosa and her fellow thieves would not have failed to detect. "Yes. Your brother. I know about him too. Him and your Spanish father, Castellanos. Spain beats in our hearts too."

"What about my brother? Tell me."

The gypsy's penetrating black eyes

fixed on her. "How much do you love this brother you have no memory of? Do you love him so much you'd be willing to save his life? How much would you sacrifice for him?"

Isabella's face drained of color and her mouth was shadowed by pinched white lines. "I don't understand. I mean, yes, of course I would do anything I could to save Alejandro ... But how is he in danger?" She shook her head, as if trying to dislodge a repugnant thought. "Preciosa, how do you know these things? Why should I believe you?"

Preciosa turned her dark expressive eyes on Isabella and gently traced down the side of her cheek with one hand, pushing back a stray lock as she caressed. "Ah, little one, I have already said. I have the second sight. The wit of a gypsy girl steers by a different compass from that which guides other people. I see things others don't."

Isabella shook her head again and made as if to rise from the bench. Preciosa held on, subtly forcing her to stay. "Walk away now and you will never know what the consequences will be. Listen to me, and I can help you save Alejandro and ensure a long life for yourself."

"No. That is ridiculous. Unbelievable. It can't be true."

"What if it is? Are you willing to take that risk? Especially when the cost is so small."

"Then tell me. Stop playing games. What is this risk, this cost? Tell me!" Isabella had dropped all pretense of nonchalance.

As they'd been talking the children had vanished and the scowling woman from the Fort and the two men had crowded in. Now Preciosa stood and took a step away, leaving more room for them to muscle in. Sebastian shot an anxious glance at Rosie. Her head was set at an alert tilt, whip-smart eyes not missing a detail. He grimaced. *Get ready.* He inwardly cursed himself for letting this confrontation happen. Even with the revolver he carried he couldn't take on four attackers, not when neither Rosie or Isabella was armed. It would be sheer folly and bound to end badly.

As if on cue, the sombrero-wearing heavies stepped closer, casting a threatening shadow over Isabella. She shifted nervously and shot a sharp look at Preciosa. "Are these your friends?"

"No need to be frightened, little one, they won't hurt you. They are simply here to ensure your safety."

"Oh? I was not aware I was in danger. I am a few steps from my hotel, and it is the middle of a bright Sacramento Sunday. What can there be to fear?"

"Ah, chiquita, if you only knew. This quest of yours to find your brother, it is not good. It will bring danger for you and him. But I cannot help if you do not trust me. And I will need payment before I am able to tell you more. You've already told me you'd do anything to keep him safe. Isn't that what you said?"

Isabella's hand flew to her open mouth, and she tried to stand, alarm etched across her brow. Sebastian reached for his weapon, but it was only half-drawn when the heaviest and oldest of the enforcers shoved Preciosa aside and grabbed Isabella by the arm, waving a knife in his other hand. In the blink of an eye he was joined by his accomplice, a younger man with mean eyes and an ugly scar down one side of his face. He snapped his fingers in front of Isabella's face and then rounded on Preciosa with a long harangue in their own tongue. The words were a mystery, but his dark flushed face and emphatic manner showed his increasing anger.

Sebastian dreaded the next step because it was already certain what they intended. They would retain Isabella 'for her own safety' while the money to pay for the release of her brother was delivered to some shady rendezvous. He raised his eyebrows at Rosie and slipped the gun back into the inside pocket of his jacket. Timing was everything.

He slid in front of Rosie, who was melting back behind the fountain, and gave the courtyard area a quick survey. It was secluded, but not completely cut off from K Street, and a nub of curious onlookers had gathered to listen to Preciosa's spiel. Now people were edging away from trouble, moving quietly so as not to attract unwelcome attention, but sneaking away from danger.

With one exception: a big, sandy-haired man with military bearing who was slipping thorough the dissolving flock like a wolf in the sheepfold. The smooth slick gait was familiar, the carriage of a man who went after what he wanted and was used to getting it. He already had his Union army-issue revolver drawn when he hauled up and leveled the barrel at the man holding Isabella. "Drop the knife, Garcia," he said. "Suelte la. Drop it."

The heavy-set man froze, and slowly turned to face Corporal Edmund Quincey.

Sebastian had simultaneously drawn

his weapon and now stood facing Edmund, putting the gitano thieves in their cross-fire.

"Let the lady go. And then get going yourselves. Understand?"

Garcia's head jerked in acknowledgment. He tucked the knife back in the folds of his voluminous pants, gestured to his fellow crooks, turned on his heel and left, the rest of the band following.

Preciosa was the last to go. She took Isabella's arm and stared into her eyes. "Don't forget what I said, or you'll regret it." Then she too wheeled around and disappeared onto K Street.

# Twenty-Four

It was just as well the Ebner was only a few steps further down the street from the confrontation with the gypsies because Seb doubted if Isabella could have held together for much longer than the time it took them to get back to their suite. She was drawing on her last reserves of strength and stoicism, he could see that. Her expression was curtained and blank; her eyes skated away into the middle distance, so different from her normal direct, crystal-clear gaze. Her balance was tentative and bumbling, lacking her assured grace.

"Sit down here, Isabella, and we'll get

some coffee. You need a boost after that ordeal."

She sank into the chair, white-faced and distracted, seemingly deaf to his reassurances, staring at a spot on the floor. When she spoke it was in a plaintive, musing tone, seemingly addressed to herself. "How did she know about Alejandro?" She looked around desperately, as if she expected to find something shocking in the hotel sitting room. "Is that where he is, do you think? Did the gypsies take him, all those years ago? Is he with the gypsies?"

She turned and pulled at Seb's sleeve. "Do you think that's what's happened, Sebastian? Is my brother with the gypsies?"

Seb was about to reply when Edmund cut across their exchange. "Nothing like that, Miss Wilmington. Not likely. A blatant attempt at extortion, more likely."

She glanced up at him with a bewildered frown, as if he was a stranger to her. "Extortion? I don't know what you mean."

Sebastian stepped in front of her and crouched down, taking one hand in his. "Izzy, they don't know anything about your brother. They've just heard about the scandal through the vagabond grapevine and stepped in to capitalize on it. I am sorry, but the worst thing would be to put any stock by it. That's exactly what they want."

She shook her head as if wanting to reject his words.

Edmund towered over her. "He's right. They're a band of thieves and beggars, preying on decent people. It's a great pity you got mixed up in it." His voice was too loud; it boomed in Seb's ears, and Isabella flinched.

"Thieves?" She stared questioningly into Seb's face. "But she knew his name. She called him Alejandro."

Sebastian squeezed her hand consolingly. "No, Izzy, she didn't know his name. Not until you told her."

Rosie proved worth her weight in gold, calming and reassuring her friend, and after a subdued coffee she encouraged her off for a daytime nap. The two young women withdrew, both looking exhausted, and Seb was left with Edmund.

"Jolly fortunate you chanced along when you did. I must thank you. It could have turned nasty there if you hadn't had intervened." It stuck in Sebastian's craw to say it, and he wondered just how much of a coincidence Edmund's appearance had been, but he muted those doubts and gave his former soldiering companion the benefit of the doubt.

A familiar expression flickered across Edmund's face and was gone almost as soon as it had appeared, a gloating "I'm always one step ahead of the action" self-congratulatory smirk that was reflected in the way he stood, legs apart, weight balanced on his heels, pelvis thrust forward, arms folded. How often Seb had seen that self-regard splashed around, and how often people — well, women and commanding officers — seemed to be taken in by it. The full memory of his loathing for this man flooded back so strongly he turned away in case it was betrayed in his face.

"Sheer good luck old chap. Just happened to be in the area and thought I'd call in."

"Met that gang before, have you? You seemed to know them."

"Came across them when I was doing another surveillance job. They were accused of extortion that time too. Not enough evidence to prove it, but I know enough to know they're bad news."

"I think we all know that."

"Thing is, they do have some surprising friends, if you know what I mean. It pays not to get too far on the wrong side of them."

"What's that supposed to mean?" Sebastian's skin itched and he rubbed his forearm in irritated small circles.

"Well, I wouldn't be surprised if they had heard something about the missing brother on their 'gitano wire'. They have amazing networks stretching right back to Spain and down into South America. I'd go carefully if I were you."

Sebastian stared at Edmund, examining the bold masculine planes of his face, searching for the truth behind the counterfeit. Under his gaze Edmund preened like a bantam rooster.

*Just like a farmyard bully — shuffle his feathers to increase his size and control.*

"You're serious. You want me to go slow on looking for Isabella's brother — and what, searching for Mrs Stockton's killer too? So who's crossing *your* palm with silver? Whose nark are you?"

Edmund's face darkened. "I'm just trying to help an old friend." He picked up his hat from where he'd casually cast it on the dining room table. "I'll see myself out. But don't say I didn't warn you."

He seemed to be making a habit of this lately. Peering into his cups, disappearing into burrows like a ground squirrel, though this time he was trying to read the coffee grinds, not the foam on his beer. What he needed was a fortune teller, he mocked. That would do it. Sebastian groaned inwardly. After Edmund had departed he couldn't move. His legs were like tree trunks, heavy and inert, and he didn't have the power to lift them. He was immobile in body, but ranging far and wide in mind. Hiram. Burton. Polk. How did each fit into this murder tree, and was it going to lead him to Alycia's killer, or Alejandro, or both?

What had today's bizarre turn of events shown him? That he couldn't trust anyone? That this whole business was far more complicated than he'd understood? That although in his eyes he'd barely begun to make serious inquiries, he'd managed to twist the lion's tail?

Just who the lion was, and how its tail was being twirled, he had no clue, but he was going to make it his business to find out. Hiram, the poor beggar, had been lucky to survive his apoplexy attack, but the doctor said he needed total bed rest. He would be out of bounds in terms of questioning for some time. Polk was already dead. That left Burton. He'd be as welcome as a tornado on a trail drive, but he would go see Burton again tomorrow.

# Twenty-Five

Seb returned to the Purdy home in Tong Yung Gai — the Street of the Chinese — early the next day, intent on getting to Burton before he had a chance to get drunk or simply run out of daily steam. But when he got there, his long-suffering wife explained he was in one of the joints that lined the Front Street Embarcadero on the Sacramento riverfront.

Seb found him in the third place he tried, sitting alone at a corner table staring into his glass. When he saw Sebastian his jaw dropped, but Seb quickly tried to reassure him. "I'm not here to cause grief, Buffalo, I promise. I just want to satisfy myself about something from back then — something I've been too much of a coward to face up to. I think the time has come."

There was a spark of the old calculated intelligence in Burton's unusual dark blue eyes, a dark blue that verged on black. "Not too much about the old days I care to remember, or even can remember, but fire ahead." Burton took a long gulp of his light ale.

"There were rumors that Edmund got too friendly with the women who hung around the bars in town where the officers drank — and that he didn't mind his mouth enough," said Seb. "You had a better chance than me to know whether that was so because you were on the road a lot searching out supplies. Did you ever see any evidence of that?"

Burton waggled his head from side to side like a grandfather-clock pendulum.

"Maybe, maybe not. Maybe, maybe not." He shot a wry grin Sebastian's way. "You know how it is, Tiger. He was a slippery gaffer. He certainly went for the ladies — and some of the worst of them. Whether he exchanged anything more than sweet nothings, or whether he was tempted to indiscretions in return for female favors, I wouldn't know."

He chewed his bottom lip, as if recalling some long-past conversation. He took another long draught of ale and banged the glass down with a satisfied thud. "Old Johnny Turkey now, he'd be the one to ask. He knew all about it. Shame he's dead."

Sebastian frowned. "Johnny Turkey? What about him?"

"Oh, old Johnny was convinced that Quincey had rubber lips. Worse than that. He reckoned he sold information.

Must say I've always wondered about that surprise attack where I got taken prisoner, along with all our food supplies. The Rebs were starving, everyone knew that. And we had loads of grub. Everyone knew that too. You'd wonder what they'd pay for the keys to the larder. And course Johnny got killed in that same raid, so he wasn't around to moan about it afterwards."

An icy chill ran up Sebastian's spine as Burton Purdy talked on, seemingly disengaged and disconnected from the impact of his words, staring at the table, fingering the line of froth around the rim of his empty glass. But when he did finally glance up at Sebastian his eyes were focused and fierce. "That's not the worst of it, though."

"What do you mean? What could be worse?" Sebastian reached out and put his hand on Burton's forearm. "Tell me, Burton. What else is there?"

"He was up to his eyeballs in the contraband trade. Remember around Gettysburg? Blacks who'd been freedmen for years were rounded up and sold back into the South as slaves. They tried to hide, tried to run, but most nights they were rounded up and driven back across the border. There was big money in that trade. Big money... Thousands of dollars, for sure. And our gaffer Quincey made sure he got his cut. That coot is slicker than a slop jar."

"You slay me, Burton. I don't know what to say." Sebastian's head was swimming.

"Oh yeah, Tiger. He's as crooked as a Virginia snake. Too late to do anything about it now, though. I'm surprised he isn't a lot richer than he is, what he's done. Tell you who did know a lot about that contraband business — Johnny Turkey's mate, the chaplain. Forget his name. I've got no idea where he is, or if he's still alive, but he'd know."

Sebastian left Burton starting on his next beer and went on out to the Louisiana Race Course, hoping to talk to the groom who'd saddled up Isabella the day before yesterday, but the man wasn't to be found. As he ambled the Sacramento streets in the bright sunshine he mulled over what Burton had told him. It gelled with other small hints he'd heard over the years, and he had no difficulty in believing that what Purdy said was true.

The man showed remarkably little bitterness. If his capture had been directly related to Quincey's betrayal, then his broken health and all of the suffering he and his family had endured could also be laid at Quincey's door. Seb thought of the threadbare shanty Purdy shared with his wife, whose complexion and physique spoke of African forefathers. Should he have a quiet word in Caroline Studebaker's ear, or at least arrange somehow for her to learn the truth about her suitor's past? Or should he keep out of it? He thought of the old verse: how did it go? 'Vengeance is mine, says the Lord.' Maybe he'd be better to make sure Mrs Purdy was looked after.

He arrived back outside the Purdy's home in the foul-smelling air of I Street late in the afternoon, loaded down with enough supplies to keep the family in food for a week. A side of cured pork, fresh vegetables, bread, beans, watermelon, cheese and honey — all procured from the stalls under the massive oak near the Horse Market on J Street, the liveliest part of the city for most of the day. Leaving some of his haul on the street, he hoisted the pork on his shoulder and made for the front door. No one responded to his knock, and he was about to thump again more loudly when he smelled smoke. He gingerly opened up and put his head inside, and the small room where he had sat with Mrs Purdy the day before erupted like a fireball that was just waiting for a fresh draft of air to get going.

Sebastian threw open the door and yelled, "Mrs Purdy!" He edged into the seemingly empty space, calling as he went, "Anyone here? Anyone home?" He recalled there was no pumped water, and he had no idea where they went to get bucket supply, so there was little he could do to douse the blaze that flickered near the base of the stairs.

At first he could hear nothing but the crackling of the flames as they licked up the wall and began a race up to the next level. Then he heard a heavy thump and a woman's scream from overhead. He charged up the narrow passageway. He thrust his head into Burton's room and saw his wife bent over his prone figure, half-in, half-out of bed. She pointed feverishly to the few steps that led to the next landing. "The boys! They're upstairs!"

He cast a doubtful look towards Burton, and she shook her head. "I'll get him. You get the boys." He stumbled up rickety stairs to the next level. The smoke had become so blinding within the few minutes he'd been inside he had to feel his way the final few feet to another door. He hesitated for a second, worried that opening it would send a gust of fresh air that would ignite any smoldering material, but he had no other choice. He had to get in there. The door resisted his first attempt to open it, but gave way when he put his whole weight against his shoulder and charged.

The room was already well alight. A smoldering board had fallen across the entryway, blocking the exit. Through the heat and haze Seb could just make out a small figure, a boy, desperately trying to drag a larger boy out backwards. He grabbed the child by the arm. "Here, I'll take him. You run. Get yourself out! I'll be right behind you."

The boy stared up at him with huge, frightened eyes, then dropped his burden and whirled to the door. Seb threw the other boy over his shoulder and raced downstairs. They pounded through the tiny living space and out into the street. He gave each boy a cursory check — clothes smelling of smoke, a couple of mild burns, maybe some inhaled smoke to hinder their breathing, but they were both essentially safe.

"Stay here. Don't move," he told them, and could see they needed no further instruction. They sank in a huddle to the ground and hugged each other, streaks of white ash showing up on their dark cheeks. He swung back into the house. The heat was much fiercer now, and the stairs were disintegrating. He had to take two huge steps to broach the gap to the alcove where he'd last seen Mrs Purdy and her husband.

He felt his way through the smoke, calling as he went, "Mrs Purdy, where are you?" His foot came into connection with something soft and he leaned over, feeling with his hands. Mrs Purdy was crumpled on the floor beside the bed, semi-conscious and moaning. He scooped her up in a fireman's lift across his hip and lumbered down the gap where the stairs had once been and out into the smoke-filled street. By now people were gathering on the curb in silent knots, looking up at the house, awestruck.

"Is there anyone else in the place next door? Can someone check?" He grabbed the nearest man by the shoulder and pointed him towards the Purdys' neighbors. "Go and look. It's urgent!"

Seb spun round and veered back up the path to the Purdys' front door, but as soon as he got there, he knew he was too late. He was met by a sheer wall of flame, and the walls, the modest table, the rickety stairs were already turned to glowing ash. He stood wavering on the threshold for a few seconds, and then the floor above caved in with one mighty roar. He backed away, tears streaming down his face, vaguely aware his clothes, the hair on his head and arms — all smelled of burning.

Two units of volunteer fire fighters were pulling up outside. He stumbled down the path out of the way of any falling debris and headed straight for the closest engine. "I was too late for one poor sod in there. There's at least one dead. Maybe more, I don't know."

Mrs Purdy was being given sips of water from a cup by a woman Seb assumed was one of her neighbors. He went over and crouched on the ground next to her. "Mrs Purdy." She looked up at him, grief etched in every sooty line on her weary face. "You couldn't get him, could you?" She shook her head in despair. "He came home so drunk. It was impossible to make him get up and walk. He just laughed at me when I tried."

Seb took her hand. "You did your best. I know you did. You were stupendous. You kept on trying until you passed out. Another half a minute and you would have been lost too."

A woman in a nurse's uniform leaned over them. "Any help needed here?" she asked.

Seb nodded. "Yes, you'd better check out Mrs Purdy here for any burns." The boys sat clutching their knees to their chests, eyes wide and staring, unnaturally quiet. "And the boys probably could do with blankets around their shoulders and something sweet to suck. They look like they're in full-blown shock."

"We didn't have much before, but now we've got nothing," Mrs Purdy said to no one in particular. "Begosh, Burton Purdy. You know the little man never wins. Now look what you've gone and made them do."

# Twenty-Six

"Mmm. Nice cookies." Isabella smiled at the small ebony-skinned boy with liquid dark eyes who gazed at the shortbread he held up between delicate fingers, as if anticipating it might disappear before he could bite into it. "Nice cookies." The only words either boy had uttered in the forty-five minutes since they'd arrived at the Ebner suite, smelling of smoke and hanging off Mrs Purdy's arms for grim death.

Sebastian had given her the briefest of explanations: they had been rescued from a raging house fire; Mr Purdy was missing. He instructed her to make them as comfortable as she could while he returned to see if he could locate her husband in the ruins.

The copper hot tub had washed away the stink of the smoke, the charcoal smears of ash and cinders on their faces, arms and legs, but she knew hot water did little to remove the frozen shock that suffused their angelic faces.

Now they were sitting up at the table drinking hot chocolate and eating cookies, all cleaned up in the new shorts and shirts she'd sent Rosie out to buy, while Mrs Purdy used the bathroom for her own ritual of cleansing and restoration. About all she'd been able to get out of their mother was their names: Sam and Sol, short for Samuel and Solomon.

"They're shortbread," said Isabella, flicking a look at Rosie who sat quietly alongside them. "There's plenty more if you're hungry."

"Thank you, ma'am." They chorused together like little chicks on a wire, and Isabella felt tears welling up. Mrs Purdy seemed to be doing a great job at raising these boys, and she'd now likely be destitute. She heard a slight cough behind her, and the boys put down their cups and fixed their eyes on the stocky, strongly built woman who came in, the fragrance of lavender soap with her.

"Samuel, Solomon, are you being good boys now, not causing the lady any trouble?"

It was a statement rather than a question, and their little faces wrinkled with concentration. "No, ma'am." The chickadee chorus again.

Isabella smiled. "They've been perfect angels, Mrs Purdy. Now you sit down and take time to recover from your ordeal. Would you prefer hot chocolate or coffee?"

The look of disbelief on Mrs Purdy's face spoke louder than words. It had been an eon since anyone had ever addressed that question to this capable matron. Perhaps she'd never heard it before. Her mouth opened and closed without sounding, and then she took a few faltering steps to the closest chair and sat down.

"We've got hot chocolate, Mimi." Sam's huge dark eyes shining, the boy who hadn't spoken so far — apart from the chorus — thrust his cup forward. "See?"

Mrs Purdy patted his tight black curls and smiled at him. "It smells good, Sammy."

Isabella nodded. "Hot chocolate it is."

Rosie stood. "I'll get it. Won't be long."

Isabella cleared her throat. "Mrs Purdy, I'm sorry you've had this dreadful experience, but I'm sure Sebastian will see to it that you've somewhere to go."

Mrs Purdy put the flats of her palms over her eyes and turned her head slowly from side to side. "Thank you for your kindness Miss …" She stopped and gave a huffing breath. "I don't even know your name."

"Isabella. It's Isabella. Izzy for short."

Mrs Purdy nodded. "If we're going to be on first-name terms, my name is Betty. Betty Purdy."

"Oh? I thought the boys called you Mimi."

She chuckled. "Oh, that's just what they call me. A pet name. They're not my boys. I just care for them."

When Sebastian returned an hour or so later, his eyes hollow and ringed in shadow, his shirt pockmarked with black burn holes, Betty Purdy and the boys were fast asleep.

"They were wrecked. They needed time to recover, so we put them to bed." Isabella's eyes crinkled in concern. "Sebastian, you look dreadful. What do you need first — food, a bath, or sleep?"

He slumped into a chair at the table and put his head in his hands. He could smell the smoke, the dirt, the death, on him, and hunched his shoulders in despair. He'd spent the last few hours working alongside the fire fighters, dousing down the coals and combing through the rubble in a hopeless search for Buffalo Purdy. He knew it was hopeless, but an inner drive to find his old friend, to ensure he was treated with decency in death, would not let him go.

"Food or sleep. I can leave a bath till last."

Isabella chuckled. "Food it is. We'll rustle up something from the kitchen."

His eyes flicked around the room, unable to settle on anything. Isabella rested with her elbow on the table and head cupped in her hand, watching him, holding back on her questions. He knew she'd have questions, but she was being patient, giving him room to come back to reality. A deep sense of calm, of grounded good sense, emanated from her.

She'd packed away the mourning clothes, he noted with a jarring lurch of his heart. She wore a pretty apricot dress, some kind of filmy fabric covered in botanical designs — sprigs of blue-and-green branches, deep pink birds. And the apricot color set off the golden sheen of her hair to perfection. His mood lightened as he drank in the sight of her, like getting a hint of spring in the middle of winter.

"You managed Mrs Purdy and the boys all right? No problems?"

"Yes, everything was fine. The boys are total darlings. Very well-behaved. I suspect they had hot chocolate for the first time in their lives. Sad isn't? 'I'll never forget the day my father died, and I first drank hot chocolate.'" She sighed and looked pensive. "Though I wonder if Mr Purdy was actually their father. They seem to call her Mimi, a pet name, and she said they're not her boys, she just takes care of them." She sighed. "I guess you didn't find him alive?"

Sebastian shook his head. "No. I knew it was impossible but until you try … At least he will be given a proper burial."

"Did you know him well?"

"He was the quartermaster, so he

wasn't alongside me in battle like Robert was. But we all appreciated his work because he kept us fed and provisioned so well. One of the best in the whole army, I reckon. Until he got taken captive. That broke him."

His mind flew back to the last conversation they'd had — when was it? Heavens to Betsy, it was today, earlier today. Over a beer on Front Street this morning.

He allowed his mind to wander to the place he most dreaded going to. Had his pursuit of information from Burton led to the fire, to his death? The firemen had been equivocal in deciding on a cause for the blaze. The building had been derelict, the owner a hated slum landlord. It was possible it had been deliberately lit, by him or one of his enemies. But it was equally likely it was sheer bad luck: an unattended cooking pot or a smoldering cigarette end. Could he accept it was simple coincidence, or did he have to acknowledge he might have caused Burton Purdy's death?

"Calling Sebastian ... Sebastian ..."

He opened his eyes and his stomach somersaulted. Isabella was regarding him with a soft, warm expression. She'd been trying to call him back from his wool-gathering — without success. "Methinks thy wits run the wild-goose chase," she joked.

"My what?"

"You were miles away. Lost in thought. It's a line from *Romeo and Juliet* I learned in school."

"And you played Juliet, I suppose."

"How did you guess?"

He shook his head and smiled. "How could you possibly be anyone else? You did a great job here today, but I hardly see you as the nurse."

She laughed. "Speaking of which, here comes your food." Rosie had returned with a tray of delicious-smelling hot soup and warm bread.

"Thanks so much, you two. You've been so much help."

"Seb, truly, it's nothing. I just want to help you make sure this poor family is looked after."

He caught a whiff of the food — a beefy stock with lots of vegetables — and his gastric juices kicked in. He was starving, and he needed to eat. All the rest could wait.

As he dipped his spoon into the rich gravy, he glanced up and caught Isabella's eye. She blushed faintly and quickly diverted her attention to Rosie. Whatever she'd been thinking at that moment, she was embarrassed to have been discovered. He took in his first mouthful and as the salty, warm, potato taste filled him another thought penetrated his pleasure.

*She really is a remarkable nineteen-year-old, with a maturity and understanding well beyond her years.*

Followed immediately by the riposte he'd made to Edmund a few days ago: *For goodness sake, she's just a kid. Find someone your own age.*

He felt his face getting hot, and knew it wasn't because of the good soup. Now he was the one turning red.

# Twenty-Seven

Caroline Studebaker wasn't pleased. "Corporal Quincey, I thought you could do better than this. I really did." Her full red lips turned down at the corners as she calculated her cards with glinting eyes. His temples throbbed with a burst of anger at the thrust-out, petulant bottom lip. For the first time since he'd been romancing Caroline Studebaker he noticed how her jawline sagged over her expensive pearls in puffy, froggy pouches. Funny it wasn't so evident the other night, when she was into the merry-making.

It was fast becoming obvious why Caroline was reckoned to be the richest merchant on I Street. It wasn't just because of her deceased husband's craftiness, although that no doubt had helped: she was a match for any man when it came to bluffing, bargaining and bullying. Edmund braced himself mentally. *You're a match for her anytime*, he told himself. *Together we'll be dynamite.*

He was not feeling at his most suave tonight, and wouldn't it just be like Caroline to pick up on his rattled mood and home in on it. First the chair had been too hard. Then the punch too warm. And now the card game was *so* boring. "I'd rather be back at the store going over the ledger. I trust my people, but you can't be too careful." She gave a discreet yawn behind the back of her hand. "Oh my goodness, these early starts are getting to me. I don't think I can stay up much longer."

He hadn't been as attentive tonight, and Caroline was alert to the smallest changes in body language or voice. He'd have to remember that. He gave a sigh. It looked like the 'honeymoon phase' of their relationship was already over — and they'd barely begun.

Truth was, he couldn't get that cussed Sebastian Russell out of his head. He'd tried to warn him off. Steer him away from poking into things that didn't concern him, but he wasn't willing to take a hint. He'd had to go and pester Burton Purdy. God's honor he didn't know what they'd talked about, but he couldn't afford to take any chances.

Caroline was like her late, lamented Armin, a committed supporter of 'liberty and fraternity', leftovers from the youthful radicalism which had got them into trouble in their German homeland. They'd paid for the setting up of the Sacramento Hussars and had been staunchly on the side of preserving the Union and abolition of the war. Any hint of his extra-curricular activities would sink his chances of drawing her into his plans to set up in partnership with Hector de Vile. De Vile was interested in him partly because he figured he might be close to marrying the Studebaker woman. He had no illusions about that. What was it they said about the big rollers who were making their fortunes in railways, all through the public purse? You had to have money to make money — and thanks to Delia's green-eyed wittering he had none.

He couldn't afford to let this golden opportunity slip through his fingers. He especially didn't want any details filtering through of his past lives — with Delia, in the unit — none of it. A clean slate. That's what he needed. Caroline looked up from her cards sharply. "Are you all right? You're quiet tonight."

"Just a bit tired, that's all. Been a busy few days. Perhaps you're right, maybe we should call it a night."

"You're looking decidedly peaky." Caroline laid her cards down and gathered up her skirts ready to leave.

"I'm fine. Just tired. We've got de Vile's dinner tomorrow, remember. I promise I'll be better company there."

He screwed up his fists in his pockets, and a conversation he'd had with Delia rang in his head. She had accused him of not loving her, of only marrying her for her money. Not that it was hers, exactly — it was at her father's disposal, as he'd found to his cost. As the only child of a wealthy landowner she'd be in for a great handout when her old man croaked. But she'd looked so pitiful, wringing her hands and complaining about his infidelities, that he'd let her have it. He was tired of tiptoeing around. Told her she was lucky to have him. That at least a dozen women prettier than her and much better in bed would give their last petticoat to be where she was. That had shut her up. It had almost been worth it to see the appalled look on her face.

Almost. But not entirely because she'd gone tattle-taling to her Daddy. So when she died a few months later, Colonel Meredith called him in straight after the funeral and told him he could pack his bags and be gone. There was no patrimony coming to him there.

He shivered as he remembered the

confrontation. Well, Caroline was no Delia, and he wasn't going to make the same mistake twice. She was a shrewd operator who understood both the value of a dollar and her own worth. He wasn't going to risk the most promising opportunity he'd seen in many a year just because some black sozzle had whispered her husband's drunken stories abroad. He'd make sure she — and anyone else she might have talked to — were silenced.

And meantime, he'd better get Caroline smiling again.

# Twenty-Eight

"A most remarkable record of service. No doubt he's been too modest to mention it to you, Mrs Studebaker?"

Hector de Vile gave Edmund a sly wink and topped up Caroline's wine.

"You're right, Senator, as usual." Caroline smiled at both men.

She was looking quite attractive tonight, Hector thought, in a green-and-white off-the-shoulder evening dress and matching emerald necklace and earrings. Not beautiful — Caroline Studebaker would never be that. 'Handsome' might be a better word. Her arms were sculpted and strong — from years of moving boxes in her warehouses, he supposed — and her brown eyes had a steady penetrating glint. The candlelight from the dining table lit up the deep copper tint in her wavy brown hair. It came to him in a rush that it would be a foolish man who underestimated her.

"Of course, I knew he fought bravely, but I know nothing of the particulars."

"You'll have to get him to tell you sometime. He was the hero of more than one battle, or so I've heard."

"Hector, no need to drag up old history." Edmund's palms were upturned in a gesture of surrender. "Mostly we old vets don't want to remember the war. Too many painful memories. But yes, it was my privilege to serve with General Sherman. Now *there* was a remarkable soldier."

Caroline's face lit up with pleasure. "Sherman was here in Sacramento, did you know? My father always talked of him. That's one reason Armin and Father were determined to support the Sacramento Hussars." She turned to Edmund. "The Hussars were the only cavalry unit in the county. Armin was a member from when they began ten years ago until his death." She took a sip of wine and her face softened to a dreamy nostalgia. "They looked so splendid in their dashing gray uniforms on their beautiful horses, and they always did everything so well, all ship-shape and military." She sighed deeply. "Forgive me. Living in the past." She gave a tinkling laugh — no nervous bray evident tonight — and adjusted one of her earrings. "I still love to see them on parade, even without Armin."

Hector raised his glass and clinked it against the one Mrs Studebaker held.

"You'll have plenty of splendid occasions to look forward to in the future, I'm sure. The opportunity we're here to discuss, for example. Edmund might have already mentioned it to you?"

The light humor gone, Caroline regarded him with serious eyes. "Just a mention. No real detail. He said you'd give me that." She flashed a look at Edmund. "I've been honest with him. I don't know much about business beyond my own retail area. And I'm a conservative investor, so it will have to be a convincing proposition."

"I wouldn't expect anything else of you, Mrs Studebaker."

Hector steepled his fingers and for the next forty-five minutes outlined the proposition he and Quincey had hammered out together. Correction. He told her the parts that she needed to know. How much it would cost her, and what profit she could expect. Why it was a great proposition, and how he could be trusted to ensure it all went smoothly. He didn't tell her about the commission he was paying Edmund for bringing in her money, or the offer of other incentives if he steered her into further investments to the de Vile Corporation. Edmund could tell her about those side deals if he wished, but it was none of Hector's business.

Caroline Studebaker might be immured in her own business but she was a quick study and asked some penetrating questions. De Vile was impressed. *She thinks like a man. Goes straight for the jugular.* The more time he spent with her, the more engrossing he found her company. It was plain she valued strong lines of command and a disciplined work ethic. He could see why the Hussars' precision drills would have appealed to her preference for knowing exactly where she stood.

He glanced across to Quincey, who'd been quietly observing, and just occasionally boosting, the business opportunity under discussion. He hadn't known Quincey long, but given a choice between doing business with him or with Caroline Studebaker, the woman would win hands down. Quincey had a slickness about him that always left him questioning his reliability.

Caroline had taken out a notepad and elegant propelling pencil from a small evening bag and was making meticulous notes as Hector spoke. Now she closed the notebook and stowed it back into her bag with quick, neat movements. "It's getting late, and I'm not fresh enough to digest all this new information. I need to sleep on it."

Hector became aware of a dull ache in his chest. The sense of disappointment deepened as she snapped her bag shut and made to rise. This woman had a lot more to offer than her money. Edmund was maintaining his carefully groomed insouciance, but he could sense tenseness in the set of his shoulders under the dinner jacket.

Hector was slightly let down that Caroline had not immediately taken the line hook, bait and sinker, straight out of the boat, but he knew there were other fish. She wasn't his only likely catch. Not so for Edmund Quincey. As they began the rituals of thanks for hospitality and farewells, Hector didn't miss the famished look in Quincey's yellow-green eyes. He was keen, but Quincey was *desperate* to score the deal, no doubt about it. And Hector was guessing he'd go to any lengths to seal it.

# Twenty-Nine

"Surprise!" Sir John Russell, Seb's oldest half-brother, and his wife of three months, the Maori singing star Pania Hayes, stood arm-in-arm in the hallway of New Gold House and beamed at the circle of bright smiling faces around them. Their return after several months away on an Australia-New Zealand stage tour was fully expected, but none had known exactly what day they were due, and now they were here no one could believe it.

Seb's face ached from the wide grin that had started at the sound of John's foot on the front door step. Married life and the time away had transformed him.

The gaunt, haunted look he'd developed over a terrible period last year when he faced extreme business and personal dangers had vanished. He stood, over six feet in his socks, his stance casual and easy, his sun-tanned face smiling. He looked years younger than his thirty-eight summers.

Isabella's mother Huldah stood out front in one of her 'impossible to miss' tangerine creations, clapping her hands and smoothing her cheeks with the back of her hand. Next to her was Mrs Snively, John's long-time cook-housekeeper, wiping her hands and eyes on her apron. The pair had been hard at work planning this 'welcome home' gathering for days now, Huldah having returned to Grass Valley after Alycia's funeral ahead of everyone else for this very purpose.

The newlyweds had moved into New Gold House — 'New' because it replaced the original, which burned down last year in an arson attack — a couple of weeks before they went overseas. John was a seriously wealthy business magnate who had spared no expense to make his home a showcase of comfort and style. Along with the builders and architect, he'd created something glorious to see yet still homely to live in.

And sparkling. Huldah and Mrs S. had done a great job: the beds were all made up with fresh linen, there were flowers in the well-aired rooms, and the hallway was permeated by the onion-and-gravy smell of one of Mrs Snively's renowned beef stews. "Come on in!" Seb embraced his brother. "Don't let's stand on ceremony!"

The 'family' included Rosie and

Isabella; Sir John's groom and handyman Nelson; and John's Chinese house manager and general factotum Mr Lee and his wife. The only important ones missing were their other half-brother, Nathan, and his wife Graysie who were still away in Sydney.

"We've got so much to catch up on! We hardly know where to start!" Pania stood with her hands laced in front of her, her husband's protective hand across her shoulders. "We're devastated about Alycia, of course, and so sorry we weren't here to support you and give honor to an unforgettable woman. We want to make up for our absence. But right now, I do believe it's dinner time. And I guess you're all starving."

The meal was one of Mrs Snively's best. Nothing fancy: homegrown carrots and potatoes in a rich meat gravy bringing with it the deep earthy comfort of the soil and sun that satisfied a man's bones to the marrow. Seb glanced around the table and guessed from the collective hum that hovered over them that everyone seated there shared the feeling. Eating rather than talking was the priority of the moment. Alycia's loss hovered in the subdued talk, which was not the usual Russell raucous chatter. But there was no doubt that having at least some of the family back together again brought a peace and comfort he'd been missing. He'd had it so rarely after his father died and he and his brothers were separated so many years ago.

They were the three sons of a Scottish-born Hongkong taipan's three wives, and when Sir Robert Russell died the two youngest — Nathan and him — had returned to their maternal families:

ten-year-old Nathan to Sydney with his mother, Seb to his dead mother's brother in Boston, while John had struck off to San Francisco to work for the family business. They'd finally closed the thousands of miles that separated them with a California reunion last year.

He didn't think he was alone in his deep pleasure at John's return. Everyone lingered over dessert, reluctant to end the occasion, eagerly catching up on all that had happened. John and Pania had a new solidarity in the way they deferred to one another: often before one spoke they hesitated as if giving the other a chance to speak first, a slight pause of acknowledgment that said more than words could about their high regard for one another.

Finally the household broke up, and the brothers sat on the veranda nursing a brandy each in the deepening dusk. Over dinner they'd limited themselves to the barest of outlines — what happened and who had been responsible. They sat, enjoying the cool freshness of the evening, silent apart from the stirrings of night birds in the orange grove.

"Murky situation." John pulled on his cigar and stared out over the purple-gray garden. "We know Polk pulled the trigger, but we don't know who paid him to do it or why."

Seb nodded. "That about sums it up. And with Hiram the way he is there's no chance we can take it any further with him right now."

John got up and tapped his cigar over the veranda edge, the ash falling with a slight hiss into the garden below. "The thing you have to wonder about is motive. Alycia could be imperious, but her conduct was beyond reproach. Why would she be the target of a planned attack like that? It beggars understanding."

"You'd have to say it's either something to do with Basil's business dealings — though if that's the case why not go after him? — or, and I'm reluctant to admit it because at first I couldn't see it, something to do with the way she backed Isabella's search for her twin brother. She's been beating that drum ever since last summer, and seemed unwilling to give up on it, even though nothing's come to light."

"Reluctant to admit it? Why?"

The candle holder set on the table between them was attracting a cloud of small lavender-winged moths. One now dive-bombed and drowned in the pooled hot wax.

"I disagreed with Isabella about it right from the start. It seemed too far-fetched. I suppose just for that reason. There's no hint Hiram ever uncovered anything new. So if someone didn't want the boy found, you'd think he or she wouldn't have any reason to be worried anyway. Why go to such lengths, when you're in no danger of being found out?"

John grimaced and took another puff. The smoky aroma tamped down Seb's prickling unease. *What am I missing?*

John cleared his throat. "Maybe we're not as far off the mark as we think. How has Isabella been taking it all, anyway?"

Isabella. Seb was embarrassed to acknowledge how readily he'd discounted her as an overwrought teenager barely a week ago. He didn't think of her as an indulged ingenue any longer.

"She's been remarkable. I must admit

at the beginning I couldn't see the link with the brother, and I told her so, but I'm starting to think she might be right. I didn't want to get into it at dinner but there have been a couple of nasty incidents with her — suspicious goings on. Not-so-subtle attempts to frighten her off, I'd say."

He told John about her riding accident and the gypsy threats. "She's shown herself to have quite a capacity for absorbing disaster. Way beyond what you'd expect for her years. She was tremendous with Mrs Purdy and the boys, too. I had no idea she had it in her." He could hear the admiring warmth in his voice and his neck heated with a matching flush.

After a long pause John asked, "What do you see as the next step? If Hiram is off-limits, what or who else is there?"

Seb adjusted his position, suddenly

uncomfortable. "It's fragile. The weakest of possibilities, probably. But I've got a feeling that Mrs Purdy knows something she's not telling. She was the one Hiram gave Polk's payout to, remember. I've already tried Mrs Polk — you'll not get any sense out of her. She's well and truly cracked in the filbert.

"And what about Mrs Purdy?" John was frowning over his cigar. "Where is she now her house is gone?"

"I understand she has family in Grass Valley and was going to stay with them."

"And what about you, Seb? How have you been? I'm sorry you've had to handle all this drama without any back up from me or Nathan."

"Me? I'm all right. Alycia, the gun going off at close range, brought back unwelcome memories. But I'm getting over that."

"You knew Burton Purdy from the war? That's a bit of a surprise."

"Yes. The war was very hard on him. He never fully recovered. Still had his wits about him when he wasn't foxed, but most of the time I'd guess he was buried in his cups." He stubbed the toe of his boot a couple of times on the painted wooden deck. "Seeing Burton reminded me all over again of the toll that war took on ordinary men, and the women who loved them. A different stroke of the clock, and it could have been me. Lately I've been thinking a lot about things that happened back then."

"Oh? Like?"

Seb liked it that his brother wasn't wordy.

A night bird called. His arms felt cool — must be the breeze which had sprung up — and a light shiver went through him.

"Ah, a lot of stuff that happened in the third year of the war. Just when we thought we knew what we were doing. That's when my buddy Robert Kingsley got killed. His sister died not long after. They'd both been close friends from my first days back here from Hong Kong, a time when I desperately needed friends. I really thought we were all going to get through it alive. Silly of me. Shows how wrong you can be, doesn't it?"

John shifted position in his chair, stretching his long legs out in front of him and crossing his ankles. He slouched back and let his brother's soft voice filter into his mind, his soul, leaking into all the vacant places and filling him. He'd been reunited with Seb for more than a year, but any time the subject of the war had come up, his sibling had batted it away and closed down the conversation.

Until now. He knew that old soldiers said it was impossible to explain to others what being in battle was like, and he accepted that. But Seb had a distance about him that even in their moments of most brotherly affection set him apart — and the old Seb hadn't been like that. Sure, he'd always run quiet and deep, but he wasn't disconnected.

"I don't think it's at all silly, Seb. Tell me about Robert. And his sister."

Sebastian's chair creaked and the candle between them made a spitting sound and petered out. The purple dusk had turned to dark as they'd been talking, and the black air was heavy with the perfume of night-scented jasmine.

"The 22nd were renowned for their 'skirmishing' — where we were sent ahead to harass and delay the enemy from attacking the main lines. There came a day we were sent to an area where there were supposedly only very light concentrations of Rebel troops — a good-sized advance party sent on ahead to establish safe passage and get a forward camp set up — while the rest of our unit went on the opposite flank to engage with what was supposed to be a heavy penetration of Rebs. We thought for once we'd got off with light duties."

Seb gave a short bitter laugh and twisted irritably in his chair, causing the iron legs to screech against the boards. "Turned out the intelligence Corporal Edmund Quincey claimed was watertight was a leaky bucket. Very light numbers met Quincey and they melted away at first contact, and very heavy numbers hit us. We were outnumbered and under-prepared. That's when Burton got captured. It seemed like a deliberate pincer movement to capture our supply lines — they were starving — and it worked a charm."

Even in the dark John could see the shadowed furrows of pain that scored Seb's cheeks and brow. He looked years older than he had earlier tonight — old and exhausted.

"Robert was right beside me when he got hit by one of those devilish Minié balls. Mowed him down before my eyes. Nothing I could do for him except ensure he was gathered up and given a decent burial. Something many of the other poor beggars didn't get."

John let the long silence draw out between them until Seb's breathing returned to a regular pattern. "And his sister?"

"Sarah? Funny, I guess tucked away

somewhere in the deepest corners of my heart I imagined she and I would end up together. I never spoke of it, I suppose partly because I was frightened of jinxing it. Me getting killed or some other disruption breaking the magic of what we had, a very special friendship, if she didn't see things the same way. If you're a soldier you never know what the next day might bring, and I didn't think it was fair to marry, maybe leave her in child and then die on her. We had to get through the damn war. And we didn't manage to do that."

"What happened?"

"She came to visit Robert — well, Robert and me, I guess. Called us 'her two boys'. Brought us a wonderful food parcel from home. And then Robert got sick. She stayed on, nursing him and when he recovered made herself useful in the hospital tent, reading to sick men, writing letters home if they were too weak to do it for themselves … just generally helping. It all went well until she caught Edmund Quincey's eye. He had always been one for the ladies, and Sarah was one of the sweetest ladies on earth. Quite swept her off her feet, he did. She appeared captivated."

John noted the sour edge in Seb's voice as he continued. "And then Robert was killed. That was hard enough, but there was a lot of gossip, a lot of suspicion, about how it happened. Men grumbled that Edmund had been off carousing in a beer house notorious for entertaining men from both sides of the line, so to speak. A place where drunken talk was currency. It just seemed too convenient that we'd had our supplies stolen and men killed and captured as the result of what looked like false intelligence. I tried to reason with Sarah, but she was devastated. There were rumors all about camp that Quincey had a loose mouth. I think she felt betrayed. That she'd been consorting with someone questionable and her brother was killed as a result. I'm just assuming, because she didn't confide in me. I guess Quincey's shadow had come between us.

"It didn't help that he was as arrogant and bumptious as he'd ever been. He didn't take any of the rumbles seriously, rubbished her when she tried to ask him about it, treated her in an offhand manner, I gather. As in, what would a mere woman know?"

Seb's expression was so shot through with pain that John's throat closed up.

"I think she felt completely shamed. She wouldn't talk, just cried and shook her head and said everything was ruined. I got furlough — I was at the end of my three years — and accompanied her back home after the funeral, but two weeks later she shot herself."

The near-full moon had been climbing as they'd talked and was now high enough in the sky to cast shadows of colonnaded stripes from the veranda pickets across the floor to their feet. Seb's face was lunar pale, and his knuckles were white on the arms of his chair. He was gripping it as if he would float away in misery if he let go.

John scrambled for the right words to say, even merely adequate words, but came up with nothing. *Darkness, and light, darkness, and light.* His eyes roved the striped shadows, and his head almost set up a chanting rhythm, 'Darkness and light' over and over. Was that how life always had to be? And with more darkness than light, it seemed.

"This Quincey fellow," he said at last. "Where's he now?"

"Right this minute? I have no idea. Trying to get into Caroline Studebaker's bed most likely." He shot his brother a sickly smile. "Sorry. Uncalled for. He's around. Surfaced in Sacramento last week — but he's been here longer than that. He's been married and widowed at least once since the war, but I gather his wife's riches didn't get passed on, so he's on the hunt for a replacement. He did bail us out of a spot of bother with the gypsies on K Street a couple of days ago. Once again, a bit too convenient for my liking."

After he told the story of the encounter with Preciosa and the Roma people, John observed, "It does sound rather too coincidental, given his past history. Tell me, did you ever settle the case of whether he had actually betrayed your unit with his loose mouth, or even colluded in return for favors?"

Seb shook his head. "No. It wasn't really possible to get hard facts. We moved territories soon after that, anyway. But a few days ago, Burton shocked me with dark tales of other stuff. I had no idea."

John waited expectantly, giving silent thanks for the blessing of being back home with his beautiful wife, talking to his half-brother he held so dear. He'd enjoyed such good fortune. He sent up an arrow prayer that Seb would see the same fruitfulness: he had done enough sacrificing. "What kind of stuff? Do tell."

"He said that before those battles where we got so badly mauled Edmund had been dealing in contraband. You know the old story — how some no-goods went looking for freedmen or escaped slaves to sell back across the border to the Confederates. They'd kidnap any they could find in Union territory and bundle them back across the lines at night. They were getting up to a thousand dollars apiece for strong young men."

John snorted his disgust. "You'd wonder why he had to marry a rich girl and make her life a misery. I'm assuming. He sounds the sort."

"Think you're right. At one stage I thought he might have had an eye on Isabella, but thankfully it seems she's got more sense."

John permitted himself a quick smile. Seb's voice betrayed a very slight, and uncharacteristic, waver as he tripped over the name 'Isabella'. He would take a guess that, right at this moment, Son Number Two's heart was beating a little faster. He glanced over at his brother, but his face wasn't giving anything away.

*The poor sod. He's got no clue he's already half in love with her.*

He reminded himself that this time last year he was just about as clueless as Seb.

*Here's hoping by this time next year he too will have a wife he adores by his side — one who, like Pania, is about to announce to the world she's with child.*

He stepped off the veranda and ground his cigar stub under his heel. "What's first on the agenda? Let's see if we can get this mess cleaned up before Nathan gets back."

# Thirty

"That's one thing I haven't done." Seb stopped buttering his toast.

"What's that?" John leaned over the morning paper spread out in front of him, coffee cup in one hand, toast in the other, at ease in a paisley banyan, the informal house robe men wore for relaxation over loose shirt and breeches, looking for all the world like the King of his Castle. Seb supposed he was.

"Talked to the manager at the Louisiana Race Course. Where Isabella had her fall."

The thudding of horse hooves down the grassway to the nearby stables caught their attention. "That's what made me think of it," said Seb as they watched Isabella smoothly bring the mare to a halt and hand the reins to Nelson. She spun around and headed straight across the meadow towards them.

"I called back a couple of times to talk to the guy who set Isabella up, but he was never there and I couldn't catch the manager either. I wanted to satisfy myself on what they think happened."

Isabella tramped up the steps and shed her riding boots in the hall just outside the dining room door. "Morning, all! Gorgeous day out there."

John smiled. "You sound very chirpy this morning."

Isabella slipped her lithe form into a chair next to Seb. "Oh, I am, Sir John. It's so marvelous to be back in Grass Valley and my own bed. And thank you so much for allowing me to ride one of your mares this morning. I just love to get some exercise."

John gave a wry twitch of his lips. "So Seb has been reminding me."

She turned sharply to Sebastian. "Nothing bad, I hope. I told you, that fall really wasn't my fault."

Seb made a placatory gesture with his free hand. "I didn't say it was. I was recalling that I never did get to go back there and talk to the men in the stables, find out what they thought went on there."

Isabella's eyes softened. "Oh, we ran out of time, didn't we, what with gypsies and fires and all. Such a lot going on, it's no wonder."

"John, you were asking last night about first things on the agenda," said Seb. "I spent a lot of the night thinking about that. Do you want to hear my thoughts?"

"Thoughts about what?" Pania wandered in, wearing a silk wrapping robe that matched her husband's in style, though hers was in burgundy and his in bottle-green. She put a hand up to her mouth to stifle a yawn and sank into the dining chair next to John. "Sorry, I had such a refreshing sleep. But it's lovely to wake up here." She smiled at him. "Did you sleep well, my darling?"

John flashed her an affectionate smile and muttered to the room, "Forgive us. We seem to have turned into nauseatingly gaga newlyweds. Don't know what's come over us."

"I'm just savoring precious time together." She reached over and rumpled his hair. "You recall I'll need to go to Sacramento in the next couple of days to sort out some business."

"Perfect," said Seb. "Just what we need. John can accompany you to your business, and then you can accompany him to talk to the Race Course owner where Isabella had her fall. Try to get to the bottom of what really happened there."

Pania raised her strong, dark eyebrows and flashed Isabella a determined look. "Nothing I'd like better than to help get to the bottom of all this."

"What else came to mind when you weren't sleeping, Seb?" John held up the coffee pot questioningly and both women proffered their cups. "In order of importance."

"Well, it seems to me we've reached a bit of a blind alley with looking into Alycia's death, unless we can talk to

Hiram again — which probably won't be for a while yet — or coax whatever it is Mrs Purdy isn't telling us out of her. After all, she was the one who was the intermediary between Hiram and Mrs Polk. I think just by default because Mrs Polk is a basket case, but still …"

"Sounds logical," said John. "What else?"

"Well, if you tick off Alycia and move onto Edmund Quincey, you could ask is he involved in any of this and if so, how? His appearance when the gypsies appeared seemed convenient, to say the least."

"What would be the best way to handle him, do you think?" John had the eager look of a water dog sighting up a duck.

"He's probably still in Sacramento weaseling his way into Mrs Studebaker's good graces. I think he's desperate to break into the merchant clique here in California, and he'd go to any lengths to achieve it. I sense he's getting more reckless with age, and he always was one to cut corners. He's got ten years on me, and he's still got nothing to show for it except bombast."

John's bright attentiveness sobered. "Would that include burning down someone's home with them in it?"

Seb shrugged, shaking his head. "Who knows?"

John sniffed. "Well, if I happen to bump into him I'll certainly engage him in business talk. See how far I get. Anything else?"

Before Sebastian could answer, Isabella's clear strong voice cut in. "Aren't you forgetting something?"

Seb glanced up at her over his cup.

Her complexion retained the freshness of her morning ride; her eyes sparked with indignation. "What about finding Alejandro? Haven't we agreed already that Alycia's insistence on keeping up the search is the most likely cause of her death? Her death and my 'incidents'. And what about the gypsies?"

She held her chin high and tapped her fingers on the edge of the table to release the frustration that was boiling over. She glared around the table, her lips set in a pinched line with the end of the outpouring.

*Put your head in a noose, why don't you,* thought Sebastian. *Here we go again …*

"Isabella, we haven't forgotten about Alejandro, I promise. But we come up against the same brick wall over and over. Where else can we look? Hiram is off-limits, and it seems even he couldn't find anything. And as for the gypsies — honestly, Isabella, there's nothing to be gained in trying to find them again, even if we knew where to look. You must appreciate that. It will all be about extortion. They're liars, thieves and fraudsters. We were clearly set up last time. They've got no intention to help anyone but themselves. Even if they could, and I doubt they know anything about Alejandro ... I'm sorry but there is no other way to say it."

Isabella pushed back her chair from the table with a gust of raw energy. She put her hands over her ears. "I don't want to hear it!" She glared at Sebastian. "How could you? Doesn't anybody care? Has Alycia died in vain?"

She stood frozen, her face draining of color. Then she said in a scratchy whisper, "I'd better get home. Please excuse me." Shoulders slumped, head down, she turned for the door to retrieve her riding boots. Her gait as she crossed the room was discouraged and listless. So very different from how she'd bounced in thirty minutes before.

*Yup. Put your head in a noose, Sebastian, and kick away the chair.*

Nelson would drop her back to Huldah's, but he still had to tell her he didn't want her going anywhere without his full protection. That meant him tagging along. He could imagine how that would go down, but too bad. Until they knew what they were up against, it was too dangerous to risk anything else. The last thing he could tolerate was the idea of losing her, fiery little madam as she might be.

# Thirty-One

When Pania spotted Isabella's tight expression as she stood at the entry to Huldah's drawing room, she wondered for a moment if the girl might actually refuse to see her.

The cook had answered the door and led her into the hall, but Isabella was plainly not in any mood to receive visitors. In one hand she clutched a sparkling turquoise dress close to her chest, like a shield. In the other she grasped the drawing-room door handle, and her stance indicated she was tempted to shut it in Pania's face.

Her light-gold complexion was suffused with rosy indignation, her blue eyes flashed angrily, and she had probably never been more beautiful. Pania had to suppress the urge to smile. No wonder John suspected that Sebastian was already half in love with her. She was not only lovely but she had the spirit of a thoroughbred. All fire and determination.

"Mother isn't here at present, if it's her you've come to see." Her tone was clipped, her stance rigid. "If you're thinking of trying to insist on Sebastian tagging along with me wherever I go, I'm afraid you're wasting your time. I can't stand the man."

Pania willed herself to be as soothing, as unthreatening as she could be. "Isabella, I understand your frustration, I really do. But how about we let all that drop for the moment and just catch up? I've been out of circulation for months.

I'd love to hear what's been going on."

Isabella's eyes widened in surprise and her stance relaxed. She stepped back and said in a much softer tone, "How could I refuse such a gracious offer? Would you like coffee or tea?"

"I'd love some coffee. I've been drinking nothing but tea for months." Pania smiled and the tension between them dissolved. "It's lovely to have a chance to talk without the men around."

Pania followed Isabella into the drawing room and settled in while her hostess slipped out to get coffee. Everything about the décor — squat brown armchairs and plum velvet drapes — was unimaginative, plain and comfortable. It spoke of Huldah's sober conventional values, her dedication to hard work, propriety, and definitely no rocking of the boat with outlandish dreams or a creative spirit.

It had been no surprise to discover Isabella was not her natural-born daughter: the two were so different that it rather stretched the imagination to accept that she was. But it was touching the way they'd retained a high mutual regard for one another following the dramatic revelations of Isabella's family origins last year. Isabella's mother, Elanora Grayson Travers Castellanos, was the captivating, disgraced daughter of New York society, who if she hadn't died young may well have made a splash on the stage herself.

It hadn't been easy for mother or daughter to adjust to the new reality, but Isabella remained grateful for all the years of loving care Huldah had given her. Huldah, in return, had at last understood that she had mothered a young woman who was never going to settle for being a model of docile domesticity and nothing more.

Isabella bustled back into the room with a tray and a sunny smile. "Sorry about my attitude earlier. I couldn't help it. I'm still mad as a March hare about Alejandro. I feel it in my bones. Time is running out!"

She hurled the last few words across the room, her face squeezed into a frown of desperate appeal. "I can't explain it, but I'm so scared we'll find him too late."

Pania patted the seat beside her. "Come and sit down, my dear. Let's go over it all together." For the next thirty minutes or so, Pania listened as Isabella ranged far and wide with her account of everything that had happened since Alycia's death.

"Sebastian has been wonderful, he really has. But from the very first day I got the impression he didn't take me seriously. And he certainly didn't think Alejandro had anything to do with what was going on."

Pania nodded. "Sometimes, dear Izzy, we women are more intuitive about things. And it's very hard to explain to the men why we are convinced of something. I came up against that last year with John when we had that dreadful business with Lily's kidnapping. I felt the same frustration you are now. And I've learned from all my extra years that often its best to play along with them."

She raised a theatrical eyebrow and Isabella giggled. "You really are a naughty grande dame, aren't you? So tell me ..." She sighed and adopted a faux-tone of resignation. "Tell me what I should do about it."

Pania felt a rush of warm affection for the young woman beside her. Yes, she had spirit, but she was also amenable to common sense. "What you need to do, dear Izzy, is punish Sebastian Russell by taking him on an especially long fitting session at Cressida's tomorrow. That's why you had that lovely turquoise number out, isn't it?" She gestured to the frock which Isabella had discarded on the arm of a chair. "They are right in their thinking, you know. You *do* need to take extra care at the moment, and Seb would consider it a personal failure if anything happened to you while you were in his care, so to speak. So go along with it. Let him be your protector — but that doesn't mean he has to enjoy it …"

# Thirty-Two

Seb sat in dressmaker Cressida Washington's reception room with a coffee, his third, balanced on one knee, and tamped down his rising impatience. One of the burdens of insisting on keeping Isabella safe was that he'd had to accompany her to a dressmaker's appointment at Cressida Washington's establishment. Cressida was the most sought-after fashion virtuoso between the mountains and Sacramento. Women came from the capital for designs and fabrics that were found nowhere else. Pania, for one, swore by her flair for suggesting just the right cut and color to flatter.

Sebastian was more than happy to leave all that to the ladies, but for the last hour and a half he'd been twiddling his thumbs like Isabella's fashion lackey while she conferred with Cressida about her wardrobe for a planned tour. Isabella didn't want him there any more than he wanted to be there, and he suspected she was taking her revenge by ensuring she took as long as possible to finalize the details.

When he clocked in this morning to meet her, she was as icy as a frozen waterfall and had made a fine job of ignoring him ever since. He'd filled in the enforced leisure by going over everything in his head one more time, asking himself if there was anything obvious that he'd missed, any gap he'd overlooked. The only thing that came to mind was that he had no idea where

Betty Purdy's family lived, whether in Grass Valley proper or one of the nearby towns. It occurred to him that they should provide her with extra security as well, even if she were in semi-hiding.

He could hear the muted sound of women's voices through the wall, as Cressida and Isabella chatted. He was just starting to wonder if he would be shut up in here all day when Cressida emerged with a broad smile. She was tall and strongly built, her full round face and light-chocolate skin evidence of African ancestry, but the seamstress had never been anything but a free spirit with a determined purpose to make good in life. Her husband, George Emmanuel, had died fighting for the Union, and she'd come out West to distance herself from the pain of loss. She didn't want to be reminded of the bloody conflict that had resulted in freedom for slaves, but at such a horrendous cost.

*A bit like me. A refugee from the consequences of slaughter.*

"Mr Russell! So sorry we took longer than I'd expected. I hope Jessie has ensured you were well-watered?"

"Better than a prize stallion," said Sebastian. "But I can't say I'm sorry you've finished your work. I'm not exactly at home in a ladies' salon." He looked around at the elegant couches, the fashion annuals and pattern books that sat in big stacks on the floor beside occasional tables, then past Cressida's broad shoulders to Isabella, who had followed her out of the fitting room. "Everything okay? All ready to go?"

"Yes. Fine, thank you." She didn't meet his eye and spoke coolly.

He turned his attention back to

Cressida, who lifted one eyebrow. "Isabella tells me you're from Boston. You haven't been out here long."

"That's right, Mrs Washington. I lit out four years ago, wandered all over the Midwest before ending up here. I like it here."

"You were a-fighting before that?"

"Yes, I was. Seen more fighting than I ever wanted or ever wish to again."

"I know how you feel. I lost my man George Emmanuel at Fort Wagner."

"Very sorry to hear that, ma'am. Who was he with?"

"The 54th Massachusetts."

"Fine bunch of men by all accounts. Good workers too." He hesitated. "Tell me, Mrs Washington — and please don't take offense at this question — but did your husband ever complain about the activities of the contraband men?" Union officers had been involved in the noisome trade even though it was expressly forbidden by Army rules. "Did your husband ever mention them?"

"No. He wasn't affected." Cressida gestured to an armchair. "Take a seat for a moment. No need to stand all day. I'll get Jessie to bring us some cold lemonade."

She called to her assistant to bring in refreshments and settled with the air of a woman who liked everything she did to have a measured tempo. Her bottom had just touched the cushioned seat when she had another thought, and rose again. She hollered to the shut door, "And bring those photos on the mantel. I want to show Mr Russell something."

She sank back down with a grateful sigh. "Now, where was I? Oh yes." She gazed up at Sebastian. She was not to be hurried. "As I was saying, George never said much about that bad business. How they can look at themselves in the mirror each morning, well, it's beyond me. But George's brother — my brother-in-law, the Reverend Charles Moses Washington — well, that's a different story. He was a chaplain and he came across a lot of injustice and abuse in his work. Being the kind of man he is, he tried to find remedies as best he could. I've heard him tell some hair-raising tales."

"Oh? And is he still alive?"

"Sure is. In fact, he's living not more than ten miles from here." The connecting door to Cressida's private quarters swung open and a pretty young woman with glittering black hair entered carrying a tray with three glasses and a pitcher of lemonade with rings of fresh lemon and mint leaves floating on top. She set it down, distributed a glass to each of them, and deposited several daguerreotypes on the table beside them.

"Your soda, and your photos, Mrs Washington." She gave a quick nod and bustled out.

"Speaking of the saints," Mrs Washington beamed. "The very man. Here he is."

She picked up one of the glass sheets and held it as if it were a family treasure, which it plainly was. "The brothers Washington." She handed it to Sebastian. "Here they are, George Emmanuel and Charles Moses."

Sebastian took hold of it carefully and gazed at the image. Two handsome black men, the taller with his arm across the shoulders of the shorter, stood in front of a makeshift army tent, gazing into the lens with a confidence and purpose which gave him goosebumps. One wore the familiar blue of the Union men; the other wore a tidy dark suit with a white clerical collar

"This is your husband and his brother?"

"Yes. They were so proud to have that taken. I think it reinforced for them they were free men. They could have a picture taken and send it home just like white soldiers did." Sebastian handed the photograph to Isabella, and Cressida huddled close to her. "That's George." She pointed with her index finger. "And that's Charles. Did I say he's a saint, that one? Even today his door is always open to the downtrodden, offering protection and succor to all who need it. He's got some poor woman and two boys staying at the moment. Her house burned down, her husband with it. Something like that. The usual story."

Isabella was sitting, not taking part, eyes in middle distance, quietly disengaged as Seb and Cressida Washington talked, but she'd been listening. At the words 'poor woman' her head snapped up and her eyes flashed at Sebastian. He acknowledged her with an answering dart of understanding.

*Who'd ever have thought we'd find Mrs Purdy at Isabella's dressmakers?*

Isabella leaned across to Cressida and patted her hand. "What you are telling us is fascinating. It might even help us get to the bottom of Alycia's murder, though I can't think exactly how right now. It's a long shot. I don't suppose you would know the name of the family your brother-in-law has staying?"

"Oh no, dear, I wouldn't have a clue. I don't think he mentioned it. But you're welcome to go and ask him, if it's of interest to you. He's just over the hill in Nevada City. I'd be happy to jot down a note of introduction if you want to go see him. You'll just need to remember to be discreet about it. He's doesn't want his visitors being disturbed, as I'm sure you can imagine."

The sound of boots thumping up the front steps interrupted the peace of the reception room. "Doesn't sound like a client coming for a consultation," said Sebastian.

"Not with those feet," chuckled Cressida." Unless he's carrying the client over his shoulder."

Jessie appeared at the reception room door, shifting her weight from side to side uncertainly. "Mrs Washington, there's a man to see you. Says it's urgent."

Cressida's brows contracted. "Did he give a name?"

"Mr Quincey. Sorry, I mean Corporal. Corporal Edmund Quincey."

# Thirty-Three

"What the blazes are you doing here?"

Edmund was practically tramping on Jessie's heels in his haste to enter the room. When he saw Sebastian and Isabella he stopped in mid-stride and stiffened.

"We could ask you the same thing." Sebastian's stomach tightened. The set of Edmund's powerful shoulders, the pugnacious jutting jaw hummed with aggression.

He glanced to Cressida and started toward her. "Mrs Washington, I presume."

"That's correct. And you are?" She raised one eyebrow, the model of matronly dominion, her back as straight as the three-foot ruler she used in her work, her voice carrying a deep measured authority.

Edmund halted, raised his hat and bowed. "Corporal Edmund Quincey Jnr, ma'am."

Cressida looked him up and down, assessing the newcomer, then coolly gestured to an armchair at the end of the room. "Sit, Mr Quincey. If you are no longer in active service, which I assume from your suit you are not, bringing out a moth-eaten rank doesn't impress me any more than a holey overcoat would."

Edmund flushed and flopped down in the chair. "No offense intended, Mrs Washington. I find it doesn't hurt to remind people that some of us did our duty for the sanctity of the Union. Thought you of all people might appreciate that."

She snorted. "I, of all people? You're entering treacherous territory there, Mr Quincey." She fixed him with her formidable stare.

For the first time since he entered the room Edmund seemed to get an inkling he'd got off on the wrong foot. His casual intimidation wasn't drawing the desired response. Worse, it was stirring up antagonism. "I really didn't intend—" He glanced around the room as if seeking moral support. "Never mind." He shrank back, his bravado exhausted.

An awkward silence ensued, broken only when Mrs Washington asked, "We are still none the wiser as to what brings you here, Mr Quincey. I presume not the dress-making requirements of a wife or daughter?"

Cressida didn't snort, but the glitter in her eye communicated a similar message.

"Dress-making? Oh, no." He glanced at Sebastian, as if reluctant to state his business with him in the room.

"Don't mind me," Sebastian said. "You were the one in a rush. We've still got a few loose ends to tidy up, but we have all day." He spread his hands wide, palms up. "You sound as if you're in a hurry."

Edmund gave a sigh. "I was looking for someone, and I was told you could help me, Mrs Washington."

He glanced at the occasional table, where the daguerreotypes of the brothers still rested, face up. "I very much hope that will be the case."

Cressida interlaced her fingers. "Go ahead. What is it you want?"

"I have a very generous payout to make to a woman who recently lost her husband. A veteran's widow. But unfortunately she's moved and I have no new address. Her neighbors suggested you might be able to help."

"Oh? And what is this widow's name?"

"Mrs Purdy. Mrs Burton Purdy."

Sebastian was almost surprised that Cressida's reception room wasn't smoking from the lightning bolt Edmund's statement delivered, but no, the floor, the walls were still intact.

She took a deep breath and said she didn't know of any family such as he described.

Sebastian's heart hammered against his ribs as he forced himself to stay seated and calm. Isabella, who had barely acknowledged his presence the whole day, fixed him with a galvanizing glare. When Cressida's eyes flickered with surprise and she glanced at Sebastian seeking some sort of cue, he risked the barest of head shakes. *No. Don't do it.* But he needn't have worried. Canny businesswoman that she was, she was smart enough to smell a rat when it was dropped right under her nose.

"If you don't mind me asking, what is Mrs Purdy to you?" Her dark eyes pierced Edmund's faked concern.

"Er, I don't know the lady. I'm acting on behalf of a friend." His forehead glistened with perspiration.

"Oh yes? And I'm George Washington's great-grand-daughter." She fixed him with a piercing stare. "Look, Mr Quincey, I've been around on this sad earth long enough to know no one comes a-knocking on the door offering poor widows lotsa money. Even if I did know this Mrs Purdy, which I don't, and even if she was Mother Mary incarnate, it's not going to happen."

Edmund paced to the fireplace. "Oh, but you're wrong. There's a fund for widows of veterans."

Cressida rose in response to him, and stood, hands on her hips, facing him down.

"Is that so? Well, it's one that this poor old veteran's widow never got her paws on, isn't it?"

Quincey's eyes flicked to the table where the images lay. He stepped forward and picked up the uppermost, the picture of the two brothers together, and studied it with more than casual interest. "Widow? Oh, I see. One of these fine gentlemen is your husband, no doubt. Doing a little reminiscing before I arrived, were you?" He flicked a glance from Cressida to Sebastian, a nasty sneer slashing his face. Then he switched gears back to conciliatory. "Perhaps you missed out. There can be bureaucratic bungles. Papers not signed off, that kind of thing. But there *is* a windfall coming Mrs Purdy's way." His face was red and menacing, his voice a rising pitch of insistence. His eyes were thin slits, his cheekbones highlighted by white anger spots that stood out against the flush.

Sebastian stepped forward. "Edmund, I think Mrs Washington has made herself clear. She doesn't know the woman. And it's time you left."

Edmund spun on his heel and walked to the door. "I don't know what you're playing at, Russell, but you'll live to regret it. I promise you that."

After he left, Isabella was pink-faced with rage. "That was so awful! How dare he? The horrible man!"

Cressida shrugged. "His sort aren't worth worrying about. They're yesterday's men."

"Brave words, Cressida," said Sebastian, "but I want you to be extra careful from now on. He's a dangerous man to have as an enemy. I'm most concerned about him seeing that picture. He already has a suspicion about where the Purdy family are, or he wouldn't have been here. And now he's memorized those faces. He mightn't know who's who, but he'll be on the lookout. I felt it was important for us to locate Betty Purdy and make sure she's OK. Now I know it's more than that, it's urgent. And when we find her, we will give her and Charles extra security."

Cressida's lips pinched tight. "Do you really think that's necessary?"

"You saw him, Cressida. He's a man who can't stand to be bettered. And today, without a doubt, he came off second best. At the hands of a black mama too. That's why he turned nasty. He can't stand the humiliation. And he's probably got something big — something personal to do with women or money, or both — riding on it too. No, we can't take chances on this one."

Isabella had ignored him for most of the day, but on the way home she nagged him. He instantly knew he preferred the cold-shoulder treatment.

"No, Isabella, you cannot go to the Purdys' with me. No and full stop. It's too dangerous."

"But I'd like to see Betty again. I could take her and the boys some food and toys to help them out."

"Isabella, can you just get this into that stubborn little head of yours? You are *not* coming with me!" All of the anger he'd kept tightly held in was threatening to erupt if this well-nigh irresistible young woman at his side did not stop pushing the boundaries and shut up good and proper.

"Stubborn little head." She mimicked his exasperated tone to perfection. "You're so old-fashioned!" Her musical voice, so lovely in a performance, was close to a wail. She was making small jittery movements with her fingers, flexing them, keying up for a fight.

"Guilty as judged, if old-fashioned means keeping a young woman entrusted to my care safe from harm." He sighed as John's house came into view. How huffy and stuffy he sounded. Maybe that was the trouble. He was just too old, too loaded down with responsibilities, to have any appeal for a bright young thing.

He'd thought that day at the Fort they shared some special moments, and he had been captivated by her easy wit and natural beauty. But apart from that isolated day, they'd pretty well been at loggerheads. If it wasn't one thing, it was another. Finding Alejandro. Alycia's murder. And now the Purdys. They couldn't see eye to eye on anything.

He'd briefly been attracted, he admitted that, seen her as a captivating equal rather than an annoying juvenile he'd assumed unwanted responsibility for. He shook his head. How could he have got it so wrong? When it came to women, he couldn't seem to get it right.

*How could I ever for a minute have thought this would work?*

Clearly his age was affecting his judgment.

*Don't give her another thought. She's*

*trouble, and I've already got my hands full.*

Isabella snuck a sidelong glance at Sebastian, wanting to gauge his mood without him seeing her do it, and she caught the exasperated shake of his head, as he pulled up outside Huldah's, eyes fixed on the road in front. What was his problem? She gave an irritable toss of her own head. She was the one being denied her wishes. He could please himself and do whatever he liked.

Still, there was something boyish and delightful about the way his red-gold hair, slightly damp from the midday heat, stuck to his temples, framing hazel eyes that subtly changed color with the light. The green flecks showed up more in sunlight, while in dull light the light brown was stronger. He was a chameleon, never the same from one hour to the next. The curling forelocks and sprinkling of freckles conjured up thoughts of the Hong Kong boy he once was, but that was the only thing remotely child-like about Sebastian Russell. He was tall, lean and broad-chested, and had such a seriousness about him that when he laughed it was as surprising as it was mesmerizing. She'd love to see him able to relax more, to drop the sense of duty that he wore like armor.

As she turned away, her cheeks warmed from the unwelcome admission that she was being unfair. She, along with many others, was relying on Sebastian to be the honorable, trustworthy controller: part-deputy, part-detective, and all-round good reliable fellow. The one designated to watch after others. Certainly that was part of the role Basil expected from him, but he went so much further than treating it as a job, as simply a custodian. She thought of his concern for Cressida today, and his insistence that he needed to warn and protect Mrs Purdy from Edmund as soon as he could. As far as she knew, he didn't owe Burton anything, and yet he assumed a role as his brother's keeper, however inconvenient and burdensome.

She swung her legs over to her side of the wagon and was about to descend when she glanced down and found herself looking into his tawny eyes. Today they were the color of a stormy sea. Her heart caught halfway through a beat as she gazed into his face, her movement and her speech frozen in time. *Why does he affect me this way?*

He reached up both hands, offering to help her over the uncomfortably long drop step to the path outside Huldah's house. "Are you OK?" A crease of concern notched between his eyes. "It's been a stressful day. Good to get home."

She put her hands into his outstretched palms and felt a sizzle run through her fingers as they touched. She drew in a sharp breath, then quietly exhaled, hoping with all that was within her that he hadn't noticed.

"I'm fine, Sebastian. Thank you for being Cressida's champion today. It could have got really nasty if we hadn't been there." She felt his steadying brace as her toe hit the ground. "Thanks." She quickly let go of him and brushed her hair off her face. Now they were no longer touching she felt it as a loss.

His glance was questioning. "I'm sorry

we had yet another disagreement. We don't seem to do much else, do we?"

She narrowed her eyes, her arms stiff by her sides. "I know coming to Cressida's was a drag for you. But getting my stage wardrobe sorted out is an important first step in getting back to work. Of getting out of your hair."

"Sure," he said. "No problem. Anytime."

She laughed. "I suppose you'll insist on tagging along whenever I go out, even though it's such a chore for you. Just in the meantime ..."

"Just in the meantime," he echoed. "And it isn't a chore at all."

She didn't protest because she didn't want to appear to be milking him for compliments. But she knew the truth. Sebastian Russell was too conscientious for his own good, and she was just one more obligation in a long line of them. Well, she didn't want to add to his load, and she regretted now being so insistent about accompanying him to the Purdys. Of course, that was a *stupid* idea.

She stepped away, resisting the urge to take one last gaze at Sebastian, though she'd love to study every line and freckle at her leisure. She'd never known her father, and Huldah had never lived with a man while she was with her, so she didn't really have any clue how men thought or acted. For a moment she felt like a small skiff lost at sea, at the mercy of any wild current. Then she lifted her chin, squared her shoulders and reminded herself of the ambitions that burned within. She had her own stuff to do, and she didn't need to make Seb's life any more difficult than it already was.

She needed to get on with making her dreams of stage success come true. And find Alejandro while she was doing it.

# Thirty-Four

Charles Moses Washington's gray, wiry hair stood upright from his scalp as if some invisible magnetic force hovered overhead, drawing him forth with unflagging power. Despite his ash hair, his face was infused with the alert glow of a much younger man. His compact form, clad in the somber formal black suit of a religious man, exuded a vitality that promised immediate action. Even in the latter stage of life, he was a warrior for Christ rather than a contemplative preacher, Sebastian saw with a sense of warm approval.

The modest front parlor was quiet and empty. There was no sign of Mrs Purdy and the boys. Sebastian had quickly explained he'd got the address from Cressida and told the chaplain of the peril the widow might face. "I believe the Purdy house was deliberately fired, with the aim of killing all of them. Whoever is behind this was worried Burton would talk when he was in his cups, possibly without even being aware of it. Firstly about who paid Polk to kill Mrs Stockton. And secondly about Edmund Quincey's activities kidnapping and selling free black men back into slavery. Two different men, and two different motives, but they come together in a shared desire to silence dangerous talk."

The Reverend listened in silence, the dark planes of his face tranquil, his eyes fixed in rapt attention. Occasionally he shifted his weight in his seat, or stroked his neatly bearded chin, deep in thought.

At the end of Sebastian's account, he stood and gestured to Sebastian to follow. They moved from the parlor to a small study lined with old books — those spines Sebastian could read appeared to be theological texts — and Charles Washington sat down behind the desk and pulled an envelope out of a drawer.

"I've been waiting for this day to arrive, Mr Russell. And it feels like I've been waiting a mighty long time."

He slipped his fingers into the unsealed brown envelope and drew out a handful of small items that looked like army-uniform buttons and sheets of yellowed paper with tattered edges. The musty smell of old things filled the gap between them. The Reverend Washington pushed them across the flat empty desk top towards him.

"What are they?" Sebastian was

puzzled. More than a little perplexed. What did a few items of old memorabilia have to do with their discussion?

"Take a look. Read it." The Reverend's expression was as still as a windless lake at dawn. He sat back in his chair as Sebastian turned the papers and began to read. They were sworn statements, recorded in fluid, well-shaped cursive handwriting, bearing witness to the activities of a certain army corporal. The facts were succinctly stated, and in most cases well-expressed, by men who worked as ambulance attendants and non-military workers for the Army in the years before there were black regiments.

They recorded the activities of a band of men who kidnapped and sold former slaves back across the border. Too clever to threaten men when they were surrounded by soldiers and friends, they preyed on those who wandered into town for a drink in a local tavern, or who fossicked in country lanes for wild food — turkeys, berries, fruit. Anywhere they might be isolated and vulnerable to kidnappers.

Sebastian read the accounts in silence. When he finished, he put the papers down and brought his fingers up to his temples and massaged his head. "I had no idea of the scale and organization. You heard rumors from time to time, but I suppose I always dismissed it as scaremongering because I never saw any evidence."

"They were very careful to keep it secret. To buy off or threaten to keep silence. Kidnapped them and hustled them back south so smartly they never had a chance to make a fuss. Sometimes they went to a tavern and woke up next morning forced back into slavery without any recollection of how it happened."

The two men sat in silence, the tick-tock of a mantel clock keeping time with their reflections. Sebastian said, "This is a remarkable record you've collected here. A historic record. I'm sure as a clergyman you understood you were standing witness."

"I did. I saw it as a sacred duty. Quincey's commanding officer was a weak man, inclined to look the other way. He had no sympathies with abolition, but I always believed the time would come."

"You've got conviction on your side. I think the Good Book says, 'If they remain silent the very stones will cry out'."

Charles Washington's solemn face broke into a wide smile. "You know your scriptures."

"Not very well. And sadly, I'm not sure there is any way to make Edmund Quincey accountable for his actions. As you know, the law is soft on it. But if you entrusted these documents to me I could make sure the right people saw them. Quincey most certainly won't want that."

Charles hesitated. As Sebastian waited on his response, heavy boots thudded up the steps and a fist drummed impatiently on the front door. Before Charles had time to blink at the intrusion, his visitor was on his feet, pulling a revolver from inside his jacket. Sebastian had a sixth sense about who the intruder would be.

# Thirty-Five

It had been the work of just an hour or two to locate the dressmaker's brother-in-law. Not hard. As soon as he saw the photograph at the black mama's establishment he was years back. He knew that face: it was one he'd seen before, many times. The black Bible-thumper, the one who always gave him the feeling he was watching him like a hawk. The boys who worked for him warned him about him as well.

But when Sebastian Russell opened the door with a revolver in one hand — now that was a surprise. He had to give it to him, he'd got there mighty fast. Edmund wasn't sure what his interest here was. Sebastian's narrowed, flinty eyes weren't welcoming either.

"Why, Seb, you old war-horse." He mustered up a wide-eyed grin. "Didn't know you hung out in these here parts. Haven't you got better things to do?"

"Same could be said for you, Quincey." Sebastian remained planted full in the doorway, blocking entry, his gun at his side.

"What's with the artillery? I come in peace."

Sebastian didn't move or smile. "I don't think you're coming in peace or any other way. You're not welcome here."

"Come on, man, what's the problem? And who are you to be saying? Surely the man of the house can speak for himself."

Sebastian remained like a granite

boulder, his mouth set in a thin, hostile line. The front door opened onto a dim hallway, the bare wooden floorboards leading down a corridor which had several doors off it, all of them closed. The walls were hung with framed photographs very similar to the ones he'd seen a couple of hours earlier, though the light was too gloomy to make out any detail. Then a door opened, and the solid figure of a man backlit by a flood of light strode up the passage.

Someone nearby was cooking something that took Edmund right back to army days, when men gathered around cooking fires and did their best to feed themselves. A smoky aroma of pork and beans, maybe with some turnip greens in the mix. Did that mean there was a woman in the house?

The man who had joined Sebastian

had aged since he'd seen him last, but there was no mistaking the sharp, knowing glint in his eye, or the firm set of the bearded jaw. He looked just as forceful in his views as he ever did, a right thorn in the side.

"State your business, sir. Why are you here?" His voice was sonorous and authoritative. He'd drawn himself up to full height, his broad shoulders more those of a field worker than a religious man, and he fixed him with an eagle eye.

"Why, I believe you are the man I seek. Charles Washington is it? The Reverend Washington? You probably don't remember me, but I recall your work in the war. I was with Sebastian here. With the Massachusetts boys."

"I am Charles Washington, but I don't recall having any business with you, Mr …"

"Quincey. Corporal Edmund Quincey." He thrust out his hand and tried to step forward, but checked himself when neither Sebastian nor the black man budged.

Washington pointedly ignored the hand. "Quincey. I do recall an officer of that name."

His gaze was like stone.

"Reverend, can I come in and talk for a moment? It won't take long." An awkward silence followed. "Look, I know you don't think much of me. I'm not like you. I'm not a good man. But is it up to you to deny a poor woman a payout that is probably more than she has ever seen in her life?"

The Reverend bristled. "*Woman*, Mr Quincey? Who said anything about any woman?" He made a shuffling movement as if to shepherd Quincey out.

Quincey held up his hand. "All right, all right, I'm going. But just one last thing. I challenge you — doesn't your Jesus say you are to forgive many times? As many as seventy times seven times? An infinite number of times. And don't I deserve that too?"

The Reverend held Edmund's gaze for a moment, then seemed to suddenly come to a conclusion. He stepped aside to allow him access.

In the small office overflowing with dusty books, Washington sat down behind a desk and gestured to a chair on the other side. Sebastian leaned against the door jamb: he had put away the gun. The desk was littered with buttons from old uniforms and tattered yellow pages of old letters. Men reminiscing about old times. As Edmund lowered himself into the chair he noticed the black man gather up the buttons and paper and stuff them all back into a brown envelope. When he looked up again his expression was not welcoming. He might have let Edmund in, but clearly he didn't trust him.

"Reverend, I'm seeking a poor widow woman who's lost her husband recently in a fire. Got a handsome payout for her if I can locate her. Something from the pensions office."

"Oh?" The black man's face was closed and unresponsive. "Well, like I said earlier, I know nothing of any woman. What was her name?"

"Mrs Purdy. Mrs Burton Purdy."

"Oh? I vaguely remember the name Purdy from long ago. But no recent contact. None at all. Sorry I cannot be of assistance."

The statement was stiff and formal,

and Edmund didn't believe a word of it. "You're sure? Because I spoke to people in the district who thought Mrs Purdy was here."

"Quite sure. Anyone who says otherwise is mistaken. Now, if there's nothing more?" Washington got up as if to usher him back out.

Edmund flicked a quick glance at Sebastian, who was still lounging in the doorway. In one swift move he stepped away from the desk and pulled out a pistol, which he aimed straight at Sebastian. "Actually there is something more."

Sebastian's hand jerked at his side, and then relaxed again. His face showed only slight amusement. "Really Edmund? Is it so unlikely we'll agree?"

The superior tone jabbed like a hot poker. Sebastian Russell had always been a self-righteous bastard. That was one of the things Edmund had always disliked most about him. That, and his 'holier than thou' morality. He waved the gun, gesturing to Sebastian to start walking down the hall, pistol threatening his back.

The Reverend stayed planted. "What's this about, Corporal?"

"Between me and Russell, Reverend. Don't bother your old head about it."

He crossed to the chaplain's desk and swept up the brown envelope, never wavering in his sighting on Sebastian. The chaplain suppressed a gasp. "That's private information!"

Sebastian put his head back around the door jamb. "It'll be fine, Charles, don't you worry. But lock the front door as soon as we're gone. And be careful who you open it up to from now on. No more opening up to 'seventy times seven' gambits."

# Thirty-Six

It had been five days since the bust-up with his father and whenever he thought of it Alex's heart burned with a sense of having been badly wronged. He'd dutifully reported daily to his desk at De Vile's Nevada City office, but Hector was away on business so they hadn't been forced to see one another. The reprieve gave him relief because he didn't think he could keep his silence if Hex started in on it again.

'Hex.' He clicked his tongue against his teeth. The name had started as a joke after they'd gone on a 'father-son' fishing trip — announced by Hector with much fanfare — and caught nothing.

Hector's passion was horses, not fishing, and he'd plainly been out of sorts in waders. Alex had playfully suggested his lack of enthusiasm had put a curse on their efforts. Somehow the name had stuck; it surfaced whenever they were reminded how temperamentally different they were. He wondered if that was why he'd felt such a close bond with Charles Durant. He had the soul of an artist. Alex didn't know whether he was an artist himself. He just felt as if Charles understood things about him without any need for him to explain.

Charles's funeral had been an unadorned but quietly elegant affair, attended by a couple of dozen people who shared the photographer's world — the landlady and other boarders at the house she ran, some of his photographer colleagues, and the innkeepers and fellow drinkers with whom he'd shared the successes and scrapes of daily life. They spoke fondly of his gentility and sense of honor, but none of them seemed intimate friends, and it was left to Alex, an acquaintance of only a few days, to tie up the loose ends of a life that really was 'like grass'.

Alex sighed as he recalled the closure of Durant's studio. He'd retrieved everything he could — in fact, he had the beginnings of a fine little photographer's kit for himself now — but it was so sad to see how little impact the life of one good man apparently had. He'd bloomed like a flower in the field, the wind had blown, he'd vanished, and the place remembered him no more.

He glanced down to his desk, and his eyes glazed over at the columns of numbers lying before him. He ran his tongue over his top lip. His mouth was very dry. It was definitely time for coffee and some sunshine.

He grabbed his hat and trekked downstairs out into Main Street. He blinked as the bright sun hit his face. De Vile & Co was only a few doors down from a popular coffee house, and his eyes smarted as he stumbled and turned to head up the street. His shoulder bumped lightly into someone on his right, and he froze, eyes wide open. "My apologies. The sun, it blinded me."

The woman before him was probably more than a decade older than he, but she had the kind of mature beauty that endured beyond girlhood — dark hair caught loosely at the back of her neck, shining brown eyes and a light bronze complexion. Strong dark eyebrows and a wide fine mouth. Exotic — and familiar.

With a start he recalled a newspaper item he'd seen just in the last couple of days:

*Sir John Russell and his wife, Pania, Lady Russell, the celebrated singer, have returned from a very successful several months away on tour in Australia and New Zealand, and are to resume occupation of New Gold House, which Sir John has rebuilt after last year's tragic fire.*

He gave a bow, a quick smile of recognition. "Forgive me, Lady Russell. You're not hurt, I hope?"

"I am totally fine, thank you. It's easy enough to do when the sun's in your eyes." She gazed into his face. "But I don't believe I know you. That's seems unfair when you know me." She gave a playful smile to show she was having a little fun at his expense.

Alex thrust his hand forward. "Alexander de Vile, Lady Russell. Hector de Vile's son."

Pania's smile broadened. "So I've bumped into not just any street wag."

Alex laughed with her. "Delighted to meet you, Lady Russell. I don't mean to be obnoxious but I must confess immediately, I am a fan. I saw you and Graysie Castellanos at the Orleans in Sacramento last year. One of the best shows I've ever been to. You were just wonderful."

"Well, thank you."

"To make up for my clumsiness, would you join me for coffee? That's where I was heading when I so witlessly collided with you."

"I'd be delighted. I'm not long back from a time away and my engagement diary is wide open."

They'd enjoyed a coffee and exchanged social chit chat — the details of her trip, his involvement with his father's business — over their first cup and were about to embark on their second when Alex leaned across the table, his eyes drawn down in an anxious frown. He touched her hand lightly at the wrist. "Lady Russell, there is something I would like to ask you about, and it seems this opportunity is too good to pass up. Something that's important to me."

Pania looked into his finely boned face with the lick of dark hair that fell across one eyebrow. It made him look like a pirate, a risk-taker, and yet she sensed a gentleness and uncertainty underneath the debonair mask. "If I can be of help without breaking any confidences," she said as she withdrew her hand, "then of course."

"It's to do with your friend Graysie Castellanos. Well, your fellow entertainer. I'm not sure how well you know Miss Castellanos."

Pania smiled. "I know Graysie very well. In fact, we're family. Graysie married Sir John's brother Nathan a few months ago, so we are sisters-in-law."

Alex nodded. "I am not at all sure what I am going to relate has anything to do with Mrs Russell at all, but can I tell you why I am asking?"

For the next little while he related to her the story of meeting Charles Durant, the attack, Charles' death, and the historic photographic prints. "My life was affected by Charles in ways I can't really explain." He gazed at her over his cup, suddenly serious. "I feel a responsibility to follow through on looking into the daguerreotypes he left me. They are such beautiful reminders of a past age. He told me some of them at least were quite possibly the work of a Spanish photographer named Castellanos. I wondered if they might have any connection with your friend. I know Spanish surnames are common in California, but it seemed a coincidence worth pursuing. It's possible Mrs Russell would be interested in seeing them, if there was any connection."

Pania shook her head. "Graysie and Nathan are in Australia at present so that won't be possible, I'm afraid. But I have the feeling that Graysie's father was a photographer, so there may be some connection." She put down her cup and pushed it to one side. "Actually, it's slightly more complicated than that. Rafael Castellanos was Graysie's stepfather. But she was with him a long time — she took his name, obviously."

"Rafael." Alex savored the name on

his tongue as if it was nectar. "So that was his name. Rafael Castellanos. It suits the work. It's got a deep music about it, like the name."

"My, you do have a poetic soul, Alexander de Vile. What does your father think of that?"

The dreamy look disappeared, replaced by one closer to despair. "My father? Hex isn't impressed." He sighed. "You don't need to hear all about our disagreements. All I need to say is he doesn't approve of my interest in things photographic. To put it mildly. Vehemently opposed might be more accurate."

"Hex? You call him Hex?"

She thought of the imposing, self-confident Hector, always aware of his own dignity.

His right cheek dimpled. "I do. He

does manage to put a dampener on things sometimes."

She regarded him thoughtfully. Simple curiosity had played a big part in her snap decision to accept his invitation to coffee. As one of California's two Senators, Hector de Vile was widely known, but Pania knew more about the ruthless side of the magnate's activities. De Vile was a relentless empire-builder who exercised a malevolent drive to win at all costs; Pania knew he did not blush at using the services of enforcers to get his dirty work done if all else — bullying, theft, extortion, inflating or deflating share prices — didn't get him what he wanted. This open-faced, apparently guileless young man couldn't be more different from his father.

As she studied him, she could glimpse something of Hector in the young man that sat before her — impeccable manners, a handsome beautifully structured face with high cheekbones — but there the similarities ended. And there was that lingering sense of having met him before … She felt as if she knew him from somewhere.

"Alex, I'll tell you what I can do. Graysie isn't expected back for some time yet. But if you bring the photographs up to New Gold House I'd be happy to look at them and help in any way I can. My curiosity is aroused — and there's a very slight chance I may be able to help throw light on where they come from. My husband might even be interested in taking a look. He's been in California for many years and did a bit of mining himself at one time."

Alex let out a contented sigh. "That sounds absolutely marvelous. I'd so appreciate it." He pushed back his chair. "Hate to say it, but I need to see you home and get back to work. Bumping into you has made this a happy day for me. I hope that turns out to be true for everyone."

# Thirty-Seven

After Sebastian left to warn Cressida's brother-in-law of the danger that threatened, Isabella couldn't settle to anything. She tried learning some new songs Pania had passed on to her, but gave up in frustration after half an hour. Her throat felt scratchy and the notes didn't sound right. She thought about making some pancakes but there wasn't enough flour left in the bins — the cook must be out getting new supplies now.

She prowled her mother's drawing room like an outdoor cat that's shut up inside, standing and looking out windows with a funny distant feeling she couldn't define, as if she'd lost something and couldn't remember what it was. Rosie was out visiting friends. When Huldah arrived home in the late afternoon she was pleased to see her, she was so thoroughly sick of her own company. "I wonder how Sebastian, Mr Russell, got on with warning the Purdys. I hope everything's all right." She watched closely for Huldah's reaction.

Her mother shot her a knowing glance and dropped her shopping bag on the table. "I got a nice piece of beef for tomorrow," she said. "Has Mrs Williams started dinner?"

Isabella shrugged. "No idea. She wasn't in there when I was in the kitchen a half hour ago."

"And what's this about Mr Russell? I'm sure you don't need to be a-worrying about him. He's perfectly capable of looking after himself."

Isabella pouted. Sometimes her mother just didn't get it. "But what if he's met with trouble? Who's there to help if he has?"

"Well, no doubt his brother, now he's home. But there's no reason to believe anything's amiss, is there? I don't want you stirring anything up. We've caused enough trouble for Sir John as it is. You just stop worrying."

Huldah didn't like to let her forget the unfortunate escapade last year when she'd run away to join Lotta Crabtree's traveling show, and Sir John had come to find her. Isabella cringed at the reminder and felt even more down than before.

Rosie came back and they'd all just sat down to dinner when they heard determined knocking at the front door. A few minutes later Mrs Williams showed in a bedraggled Cressida Washington, accompanied by Ezra, her Mr Fix-it man. Her normally smoothed-down hair was at all angles, and she licked her lips nervously as she stood before them.

Huldah jumped up immediately, sensing something was amiss, and pulled out a spare chair at the table. "Mrs Washington, what is it? You look upset. Can I get you something? A glass of water?"

Rosie slipped from the table. Isabella couldn't move. The uncomfortable hard lump in the pit of her stomach which had bothered her all afternoon was suddenly so full and heavy she was close to vomiting. Waves of nausea rolled through her. The thing she'd been too fearful to confront was about to become unavoidable. "It's Mr Russell, isn't it. Has something happened? Is he hurt?"

Cressida shook her head. "We don't know, child. We don't know."

"What do you mean? Where is he? Hasn't he come home?"

Rosie appeared with a clean water glass. Huldah made a shushing noise in Isabella's direction and poured Cressida some water. "Let Mrs Washington have a moment. Can't you see she's concerned?"

Isabella's chest felt so tight she was fit to burst. She clamped her mouth shut to stop herself from protesting.

Cressida rocked back and forth on the lip of her chair, barely suppressing her agitation. "It's not good. Not good at all. But we shouldn't give up hope."

"Please!" Isabella couldn't stand it any longer. She jumped up and strode restlessly down the table length. "Just tell us what's happened. I can't stand not knowing."

Cressida's hands flew to her cheeks in shock. "Sit down, girlie, sit down. I will tell you all I know."

Then it came out. Charles Washington had arranged for two strong men to keep watch over Mrs Purdy and the boys while he escaped to Cressida's to tell her of Edmund's sudden arrival and subsequent departure. "He had a gun on Mr Russell. Charles says he let himself be taken to protect him. That's what he thinks."

"That's so like Sebastian," Isabella was close to wailing. "Where is he now?"

"That's what we don't know, girlie. Charles went back home — he can't be away long with all that's going on — and I came over to see Sir John, to find out if his brother had come back." Cressida looked down at her folded hands, and Isabella sensed she had to brace herself before she lifted them to meet her own.

"Sir John hasn't seen him since this morning. He hasn't returned. And it's too dark to go looking for him tonight. Sir John's ready to mount a search as soon as it's light. But right now, well, there's not much we can do. I wanted to be sure and check that he wasn't here before I went home. Told Sir John if he was here I'd send him right on home."

"No!" Isabella sank down and put her head in her hands. "Do we have any idea where he was taken?"

Cressida shook her head. "I'm sorry, dearie, we don't. We don't. But Sir John will be onto it first thing tomorrow. We'll just have to keep faith through the night."

Isabella felt as if her heart was being wrenched from her chest. *How typical for Sebastian to step in and risk himself to protect others. This will be the longest night of my life.*

# Thirty-Eight

"You don't really think anyone cares about this stuff, do you?" Edmund waved the ragged-edged yellow paper in front of Sebastian. "You must be the last man in Christendom to give a toss," he sneered. "You and the black saint back there."

He screwed up the sheet into a loose ball and threw it onto the ground at his feet. The waste pile of Washington's conscientiously sworn statements grew. When he had read and ridiculed the last one, he unhitched a tinder box from his belt, struck a match and set fire to the mound of crumpled paper. The late afternoon was still and hot, and the flame caught immediately, devouring the testament to black civic status in less than two minutes. Within another two minutes the tinder-dry low chaparral on which they stood smoldered, the green wood smoke making his eyes smart.

"Put it out, you fool." Sebastian made an ineffectual attempt to stamp on the embers, but his bound ankles and knees made him unstable on his feet.

Edmund and his sidekick Black Pete had dragged him to Sugar Loaf Mountain, the highest of Nevada City's many hills, a roughly forested dome that rose dramatically from a flat plain just north of town. Town limits did not extend into this wasted wilderness, inhabited by rattlesnakes, bobcats and hydraulic miners blasting water from pumps like long-nosed cannons. On a dry August day it would only take a spark to set alight the highly flammable shrubs that still hung in small gullies missed by the hoses, and within a couple of hours the whole mountain could be ablaze.

"Keep your shirt on." Edmund jabbed an irritated look Sebastian's way, but moved to tramp out the sparks. Job done, he surveyed the black circle left by the burning paper with a satisfied smirk. "That's what I think of arrogant do-gooders. I don't know why you people waste your time."

They'd dumped Sebastian close to where the flat-topped mountain plummeted vertically onto arid man-made cliffs, the legacy of the high-pressure flows that had stripped and denuded the domed walls for more than a decade.

The bumpy ride to the top had taken more than an hour, and now they were here Sebastian had no idea what Edmund planned next. Tied over a horse in front of Black Pete, bumping like a sack of flour while Black Pete's pack of hounds ranged far and wide, he'd berated himself for allowing things to get this far. But his frustration at his failure to beat Edmund to the draw eased when he reminded himself he'd led Edmund away from inflicting any further harm on Charles Washington or the Purdy family. As soon as Edmund pushed him out of the house, gun hard against his spine, he heard the lock turn in the front door, and satisfaction had momentarily flooded out fear.

No one on that low-rent side of town was likely to come to the aid of a man being stiff-armed up the street with a gun at his back. In these parts, people knew to keep their heads down and not invite any trouble.

Black Pete had been loitering in the shadow outside Charlie's, watching the house while Edmund was inside. Seb guessed he was the informant who'd told Edmund where Charles lived. He had no gun, but carried a lethal-looking hooked knife. An ugly scar that curved from above his eyebrow, around his eye socket and down his cheek indicated he'd had close personal experience with blades like his own, and Sebastian wasn't taking any risks. Not yet, anyway.

He stood erect by the charred circle and rolled his shoulders and twisted his hips back and forth, back and forth, ironing out the wrinkles up and down his spine. Then he went on the attack.

"Edmund, what is this all about? It's preposterous what you're doing here — holding me like this. What's it all for?"

He knew he was in a pig's wallow, but

he was unreasonably sanguine about it. He could bargain his way out, he was confident.

"What for? You know very well what for." Edmund glared at him, his eyes piggy and mean.

Sebastian shrugged. "Enlighten me."

"This snuggling up to the blacks, to Burton and his missus — it can only be to ruin me, harm my reputation. To dig the dirt, and then dish it somewhere. Why else would you do it? I know you've never got over your jealousy."

"Jealousy? You're talking in riddles."

'Let's face it, Russell. I've always been more successful with the ladies than you'll ever be."

Sebastian felt a twinge of disquiet. "Are you talking about Caroline Studebaker? Is this where all of this is leading? Let me see. You think if she knew about your unsavory activities in selling freemen back into slavery, she'd cut you quicker than a blue streak of greased lightning." He laughed. "And you're scared I'm going to split on you? Do you seriously think that's the only thing standing between you and her fortune?" He shuffled himself sideways and rested his behind on a boulder that gave him a vantage point to the valley floor below. "Do you?" He gave another short laugh.

"I don't see what's so funny." Edmund was huffy. "Caroline and I are getting on very nicely. I fully expect to announce an engagement soon. Followed by a quick wedding. It's no secret she and that last husband of hers were very hot on freedom. Well, it's the German thing, isn't it? Left over from the way they all backed the 1848 revolutions and then had to flee when they failed. I'm pretty confident, but I don't want to take the risk."

Sebastian moved his position slightly and looked out over the edge as Edmund talked. Creamy-red ribs, the fluted artificial cliffs created by the flushing, abutted great hummocks of discarded rock and geological waste that nestled against the mountain's flanks on the western side. Amid the devastation, some islands and gullies of green vegetation clung on, having escaped the high-pressure hoses.

He turned his attention back to Edmund. "How about we make a bet, a gamble for my life. I'll bet Caroline Studebaker won't marry you, even if she doesn't hear about your despicable contraband money-grubbing. She's too smart for that. I won't say a thing about your past, and she still won't marry you. A hundred on it. Have we got a deal?"

Sebastian stuck his hand out in mockery. Edmund was squatting across from him, his eyes shining with dislike, his nostrils flared, his face slowly turning a light purple. Seb had struck his pride where it hurt most — his attractiveness to women — and he was furious.

As if to confirm his reading, Edmund jumped up and began striding back and forth, taking jerky aggressive steps. "You arrogant toad-eater. You just don't get it, do you? Women adore me. They all want to marry me. All of them." He bared his teeth in a predatory grimace, and Sebastian scrambled back up from his boulder, suddenly unsure of where Edmund's mood was taking him. "You've been as mad as a hornet with me ever since your so-called childhood sweetheart killed herself. But that wasn't my fault. The silly cow couldn't seriously expect me to marry her."

The words were like a clout on the head. Sebastian's ears rang and he swayed, momentarily unable to count on his ability to remain standing. Edmund thundered on, blind to the impact of his self-obsessed spiel. "Anyway, I've nothing to fear now. No one will believe the blacks, and you won't be around to stir up any more trouble."

He glared at Sebastian, but he hadn't heard the last two sentences. "Marry her? What do you mean, she couldn't seriously expect you to marry her?" His voice sounded barking and desperate, all pretense of self-assurance gone.

Edmund gave him a withering look. "The girl, what was her name? Sally, Susan? No, Sarah. That was it, Sarah. I don't know where she got the idea that a roll in the hay equals a ring on the finger." He flicked a calculated look at Sebastian. "Or that just because she's in the family way I'm going to marry her."

His eyes gleamed with satisfaction as he landed the killer punch. "Driveled on about how I'd ruined her honor and she could never marry Sebastian now. On and on. It got tiresome." He licked his lips. "I wasn't sorry. Some people don't deserve to live."

He stared off into middle distance for a few seconds, as if recalling a last conversation, while Sebastian clicked from blind confusion to an icy crystal clarity. Sarah had not killed herself of her own free will. She'd been bullied into it. And it hadn't been about Robert. It had been about the shame of being abandoned by this philanderer. He closed his eyes and exhaled, long and slow, letting go of things he'd imagined that had never been, that he'd never understood. He couldn't change anything, but he felt a deeper calm than he'd known since Sarah's death.

He blinked his eyes open. Edmund had taken several steps toward him, his face shining with a strange, exultant glow. "I'm not taking you up on your bet, but not because I think you'd win. I'm certain you wouldn't. But frankly, I'm not willing to take the risk. Anyway, having you out of the picture serves more than one purpose. Pete, it's time!"

The loiterer appeared at Edmund's shoulder, his dogs milling in a pack around him, and without further instruction he grabbed Seb from behind and dragged him toward the cliff edge. His heels bumped on the rough ground,

Black Pete's vice-like grip across his chest crunching the air out of him. The dogs danced excitedly alongside, as if expecting to be given some sort of quarry.

"You're about to have a terrible accident. Nearly as nasty as sweetheart Sarah's." Edmund was laughing as he reached to his belt to pull out the gun. He gestured to Black Pete. "Cut the ties before we finish him off. My friend is about to have a nasty fall."

Sebastian didn't wait for the knife, or the bullet. He braced himself in a crouch and jumped as far out as he could, trusting his life to Providence.

# Thirty-Nine

For a second or two he was only aware of the rush of sweet-smelling air in his face — of pine, vanilla, a green woodsy aroma, and the glare of the sun's rays on the vertical white ribs of rock below. And further off, a brief glint of water. His feet hit the cliff face with a crunching thud. On impact he curled into a ball and rolled sideways, slowing his downward momentum, scrabbling madly for something, anything, to grab and hold. His last thought was that if he had to die, he'd seen a hundred worse ways that men less fortunate than him had breathed their last. And then there was nothing.

How long he hung draped between the branches of the small pine he had no idea. He forced his eyes open and looked gingerly around him, hardly daring to twitch a muscle in case he set himself in motion down the cliff again. The impact of his fall had half-flattened the fragrant conifer crushed under him, but its deep roots clung on, holding him in its arms. He let himself rest there, listening first to his own breath and then, as his consciousness expanded, to the fluid notes of a lark rising high overhead in extravagant song.

*Singing at the sheer joy of being alive. If I could sing like you, I'd join you.*

Strangest of all, when he looked out, the near-full moon had already risen, although it was still only late afternoon, and as sunset approached it climbed high in the eastern sky, casting an eerie glow over the land below.

With hesitant, testing movements he drew his legs tightly behind him and reached with his still bound hands for the knife stowed in his boot. As he stretched down he became aware of a stinging pain on the outer edge of his left shoulder. The frayed cloth was red with blood. Damn. He hadn't dodged Edmund's bullets completely, but he was cheered to see he'd got nothing more than a deep graze — a superficial wound.

His head jerked upwards.

*Edmund. Where is he? Can he see me from the top? Does he know I'm still alive? Is he coming after me?*

He saw that he'd rolled back in against the cliff face and the top was obscured from view by an overhang. With any luck Edmund would not have been able to gauge how far he'd fallen.

Dusk was closing in. The daytime temperature was fast cooling, and it came to him in a sudden rush that the mountain was home to animals — deer and squirrels, but also mountain lions and bobcats which he'd prefer not to meet unarmed. He needed to get out of this tree and find somewhere safer to lodge.

*Get the knife from your boot and cut the ties on your legs.*

Thinking it was easy; doing it was close to impossible. Getting the knife from the boot was tricky, but doable. Jack-knifing his legs to bring them within reach of his knife, that was another thing.

He clenched his jaw as the iron claw of cramp gripped him. It felt as if every sinew from toe to thigh tautened and strained at the stretch. The moon was sailing high overhead by the time the task was completed.

*Now for the hands. But first, get out of this tree.*

He wriggled with painstaking care until he was clear of the saving pine, and then he saw it. His fall had smashed down one of the juvenile pine's side branches, and the jagged line of the break was within reach if he could position himself carefully.

It took a long time. A very long time. But by dint of determination and unflagging will, he positioned the ropes over the tear in the wood and pulled the hemp fiber back and forth, repeating the sawing motion again and again.

Finally the rope parted, and his fingers tingled as he moved his hands after the tight constriction. He scuttled backwards, digging in his heels to avoid sliding down the forty-five degree slope, which was made up of hard rock blanketed in loose shale which he knew could make a deadly slide. He anchored himself between the vertical cliff face and a tough red-barked bush covered in berries that locked him in; then he lay back and tried to think through his options.

Edmund wouldn't be able to leave this business unfinished now he'd begun it. He would come looking for him to finish him off, but he couldn't do much in the dark, so that wouldn't be till morning. That gave Seb eight or ten hours to get far enough away that he'd be impossible to track down. And he hazarded a guess that if he didn't make it back soon, John would be alerted and would come looking.

The bullet wound on his shoulder bothered him with a constant dull ache, but other than that he was fit to move. But which way? He recalled the glint of water he'd glimpsed as he fell. A pond of some kind, maybe even with an outlet to a stream or river. He didn't know the area well and wracked his brain to recall the local geography. If he made his way carefully down this spur to the base of the mountain, he might be able to follow the watercourse out; even float downstream. Was that feasible, or was he going a little crazy?

He lay there in the teeming night, with a sense that all around him green life endured; he heard the yapping of foxes in the distance and from far below he thought he caught the croaking of frogs. Life went on, regardless of his or anyone else's vanities. All one big circle, birth to death. He thought of Sarah, caught in the paws of a man like Edmund Quincey, an innocent little bird in the jaws of a big cat. He opened his hands, palms upward, submitting to some invisible force.

He finally saw what he'd been so reluctant to admit till now. Sarah had made her choices, wise or unwise, and he had no place, no truck, with any of them. He released the guilt he'd been carrying that he'd somehow failed her, or that he could have intervened. He saw with a clarity he'd never reached before that it was none of his business, never had been, even though it was unfair, a personal tragedy. A great weight lifted from him. Even the ache of the bullet graze seemed to ease. What replaced the guilt was a clean sadness, unburdened by guilt. So clean it was releasing. It came to him that for the first time since Sarah's death, he was finally free to grieve.

He didn't know how long he lay there in a half-trance of nostalgia. The weird idea came upon him that the green life that pulsated around him was infusing him with its energy, healing and restoring him, and when he finally began his cautious descent down the chaparral in the bright moonlight, he felt more whole than he had in years.

By the time he reached the marshy pond at the mountain's base, the moon had set and the pre-dawn was bringing a subtle, pearly, fast-changing light. He'd had some terrifying moments coming down, and more than once he'd thought his time might be ended, as he stumbled and slid from spur to shelf, and from the shelf to the next shingle escarpment. Once he had not been able to stop his slide on the loose rock and had shot right over the edge, like a piece of disposable material caught in a flume. He hung in mid-air, unable to see where he was going to land, and he did the same thing he did with his first dive, rolled sideways the minute his feet touched solid ground and grabbed for any handy vegetation to anchor himself. Apart from some gravel grazes, he'd held on without injury.

And once he could look up at the looming dome from its bottom, the anxiety of not reaching this spot was replaced by another greater fear: had Edmund already come down the mountain and was waiting somewhere close for daylight? When he heard hounds baying somewhere close by, his blood ran cold. As soundlessly as he could he plunged forward into the sedge-like bulrushes that rose like a murky screen in front of him, seeking water that would cut off his scent and hopefully carry him clear. As the cold mud sucked his boots under, he knew he was trading the risk of dying from drowning, exposure or exhaustion for the slim chance of escape. But anything was better than having to face Edmund and a pack of dogs, alone and exhausted.

# Forty

"Your brother, Sir John, he acted like he was going for an afternoon stroll in the sunshine. Wasn't concerned in the least. I'm sure he was distracting that spawn of Beelzebub from us. Drawing him right away from the house, he was."

John was standing just inside the chaplain Charles Washington's hallway. The old man was clad in soft slippers and had a woolen rug thrown across the back of his neck; his head was about level with Russell's shoulder, and he was blinking away sleep. He and Nelson had banged on his door until he shuffled out and opened up to them after a lengthy checking process. Dawn was barely breaking, but he was impatient to get on Sebastian's track as soon as he could. They'd already wasted a whole night.

"Sounds like Sebastian, Reverend. He wouldn't have wanted it any other way. Especially when he was worried he'd led Burton's killers to him. You know he felt responsible for Mrs Purdy's loss?"

"No, sir, I didn't, but it figures. She's sure glad he was there, don't you worry about that. Says she wouldn't be alive today if he wasn't. Nor those boys she takes care of."

John nodded and took in the clean but modest dwelling; the bare floorboards, a snatch of a threadbare sofa through a half-opened door, the stuffing spilling out of one of the seat cushions. Charles Washington didn't look as though he had a lot of excess to share with a woman and two children, but he showed no sign of being bothered by that lack.

John pulled at the bag he had slung over one shoulder down and handed it to Washington. "Some food my cook packed for you and your guests. Just a few bits and pieces she had in the kitchen. She's insisting she'll bake for you next time, when she gets more notice." He grinned. "She loves feeding people, so don't spoil her fun. And I've brought a couple of extra men with me to make sure you are all safe here while Nelson and I go and search for Sebastian. We don't want to risk any more mishaps."

"Appreciate that, Sir John. Really do. Wish there was more I could tell you. But the last I saw of Sebastian was his back disappearing out my front door. I was too gob smacked to do or say anything much."

"That's fine. We've got it under control. We'll check back with you later." He stepped out into the fresh morning and sniffed the air, so dry it caught in his throat.

Manzanita Hill was still in pre-dawn gloom, but through the thin board walls of the little house John could hear the stirring of birdsong in the oak forest and chaparral scrubland that stretched up Coyote Street onto Sugar Loaf Mountain. He'd left Nelson to reconnoiter the area and see if he could find anyone who had seen Edmund and Sebastian leave last night.

"Damned nuisance we had to leave it so many hours before we could get out here," he said to Nelson when he found him up the street a way. "Have you had any luck?"

"As it happens, I did. The soap factory

not far from here goes all night, and some of the young varmints who work there nap between shifts on the veranda overlooking the street. Some of them don't have anywhere else to go. They report seeing a man being pushed up Coyote Street in front of a gun, heading towards Sugar Loaf. Say he had Black Pete with him — he's one of the ne'er-do-wells known by everyone around here. Had Black Pete's bloodhounds with them as well."

"Bloodhounds? That doesn't sound good."

"No, it doesn't. They're generally only brought out when a man's wanting to keep track of another man. Or quarry"

"Then what are we waiting for? Sugar Loaf Mountain it is."

They turned their horses and followed Coyote Street outside of the city limits and into rough bushland. They had only gone a mile or two when they heard the distant sound of dogs barking. John immediately reined in his stallion and bent his ear to the slight breeze that had sprung up. "Dogs. Listen!"

Nelson did the same. "Seems to be coming from over there." He gestured to the lower reaches of the distinctive dome-shaped mound, which rose more than 3000 feet above the surrounding countryside. "If it's them, if they took him to the top, he's somehow got back down again."

"Who else is it likely to be? It's not as if they do a lot of hunting out here."

They walked their horses through a wrecked barren landscape, past mounds of hydraulic-pump debris, threading between lumps of dense scrub and tough, dry-leaved chaparral grass. The birdsong had faded, and John wasn't sure if the occasional cracking noise he heard — twigs or branches being broken — was really happening or something his imagination was dreaming up. At each bend in the twisting route he pictured coming upon Sebastian's bloodied body. A wave of anguish sluiced through him: his middle brother, whom he'd only just started getting to know after all their years apart. Please God don't let him be dead.

After the first bloodhound calls announcing they'd picked up a scent, there had been no more canine talk, and they'd turned off the main road more than thirty minutes ago. Up ahead he could see the rising rusty red stalks of swamp grasses, bulrushes and the like, their velvet sausage-shaped heads spilling out a kapok-like filling that caught in his nostrils and made him sneeze. The once-pristine Sugarloaf Springs, flowing out into the Sugarloaf Stream, was now a stagnant swamp, half-filled with mining tailings and the toxic metals like mercury used to separate the gold from the rock. In a few places he could see the glitter of water as the springs continued to push through the mud, but what had once been a productive fishing ground for the local Nisenan people was now a smelly, muddy wallow.

A bare stretch of muddy track caught the sunlight up ahead, the mud churned into soft ridges by what looked like men's boots. John drew up fast and put out his arm to halt Nelson, who was following. "Look at that up ahead. Looks like footprints."

They both dismounted and John pulled out his side-arm and took the lead, stalking through the low brush to get closer to the disturbed ground. He had his head cocked, listening intently for any sound, any whiff of a different scent or the tiniest movement. When they got within a few feet they stopped and considered their surroundings, surveying the ground in a 360-degree circle.

"Definitely boot marks, and fresh ones. Doesn't look like the mud has dried on the ridges. It's still damp enough to gleam in the sunlight. I'd say no more than thirty minutes old." Nelson gazed around him. "Probably about the time we heard the barking."

John nodded. "Think you're right. A good guess, anyway. Looks like quite a tussle went on by the number of prints. At least two, maybe three different men." He handed his reins to Nelson. "Take my horse and keep me covered. I'll do a wider circle around the prints and see if I can see anything else further up the track. I won't go far."

He skirted the mud. The swamp, which until this point followed a rounded bowl edge, fissured into a narrow gulch, once a spring bed, now a drainage rill from the mountain. The sides were steep, the bottom deep and murky, and it was too wide to jump in one stride. John peered up and down it, trying to decide the best place to cross on foot, or whether to return to the horses and jump it on horseback. That's when he saw it. A man's hand like a claw, desperately reaching out of the murk. His body froze. For half a minute his legs refused the mental urging to go closer for a better view. Then he stepped forward.

"What is it? Have you found something?" Nelson called, urgency in his voice.

He ignored the query and looked deep into the trench. The arm was attached to a bloodied torso and head that showed the caved-in fractures of a major bashing, buried face down in the mud. His guts erupted, bile racing up his throat, and he bent over and spat. When he could stand upright again, Nelson was beside him.

His sturdy steward stood in a rigid stance, bent forward to get a clear view. "Poor beggar! Don't know who it is, but it's not Mr Sebastian. Even with all the blood it's clear he's got black hair and dark skin. Mr Sebastian is pale with freckles."

# Forty-One

Isabella's spine tingled in anticipation of the scorcher of a day that was coming. It was barely six in the morning and already the air had that electric feeling of late summer heat. She shifted contentedly in her saddle, glad to be breathing in the puffs of fresh breeze after a night spent tossing and turning, worrying about Sebastian. Had he managed to talk Edmund down? Was he safely back home?

She'd slipped out early while Huldah was still sleeping and collected a mare from the Excelsior Stables and headed out of town on the Nevada City road, rejoicing again in the yeasty, horsey aroma. She planned to ride for an hour or so and then return. Hopefully by then it would be an acceptable time to call on Sir John and Pania and see if they had any news.

The road was quiet at this hour, and the steady roll of the horse's stride was lulling her into a pleasant reverie, when she heard the graunch of cart wheels on rock and looked up to see a procession of three or four brightly colored caravans heading her way, with children dancing alongside while their mothers and smaller babies rode beside them. Her hand strayed to her riding-skirt pocket where she carried a muff Derringer as protection, but she rode on boldly. Mexican merchants selling exotic foods and other niceties were common visitors through the small towns of the Sierras, and she had often bought Mexican popcorn in a twist of paper or a pretty Spanish handkerchief from passing wagons.

"Isabella!" Her name floated to her from the crowd, with a Mexican inflection: *Eezabella!* Her head jerked toward the sound and she saw Preciosa's willowy arm waving gaily, colorful wrist bangles jangling. She bounded forward to come alongside Isabella and took the halter of her mare, smiling up at her brightly. "So good to see you! It was meant to be!" She danced gaily for a few steps. Her strong white teeth flashing as she laughed, and Isabella was struck again by the young Roma's vitality and strength. Just being alongside her infused her with energy after the creeping fatigue of her sleepless night.

"Preciosa! This is a surprise!" A good one, she hoped, her mind flicking back to their last encounter on K Street. That hadn't ended well. Her eyes searched the crowd for the bulky form of Garcia — that was what Edmund Quincey had called him — and his swarthy companion. *Not immediately in evidence.* She smiled down at Preciosa. "Why don't I ride with you a way? You're heading out for Nevada City, are you?"

Preciosa returned the smile. "We are. But walk, rather than ride. There's still much to say, and it is for your ears only." She scanned the crowd while Isabella slid from the mare and fell into step beside her. "I think we can talk without disturbance for a little while." She stopped suddenly and drew Isabella's upturned palm to her. Her touch was warm and dry, the fingers that held her supple and strong. "Oh dear, something of silver."

Isabella drew her hand away and detached a silver hoop from her ear. "I carry no coin, but my earring may suffice."

"You remember well," said Preciosa, eyebrows raised in approval. "In your few years you have accumulated much wisdom."

Isabella laughed. "May it be so." Momentarily she was touched by an inner effervescence. Anxiety, lassitude faded away under Preciosa's novel touch. She took a deep breath. *Don't get ahead of yourself!* "Last time we met you were going to say something about my brother."

"I was, Chiquita, I was. And I still will, but there are more pressing things right now." Her strong dark brows contracted. "That man, Garcia's friend, the one who took you away from me last time. Take care with him. He's a snake in the grass."

She took another long hard look at Isabella's palm. "The man you were with then, the redhead, *el pelo rojo*, he is in grave danger. And there's also a man who can help you. He is close to death. The darkness is not far away."

"Death? Who is close to death? Not Sebastian?" The name caught in Isabella's tickling throat.

"Sebastian? Perhaps. Hiram? Certainly."

"Hiram? But he told me he couldn't help me. He said he knew nothing." Isabella heard the plaintive chord in her voice even as she struggled to comprehend what the gitana was saying. "I know Hiram. He performed a service for me."

"There is still more for him to do. And

he is waiting to do it, but his time is running short."

"But I don't even know where he is."

Preciosa thrust her hand into the pocket of her skirt and brought out a scrap of paper. "This is all you need. I now leave you to God."

Isabella could only lift her hand in farewell as the Roma diviner was carried away amid the hubbub of her people, children and ragged-looking dogs who trailed at the end of the procession. She stood looking at the scrap of paper in disbelief. A Nevada City number and street name. Presumably where she would find Hiram. The pent-up breath she'd been holding as Preciosa drifted away came out in a sudden explosion. Her logic rebelled against it. Hiram had already resigned from working with her, and he'd clammed up on Sebastian as well. Why was he likely to have changed his mind now?

But underlying the common sense was a deeper thread that even now she was holding onto, pulling toward her, like unraveling fabric. Preciosa knew things. Of that she was certain. And what did she have to lose by listening? A Romany phrase she'd heard moons ago came to her mind: 'It is with God that we found you.' Perhaps there was a universal wisdom at work here, and she'd be foolish to remain deaf to it.

She considered riding back to New Gold House and telling Sir John, "A gypsy told me …" She could imagine how that would go down, especially if he was still engaged in looking for Sebastian. Fact was, she was already just about halfway to Nevada City. It was still nice and early in the day — not too hot for riding.

Without any further hesitation she remounted and turned into the light dust cloud that hovered on the Nevada road. Preciosa had said time was short, so she'd better not waste any more of it.

# Forty-Two

The evil-smelling, thigh-deep mud might just prove his slimy grave. He moved with infinite caution, maintaining intense discipline so as not to make any noise that would attract his pursuers. And as he moved, the years slipped away. He was skirmishing with the Massachusetts infantry, on a special assignment to reconnoiter enemy advance positions.

He slipped back into that world, taking on the eyes and ears, the heightened senses of an animal in the wild. He noted tiny signs on the breeze, and in the air: the whiff of charcoal from a doused fire not more than eight hours old, the soft rasp of a man hoiking phlegm in a wake-up time throat-clearing, the faintest scent of unwashed flesh.

Sugar Loaf Mountain had a dubious reputation as a hangout for thieves and renegades. That's why on the night of the Big Scare three years ago — when secessionists were rumored to be about to raid the town's banks and armory in the dead of night — many of the town's women and children were sent to hide out there under heavy guard. The fact that it had been a false alarm that made the sheriff a laughing stock for years after didn't change the fact that Sugar Loaf had an unsavory reputation.

Sebastian's sixth sense told him that somewhere skulked a fugitive or vagrant — maybe a group of them — who were using the wilderness close to town as a hideout. If he could draw Edmund and the dogs across their scent trail, the dogs might get so confused they'd be thrown off altogether. It was a tactic, anyway. He knew he'd need to keep moving as fast as he could because any time he spent standing around was time he was gifting the dogs to catch up with him.

As he moved further into the swamp, water levels increased and mud reduced, so that by the time he was fifty yards in the water was up to his shoulders and his legs moved freely. He looked around, gauging the most likely location for a villain's hideout.

A hundred yards upstream and upwind of him, a slight promontory jutted out, sitting on a bank of shells and shale, conveniently cloaked in dense scrub which it was impossible to see into. Upwind — so it was highly likely that those faint hints he'd picked up had come from there, even though the movement of the air current was barely discernible.

He stopped walking and turned slowly in a circle. As he turned, his eye caught the bobbing outlines of Digger Pine cones floating around him. The fat nutritious seeds were popular with mountain foragers, and at this elevation the pine's droopy, twisted branches overhung any ravine or gulch with enough soil to allow it to put down roots. The flanges of the ripened cones had burst open in the summer's heat until many were double the size of a man's clenched fist: perfect hand grenades of buoyancy and lightness.

Sebastian considered the scene again. The swamp edge on the other side was a couple of hundred yards away, and the wind was blowing away from him. It seemed a good gamble to pepper the bank with cones, creating a rustle, a disturbance, at numerous conflicting spots along the bank, and see how Edmund and the dogs would respond.

First, though, some camouflage so he wouldn't be easily spotted if anyone stood on the edge and looked out. Within a few minutes he'd draped his head and shoulders in pine branches caught in a logjam of debris. If he bobbed down so only his head was out of the water, he could pass for an island of floating debris himself.

He loaded up his arms with cones and got to work, lobbing them to the mudline, and then moving on, always keeping a low profile and going with the current whenever he could. He quickly saw results. Birds prodding the mudflats for food took to the air with startled cries. A hare froze for seconds and then fled, sparking a satisfying shriek of hounds. Soon he saw white-shirted figures emerge from the scrub on the promontory and cast around as if trying to discern what was upsetting the wild life. And then he saw them, Edmund and Black Pete, stumbling to the marsh edge, the dogs milling around them.

The men on the scrub bank scrambled inland, seemingly unaware of the presence of Edmund and the dogs, or worried perhaps about being snatched by a sheriff's search party out on an early hunt. At practically the same time the dogs heard or smelled them and shot off, Edmund hard on their heels. Sebastian could see the rifle he carried, waving as he ran to try and keep the dogs in sight.

He stood stock-still, the water warming around him as the sun rose, and listened as the sounds of hell shattered the early morning quiet. The eerie howling of dogs who've found their quarry. The raucous yells of the dog's handlers, urging them in for the kill, the dreadful screams that reminded Sebastian of the battlefield, and then the ear-ringing volley from guns at close quarters.

For a long time after the noise stopped, Sebastian remained anchored where he was, awaiting he knew not what conclusion, reluctant to walk into some 'welcoming' party. Edmund must know now that he'd flushed the wrong prey. What would he do? Stay and keep searching, or run?

But after hours in the water, his bullet-grazed shoulder was stiffening up as the bruising made itself felt, and he was fighting a losing battle against numerous itchy places where ticks from the murk were making themselves at home on his legs and torso. He was on the point of concluding he needed to get out of there when he caught a new sound of men's voices in the air.

He set off for the shore, moving at the same time in the direction of the voices, the points where he'd peeled off ticks showing as little bloody spots on his pale skin. He'd reached the bank and was pulling himself up through the scrub when a voice he recognized came to him, the deep baritone voice of Nelson, John's go-to man for tasks big and small, who sang in the local choir. And if Nelson was here, it was pretty well ninety-nine per cent certain his brother would be too. He broke cover in the waist-high scrub. Twenty yards or so away John's tall form was unmistakable, leaning over a gulch, shaking his head in disbelief.

Seb started forward but found his legs had turned to rubber. He pitched onto his front with a cry. John's head jerked up. He wheeled around and as Sebastian floundered on his hands and knees to get upright his strong warm hand was on his shoulder. "Take it easy, old man, we're here now." He stepped around him and, slipping his arms under his armpits, hoisted him up in a fireman's lift.

"I'm OK. I'll be all right."

Sebastian was gasping and smiling and crying, all at the same time, too happy to feel embarrassed. His brother pressed Sebastian's face against his shoulder — hard to do when the younger brother was the taller — in an urgent fraternal embrace, and muttered into his hair, "Sebastian you look a sight, you really do." He held him at arm's length and gazed in disbelief. "Pine twigs in your hair, tick spots all over your hands, but walking, however unsteadily, on your own two feet."

The brothers regarded one another in unabashed affection. Then Sebastian broke eye contact and turned to the trench where he saw men's bodies lay. "S'truth, John, there were so many times last night when I didn't think I was going to make it. I could so easily have ended up like those unlucky beggars there."

# Forty-Three

Isabella found Hiram Williams in a boarding house in the least desirable part of town, and the stink of sweat and cigarette smoke that hit her in the face as she followed the tough-faced manager into Hiram's room left her in no doubt he was occupying one of the least desirable corners.

He was propped up on stained pillows, his yellow-tinged horny nails grasping grubby sheets up to his neck, gnarly fingers clutching the fabric. The face that peered over the linen was ashen and furrowed with dark lines; sweat beaded his brow. Maintaining his breathing was laborious work, and the noise of it filled the stuffy room that was not much bigger than a coyote hole, a steam train sound of wheezing and puffing that ground on without respite.

The proud man with tired eyes who always gamely concealed his limp under a determined forward thrust had been stripped down to the barest relic. He was a beached carcass, expiring unnoticed on the high-tide water-line. Isabella wasn't sure he would even remember who she was. She stretched out her hand and said as gently and clearly as she could, "Mr Williams? I am Isabella Wilmington. You did some business for me recently. Do you recall?"

His eyes snapped with fear as he hitched himself higher on the pillows and stared. "Miss Wilmington?" The voice was no more than a scratchy hiss. "What do you want?"

Isabella turned to Mrs Roach, who doubled as a nurse aid as well as house matron. Her hard eyes and tightly set mouth announced her disapproval of this whole exchange. "Could you leave us for a time, Mrs Roach? I'd appreciate the opportunity for a private conversation."

Mrs Roach turned toward the door with a humph. "Please yourself. I've got better things to do anyway." She strode out, leaving the door into the hallway ajar so a sliver of daylight lit the dim room from a window on the first floor landing that opened onto a small wrought-iron balcony.

"I am sorry to see you unwell, Mr Williams. Very sorry. Is there anything you need that I might be able to get you? Are you eating well?"

Hiram made something like a cackle deep in his throat and shook his head.

"Won't be needing food for much longer, Missy."

Isabella regarded him quietly. He did not want the conventional response, the denials. *Oh no, you'll be well right and soon.* No, he didn't want that.

"Then if our time is short, we'd better make the most of it." The statement was gentle but direct and clear, and she could see by the way his eyebrows lifted under his lanky blond-gray hair that he respected her honesty. "When we last met you told me you had nothing to report on the situation with finding my twin brother. Could I ask you, is that how things remain today? Entirely for my ears only, of course. I just had the feeling …" She held her breath as she gazed into his face. She felt a surge of tenderness, of benevolence, for the man before her, a basically decent man. "I thought there was something you weren't telling me. It was just a feeling. And please, take your time to answer. What you say may affect me for the rest of my life."

Hiram shuffled his hands uncomfortably along the edge of the sheet, and Isabella had the oddest urge to reach out and take his right hand in hers. She held it between hers and stroked it as she waited for him to speak. His breathing, while still rasping, quietened.

"You're giving me a chance. A chance to make a clean breast of it."

His eyes flicked to the overflowing ash tray and the empty water glass on the bedside table. "We never know where we're going to end up, do we? And if I'd ever had any idea I'd end up working for Senator Hector de Vile, well I'd never have begun, would I? Seems such a grand fellow. You think you're making the big time, working for someone like him."

Isabella nodded. "The Senator? You worked for him?"

"That I did. Same time as I was working for you. Saw no trouble in it. He wanted me to follow his son, keep an eye on him, make sure he didn't get into any trouble."

"His son? I don't know much about him. What's his name? Alexander, is it?"

*No idea where this is going but I'll play along. See where we get to.*

"Alexander. That's right. Saved his life I did. That's the good part. The bad part was setting those thugs on the photographer. Shouldn't have let Knuckles loose there. Should have known how it would turn out." The old man's cheeks were wet with tears, and he dragged his hand free of Isabella's and angrily swiped down the side of his face. "God forgive my soul." He was whispering to himself. For a moment Isabella wondered if he'd forgotten she was there.

"Thing is, that boy had some photographs. Important photographs." He cast a level look in her direction, and Isabella saw he was still fully in control of his faculties. He wasn't confused, but she didn't have a clue what he was talking about.

"You need to tell those Russells — Sir John and all that lot — that de Vile's son has got daguerreotypes they might be interested in. And old man de Vile don't want anyone to know about them. Didn't like that Mrs Stockton getting involved either."

Isabella's hand flew to her throat. "Mrs Stockton? Alycia?" Now she was whispering, unable to comprehend what he'd said. "Senator de Vile was tangled up in that? Was he the one who paid Polk?"

Hiram stared down at his hands and then looked up. Straight in her eye. "He paid Polk. I know because I was the messenger boy who delivered the cash. As to why? That I don't know. I'm not privy to the Senator's dirty secrets." He cackled as if he was actually enjoying the joke. "I did his dirty work, God forgive my soul, but I never gave Polk that rope. That's like putting a loaded gun in the hands of a madman. I never did that."

His mood swiftly snapped back to somber. "Dangerous man to get involved with, the Senator. I wish with all my heart I hadn't gone along with him."

"And Mr Purdy? Burton Purdy? Was he mixed up in it too?"

"Nah. That's one thing I can say. Had nothing to do with that there fire. That was all that other joker, Quincey. Edmund Quincey. Polk too. Had his own reasons for playing dirty."

Hiram's hands flew to his face and he began coughing violently. In between coughs he gasped, "Sick. I'm going to be sick."

Isabella jumped up. "I'll get a bowl." She flew down the stairs, seeking the kitchen, an office, anywhere there might be someone who could give her a bowl or bucket. She spied a bucket in the hall near the front door and was racing back upstairs when she heard the front door slam open against the hall wall. There was the sound of a heavy male tread on the stairs. She paused on the landing and peered cautiously over. Edmund Quincey's glossy black head loomed into view, his head down watching his feet so he didn't see her bob back out of sight. He was coming upstairs. Not to Hiram's room, surely?

She whirled and stepped through the open window onto the iron-railed balcony, shrinking back behind the wooden shutters. She stood stock-still, holding her breath, clutching the bucket to her chest. Edmund reached the landing, and the steps stopped, as if he was pausing to look around him. The steps moved on, quieter, stealthier. The door hinge of Hiram's room groaned as he entered.

Then she heard low riffs of murmuring conversation, but few coherent words. Hiram's voice was momentarily raised in dispute: "No, I didn't!" She heard a muffled cry, and then silence. She clutched the bucket even tighter, willing herself to not make a sound. For what seemed like an age, nothing moved.

Then there was a rustling, a thumping noise, the sort of noise an old man might make falling out of bed. She remained frozen in place, becoming increasingly aware of her exposure. What if the matron saw her from the street and challenged her? She was wondering how much longer she might have to stay huddled there when she heard Edmund come out, banging the door shut behind him. He clumped downstairs. She timed her exit from the balcony precisely with his leaving the building.

She tiptoed across the landing to Hiram's door and stopped. She did not want to turn the handle, fearful for what she might see. Maybe Hiram was neither harmless nor innocent — but he was defenseless. Had Quincey killed him?

The door whined open at her reluctant touch, and she looked in. Hiram's body lay sprawled, partly in bed, partly out of it, in a tangle of grubby sheets. A pillow imprinted with a damp ring of saliva lay beside him. The sickly smell of vomit mingled with the familiar odors of sweat and cigarettes. She placed the bucket down, tiptoed into the room to grab her bag, which sat undisturbed at the foot of his bed, and turned and ran. Never for a minute did she stop to ask herself how Quincey hadn't seen it.

# Forty-Four

Edmund Quincey sat at a window in Blazes Saloon and nursed his whiskey. It wasn't often he killed three men before lunch — not since the war, anyway — and he needed to calm himself. The infuriating thing was that only one of them was intended, and the one he wanted most had got away, damn his soul. He focused all his attention on the liquor in the glass on the table in front of him, and on Sebastian Russell.

How had he done it? First that precipitous drop to the base of the mountain. That should have done for him there and then. Perhaps he was still up there, his mangled body in some crevice, and he just hadn't been found yet. But even if by some remarkable feat of daring he'd got to the bottom, they'd had the dogs there. They should have picked up on him long before they had the misfortune to cross paths with those stinking outlaws.

His heart raced as he recalled the men's torn bodies, the dogs' blood-flecked drool. True, his rifle had finished them off, but the dogs had a good go first.

The saloon sat at the corner of Pine and Commercial streets, and normal Friday street activity showed a peaceful summer day in progress. Housewives entered Cooper's General Store and left sometime later, baskets on their arms filled with provisions for the weekend. A small boy with a bucket and shovel scooped up hillocks of horse dung, the green, heady smell of equine business hanging like a small cloud over the stables a few doors down. Music tumbled from a barrel organ, its handle turned by a wrinkled old peddler who offered his hat to anyone feeling generous enough to share their pennies. A day like any other September summer day in Nevada City.

He gazed out in a semi-trance. Fatigue seeped into his bones from the night on the mountain: the extreme excitement of having Sebastian Russell in his grasp, and then the intense frustration at losing him. As for Hiram? He was a consolation prize. He'd intended to get both of them sometime, but when he missed out with Sebastian it became imperative to at least settle the score with Hiram. He needed, craved success. To get his own way. To drive his will to achieve what he deserved

— to be a man of substance. And anything that stood in his path he crushed.

He couldn't afford to have Hiram ratting on him, especially when he'd heard he was on his death bed anyway. There was always a danger with a basically decent chap like him that he'd have an attack of conscience and confess all. He couldn't afford to take the risk.

Senator de Vile would be glad he'd taken the initiative. Not only was he now certain no one would know who had paid Polk, but no one need ever know about his wartime activities, not with Burton Purdy out of the picture as well.

And really, those guys this morning? The sheriff should give him a commendation for ridding the town of no-goods like them. He wouldn't be surprised if they were wanted for murder.

He glanced across the street to the boarding house where Hiram Williams lay. A willowy young female slipped out the front door and looked nervously up and down the street. She was very pale; and as she hesitated on the door step she clasped her hand across her stomach and bent over, as if in pain. Straightened up again, she half-huddled into the door jamb as if not wanting to be seen, and then, mind made up, set off at a good pace across the street to the stables. She was dressed for it, a smart young woman in a deep-blue riding outfit who looked just like Isabella Wilmington. And she had a black purse squashed against her body that looked very like the one he'd seen on the floor in Hiram's room.

Isabella Wilmington! He shot to his feet with such force the table rattled as his thighs connected with the edge. He grabbed his teetering glass and swigged the final dregs. Then he was across the street and into the boarding house, banging on the landlady's door. "A sheriff. We need the sheriff. Something terrible has happened!"

The boarding house matron was slow to react to his alarm, but when she followed him upstairs a few minutes later and saw the mess of death, her attitude changed. "This is shocking!" Her hard black eyes bored into his. "You found him, you say? He must have had another attack of apoplexy. Doctor said he wasn't to be disturbed." She ran her tongue along her upper lip, staring at the disorder around her. "Why it wasn't thirty minutes ago I showed a young miss up there. Said she wanted a private talk."

His heart surged. He'd guessed right! "A young miss?"

"Some young thing. Didn't give her name. I thought it was strange. Looked like she'd ridden here. Well, that's not right for starters, a young woman out riding on her own. I knew there was something wrong."

"Would you know her again if you saw her?" He affected a sad expression. "She's probably the last person to see Hiram alive. Such a lovely old man, too. I wonder why she'd bother him."

"I'm Mrs Roach, by the way. Wilhelmina Roach. And would I know her again? Most certainly."

"Well, Mrs Roach, I'll call the sheriff. Meantime, I'd suggest keep this door closed and don't allow anyone else into the house until he gets here. Protecting your reputation and all that. As a woman running a boarding house, well, you don't want any nasty rumors, do you?

Chaps might be reluctant to flop here."

He stalked across the street straight to the stables. A groomsman was handing Isabella Wilmington a fine brown mare. She stood on a mounting block, wiping a strand of hair off her face with a distracted air, her eyes disengaged and staring into middle space.

He strode up and grabbed the halter. "Miss Wilmington, I believe you have some questions to answer before you go anywhere else today."

She jerked in shock and her hand flew to her mouth. "Questions? What do you mean?"

"You'll find out soon enough. The sheriff will be here any minute."

"The sheriff? I don't understand."

She rubbed one side of her face, as if easing a headache, and stared at him. "What's all this about?"

He gave her a disparaging 'don't play games with me' smile. "I think you know very well what it's about. Does the name Hiram Williams ring any bells?"

She pitched over against the horse's flank and hung there. She was clinging to the saddle with both hands, her knuckles white against the brown leather. Her breath came in racing gasps. With what he could see was a supreme act of will, she pulled herself to her full height and let go of the saddle with one hand, though she still braced herself against it with the other. "I want a lawyer." She stared him. "A lawyer, or Sir John Russell. Preferably both."

# Forty-Five

She was shivering so badly that her teeth were chattering, and it was a hot summer's day. She perched on the front edge of a chair, facing the iron-faced bat she'd been told was Mrs Roach and fought to keep control.

The shock of finding Hiram dead, and then immediately afterward having Edmund entrap her, was taking a goodly time to digest. She'd barely said a word since she made the demand for Sir John to be called. She recognized that even though the accusation was ridiculous, her situation could be perilous. And she certainly would not be telling anyone the incendiary incriminations Hiram had made against the Senator. Tell them any of that and it would confirm their suspicion she was a madwoman.

Mrs Roach sat glowering on the other side of the desk in a stuffy sweltering room that felt more like a cell than an office. The shutters shut out light from the street, but the room still radiated its heat.

"I knew there was something wrong when a girl turns up alone — and on a horse, no less — and demands to see an old man. I should have known." She curled her thin lips in a gesture of disgust.

Mrs Roach. Such an appropriate name for this scuttling horror of a woman. Isabella wagered you wouldn't have to look too far in the dive she ran to find some of the six-legged kind. When Edmund had dragged her by the arm from the stables she'd been waiting just inside the front door, hands on hips.

"Is this her? The woman last seen in Mr Williams' room?" Edmund was all gentlemanly indignation, and Mrs Roach fell right in with his mood. "It most certainly is. Who would have believed it? She looks such a mild little thing."

"I didn't … When I left Mr Williams he was alive in his bed."

The protest brought another scowl. "Yes, sure. And five minutes later he's dead. What kind of a skunk cabbage upsets a poor old sick man who's on his deathbed? What did you say to upset him?"

Mrs Roach came around from behind the desk. thrust her face into Isabella's and glared at her through narrowed slits. "Stand up and put your hands above your head."

Isabella reared back. "Pardon?"

"I said, stand up put your hands above your head."

With a screech of chair legs, Isabella complied, and beginning at her armpits the woman patted her down with hard flat palms. When she came to the Derringer in her pocket she stopped. "Aha. So what's this?"

Sheriff Kinghorn was a stout, full-bellied man with squinty eyes who stank of hard liquor at ten in the morning — whether from a hangover or a breakfast booster she couldn't tell. Either way, he wasn't the man to tell combustible allegations about a favored local son.

He waddled in with the stiff bow-legged gait of a man who spent much of his day in the saddle. He wore the aggrieved air of someone of whom too much has been demanded.

"Bodies everywhere today. Must be the full moon."

"Oh?" Mrs Roach raised her thin-penciled brows. "Where else you bin?"

"Out at Sugar Loaf. Two stiffs in a ditch mauled by dogs. Hard to tell who they are."

Isabella's stomach cramped and she gripped her sides to control the pain. "What's wrong, girl? If you've done nothing wrong you've nothing to fear."

Mrs Roach gave a grim smile and pointed to the Derringer she'd placed on the desk. "She was carrying this. Not exactly an innocent cherry."

The sheriff squinted at Isabella and shrugged. "You'd better show me the damage. And bring the girl."

Mrs Roach led the way in a triumphant march upstairs to Hiram's door. Isabella grabbed hold of the stair rail and refused to move any closer. "What? Don't want to view your own handiwork?" The cockroach flashed an evil grin at the sheriff.

He stepped inside, took one look and quickly drew the door shut. "Nasty. Leave the girl. Don't want everyone tramping through. I'll see you downstairs."

Kinghorn was back in the office before they'd hardly got seated again. He spent a few more minutes hearing accounts from Mrs Roach and Edmund, the biggest roach of all. Isabella stared at a spot on the bare floor and said not a word. Then the sheriff took her roughly by the arm. "Jail for you, little lady. Until we sort out what's gone on here, you're going nowhere."

# Forty-Six

A luxurious soak in a Broad Street bathhouse and a new set of clothes John acquired from a men's outfitters up the street, together with a hot and filling buckwheat pancake breakfast, and Sebastian was a new man.

They'd hung around on Sugar Loaf until Sheriff Kinghorn arrived. "The only goods on Sugar Loaf after dark are no-goods," he said with a sickly grin. "Wouldn't be surprised to find these are wanted men — when we finally identify who they are. The dogs have made that more difficult than it should be."

At Charles Washington's house the men John had put on watch reported all quiet; Mrs Purdy and the boys were in the kitchen with the chaplain having a mid-morning coffee. "Sebastian! Am I glad to see you?" The Reverend clapped him on the back. "Sit down and have a coffee with us."

Sebastian grinned. "Just wanted to make sure you were all OK and let you know I'm fine. Sadly, the same can't be said for a couple of others."

They sat around the table and shared straight-from-the-oven caramel biscuits while Sebastian filled them in on the night's events, including the fate of the Reverend's carefully documented witness statements. "There was nothing I could do about it."

They were standing on the front porch saying their farewells when Pedro the organ-grinder came wandering up the street, his arm working the handle churning out the merry tunes, a group of cheeky urchins following in his wake. He stopped outside the Washington house and dipped into his pockets for sweets, which he passed around the street boys and Mrs Purdy's two. "Right now, you lot, get lost."

He made a scattering gesture and looked up the steps to Mr Washington. "Mornin' to you, Reverend. Reckon they're going to be needin' your services down the street before the day's out." He doffed the Italian cap that shaded his eyes and pulled his big mouth down into a grimace. "Yessiree, Sheriff's got his hands full today — old Hiram's dead. Not too sure how it happened."

A stunned silence engulfed the happy group on the doorstep, and then Betty Purdy raised both hands to her face and uttered a keening mourning cry. "Hiram

Williams? Nooo! He was an old rogue, but he looked out for the poorest on the street."

Sebastian drew a comforting arm around the stocky widow. She drew a deep breath and looked him straight in the eye, her cheeks shining with her tears. "It frightens me, Mr Russell. If anything happened to me, what will become of those boys?" She gestured to the lads who were kicking a ball back and forth in the street in front of the house. "Where will they stop? First Polk, then Burton. And now Hiram." She gave a chest-heaving gasp. "It's got to end. If I had the means, I'd leave California."

"Hang on, hang on. We don't have any details about what happened to Hiram. You know he wasn't a well man."

Mrs Purdy looked sickly pale under her dark skin. She turned to the doorway. "I don't feel comfortable talking out here, Mr Russell. But there's things I need to say, and I do believe the time has come to say them." She turned back to the organ-grinder. "Good day to you, Pedro. It's a sad day to hear such news."

The music man nodded. "Isn't that the truth. Died in his own bed no more than a couple of hours ago. Sheriff Kinghorn's been there. The boarding house opposite Blazes, if you know it." He looked around as if checking for anyone loitering to listen in, and stepped up one set of boards to get closer. "They say it was a young woman wot caused it."

Mrs Purdy gave a wave and turned to go inside, Sebastian trailing behind her. A young woman? That sounded unlikely. He rubbed around his ears uneasily.

Back in the hallway she stopped and

closed the door, leaving John and the chaplain on the porch supervising the boys. "Thing is, Mr Russell, I've got a sick feeling about all this, have had for a long time. It's time I spat it out."

Sebastian said gently, "Go on, Mrs Purdy. You've nothing to fear from me."

"It just sounds so queer as to be unbelievable. But I wonder … Well, I think … Look, I know you'll not believe me, but I can't get out of my head that the Senator has a hand in all this death. Has to have."

If Betty Purdy had said the Pope had shot Hiram Williams he couldn't have been more surprised. "Senator de Vile? Oh Mrs Purdy, I know he's got a tarnished reputation, he's been involved in some unsavory dealings, but why should he be interested? Alycia. Polk. What do they have to do with the Senator? Basil isn't even in business with him."

She regarded Sebastian steadily, a calculating gleam in her eye. "You don't understand what went on years ago. That son of his, and how he came by him. He had Hiram spying on that boy. Watching his every movement, checking up on his doings. Does that sound like a normal fatherly thing to do?"

Sebastian's stomach began to churn. "And what else? There's something else."

She flashed him a brilliant smile and sighed. "You don't miss much, do you, Mr Sebastian." She walked into the kitchen and leaned with her back against the bench. Sebastian lounged in the doorway, the increasing tom-tom drum of his heart belying his casual stance. "When I was a young thing, fresh out to California, I knew Bertha von Werther.

You know who I mean — the scoundrel who became Madam Ring. I knew her when she was young and beautiful, but she was a dangerous dame even then. One day she appeared with a child. He was walking, must have been around two years old, a boy. She said he was hers. Said she'd married young, her husband had died and her sister had been looking after him for her. I didn't believe a word of it, but she insisted the story was true. She'd started romancing this railway baron — she went about town with all manner of men — but next thing she's off to New York to marry the railway man, taking the boy with her."

Sebastian was nodding vaguely, wondering where this wild-goose chase was leading, no closer to understanding how it involved de Vile, or Polk, or Burton, let along Hiram.

"I don't believe she ever did marry the man. And after a few months she tired of him. Moved on to some other feller — a vaudeville singer or gambler or some such. She considered that a more glamorous life than being a Mrs Somebody with a husband always away on business and a small child in tow."

She glanced up and Sebastian guessed she saw the glazed bewilderment in his face. She broke into another big smile. "Don't you worry, Mr Sebastian, we're getting there." She turned and poured two glasses of water from a jug on the bench. She handed one to him and sipped the other herself, as if enjoying prolonging the tension.

Sebastian chuckled. "Yes, well, so far it's all as clear as mud. Do go on."

"Can you take a guess at the name of that railway king who got left with the small boy? It was said by those in the know that it suited him to keep the boy. He wasn't too sad about saying goodbye to the dame. Something to do with a family inheritance. He needed proof of a son to collect, or some such wild yarn."

"You're not suggesting ... You *are* suggesting! The railway man was de Vile?" He'd begun the statement tentatively, barely able to breathe and speak his chest was tuned so tightly. Halfway through the sentence, a wind of conviction blew through him, so by the time he finished speaking he knew in his bones that what Betty Purdy was telling him was true. "So the mother of de Vile's son was Bertha Von Werther."

One look at Betty Purdy's face and the doubt was back, lodged in his gut. "No? Bertha Von Werther was not his mother? Which is it?"

"Truth is, Mr Russell, I don't know. You could never believe a word she said. She lied all the time. But what I'm wondering is why he had Hiram tailing him, if everything was as simple as you like. And why he paid Polk to kill Mrs Stockton."

Sebastian looked at her sharply.

"I haven't got proof of that, I admit. But someone paid Polk, and Hiram was the middleman. That's why he delivered that money that day. Hiram worked for de Vile. Something happened and he got very frightened — he told Burton to stay clear of him. And just how many rich men are there around town paying desperate men to kill?"

Sebastian flopped onto a hard-backed chair at the table and buried his head in his hands, all pretense of relaxed indifference forgotten. "De Vile. Hector de Vile …"

The conversation he'd had with Isabella the night after Alycia died sounded again in his head; their sharp disagreement as to possible motive. He'd pooh-poohed the idea of Alycia's death being tied in any way to her search for her twin. Isabella had been so upset at the way he'd played it down. He hadn't taken her views seriously, he admitted now. And perhaps she'd been right all the time.

"By the heavens, Betty Purdy, I think you've given us the answer we've been seeking ever since Alycia died. It's so big I can hardly get my head around it. There's still a lot we don't know, but I think you might have put us on the right track at last."

He stepped quietly to the kitchen bench and lightly wrapped Mrs Purdy in his arms. The big woman had the quality of one of the pines that stood like sentinels on the mountains that surrounded them: anchored, enduring, and easy to take for granted. She smelled of cinnamon and butter. He understood why the boys she mothered felt secure around her and her flour-peppered black hair. "You've been such a tower of strength through it all, Mrs P. Staying strong for your boys. '

Betty Purdy laughed. "My boys. Ah yes. They're just like the rest of us. Little orphans looking for a safe home."

# Forty-Seven

It wasn't hard to pick out the boarding house opposite Blazes. The popular night club was a magnet, known by everybody. A small crowd had gathered in the street outside, and one of the town's policemen stood guard. "Officer William Scott reporting here, sir. Sheriff's waiting for the deputies to come and remove the body," he advised Sir John when they shouldered forward. "I'm afraid no one's getting admission before that."

"This is a sworn deputy from Grass Valley," said John, "and we've reason to believe this may have links to another case he is working on. Perhaps if we agreed not to go near the deceased he could survey the scene?"

Scott shifted uneasily, and his eyes jittered over the crowd behind them. Sebastian produced his silver deputy's badge and waved it in front of Scott's nose. "Ah well, if you're official, sir, that's different."

The graying cop looked at them over his wire-rimmed spectacles, more bank clerk than law-enforcement officer. He opened the door and let them slip through the slim gap into the dark stairwell. A boxy-shaped woman with hard eyes came out of a side office and stopped their progress, arms akimbo. "Where do you think you're going?" The question was sharp and peremptory.

"To see Hiram Williams' room, ma'am. I'm Sir John Russell and this is deputy sheriff Sebastian Russell. Now if you don't mind ..." He glared down at her from his superior height.

She wavered and stood aside. "Top of the stairs, first door on the right." She eyed them coolly, then thrust forward her hand. "Mrs Roach. I run the boarding house, and I can tell you nothing like this has ever happened here before. It's shocking. And to think a girl was involved! A slip of a girl. I don't know what the world is coming to."

"A girl? Where is she, this girl?" John had spoken first, but he was voicing Sebastian's sentiments exactly. Where was she?

"Oh, the sheriff's taken her off to jail. Luckily a right sharp feller came along — Edmund Quincey, I believe he said his name was — and he got onto it. Seen her skulking around here right at the time Mr Williams died."

She led the way upstairs, apparently reluctant to miss any of the excitement. "Quincey was in the bar across the street, apparently. Saw her rush out of here white as a sheet and go over to the stables."

They followed her up the narrow bare wood stairs and paused on a landing outside a closed door. The smell of death was already filling the air, leaving Sebastian in no doubt as to what lay the other side. "In there?" he asked. Mrs Roach nodded.

Hiram Williams had pitched headlong from his bed. His body lay draped across the bed edge in a tangle of soiled sheets, and the mingled smells of vomit, urine and sweat told the sad story of his undignified end. Already a black carrion fly was clumsily cruising, circling to land on Hiram's gaping face.

Sebastian gestured to the pillow that lay on the floor. "Suffocated, I'd say." He glanced up at John. "See the mottling of those tiny dark red dots on his face? Like a rash? Evidence of asphyxiation." John's face had drained of all color, and his Adam's apple was pumping in his throat. He looked close to collapse. Sebastian said, "We don't both need to be here. You wait outside, pump Mrs Roach. I'll only be a few more minutes."

His brother needed no second invitation. He whirled and with his hand to his mouth went back out into the hall. His feet thumped on the stairs as he retreated.

Sebastian stood quietly, reading the disordered mess before him. Looked like the old man had been sitting up in bed, probably hunched forward. Someone had entered the room and frightened him.

He'd made a desperate attempt to get out of bed, but his legs had tangled up in the sheets, trapping him where he was. In his weakened state it had been easy for that someone to step forward and finish him off.

He glanced at the floor. Imprinted on the dusty bare boards was the outline of a man's shoe, but it was impossible to tell when it had been left. How carefully had the room been guarded? He suspected not particularly well. Still. He took one last careful look around him, turned to leave and almost collided with a sandy-haired deputy. A local man, Bob Patterson if he remembered correctly. The sheriffs ran higher-level investigations, while the police dealt with local squabbles. He dipped his head as if he was tipping his hat and stepped aside, saying, "All yours, Bob. A sad mess."

Patterson was young and inexperienced, but from what Sebastian had seen of him was smart enough. He brought up short and, like John's, his white face was slick with a nauseous sheen. He wiped his hand across his mouth. "What do you make of it, Russell? Interested to hear your thoughts."

Sebastian gestured to Hiram's slumped form. "An educated guess? The man's been asphyxiated. Proving it when he's had a history of apoplexy? Not easy."

Downstairs in Mrs Roach's office, John was in labored conversation, but his face had regained its healthy color. When Sebastian entered he picked up his hat in what looked like relieved haste and said, "Well, here he is. We'd better be going, Mrs Roach. Thank you for your valuable information."

Outside, as his sight adjusted to the glittering midday sun, John screwed up his eyes. "Dreadful woman."

After the decaying corruption inside, the air tasted of rosewater and fresh green hay. Sebastian raised his eyes to look across the street and sure enough a few doors down a rambling rose cascaded in blossom over the stable arch. He shook his head. "By Jove, I'm glad to be out of there."

John touched his elbow and gestured to the doorway of a boarded up shop next door to the Roach establishment. "Let's just stand here out of the sun for a few minutes. There's stuff I need to tell you."

They stood shoulder to shoulder and John spoke urgently. "The young girl that's supposed to have visited Hiram? From what that cockroach of a woman next door said, there's a very good chance that it's Isabella. God knows why — or how."

Sebastian's throat had constricted so tightly he could hardly force any words out. "Isa—" He coughed. "Isabella? For goodness sake."

"Exactly. I was flabbergasted too. Apparently she was carrying a Derringer. Mrs Roach took that to be conclusive evidence she had nefarious intentions, that she was threatening him somehow."

"We'd better get to her. Where is she?"

"I was waiting for you to say that. She's in the jail. Let's go."

As they turned to leave Sebastian caught his brother's arm. "One thing that doesn't fit here. How did Edmund know anything was amiss in the boarding house if he just happened to be across the street having a quick one? And why did he have any reason to question Isabella's presence. It wasn't as if anyone had sounded an alarm — unless he already knew Hiram was dead."

It was a one-minute walk from Blazes to the Courthouse, a granite-and-brick temple of justice built three years ago after two previous wooden Courthouses were consumed by fire. As was only appropriate for a building purpose-designed by San Francisco architects at great expense, the second (and top) brick story was fronted by imposing Greek columns, and the whole edifice sat on a raised site ringed with palm trees. The granite-walled jail sat contiguous to the main building.

"Here's hoping justice isn't just seen to be done in this monument to civic ostentation," John drawled as they circled around the back to the jail entrance. "Fine buildings are all very well, but a modicum of logic and science are even better."

Sebastian smiled weakly and followed his brother into the tomb-like quiet of the jail. Sheriff Kinghorn regarded them with narrow-eyed suspicion when they entered and asked to see Isabella, but his attitude moderated at the mention of 'Sir John' and 'Deputy' Russell. "She's through there in the holding cell. Luckily it's a quiet day so no one else in there. Too early in the day." He grinned — Sebastian caught the whiff of alcohol — and unlocked the cell.

Isabella sat on a hard bench, her knees drawn up to her chin, her arms clasped around her legs, staring at a patch on the stone floor, seemingly far,

far away. She glanced up stony-faced as the door opened, but when she saw them her morose expression vanished. She jumped up so quickly she had to put out an arm against the wall to keep her balance. "John! Sebastian! You came!"

"Yes, and now they're here, I expect you to talk." Kinghorn's face flushed scarlet. "She demanded to see a lawyer and you, Sir John, and she's refused to say a word since. What's a lawman to make of that kind of nonsense?" He stroked his protruding belly as he spoke, as if anticipating his next drink.

"Not such an unreasonable request." John's tone was mollifying. "It's fortunate we heard about Hiram's death — and your dilemma, Isabella — so soon."

Isabella fixed her gaze on him. "My dilemma?" She eyed Sheriff Kinghorn.

"Yes, I suppose you could call it that. I'm so pleased to see you. How did you find me so quickly? I thought I might be in for an awful long wait."

"We were at Charles Washington's and Pedro came by with his organ. Hiram's death is today's talk of the town," said Sebastian.

The corners of Isabella's mouth turned down. "It was terrible." She'd gone a chalky white. "But Sebastian, it's wonderful to see you alive and in one piece. We have a lot to talk about." She flicked another dubious glance in the Sheriff's direction. "Sometime."

Kinghorn pushed his rotund form into the space separating Isabella from the Russell men, as if asserting his authority. "Now, Miss Wilmington, I've had enough willful nonsense from you. You will answer the reasonable questions of an investigating officer."

Isabella shot an appeal to John, and he nodded. "That seems a reasonable expectation, Isabella. Sebastian and I have some pertinent information to share with the Sheriff as well."

They sat around a table in the Sheriff's office and went through the facts as they knew them. Isabella began with a brief description of her encounter with Preciosa, her mysterious instruction about Hiram; the spontaneous decision to go straight to him. "Preciosa said time was short."

She glossed over the conversation with Hiram — "he just wanted to reminisce" — and described how she'd gone to find him a bucket because he was threatening to vomit. She described the man arriving while she was absent, and then glanced uncertainly across to first John and then Sebastian.

"Did you get a good look at him?"

Her eyes flicked to Kinghorn and then to John. She nodded. "Yes. Yes, I did."

"Then who was it?"

"It was Edmund Quincey."

Kinghorn let out an explosive guttural sound, throaty and dismissing. He wriggled in his chair. "What nonsense. The girl's lying."

John's hand went up. "Tell me, Sheriff, did you notice the pillow? Did you have any thoughts about what might have happened in there?"

Kinghorn's bushy eyebrows shot up. "Lot of vomit. That's about all I noticed."

"Vomit, yes," Sebastian joined in. "And clear signs of asphyxiation."

Kinghorn glowered. "So you're an expert, I suppose?"

"Expert, no. But I can recognize the red rash that's common when someone's breath is forcibly stopped, either by strangulation or asphyxiation. I saw no signs of any bruising to his neck, but definite signs of trauma around his mouth and nose. I'd suggest that even though Hiram was unwell, suffocating him would take more physical strength than possessed by a nineteen-year-old woman of slender build. He was a durable old coot. For starters, not many survive what he had already survived."

Kinghorn made a gargling, throaty protest. "What would you know?"

John intervened. "I think, with his experience as a soldier, he's in a better position to judge than anyone else here."

Kinghorn sneered. "And you believe her story about gypsies?"

John ignored him. "One other thing that's got me puzzled, Sheriff. Mrs Roach says Edmund Quincey saw Miss

Wilmington leave the boarding house and he came straight across to raise the alarm. Did she tell you that?"

Kinghorn nodded reluctantly.

"How did he know there was anything wrong upstairs, unless he'd already been there and seen it for himself? And if he had, why didn't he raise the alarm straight off, rather than sloping across the road for a drink? Wouldn't you agree there's a degree of opportunism about the way he rushed over to 'raise the alarm' when he caught sight of Isabella? He probably realized she might have seen him — might be able to identify him."

The tips of the Sheriff's ears turned red. He pulled at his collar. He shuffled uncomfortably in his chair once again. "It's just the word of an emotional chit against that of a mature man," he protested.

John shook his head. "Not 'just the word'. We've given you sound logic and hard evidence — the timing, the sequence of events, the likely weapon — and none of it stacks up to Miss Wilmington being capable. I suggest you get Quincey in for another chat, straighten out his account. Meantime, I see no grounds for holding Miss Wilmington any longer. "If you quibble on that, I will call in a solicitor on her behalf immediately. But I hope that will not be necessary." John pushed back from his seat and leaned across the table, planting his big hands flat, one either side of Kinghorn's chair. "Will it?"

Kinghorn bared his teeth and gave a bitter laugh. "You big guys always get your own way, don't you?" He pushed back from the table in a move that mirrored John's. "I know when I'm beat.

Take her with you." His face curved up in a snarl. "And stay the hell off my patch."

He glared at Sebastian, his beefy cheeks pinched in resentment. "For a lawman you sure as hell get yourself in a lot of trouble."

# Forty-Eight

Senator Hector de Vile glanced over the Bourbon Lodge choices for the day and clicked his fingers to get the waiter's attention. The private men's club in a villa on Aristocracy Hill in Nevada City offered private meeting rooms, an extensive library, convivial poker games, and a small but generally very good food selection. This evening, the choices were venison stew or baked salmon, both locally sourced. To his annoyance, his guest for the evening was late, and he was about to order for both of them anyway when Corporal Edmund Quincey bustled into the room on a rush of urgent energy.

"Sorry, Hector. I really am. It's been one of those days."

The waiter scuttled over and pulled out a chair which Quincey sank into. "You wouldn't believe what I've had to deal with."

Hector held up a hand. "Whiskey or wine?"

"A whiskey please. Maybe a glass of wine with dinner."

"And venison or salmon?"

"Venison. Thank you."

De Vile gave the waiter his new instructions and waited until he'd returned with Quincey's whiskey. "So what's all the excitement?"

"Oh, just working on a bit of damage control with regards to Alex and your wish to keep him as far as possible away from any chance to follow up on his roots. That old codger you had working

for you — Williams, was it? — kicked the
bucket today."

"Oh?"

"Yes, so there's no chance now of him
giving Alex any clues as to his origins.
Whatever he knew — and I for one have
no idea what that might be — has gone
with him."

De Vile nodded. "Uh-huh. What else?"

Quincey tilted his head back and
stretched in his chair; a gesture of
comfortably filling his space. It didn't
take him long to puff himself up, Hector
thought. He glanced around him. Apart
from the one they sat at, four other
tables were set with crisp white linen
cloths, silver cutlery and fine white
china, the centerpiece candles on each
unlit until occupied. Red velvet curtains
were drawn across French doors which,
in the daytime, opened onto a pleasant

garden; at night the rich color wrapped around them, providing a sense of succor and more practically, protection from a bombardment of insects attracted by the warm amber glow of the wall-mounted gas lamps.

They had the room to themselves at this early hour on a week night, but later it would fill with ten o'clock diners eating before jousting into the wee small hours at the poker tables. A faint smell of cigar smoke and brandy hung in the air. Bourbon Lodge was just the sort of male sanctuary where de Vile felt most at home.

He realized with a start that Quincey was still talking. "Sorry, I missed that. What did you say?"

"I said I'm still working on locating Mrs Purdy."

"Remind me, why are we interested in her?"

"Just a precaution. If her husband talked she might be able to trace Polk back to you."

Hector frowned. "That seems such a long shot it hardly warrants consideration. Much safer to let bygones be bygones."

The smell of hot meat and vegetables announced the arrival of their meals, and conversation once more hung in abeyance. Hector ordered a bottle of good Californian red and they tucked in.

"And how are things coming along with Caroline Studebaker? Has she given any further thought to our proposition? Any closer to making a decision?"

Quincey pressed his lips together in a slight grimace. "She's still thinking about it. Very cautious woman, that one."

"And your personal suit? Making any progress there?"

The lips puckered into a pinch, and Quincey's glittering eyes narrowed. "Small increments. I will win in the end." He fingered his wine glass and cleared his throat. "It might work a bit better if she got a personal invitation to your testimonial dinner. She tends to be impressed by that kind of thing."

Hector took a sip of wine and nodded agreeably. "No problem at all. Consider it done."

Quincey raised his glass and made a toast. "To Mrs Studebaker and her bank." He laughed out loud. "She's one woman who's worth waiting for."

Hector was wondering if it was the woman or her bank that Quincey considered worth the wait when the dining room door opened and their peaceful seclusion was shattered by loud jocularity. A group of six or eight men —

Hector recognized most of them as local merchants and professional men — flooded in, their red-faced volubility indicating that they were already well-primed for a night out.

The Nevada City sheriff — what was his name? Kinghorn? — glanced their way and tipped his hat. "Senator, Mr Quincey. Good evening."

Hector nodded. "Evening, Sheriff. Hope you've been enjoying a quiet day at the jail."

Kinghorn hesitated, then approached their table. "Unfortunately, Senator, far from it. Three bodies in the morgue even as I speak. Two died in a bullet storm. Not what we like to see."

"Goodness, Kinghorn, I thought the bad old days were behind us. California is a civilized state. What's going on?"

"Your companion can probably tell you

more than I can," he replied, glancing at Quincey. "I'll be needing you to come in tomorrow and clarify your statement, Corporal. Just don't make it early." He laughed and turned to go, then changed his mind and turned back. "Two of those deaths are almost certainly rapscallions already wanted for murder. We're trying to identify them from what we know. The third one is a bit of a mystery."

De Vile fingered his glass. "Why is that?"

"Harmless old chap named Hiram Williams. Walked with a cane and in very poor health. Not a threat to anyone. Seems like he might have been suffocated. A very odd set-up." He glanced again at Edmund. "The deputy from Grass Valley, Sebastian Russell, has raised some questions that need to be answered." He took a step back. "Well, enjoy your night, gentlemen. I'll return to the fun. "

As soon as he was out of earshot and swallowed up in the boisterous camaraderie at the neighboring tables, Hector fixed Quincey with an eagle eye. "What was all that about? Sebastian Russell? What's he got to do with it?"

"Nothing. Nothing at all."

Quincey's jawline tensed and his head sat at a rigid angle.

"It can't be nothing if he wants to see you." Hector felt heat flushing through his body. Nothing infuriated him as much as slipperiness, deviousness. He always preferred to meet buster storms head on. 'Hope for the best but prepare for the worst.' The old proverb had always been his motto, and look where it had got him.

The table Kinghorn had joined was all

fully taken up with ordering food and drinks and ragging one another. Hector dropped his voice until it was barely more than a hoarse whisper. "Did you have anything to do with Hiram William's death? Tell me."

Quincey convicted himself before he opened his mouth. His head jerked from its former rigid set, and his face contorted with a look close to panic. "No! I just found the body. I just happened to be there. *That's* why the Sheriff wants to talk."

Plain as daylight, the man was lying. Hector withheld any response except silent regard.

After a long minute Quincey broke. "That girl, the Russell's new-found relation. She was there. Kinghorn took her in for questioning until Sir John and his brother turned up with their demands. If you ask me, that's where he should be looking."

Hector felt a sick nausea settling at the base of his gut. He'd been here before. His reputation endangered by some ambitious madman who went rogue on him in the hope of earning special favors.

"Quincey, when I asked you to act on my behalf in obstructing my son's efforts to find his family, or them to find him, I did not intend you to do anything unlawful. You know that very well. As a newly elected Senator I cannot take any risks with my reputation."

OK, he'd orchestrated Polk's attack, and he was beginning to regret that. He'd encouraged the attack on the photographer, but he never intended for him to die. With a terrifying clarity he gazed into the future. If ever there was a day when Alex discovered what he'd done to frustrate and deny the desires of his heart — how would he react? Would their relationship survive, if that day ever came?

"Quincey, I'm certain I told you Alex was to be protected at all costs. Nothing was to be done which was likely to harm him or his future."

Edmund nodded. "Of course. I understand."

Hector shook his head. "I don't know that you do. I want you to drop any further activity on this account. Nothing more. Do you understand? And I will live with the consequences. 'Hope for the best and prepare for the worst.' Remember that. You'd be very well advised to observe the same."

# Forty-Nine

"Great! So we're all agreed?" Sebastian looked around the spacious New Gold House drawing room and grinned. After the hell of the night on Sugar Loaf, and then the horrible shock of Hiram's death and Isabella's arrest, tonight's homecoming dinner had been as reviving as a hot, fragrant bath.

"What about Alejandro? Don't forget about him."

He felt as if he'd been suddenly thrust into a cold shower. He sighed, and was about to answer when his brother spoke up.

"No, Isabella. We haven't forgotten about Alejandro." John had perhaps sensed that the issue of Isabella's twin was still contentious between them. Isabella gave the impression pretty well everything else was irrelevant. As far as Sebastian knew, they had all the time in the world to look for the young man once they'd settled the real work at hand, which was seeing that Edmund Quincey got what he deserved.

They'd thrashed it out over a delicious dinner — crown roast of pork madeira with scallions and mushrooms and candied sweet potatoes and creamed spinach, followed by cherry pie and crème brulée — and agreed that the priorities were justice for Alycia and stopping Quincey. Well, almost all of them agreed, he corrected.

And because it was clear they didn't have enough evidence to convict him in a court of law, they'd have to be a bit devious about how they went about their mission. No, not devious, he corrected himself again. *Creative*.

In military terms, it was like an unconventional siege strategy. Not a simple matter of 'surround it and starve it out', but more a brilliant tactical maneuver — like Grant at Petersburg. And as far as Edmund Quincey was concerned, that meant cutting him off from his supply lines and making sure he didn't have the opportunity to build new ones. Only in this case, the supplies weren't coming in by rail.

They must convince anyone thinking of aligning themselves with Quincey that they'd be making a very foolish move. Starting with Senator de Vile and Mrs Caroline Studebaker. If they could make him persona non grata everywhere west of the Sierra Nevadas, he wouldn't be a stench in their nostrils.

Isabella's beautiful face pinched up in dissatisfaction. "I know it's important to get justice for Alycia, but she's dead. Nothing will bring her back. Alejandro might be in desperate need. He might be ill or starving. I'd hate to find him when it was too late." As she spoke, her light musical voice rose in pitch and sounded increasingly stressed.

Pania glanced at her husband. "We understand your urgency, Isabella, we really do. And I'm sure the menfolk will push on with that along with everything else."

Sebastian chimed in, "Sure we will, Isabella. It's also important to get to Caroline Studebaker and the Senator as soon as we can to explain the situation."

"Mrs Studebaker, because Quincey is angling to get his hands on her money," said John, "and Senator de Vile because he's given Edmund some work and may be planning to give him more."

"It's just a shame we can't get the rotter hung," said Isabella vehemently. "I'm certain he suffocated poor Hiram in cold blood. And then he tried to frame me!"

Sebastian nodded. "I know. It's tough. But as we've said over and over, we don't have enough evidence, especially with a sheriff who isn't too fussed about getting to the bottom of things."

Pania stood and stretched. "It's a pity the Senator himself can't be made to answer for his actions. But once again, he's got other people doing his dirty work. It's impossible to prove he's had any involvement at all."

Isabella swiveled in her chair to face

Pania. "I know. Even if poor Hiram Williams hadn't been killed, I doubt his evidence of de Vile's involvement would have been believed. The man is untouchable."

"Not entirely," said John. "He'll fly too close to the flame one of these days, and who knows, he might have already done it. Or rather, we might be able to scare him into believing we have something on him that proves he's done it. Wouldn't that be a triumph?"

Isabella gave a pealing laugh. "Glad to see you're an optimist, Sir John. Always good to have one in the family. Optimist, rhymes with dramatist." She leaned forward in her chair with her hands clasped together, bright-eyed with anticipation. "I've been stuck at home not working for long enough. If we have to catch the Senator off-guard by stealth and guile, I've got a few ideas. Why don't I work up a little entertainment we could present at this coming testimonial dinner? It's being advertised in all the local rags, and everyone who's anyone will be going. What do you reckon? Can I be allowed a little fun?"

Sebastian looked uncertainly at John. What to make of this craziness . . . and yet, it just might work. "Go for it, Isabella. I'm sure it will provide you with hours of fun — and it might be the Trojan Horse we're looking for."

Pania, who had wandered over to the French doors that led into the garden, turned to her husband with an adoring look. "I'm feeling like a little turn around the garden before bed. Want to come for a stroll, John?" He was at her side, whisking her by the elbow down the steps onto the lawn within a few heart beats.

"They make a wonderful pair, don't they?" Isabella looked wistful.

Sebastian was about to take his leave as well when John's trusted steward Nelson tapped on the door and stepped in. "Took the letter to the Senator's as you requested, Mr Russell, but his man said he's not making any appointments for him just now. He's out of town and not expected to return for some time. He said check back again in a few days."

The bonhomie that had buoyed them up fizzled away. "Damn nuisance," said Sebastian. "That will slow things down. Ah well, he has to be back here by Wednesday or Thursday in time for his big shindig. I can go and see Mrs Studebaker in the meantime, and Isabella, you can work on your Trojan Horse."

# Fifty

Seb didn't know whether it was Nelson's announcement that de Vile was out of town that had demotivated him or what, but after all the others had withdrawn, neither he nor Isabella made a move to leave. She quietly poured him a second coffee without asking him if he wanted it and refilled her own cup with the last dregs from the pot.

As she nestled into the corner of the sofa, the slanting rays of the setting sun picked up the golden fall of her simple day dress. Nothing fancy: a restrained skirt in a fabric that had a light sheen to it, the top in the same fabric with a scooped neckline that revealed her rounded shoulders and enhanced the smoothness of her caramel skin and wheat-golden hair. She glanced up at him, and he sensed that her irritation had mellowed to a thoughtful melancholy, though he didn't really understand what had brought it on.

He finished his coffee in silence, treasuring the peace of the moment. It was almost as if time had stood still. He reined in his wandering thoughts. What drivel was he getting into? He made to rise from his chair and bid her goodnight, and as he stood he was hit with a gorgeous fragrance from the garden — night-scented jasmine, perhaps. He luxuriated in the keen aroma, picturing the nondescript little green flowers powerful enough to perfume a room.

"Lovely isn't it?" she said. "They've created a beautiful home here. And it's wonderful to see them so happy together." She drained the last of her coffee and replaced the cup on the table in one decisive movement. "Sebastian, there is something I would like to talk to you about." She gazed at him in full-on challenge. "And I don't want you to get mad at me till I've finished. Can we make a deal?"

He gave her an amused grin. "Me get mad at you? What do you think I am? Some grumpy old uncle who thinks he knows best about everything?"

She grinned back. "Maybe not 'old' but the rest isn't too far out." She tinkled her musical laugh, and then sobered. "Just teasing. But I'm not sure how you'll take what I'm about to say. It might be contentious — but here goes." She drew her legs up under her skirt, hands clasped in front of her. "You know that old expression that's so common out here it's almost corny? The one about seeing the elephant? The old gold rushers used it to explain the remarkable things they saw here that couldn't be seen anywhere else."

Sebastian nodded. He wasn't going to interrupt her flow.

"Well, I feel as if I understand what they were talking about because I think I've seen the elephant."

Sebastian smiled. "And what did this elephant look like, sweet lady?"

"It's taken shape as I've had time to absorb the new things we've learned over the last few days — and the picture is so astounding I almost frighten myself with it. I am scared to put it into words." She swung her legs back to the floor. Elbows on her knees, she leaned forward confidentially, her voice quiet and low.

"First, there was Hiram. He told me Senator de Vile paid him to spy on his own son. And that the son had found some old photographs, which upset de Vile so much his reaction frightened Hiram. He lost me with the next bit, rambling on about some photographer who got beaten up. He got very upset, but he wasn't confused. It was just that I didn't know who he was talking about — he didn't mention any names — nor did I have a clue how it all fitted together."

She cupped her chin in her hands. "With Hiram's death and all the other horrible stuff that's been happening, I pushed all this to the back of my mind. But last night when I had a chance to have a quiet talk with Pania, she told me the strangest story, about how Alex de Vile, the Senator's son, had bumped into her in town and insisted on taking her to coffee as an apology for his clumsiness. Pania said he was totally charming. And then, when he'd got her confidence, he ventured to ask some quite personal questions about Graysie and the Castellanos family. He said he'd come into possession of some old daguerreotypes that captivated him, and he'd noticed a faint trace of the name Castellanos on a few of them. *Castellanos*, Sebastian. That was my father's name."

She stood suddenly, as if the nervous energy that was coursing through her could no longer be suppressed. She paced five, eight steps in one direction and then back. She crossed the room and seated herself right next to him, so close he could feel her warm body with its fresh lemony smell though she seemed barely aware of him or the golden room. "The thing is, Sebastian, when Pania was talking I suddenly remembered another thing Hiram said, which I'd shoved aside because it didn't seem to make sense. He said something about how he'd saved de Vile's son's life."

She stared into his eyes and took a big breath. "Sebastian, what if Alex de Vile is connected with the Castellanos family somehow? He seems to be passionate about these old photos. Pania was really struck by how enthusiastically he talked about them. So, Sebastian . . . what if he is Rafael Castellanos' son? What if he is my missing brother?"

As she spoke her cheeks bloomed rose, her eyes lit up and she combed her hair distractedly with the fingers of one hand. Her voice had grown louder and stronger as she progressed. When she stopped talking there was a sudden, pregnant silence. Sebastian knew the next words that came out of his mouth could bind or break the fragile bonds that joined them, but it wasn't that which paralyzed his tongue. The proposal was so wild, so unexpected, so barmy, that he was genuinely at a loss for words. It couldn't be true, she couldn't be right — and yet he had to admit she'd woven together disparate threads and made a convincing cloth.

"Isabella, it's suddenly coming back to me!" Sebastian was on his feet, leaning toward her, gesturing excitedly with his hands. "Something Mrs Purdy said which seemed so extreme — and then with the shock of your arrest and everything it went out of my head. But you're onto something here, I can feel it." He sank back down on the sofa beside her. "Mrs Purdy told me a remarkable story about de Vile and your aunt, Bertha Von Werden. She knew Bertha in those days as a party girl who lived in the same San Francisco boarding house — a popular place for single women, I gather. She said Bertha turned up one day with a little boy, a toddler she claimed was her own child. Said she'd been widowed and her sister had been looking after him for her. She got into a scene with Hector de Vile, went off to New York with him and looked set to marry him, but then she suddenly up and went, leaving him with the child."

Isabella's pretty mouth had dropped open and she slapped her hand over it. She jumped to her feet. "I don't believe it — that's it! It's not a wishful tale I've dreamed up — it really happened! Of course! Huldah never knew any of this. She didn't see her sister from one year to the next. But if Bertha took me, why not Alejandro as well? Double the profits." Laughing, she shook her head. "I hate to be an 'I told you so' but didn't I say right at the start that maybe Alycia was killed because of our search? It all fits. I just wonder why it was so damned important to Senator de Vile to prevent Alex from knowing his origins."

Sebastian cleared his throat. "Betty Purdy said there was something about de Vile's father's estate. He had to prove he had settled down — married and with son — before he could inherit, something like that." He stared at her, his wide eyes mirroring her own expression of amazement. "I can hardly believe it. But now it feels like it's been staring us in the face all the time."

Isabella's gaze slid away, to the floor, and she said quietly, as if the sound of the words would make them believable: "The Senator's son . . . And I've never met him. I wouldn't even know what he looks like. My brother . . ."

A cascade of impulses bombarded Seb's shocked numbness and demanded attention: Was there any way the Senator could be made to pay for Alycia's death? What was the best way to proceed? How to go about approaching de Vile and his son? Would de Vile acknowledge the history or would he deny it all? Was there something else buried here, some secret de Vile was desperate to conceal?

He took Isabella's hand in his. "Isabella, we have to be careful with this. We have to take it very slowly, work out our strategy. De Vile is pretty well untouchable — and you're theoretically still under suspicion of murder. He's probably got the sheriff in his pocket.

What if he's got some reason we don't know about for keeping Alex's origins a secret? He might be willing to keep killing to keep the secret. And he's already had a go at you, at the race course, remember?"

Isabella pulled back her hand in shock and stared at him. "Surely not! All I want is to meet my twin brother after all these years. That can't be too hard, can it? And as for murder, I thought you and Sir John had cleared all that up?"

"We hope we have, but you can't be too careful. If Hector was intent on stirring up trouble . . . And he appears to be in cahoots with Edmund, so I'm advising extreme caution."

Isabella put her head in her hands for a long minute, and when she looked up her expression was bleak. "I can't believe it. I've just found my twin, and I can't go near him in case I'm falsely charged with murder. Is that what you're saying?"

He cleared his throat again. "Put that way it sounds far-fetched, I agree. All I'm saying is we need to take this slowly. You've done a remarkable job here, Isabella, really, piecing it all together, jogging my memory. Your determination to keep pushing has really paid off. But the Senator is a very powerful man. When we decide to take him on, we need to have all our ammunition primed. That's all."

She smiled ruefully. "You sure know how to spoil a girl's fun. From elation to deflation in three short minutes. 'Yes, Isabella, he probably is your long-lost twin, the brother you haven't seen for nearly twenty years, but let's not rush it.' Well I don't know what you've got in mind, Sebastian Russell, but I'm not willing to wait too much longer. I don't care what *Senator* de Vile thinks."

# Fifty-One

Caroline Studebaker stood among the household goods, miner's tools and general supplies in Armin's Emporium on I Street with the self-possession of an empress governing her empire. She was a short and stocky woman with a plain but pleasantly full face and penetrating dark eyes he was certain missed very little.

The dimly lit cavernous space smelt of oats and candlewax, of paraffin oil and tar soap. Reputedly one of the most profitable general stores in Sacramento, it appeared to be also one of the best stocked. Every available inch of wall was covered in display stands piled high with goods for sale, from miner's picks and shovels, cooking utensils to bedrolls, fish hooks to liquor.

"Anything I can help you with, sir?" A fair-headed, pale-faced shop assistant with a fleshy nose was standing next to the cash register, "Milton at your service. John Milton."

Caroline Studebaker had evidently delivered whatever instructions she'd just been imparting to her worker. She glanced at Sebastian without seeing him, already intent on moving back toward the glass-windowed office which sat in the middle of the retail floor. From here it was plain she could keep an eye on every piece of her business.

Sebastian took a deep breath and launched into his story. "If it's all right with you, I'd prefer it if I could speak to a female. I need advice on buying something for a young lady of my acquaintance, you see, and I'd really welcome a woman's advice." He glanced around the voluminous shelves that hung with buckets, heavy-fiber rope, saddles and equestrian supplies. "That's if you cater for that sort of thing."

He didn't have to fake being out of his depth. Why had he thought it would be a good idea to approach Caroline Studebaker this way, in her general store in the middle of the day? Isabella was the performer. Maybe he should have sent her in here to win the merchant's trust. But Isabella wasn't in any mood to show him favor, not after their stalemate on approaching Alex de Vile. And anyway, it was a lot safer for her staying in Grass Valley under his brother's fatherly eye.

John Milton's helpful expression closed

down. "A woman? There's only one woman around here, but I'm not sure if she will be able to see you. Wait here." He crossed the floor and knocked on Mrs Studebaker's door. She looked up questioningly and they conferred for a minute, before she got up and followed him out of the office.

When she got within handshake range Caroline Studebaker's face broke into an understanding smile and her brown eyes twinkled. She gave the impression of being a good-natured, understanding woman, but by all accounts she was mighty shrewd as well. "Most men do feel a little out of their depth on this sort of mission," she said. "Luckily for you, we have an area set aside out of the hustle and bustle, in the corner back here. That's where we store the items that are less utilitarian, shall we say, and more devoted to the principles of beauty and pleasure." She flashed him a bright smile. "Follow me and I'll be happy to show you, sir."

With a sweep of her teal skirts she led him towards the back of the store. They passed the shelves stacked with scales, with enamel jugs and iron pots, Tilley lanterns and hand-operated sewing machines, into a corner that smelled of lavender and patchouli. Bolts of shiny cloth in a rainbow of colors and patterns, shelves of glass jars containing skin creams and perfumes, and a cabinet displaying dainty earrings, bracelets and lace trimmed handkerchiefs. She paused in front of the display and asked, "What sort of thing did you have in mind, sir? Any idea?"

Sebastian had never felt at such a loss in his life. He'd never purchased a gift for a lady. His life it seemed, had been war: surviving it first of all, and then getting over surviving it. He'd never bought anything for Sarah; they'd never got that intimate. And suddenly buying something pretty for Isabella seemed something he had to do, a token of the new life he wanted to start, a sign he was leaving the bitter destruction behind.

He gave a wry smile and shrugged. "Honestly, I don't know. What's popular with young ladies right now? A length of fabric for a frock, perhaps, and earrings to match?"

Caroline Studebaker looked at him intently, as if reading his soul. "A frock, and earrings to match? Any young lady would be over the moon at such a gift. Give me an idea of the young lady's coloring. Hair? Eyes? Skin?"

Sebastian felt himself blushing. Not

because he couldn't remember, but because he could recall Isabella's beauty only too well. The deep blue eyes with tiny flecks of gold. The caramel skin that reflected the glow of her blond hair. The curved, naturally red lips. The hair might have come from her mother, but the Castellanos blood had imbued her with a señorita's passion. He felt a sudden rush of recognition, as if embracing her heritage made her come alive in ways he hadn't understood.

"Her father is, was, Spanish. Her mother Americano. She has the best of both of them."

"So dark hair, flashing eyes, a strong stage presence?"

"Fair, not dark. Otherwise . . . you already know her."

Mrs Studebaker smiled again. "A good guess."

It took very little time to choose an emerald-green length of shiny cloth, and turquoise and gold earrings to match, and by the time the buying decisions were made, Sebastian thought of Mrs Studebaker as a friend.

As she was wrapping the gift in brown paper and insisting on adding some sweet-smelling bath salts as a gift, he leaned into the counter and said quietly, "Mrs Studebaker, there is another matter I would appreciate being able to discuss with you, if you had a spare moment. Preferably somewhere with more privacy than the shop counter."

Her head came up sharply and she eyed him keenly. "I thought you looked familiar. I remember now where I've seen you. You chaperoned the young woman who was dancing with Edmund the night of the Hospital Benefit a week ago. But she's not the one you've bought these gifts for."

"Very observant of you. No, that wasn't her. Edmund, though . . . It's him I would like to talk about."

She nodded, completed the transaction, called to Mr Milton that she would be in the office if anyone needed her, and led Seb into a glass-fronted rectangle where they could see and be seen from the shop but could talk without being overheard.

She sat one side of a big mountain-oak desk and gestured to him to sit the other. "So tell me, what is all this about, Mr . . . Well, I don't even know your name, a distinct disadvantage as you clearly know mine."

He stumbled to his feet, proffered his hand, and presented his credentials, such as they were. "Sebastian Russell.

Brother of Sir John Russell. Working for Basil Stockton. Four years in the infantry." She nodded her acceptance and he sat down. "Mrs Studebaker, I don't want to invade your privacy, and I appreciate I have no right to speak into your life. But I know the former Corporal Quincey exceptionally well — a lot better than I would want to — and I feel I have to offer a warning, as one decent person to another." He glanced up at her serious face. "I am certain you are a very good judge of character, but Edmund can be extremely charming and persuasive, as many young women have discovered to their cost."

Mrs Studebaker gave him a hard smile. "And you think I need protection from his wiles. How very unasked for."

"He's not the man he presents himself to be. And even I, who fought alongside

him for three or more years, didn't know
the full story till very recently — so will
you bear with me? I understand your late
husband was one of the Sacramento
Hussars and you both had a strong
commitment to the ideals of freedom.
What I have to say has a bearing on that."

Caroline Studebaker raised her
eyebrows, nodded, and he told his story.

When he was through they sat in
silence for some time. Her face had paled
when he related his recent escapade on
Sugar Loaf, Edmund's involvement in
Hiram's death. But she'd seemed most
affected by his account of the renegade
Unionists who'd captured and sold
contraband soldiers back to slave
masters.

"Completely against everything the
1848 revolutions stood for," she'd
muttered, as if her dead husband was

there and could hear her. "We didn't fight for the world to allow travesties like this."

She leaned back in her chair, arms resting on its encompassing wings, the picture of a successful burgher. "What is it you want of me, Mr Russell? Interesting as all this is, I don't think you are here just to save an old widow from making a fool of herself over a murdering Lothario."

Sebastian nodded respectfully. "Astute of you, Mrs Studebaker. I'd expect nothing less."

He turned to look out over the store floor. Business was brisk; the clerks kept busy serving their customers. "You don't reach the position you have without having acute judgment. Edmund is just a small player in a much bigger picture, which I can't confide in you just at the moment. I guess I am asking two things of you. The first is rather personal and can't be avoided. Edmund has been fairly blatant about the attraction of getting his hands on your estate. I would presume, would earnestly hope, that after what I have just told you there no likelihood of that ever happening?"

"You most certainly can presume that. Even before I heard your tale, the chances of it were highly unlikely. Now they are zero."

"Good. Then the second request I have is this. I anticipate that you will get an invitation from either Edmund or Senator de Vile to attend a testimonial dinner later this week. Could you agree to go, and act as if everything is as usual? And then when you get there, if the opportunity presents, publicly disassociate yourself from Edmund's affairs? Make it clear, if asked, that you are there as a guest of the Senator, if necessary. Maybe even hint that Corporal Quincey is nothing more than an acquaintance, a mere bagatelle."

Caroline Studebaker's braying laugh echoed around the glass walls. "Turn the tables, you mean? Give Lothario a little of his own medicine? Nothing would please me more."

Sebastian was just rising to leave when Milton presented himself at the office door. "A gentleman to see you, Mrs S. Corporal Quincey? I think he's been here before."

"Thank you, Milton, I'll be with you in a moment." She turned to Seb. "He'll be glad to see you here, I'm sure. You are carrying?"

He tapped his breast pocket.

She smiled. "Good. Then let the games begin."

# Fifty-Two

"What was he doing here?" Edmund scowled.

"Who?" Caroline raised her eyebrows in innocent inquiry.

"Sebastian Russell, that's who. Don't tell me you don't know him."

"Oh, him. I believe he came in to buy a gift for a lady."

"A lady? What lady."

"I didn't ask him her name, Edmund. I had no idea it was that important to you." She flashed him a scorching look. "You seem rather out of sorts today. Is something wrong?"

"No, not at all. He just gets on my nerves. In fact, we're in luck. Senator de

Vile has invited us to his testimonial dinner. Indicated he'd be honored if you would sit at his top table with him. I presume that includes me. He specifically mentioned you."

"Really? Well, that is something. When is it?"

"This coming weekend. At the National Exchange Hotel in Nevada City. Same hotel where Vice President Colfax dined recently. Same dining room, even."

"My word. You are moving up in the world."

"Aren't I just."

"I'll need to book a room at the hotel. Where are you staying?"

Edmund felt an awkward, muddied sense of being sidelined. He didn't have money to stay in hotels. "Not sure. I've got temporary rooms in Pine Street at present. Which reminds me, Caroline.

I've been wanting to talk to you for some time about regularizing our friendship. I mean, we are getting along very nicely, aren't we? We make a great team. So I would be much honored if you would consider giving me your hand in marriage."

He'd anticipated that when this moment came she'd be overwhelmed with delight, throw her arms around his neck. Or sink to her knees in gratitude. Instead a fleeting shadow flicked across her face and was gone before he could identify the emotion — was it close to distaste? Impatience? Triumph? No. Not what he expected at all . . .

"But of course, I understand you may think it's too soon after the loss of your beloved husband. You may prefer to leave it for now."

"You are so understanding."

Now he saw the shy smile, the pleased flush to her cheeks. Ah yes, he'd pushed her too hard. He needed to back off if he was to catch the quarry. Never mind, he was confident she'd be won over by the Senator's hospitality.

*She'll see what I can offer her that the poxy Armin couldn't, devil take his soul.*

He felt a rush of irritation at Caroline's faithfulness to a corpse. Didn't she understand that life belongs to the living? That there's no point in hankering after what was?

Sebastian Russell. Now there was a man who lived in the past, hankering after that bit of muslin. And look where it had got him. Accepted, he did manage to get out of Sugar Loaf, God only knows how, but no serious loss.

*I don't know why Russell gets to me. He's irrelevant, really. Just wait until*

*Caroline and I are hooked up as one of Hector's backers. Then we'll be the power couple. Just like John and Jessie Benton Fremont.*

*And when de Vile runs for president I'll be right there on his coat tails. I've already proven my willingness to be a fixer, haven't I? No job too dirty. Yep. My future is secure.*

He sank back into the chair in Caroline's office and lit a cigar, took a satisfying draw. He couldn't wait for the testimonial dinner. That's when he'd see his payday.

# Fifty-Three

Isabella frowned as she pored over the script in front of her, the outline of the entertainment she was to present at the testimonial dinner, which she hoped would sink Edmund Quincey in California society once and for all. She loved doing it — in fact, she thought if she ever gave up performing she might even endeavor to produce her own shows. But that was for another day. Right now, Sebastian was back to talking to her like a concerned uncle, and she hated it.

He'd come back from seeing Caroline Studebaker in Sacramento looking awfully pleased with himself, though he hadn't given her any details of what was planned except to say she'd been more than happy to agree to denounce Edmund at a time to be arranged — or when she saw it was appropriate. They hadn't worked out the details, but in spirit she was with them.

But he'd no sooner shared that triumph with them all than he was back on his hobby horse about how he needed to clear her name with Sheriff Kinghorn. How it wasn't right for her to have to wear the notoriety of being linked to an unexplained death. How it could affect her good name when it came to her future — either for getting stage engagements or even, God help us, when she wished to marry.

That made her so antsy she could hardly sit still. And the reason it made her so mad? That was even more embarrassing. She felt her cheeks flush at the very thought. She'd secretly hoped he might have an interest in her himself. There were moments when she could have sworn there was something special between them. But it was patently clear he didn't feel it. He saw her as a kid, and himself as the kindly elder who was protecting her from harm. How she hated that!

# Fifty-Four

Alex de Vile could hardly contain his rising excitement as he strode to Sir John and Lady Russell's front door. After five days of 'enforced' holiday — that's how it felt — with his father in San Francisco, he finally had the opportunity he'd been waiting for, the chance to show Lady Russell the old pictures he'd mentioned to her when they so fortuitously bumped into one another in town nearly a week ago.

He'd planned to come much sooner, but his father had suddenly appeared in his rooms at the Holbrooke, falling over himself to retract his high dudgeon and start talking again. Hex never apologized, but he did the next best thing in his own mind — he insisted on taking Alex on a five-day jaunt to San Francisco. His father rarely did anything without a personal agenda: Alex couldn't flush out what had sparked Hector's sudden change of heart, but it seemed genuine.

He walked up the path that led from the front gate through a rose-covered pergola that hummed with nectar-gathering bees and rapped on the door with a sense of anticipation. He felt it in his bones — Lady Russell had the answer to the packet of glass frames he carried in Charles Durant's leather case.

The door was opened by a matronly housekeeper with flat cheeks and wide expectant eyes, but when he asked for the lady of the house she shook her head kindly. "Oh no, I'm sorry sir, Lady

Russell is not at home. Otherwise engaged, I'm afraid."

Until that moment he hadn't realized how much he'd invested in the idea of showing the historic images to someone who might know something about them. At the prospect of being thwarted yet again, his heart shrank.

"Oh dear, I knew I should have made an appointment. Can you give me any idea of when she might be available? I spoke to her a few days ago and she expressed a willingness to meet with me."

"Who is it who wishes to see her?" The woman's brow folded into a doubtful crease.

"Oh, my apologies, I should have said. Alex de Vile, Senator de Vile's son. I met Lady Russell in the village last week."

The matronly Gold House guardian

gestured to a bench on the porch. "Sit there, Mr de Vile, and I will make inquiries for you."

When she returned a few minutes later, she had a rangy freckle-faced chap with her who looked to be about ten years older than Alex. He stepped forward and thrust out his hand. "Sebastian Russell. I'm afraid Lady Russell will not be receiving visitors today, but I would be very happy to pass on a message for her. Why don't you come inside and join us for a coffee. My brother and I are just enjoying a fresh brew."

Alex followed the athletic Mr Russell into a serene interior, the pale gold walls in hall and morning room reflecting the light from the windows. At a round coffee table a much darker man, only slightly shorter than the first, looked up at him with sharp black eyes. He stood slowly as they entered, and nodded. "Alex de Vile, I presume? Sir John Russell. I gather you wish to see my wife."

Alex offered his hand, and Sir John shook it before gesturing to an empty chair. "Do sit down and Mrs Snively will see to your coffee." The woman who had answered the door bustled in with a tray on which sat an extra cup, cream jug and a plate of biscuits.

"I happened to meet Lady Russell in Grass Valley a few days ago," Alex began, "and mentioned some historic photographs that have come into my possession. She expressed interest in seeing them."

Sir John raised his dark eyebrows. "Really." The cadence of the single word was downward, expressing skepticism rather than interest. "May I ask about the provenance of these pictures?"

Alex felt those penetrating eyes rake his face and the temperature in the room drop by several degrees. This man already guessed this was more than some hobbyist's casual inquiry. "You certainly may, Sir John. And I might begin by saying I believe the provenance could well involve matters of life and death. A very fine photographer has already been violently slain for I know not what reason. Whether these images are a factor, I do not know." He patted the leather case, which rested beside his chair, and told the Russell brothers the whole sad story of Charles Durant's death.

They listened with the rapt attention of men prepared to take his words with utmost gravity: it felt strange after battling his father's dismissive attitude.

When he mentioned that some of the work was from a photographer called Castellanos, he sensed even greater attention from both men, but particularly Sir John, who asked, "Why don't you show us some of his work?" His voice was cautious and moderate, but Alex once again sensed taut expectation.

He drew out the sepia-tinted masterpieces and placed them face up on the table: the ethereal woman with her three children, their faces full-cheeked, their little legs in their romper suits and soft baby shoes plump and cuddly. Of all of the pictures, this one seemed to capture a golden moment. The woman seemed preternaturally aware. Her radiant eyes gazed out at the cameraman, shining with a wistful gleam that reached out of the frame and into the present. Alex was convinced that if he lived to be a hundred, the power of her appeal would remain. It was if she was rising up from the rose-tinged glass and whispering to him, to the man behind the lens, to the world, "Nothing will ever be this wonderful again. We watch, we wait, trusting you to make of us something that will last forever."

It came to Alex in a flash that this woman understood the magic of stage presence, whether or not she'd ever been in a spotlight.

In the moments after he placed the images on the table — there were several in varied poses — the room was so still it was as if they'd all three held their breath. The soft release from Sir John confirmed that he, for one, was riveted by the work.

The silence hung on, as if none of them wanted to end the moment. Then

Sir John leaned back in his chair, stretched his long legs out, and said quietly "Alex — I hope I may call you Alex?"

Alex nodded. "Of course."

"I have something of grave personal import to share. You'll need to take a very deep breath before we start." He glanced at his brother and their eyes met in a silent communication. Sebastian barely nodded, but Alex was certain they'd already agreed on something before he'd come in and were now confirming it.

"A very long time ago, when I was a young man of about your age . . ." Alex had no idea how long John Russell took to tell him the story of his birth, to tell him that the woman with the angel eyes was his mother, Elanora Castellanos; that the photographer who captured this timeless image was, almost without a shadow of doubt, his father, Rafael Castellanos; that he was the plump cherub under his mother's protective hand; and on her left was his twin sister. *His twin sister.*

He fingered the edge of the image as if it was anointed — and of course in a sense it was, infinitely more precious to him now than it had been when he'd walked in to the room a short time ago. To wait twenty years, and then to discover all this in what — twenty minutes? He was hollow on the inside, digging into himself, trying to locate the boy who'd lived every waking moment believing he was Hector de Vile's only son, his mother a fickle European his father didn't like very much, forget about love . . .

His mouth, his lips, felt so dry. "Could

I . . . A glass of water, please?"

He gulped greedily at the ice-cold water Sebastian brought from the kitchen. "I don't know what to say." He looked from the older to the younger Russell. "I just felt a connection with these works and with photography in general, but I had no idea why." He stood jerkily, as if testing whether his legs would still hold him up. "And Hector was so angry about it — it was weird how much it upset him. Does he know all this?"

John Russell shook his head. "That is a conversation you will have to have. But I suggest not right now. He knew some of it, maybe, but I think there is still a lot he probably doesn't know. Until we saw these pictures, we hadn't quite fitted it all together either."

He pointed to one of the lesser

images. "This woman here, Bertha Von Werther. I believe she is the woman who brought you to Hector, who briefly posed as his wife and your mother before flitting off to richer pastures. She callously used you and your sister for her own ends."

Alex ran his hands through his hair. "My twin sister. It's shock enough to discover your father is not your father. But my sister — what about her? Is she still alive? Do you know where she is?"

For the first time since they began the conversation, John Russell seemed to relax. His face broke into a warm smile. "We know exactly where you can find your sister. In fact, my wife and she are together right now. But I'm afraid you will have to be patient a little longer." He picked up the carafe and refilled their water glasses. "I presume you are planning to attend your father's testimonial dinner tonight?"

Alex nodded. "Now I am, yes. A few days ago it was far less certain I'd be welcome." He gave them a rueful grin. "But that's another story."

# Fifty-Five

"It's as though Christmas has come early!" Isabella gave Seb a quick smile and glanced around the National Exchange Dining room. He knew exactly what she meant. The dining room shone like a Christmas tree, with red napkins and green table centerpieces bathed in the soft incandescence cast by the overhead gas pendants.

"I love the red-and-green decorations," said Isabella, gesturing to the glossy leaves of the table centerpieces. Her voice vibrated with a faint anxiety.

Seb gave her a searching look. "I do believe the intrepid Miss Wilmington is showing a trace of nerves. I know I am, and I'm not about to perform. Are you ready for later?"

Isabella laughed. "We're as prepared as we'll ever be. We really will need to play it by ear — the unexpected could and probably will happen."

The National was a behemoth of a hotel, its multi-colonnaded three-story promenade taking up a good stretch of Broad Street. Built sixteen years ago, it was ancient in a town where buildings were regularly ravaged by fires. It had managed to escape several fires which had consumed whole blocks, the most recent just six years ago. The 1863 fire had been particularly damaging because, as one local wag told it, history would show that the chief engineer charged with commanding the fire fighting was, "when his services were needed, engaged in saving the duds of his strumpet". Sebastian had laughed when John related that tale over breakfast this morning.

The spacious dining room, with floor-to-ceiling windows at one end, had the air of a rich man's private lounge: formal oak wainscoting around the walls ended a third of the way up in a floating wood panel with beveled edges on which rested the series of large oak-framed mirrors that circled the room. Everything — including the guests' faces — glimmered in the pink light reflecting off the deep-peach flocked wallpaper that stretched from the warm oak paneling to the dark-apricot ceiling.

On the dozen or so tables that were rapidly filling with diners who'd eagerly paid fifty dollars a head for the privilege, branched candlesticks sent the flickering light of sixty or more candles into the shimmering mirrors' reflecting sheen.

"Yes. Just magic." Isabella's hands were clasped tightly together, her knuckles showing white. Sebastian thought back to his meeting of a few hours ago.

*Just as well she has no inkling Alex will be here. She's barely holding it together as it is.*

Their attention was distracted by the arrival of Caroline Studebaker on Edmund Quincey's arm. As Quincey confidently thrust Caroline forward, one of the stewards who was seating the guests consulted his sheet and looked up. "Mrs Studebaker, of course," he smiled. "The Senator has requested that you grace him with your presence at the top table." He led her towards a table in center-front position before the makeshift stage for the later entertainment.

Quincey trailed in her wake. As the steward seated her, Quincey confidently reached for the back of the chair next to her. The steward stopped him: "Excuse me, sir. That seat is reserved."

Quincey flushed a deep red. "It's what?"

"The seat is already allocated. To one of the Senator's guests."

"So where do you want me?" Quincey's eyes narrowed in fury. "I am the lady's escort."

"I'm instructed that the Senator is escorting Mrs Studebaker personally, sir. There must be some mistake." He gestured vaguely a few tables over against a wall. "There are some spare places over there, sir. I'm sure you'll find something to suit."

Sebastian glanced away quickly so as not to catch Quincey's eye, and saw that Isabella had also been drinking in the rejection. "You don't have to be a psychic gypsy to guess Hector's got him on the skids," he half-whispered into her shoulder. "Little does he know far worse is to come." Quincey was now huddled at a table alone. "He can't be too happy with Caroline, either. Not exactly loyal protests bursting forth, you notice." He was taking an absurd pleasure in seeing it all.

At their own request they'd been seated at a table off to one side, partly shielded by curtains that enclosed the artist's backstage area — a position which gave Isabella easy access for her role in her and Pania's 'pleasure confection'. That's what Lady Russell had told Hector de Vile's agent they would be offering. His mouth twitched.

*Infection more like it, and a fatal one at that.*

Isabella would slip out early during dinner to prepare herself and her troops for the fun — one good reason for sitting somewhere unobtrusive. Sebastian had a churning nausea in his stomach. He didn't think either of them were going to be able to eat until much later. So much hung on the next couple of hours.

The room took on a subtle heightened charge: the Senator had arrived. Alex was at his side as they entered but immediately peeled away to stand at the back, like a junior manager whose services were no longer required. "Ladies and gentlemen, please be upstanding for our guest of honor, Senator Hector de Vile."

Every head turned to the door. Two

drummers and a lone fife player slipped in ahead and played a measured colonial air as they walked de Vile to his seat. Seb glanced to Isabella. "Nice touch. One of yours?"

She nodded, eyes dancing in delight. "Indeed. We'll be seeing more of them later."

And then there were speeches of welcome and a prayer of thanks for the food and then everyone except Seb and Isabella tucked into mountains of roast beef and Yorkshire pudding, and the room smelt of caramelized onion, apples and cinnamon. From the comments around him, Seb concluded that the chefs had excelled themselves. And then it was time for the Trojan Horse.

The familiar sound of the fife and drum was the first sign to the guests, rotund in their chairs with sated bellies, half-asleep over full wine glasses, that the entertainment was about to begin. With all that had gone before, they were more than ready to sit back, relax, and — if asked — join in, like an excited crowd at a fairground, or hecklers at a political rally.

*The food's good, but what's next? What more are we getting for our money?*

The drummers and fife player proceeded in the decorous weighted strides of a colonial Williamsburg bandmaster. And on their heels came Isabella as Seb — and possibly no one else in the room — had ever seen her before: dressed as a young man, in a deep-blue jacket, white breeches and a blond mustache that looked suspiciously like the one that decorated Edmund

Quincey's upper lip. "Brigadier Squincey" — for that was what the urchins who danced around him like rats after the Pied Piper called after him — dispensed sweets and smiles with grandiose hauteur.

Following the boys were three frolicking and flirtatious young women in yellow-and-black-striped ballooning skirts with floating pale-lemon chiffon sleeves that resembled nothing so much as wings, topped off by little black hats clipped to the side of their heads. One carried a large honey pot into which they all dipped spoons, licking them with eye-rolling pleasure. Brigadier Squincey lapped up the attentions of first one and then another, licking the spoon with lascivious, long tonguing. As the girls fawned around him, the fifes and drum struck up a jaunty folk tune and the street urchins broke into a ditty, madly circling Brigadier Squincey and his harem as they did:

*Harum scarum, divil may care um,*
*With a harum scarum, diddle dum darum, diddledee dandy dee,*
*Harum scarum, divil may care um.*

At first the Brigadier appeared flattered, and the women charmed, but as the rhythm got more frenetic and the ditty turned more into a chant for blood, he swatted the boys aside, banished the women, and took command of the stage.

That's when Sebastian noticed that the Brigadier had a cushion or two down the front of his white breeches, pushing out his belly like a pot that had boiled over during jam-making. The Brigadier was the classic burlesque fool, all self-important grandiosity, blissfully unaware of his disheveled appearance. With a flourish he launched into a song of his own in a deep, rich voice:

*There are two rules in life say I,*

*The Brigadier Squincey, say I,*

*First men are valued not for what they are,*

*But for what they seem to be,*

*And the second, the Brigadier Squincey's second rule of life*

*If you have no merit or money of your own,*

*You must trade on the merits*

*You must trade on the money,*

*The merits and money of other people.*

*With a hey nonny no, and a hey noony no,*

*The Brigadier's rules of life.*

Isabella gazed out, commanding every eye in the room to attention, her irresistible stage presence engrossing every diner, the soporifics of the food and wine forgotten, all now fully awake and on the edge of their seats for what would happen next.

Caroline Studebaker lit up with a sly, satisfied smile. Senator de Vile glanced at her approvingly and his eyebrows twitched. At Quincey's table the woman on his left who'd been introduced to him as the newspaper editor's wife leaned toward her husband and whispered, "That's from that show *Money* that's just opened at the California Theater in San Francisco. It's the funny play everyone's talking about."

It seemed other guests were putting the pieces together: a small hum of conversation buzzed. Isabella raised her hand for silence, and the room went so quiet you could have heard a teaspoon chink on china. And then with manic energy she refrained the item

*Harum scarum, divil may care um,*

*The Brigadier's two rules of life.*

The room burst into thunderous applause. Sebastian chanced a stealthy glance to the table where Quincey had parked himself and saw that he was hunched over, almost in hiding, against the back wall, his chair distanced from those on either side.

As the applause finished, a second group of performers quietly filed onto the small platform, standing alongside the musicians and, a little to one side, a band of black artists. Not blackface. Sebastian recognized the wise, grizzled face of Charles Washington among them. He was certain the 'bee frocks' — which had such glamorous impact they could have graced a Governor's garden party — were Cressida's work. Everyone was getting in on the action.

Isabella turned to the newcomers, and quietly refrained 'Squincey's anthem' once more.

*Harum scarum, divil may care um,*
*The Brigadier's two rules of life.*

She paused for effect, her timing once again instinctive and perfectly nuanced. "But you wouldn't know that, would you Reverend Washington. You're too busy being good — and staying poor. Not like me, no, look at me." She thrust her cushioned stomach out, a stomach that seemed to be growing in burlesque proportions. Was she somehow manipulating it without anyone noticing? Sebastian chuckled at her audacity.

The nuggety Reverend, his salt-and-pepper hair lending him gravitas, replied, "I gotta song for you Squincey." His voice was a deep, booming bass, and he gathered the band of minstrels who'd accompanied him on stage. At the start of the banjo's first chords the Reverend paraded up and down the stage, flicking his hand in a dismissive gesture towards the Brigadier Squincey as the group launched into a rousing rendition of 'Shoo Fly, Don't Bother Me', a catchy Civil War tune that people couldn't get out of their heads from the first time they heard it:

> *Shoo, fly, don't bother me,*
> *Shoo, fly, don't bother me,*
> *Shoo, fly, don't bother me,*
> *For I belong to somebody.*
> *I feel, I feel, I feel like a morning star,*
> *I feel, I feel, I feel like a morning star.*
> *Oh, shoo, fly, don't bother me,*
> *Shoo, fly, don't bother me,*
> *Shoo, fly, don't bother me,*
> *For I belong to somebody.*

Sebastian's heart leapt to his throat. He knew the story of 'Shoo Fly'. He had been told of it by Burton Purdy during the war, how it was written by a white officer in command of a company of black soldiers from Company G after one of them dismissed derogatory remarks made by another soldier with "Shoo fly, don't bother me."

The crowd in the National Exchange Hotel was on their feet, cheering and waving and joining in the chorus. Charles let them have their head for a few rounds, then drew the song to a close with all the dignity of a man used to representing the Almighty on earth.

"Yes, we laugh. We laugh, dear people. And there is a time for laughter. As the Good Book says, there is a time for everything, and a season for every activity under the heavens."

His authoritative deep bass rolled out to the farthest corner, and suddenly the crowd sensed a change of mood. Faces sobered and to a man and woman they strained forward, riveted on him, not wanting to miss a word.

"A time to love, and a time to hate. A time to be silent, and a time to speak."

He allowed another calculated long silence, and Sebastian had a sense of every head in the room bowing toward him, like field daisies caught in a divine breeze.

"I have been silent." Another long pause, as his coal-black eyes raked the room, searching out ones he knew — De Vile, Quincey, Sebastian. "And now is the time to speak. 'For he knows what dwells in darkness, and light dwells with him.' There is a man who dwells among us" — he looked towards Quincey — "who must finally answer for his actions. No more being valued for what you seem to be, no more trading on the merits and money of other people." The room stirred, as if people realized that the hilarity was over, and proceedings were getting serious.

Charles pulled a handful of documents from his breast pocket with a flourish. "I bring, ladies and gentlemen, sworn statements from free black men, sold back into slavery, sentenced to penury and death, so Squincey could grow rich." He waved the papers. "You can read it all here, if you want to. But maybe you say that's history, the war is over, we don't want to know."

He looked around the room, his brows thunderous, suddenly more an avenging judge that a mild-mannered chaplain. "But you might want to know about murder most foul in your own town, just a few streets away and a few days ago. Yes, I'm talking about Hiram Williams. Aren't I, Sheriff?"

He fixed Kinghorn, who was sitting at a table next to Quincey's, with an icy stare. "The law moves in mysterious ways, its mercies to perform." People tittered, and Kinghorn flushed brick-red. "Less than a week ago, he abducted a man at gunpoint from my very house. Isn't that correct, Mr Sebastian Russell?"

People turned and stared. Sebastian ducked his head. Did they really have to go this far?

"Two men slain on Sugar Loaf that very night. Yes, they were probably outlaws getting what was coming to them, but who appointed Squincey their judge and executioner? And then there's the rope supplied to a condemned man, the man who assassinated Mrs Alycia Stockton, so he could end it all and not implicate the man or men who were the real perpetrators of that foul deed.

"Ladies and gentlemen, Sheriff. How much more must we tolerate before justice speaks?"

Diners exchanged nervous glances. Some coughed, others scraped their chair legs on the wooden floor as they moved awkwardly. At Quincey's table his fellow guests — Sebastian recognized the deputy he'd met at Hiram's and the town's fire chief — seemed to be avoiding eye contact with one another. At the top table Senator de Vile's blond-gray head leaned toward Caroline Studebaker's darker brunette and made a sotto voce remark which prompted her to smile and tilt her head back toward his until they were almost touching.

Quincey had seen this and was instantly on his feet, thrusting upwards with such force the chair clattered to the floor behind him. He took no notice of the racket. His face red and shining with sweat, he shouted, "I don't know what sort of game you're playing at there, Senator, setting me up to be the butt of these puerile jests. I presume this is all happening with your approval or they wouldn't be here." He gestured to the stage. "What is this about? Slandering an innocent private citizen as testimonial-dinner entertainment? Choosing some whipping boy for public amusement? Is this Nevada City's version of putting some poor Joe in the Town Hall stocks and throwing rotten tomatoes at him?"

He moved between the tables like a mountain lion stalking prey and stood directly in front of the Senator's chair.

"While I'm honored to be considered of sufficient notoriety to be entertaining, you've got it all wrong." He turned to face Isabella and Charles Washington. "I didn't do half the things you're accusing me of, and anything I have done has been at the behest of this man here. So if anyone is going to have tomatoes thrown at them this evening, why isn't it you, Senator? You were the one who wanted—"

Before he could finish whatever he was about to say, de Vile sprang to his feet with a roar. "I've heard enough of this insulting nonsense. Sheriff Kinghorn! See this man out. I won't put up with any more of his insults."

The sheriff and the deputy who'd been at Quincey's table pushed through the narrow spaces between tables towards him, while the dining room exploded into an uproar of excited babble around them. Kinghorn drew his revolver as he strode forward.

At that moment the stage crew sprung back into action, as if the whole thing had been choreographed to play that way.

*Oh I'm Squincey Incey, Devious Dincey*

*I'm a particularly wicked man.*

Pandemonium broke out at the Senator's table. As Kinghorn reached to grab Quincey's arm, he punched him hard and snatched the revolver. He spun like a child's top, checking first one exit at the back and another on the side. Both were blocked by diners, all now standing, craning their heads to get a better view of the unfolding drama. He whirled to the stage and leapt up beside Isabella, waving the revolver. "Think you're so smart? You'll find out!"

He locked his arm across Isabella's throat, held the gun to her head, and dragged her backwards to the door at the back of the stage which exited onto the first-story veranda overlooking Broad Street. "Come after me and she dies. See how funny that is!"

# Fifty-Six

Seb was on the stage in an instant. As he pounded toward the swinging door a shrill whistle sounded from outside, and when he reached the veranda deck Edmund and Isabella had vanished.

He traced the perimeter and saw straight away an obvious escape route across the hotel roof and then via the hotel's distinctive annex with its turnip-shaped dome. A hazardous iron ladder down the side of the building — an apology of a fire escape — dropped into the alley at the back of the building. The street below was dark and appeared deserted, though he could hear distant echoing footsteps, the sound of hard-soled running boots on wooden boardwalks.

John appeared at his back, breathing noisily. "Should exercise more." He gave a fleeting grin. "Any sign of them?"

Seb shook his head. "No. They got away." He looked up and saw Sheriff Kinghorn lumbering after John. The frustration that had been brewing all night burst like a dam in a ten-year flood. "If you'd been doing your job—"

His brother grabbed his sleeve. "Not the time or place, Seb. Leave it for another time. Right now we've got to find Isabella."

Alex de Vile appeared out of the darkness. "Where is she?" His face was chalk-white.

In the National's street-level lobby the hotel was living up to its reputation as the hub of commerce for the northern mines. Even at this late hour, crowds of testimonial-dinner guests reluctant to go home after the night's excitement leaned on the bar's long Honduras mahogany benchtop waiting on nightcaps or a turn at the gambling tables. Sebastian was light-headed with exhaustion, but like everyone else was too over-wrought to dream of calling it quits and going home to bed.

Hollow inside, he waited to hear what Sheriff Kinghorn planned in terms of mounting a search, as travelers loitered waiting for late-night connections at the Wells Fargo and other stagecoach offices that shared the lobby. Beneath the hubbub he could hear a faint clicking from the telegraph office. He was asking himself how much longer he could bear to wait around doing nothing when he felt a tap on his shoulder and turned to see one of the hotel's night watchmen eyeing him urgently. "A man outside. Wants to see you."

Sebastian's eyes flicked to his brother, who hovered beside him. The night watchman shook his head. "He said to come alone."

John shook his head. "Don't."

"I've got to. Any chance, I have to take it. Give me a good start."

Once out into Broad Street the hotel man pointed down shadowy National Alley, which led to the stagecoach companies' extensive stables and seedy brothels before verging into an industrial fringe and the looming stone walls of the Mining Foundry's extensive workshops. Not a part of town to be in alone and unarmed in the dark. "He said down National Alley."

Seb stumbled down the narrow alley: the smell of beer hops and whiskey fumes was fast replaced with the earthy aroma of the horse dung he tramped through in the dark. He cursed softly as his eyes adjusted to the lack of gaslight, then gradually became aware of the flicker of lamplight through cracks in the boarded-up windows of ramshackle bordellos, broken one too many times in drunken brawls.

At the corner of Spring Street, he hesitated, unsure where he should go next, and a nuggety figure appeared out of the darkness. A man he recognized from their recent encounter on Sugar Loaf.

Black Pete's expressive eyes flashed under the exuberant curls that framed his shining face. "Cap'n Quincey said you'd come, sirrah. Said you wouldn't be able to resist rescuing the pretty little piece." He cackled. "This way if you please." The little light there was shone off the steel frame of the military-style revolver he waved in one hand as though he was conducting an orchestra.

"Whoa! Take it easy with the artillery, Pete." Sebastian fought to make his voice sound nonchalant. No point in making him even more steamed up than he already was.

Pete waved him ahead and fell in a few paces behind as they turned up Spring Street. They walked in silence until they reached Pine Street, where Pete prodded him in the back with the barrel. "Down here." They were turning toward the wasteland that bordered Deer Creek, and the suspension bridge built a few years ago that spanned the canyon with a fifty-foot drop over tumbling water and rocks. Hallidie's Bridge.

After the darkened streets they were now bathed in light as they reached the bridge approach and the gas lamp that hung from the bridge arch. But even in the sudden luminosity, and the warm fragrance of the late-blooming broom below, Sebastian shivered. Were they planning to drop him off the bridge? Just a few years back two men and fifteen oxen had died when a cable snapped and they plunged to the canyon floor. He didn't fancy his chances if they forced him to jump.

Pete whistled into the dark and Quincey emerged, scrabbling up from the bank on which the bridge deck was poised with a rattling of pebbles and soil.

"Got a coyote hole or some old diggings back in there somewhere, have you?" Sebastian was playing his devil-may-care old soldier role as if his life depended on it — which he suspected it did.

"None of your business." Quincey scowled. "After that little show tonight you owe me."

"I don't know what you mean."

Quincey barked a bitter laugh. "You've ruined me for Caroline and California. You know that. Obviously that was your design and purpose. So you owe me a fresh start."

"Oh? And how exactly do you think I can effect that for you?"

Quincey's face crumpled into a familiar sneer. Contempt for others. It was one of his most recognizable inclinations. Quincey was always the only one who counted his world.

"By bringing me money, of course. I need money to get away. Begin again. A couple of thousand should do it. And don't say you haven't got it. That brother of yours is one of the richest men in the state. If you want to ever see your piece of skirt again you'll have to persuade your beloved brother to cough up the cash. By dawn."

# Fifty-Seven

Obedient to Quincey's ultimatum, Sebastian was back on the boardwalk to Hallidie's Bridge — and he was early. Sunrise was an hour or more away as he dropped the leather satchel containing John's ransom money for Isabella under his right foot and hollered for Quincey. Two hundred, hundred dollar greenbacks, issued by Lincoln's government during the war, now worth less than half their face value in gold. His brother had bought them as a patriot, supporting the war effort, and as far as they were concerned the paper money's shoddy standing made it ideal for paying off Quincey.

When he appeared from under the bridge and began to approach, Sebastian held up his hand. "Hold up! You don't get your hands on this until I see Isabella is alive and well. Show me."

Quincey sneered. "Or you'll what? Pull my hair?"

Black Pete had tracked Sebastian's every step during his return to get the money, following Edmund's instructions to keep him in sight at all times, and although he'd skulked in the shadows in the well-lit town center, it would have been asking for trouble for Sebastian to arm himself.

"Let's put it this way, Edmund. If you don't get your ass in a saddle and hightail it out of here soon, a town posse led by Sheriff Kinghorn will be on your back before you know it. Even an incompetent has his limits, and that man's had quite a conversion experience in the last hour or so. Killing me isn't going to help any. Now, go get Isabella."

"How touching. Worried about your doxy, now are you?" Quincey's voice dripped contempt. "You always were a soft touch with the ladies. Just couldn't keep them, though, could you?"

"She's not my doxy, Edmund, and beyond the simple decency of making sure she's alive and unharmed, I couldn't care less. I have nothing invested. As I've said to you before, choose someone your own age. She'd just another young girl. Nothing else to it." Sebastian's voice had turned cold and hard. The last thing he wanted was for Quincey to think he had something he, Sebastian, wanted. Experience told him that was a deadly combination for the unlucky stooge who was its target.

"She's just a decent young woman who does not deserve to be mixed up in this. So where is she?"

"Hear that, Isabella? You're nothing to him. Just a silly chick-a-biddy." Quincey peered under the bridge and yelled, his mouth curved in a derisive smile which gave the statement the echo of some big private joke. "A silly chick-a-biddy, nothing more." He waved to Black Pete, who stood behind Sebastian blocking his retreat. "Go bring her up."

The sky behind the hills to the north west was turning bright pink, but the sun's rays were not yet touching the tops. In Deer Creek ravine, water levels were low after a hot dry summer; Seb could hear only the faintest burbling of water over small rapids. If any of them fell from here they would land on bare, sharp rock. As if to mirror his anxiety, a night bird suddenly screeched, a harsh keening scream as it wheeled up from a hole in a tree, a small black shape highlighted against the pink-tinged sky.

If Quincey didn't move soon, they'd be caught in the crossfire. He detected faint sounds behind him in the streets leading here: the chink of spurs on pavement, a muffled coughing. He didn't dare look at Quincey or turn back to view the street he had just come down, in case his movement or expression betrayed him.

He stamped his foot and looked around, as if anticipating Pete's return. "What's taking so long?" He pointed at the satchel, still jammed under his boot. "You're getting what you wanted. Now cough up your side of the bargain before it's too late!"

Quincey glanced behind him. "Pete!

What's going on? I said, bring the doxy out."

Pete scrabbled up the bank, panting and out of breath. "She ain't there, Cap'n! She gone." The whites of his eyes looked huge and his mouth hung open. "I looked everywhere. She gone."

"What do you mean, gone?" Quincey raised the revolver he carried and waved it dangerously in Black Pete's direction. "You're playing me!"

Pete cringed away, scuttling crab-like sideways, seeking shelter in the bridge struts, as Quincey peppered the ground around him with shots that sent metal chips and chunks of impacted soil flying.

Sebastian took his moment. With Quincey distracted he half-ran, half swan-dived for cover on the opposite side of the bridge uprights, scraping his ribs and elbow as he landed, clutching the satchel containing the money and curling into a protective ball until he came to rest in the spindly bushes struggling to re-establish themselves since the construction. He took a quick look over the bank into the ravine and made a calculation. Better to take the risk of falling to his death while finding somewhere to hide than staying here and being an easy target. He wriggled to the edge and looked over. The bank was close to vertical, but it wasn't sheer rock. Rather it was peppered with coyote holes dug by hopeful miners testing for ore; straggling second-growth pines and oaks were poking up from the dry clay.

A third of the way down a monolithic boulder stood erect, surrounded by several other large rocks, like a forgotten talisman of some long-gone ancient worship. Head for that as a natural sanctuary, and risk breaking a bone on those rocks to stop his fall to the bottom. Either that or slide over cautiously and keep grabbing for a hand-hold — either a tree or a hole he could wiggle into for cover as he fell.

Smarting from his hard landing, he was edging toward the precipice and calculating the distance to the rocks when he heard the rumble of wagon wheels above him. A wagon was being driven full tilt at the bridge, even though road rules stipulated that vehicles crossing the bridge should proceed across at no faster than a walk.

He whirled around to see who or what approached and caught a glimpse of a covered wagon. The side closest to him was half exposed, and rifle barrels pointed out. Sheriff Kinghorn's posse had arrived. It was followed by several men on horses. Before he'd even had time to think about the wisdom of showing himself and being mistaken for Quincey he was hit by the flying body of a man whose arms clamped tight around his chest. Their heads clashed and Quincey's sour breath hit him in the face.

"I die, we both die," he grunted as he pushed off the ledge with a powerful thrust, swallow-diving, holding Sebastian underneath as a buffer for his landing.

They hung in the air for what seemed like an eternity, and then crash-landed with a bone-crunching crack. Sharp pain shot from Seb's hips to his neck, and as he tried to roll clear of Quincey he found his legs would not move. From his waist down he was numb, paralyzed. He scrabbled with his arms for undergrowth to pull himself clear of Edmund's suffocating weight. "Can't move," he groaned. "Get off me. My legs . . . I can't move."

Quincey rolled free, grabbed at the rocky ledge around the keel-like column of stone and stepped into its cover. "Too bad for you. I'm fine," he sneered. He looked wildly about him. "Where's the money?" His face was alight with a crazy bravado.

*He's having the best time of his life,* Sebastian thought, glimpsing the man he truly was, a man who got his greatest joy from challenging and beating the odds and grabbing what he wanted, wherever and whenever his greedy will drove him.

"Where's the money?" Quincey howled again. Sebastian lay, an unresponsive log of flesh, and waited for death. He almost envied Quincey his exultation. He rolled his head from side to side, mouthing, "Don't know." His chest was on fire and he could barely breathe. "Don't know."

Quincey raised his revolver, leveling it at Seb's head. The first rays of the sun bounced off the heavy wire rope which tethered the bridge overhead. Then splinters of rock behind Quincey exploded around them, small pieces hitting Sebastian's face. In his dazed state it took him some seconds to realize the Sheriff and his men were firing down from their posse above, taking aim from the shelf he and Quincey had just vacated. He made one more attempt to move his legs and then fell back, the blackness taking over.

# Fifty-Eight

He woke to screaming pain. Pain in his shoulder blades, stiff and sore from lying on sharp rocks, hot, prickling shards shooting up his legs. He rolled away from the rock that was pushing into his back and drew up his knees as he moved. At least his legs weren't numb anymore, but they were heavy as lead.

He lay dumbfounded on his side — barely any more comfortable with his hip now resting on a sharp pointed rock — and grasped the significance of that one move, no more complicated than turning over in bed.

His throat was dry, very dry. His ribs still hurt like hell and he could feel dried blood on his shirt. The sun was up, the air was warm, and getting warmer. He could hear the ear-teasing whirr of cicadas in the bushes. And he could move his legs; he could feel again.

It was enough to lie there and digest these simple facts of life. He probably would walk again, ride again. He would live.

Quincey . . . Isabella . . . What had happened while he was comatose?

Gradually, excruciatingly slowly, he pulled himself up into a sitting position, and gazed around him. He could see no one, hear no one, but he was confident that if the Sheriff had taken Quincey into custody they would have already sent a rescue party down the cliff face to stretcher him off. That meant that somewhere — possibly very near — Quincey was still lurking, ready to fire.

Painfully he edged closer to the rock pile, the big column surrounded by smaller rocks which leaned into it. Wracked with pain at every move, he worked his way into a gap in the center of the natural circle. When he was wedged in there, he was surprised to see the space opened out into a sheltered area large enough to hide three or four men. Everything about it had the sense of a hideout, somewhere desperate men — or adventurous kids — could hole up. The aspect to the east, facing the bridge, had been chiseled away so someone hiding here could see who was coming and going on the bridge. And this low-down view looking up showed Sebastian something else he hadn't known.

The bridge-builders had constructed a raw gully which ran the length of the bridge underside — a boxed-in chute, nearly as wide as the bridge itself, under the top planks, for maintenance, perhaps, or to ensure that if a plank gave way there was extra bracing underneath to prevent someone falling through. It was narrow, and not easy for a grown man to access, but it was there. He turned slowly, taking in the dimensions and dim light of the restricted space. The only light came through the gap opened up by the chipped-away rock, which made it feel like a military outpost. Was this where Black Pete and others of his ilk hung out?

Unable to support his weight any longer, he rested his back against a rock and sank to the ground, his knees folded up against his chest, groaning as the load came off his feet. From this new position he could see the ground fall away into a dark cavern in the far corner

— ideal for a fox den, though he couldn't see or smell any animal scat. He inched along on his bottom to get a closer look and saw that the ground dropped into a completely separate smaller cavern. The only noise was the shuffle of pebbles on the cavern floor as he moved — until he heard an answering stirring ahead.

Human sounds, muffled, indistinct, garbled but definitely not vulpine, drifted up from the darkness. "Anyone there?" He shuffled closer, wishing he was armed, unsure what threat might lurk out of sight. Then through the gloom he saw a familiar shade of blue — the blue of Isabella's Squincey jacket. He fell onto his hands and knees and crawled forward. "Isabella! It's you!" He scrambled forward in a rush to see her, ensure she was unhurt, that she was breathing and not bleeding.

As soon as he got close he could see she was trussed up like a chicken — bound hand and foot, gagged and blindfolded. A knee was ripped out of her jodhpurs, which were no longer white but a grimy brown. But his heart lifted for the first time in hours when a quick check showed no sign of blood. "Isabella! It's me, Sebastian. Sit still and I'll do what I can."

She made little gasping noises that sounded like a mixture of crying and laughing, through the tightly bound gag. "Take it easy, girl. Take it easy. I'll get this thing off in no time and then you can breathe properly."

His fingers were thick and fumbling, but within a few minutes he'd loosened the gag and it fell away. She took deep breaths in and out, in and out, and rubbed her eyes with her hands, then gave a beatific smile. "Sebastian! Thank God you're alive. I was so scared."

"What happened? Black Pete told Edmund you'd gone."

"He lied for me. I told him I'd pay him if he did it. Told him Edmund was going to do the dirty on both of us. We were in the same boat. That he was planning on killing us both. I managed to convince him to put his own interests first." She gave a weak smile. "Black Pete knew Edmund wasn't planning to release me. He was going to either take me with him or kill me in front of you." She shook her head. "He hates you so much. I think he sees in you all the things he isn't. He just had to have what you had." She blushed. "Not that . . . I don't mean . . . Except he thought we were close, you and I." A wistful look fell over her. "I heard what you told him, that you didn't care about me too much. I mean, nothing beyond a normal human connection. I get it — but Edmund didn't."

He looked deep into her eyes and his tongue locked in his mouth. What to say? *Oh no, Isabella, I can't go on without you and by the way I've bought you this pathetic present which I've had for days now and been too embarrassed to give you?*

The moment passed. "Anyway." She gave an embarrassed laugh. "What's a girl got to do to get out of her bonds around here?" She shuffled sideways so her wrists, tied behind her back, were before Seb. "Do you think you could get these next?"

He quickly ripped open the knots at her wrists, and then her legs and ankles. "They sure intended for you not to go far," he said. "And I'm not at all sure how far away they are, or whether they're planning to come back. I passed out for a while and don't know what I've missed."

"There was a lot of shouting and firing a while back," she said, "but nothing recently. And nothing to indicate Edmund and Pete have been taken in. I'd say we've still got plenty to worry about." She wriggled her ankles and made an attempt to stand, placing her hand on Sebastian's shoulder for leverage, and groaning as she stretched her cramping muscles. "Oh, it's good to be standing again." She looked to him with concern. "Are you OK? Can you stand up?"

"Yes, just." He shook his head with a tired grimace. "But it's going to be a few days before I'll be moving normally. I got an awful big crack on the rocks out there. I'm lucky my legs still function."

He had just levered himself up to stand on two feet beside her when they heard a shout outside. "Come on out, Quincey! We know you're in there. You're just making it worse for yourself."

They scuttled back up to the main chamber and looked out through the rock cutout. Sheriff Kinghorn was standing on the edge of the bridge shouting into a loudhailer.

Sebastian shook his head. "That isn't going to work. I know Edmund. He relishes the fight. He won't give himself up. He'd rather die first. He sees it as a glorious gamble."

"Glorious for him, that is. Not for anyone else," said Isabella. "I picked up a bit listening to them when they'd forgotten I was here. Doxies don't count, you know."

Sebastian's interest sparked. "Anything useful?"

"They were talking about some tunnel. Said if things got hot they could use it to escape. But I've no idea where it would be. The canyon is very steep. I can't imagine a tunnel anywhere here."

"No, but there could be one up there." Sebastian pointed to the bridge above their heads. "See that boxing that runs in a second layer under the planks? What's to stop them worming their way along that, under the bridge boards, and escaping at the other end when it's dark or no one's about?"

She gazed out at it. "You're right. And from the top you don't even realize it's there."

Sebastian considered it steadily. "When you look at it closely, you see how on either side, where the raised footpath has been built for pedestrians, the gap is even greater. A man could easily hide inside that boxing. I suspect Black Pete has often slipped in there when he needed to."

"Who else is up there?" Isabella asked. "Do you know?"

"Sheriff Kinghorn, obviously. His young deputy, Bob Patterson, my brother John and a few of the other men who were there at the dinner. When I went back to collect your ransom money I managed to whisper to John where we were while Pete was out of earshot. I knew they'd come. But I asked them to give us time to get out so we weren't caught in the crossfire. That part didn't quite work the way I planned."

"That part wasn't ever going to work. He wasn't planning to let us go." She screwed up her face in a rueful frown.

"What if Edmund is hiding inside that bridge? How long do you think Kinghorn would wait him out?"

"No idea. He's not the brightest star in the firmament."

"What if I got out and went and told them what we're thinking?"

"Isabella, it's too dangerous. I don't want you exposed like that. Kinghorn will handle it."

They retreated back to the underground corner as the sun rose high overhead and blazed directly in on their canyon shelter. They settled down to wait. They were both thirsty but there was no water to be had, so they tried to sit quietly, dozing off in the somnolent hot morning. Isabella searched out knucklebone-sized pebbles and amused herself playing Jacks, tossing the stones in the air to land on the back of her hand. She tried to encourage him to join in, but he put her off with a grunt.

He didn't want to tell her that as the heat rose, he could feel his strength ebbing away. His abdomen was growing increasingly painful, and by mid-afternoon he could barely breathe without checking himself under the jabbing onslaught. Then, as afternoon floated into early evening, he noticed a deep-purple mottled bruising ringing his torso, swelling even as he watched. He'd seen enough internal bleeding on the battlefield to recognize what was happening to him.

The impact of the fall onto rocks with Quincey's weight on top had done something to him that would not be easily repaired. As the sun fell lower in the sky and the heat eased, his sweating increased. When he was overcome with a wave of dizziness followed by a momentary blackout, he faced up to the unwelcome truth: he would need to prepare Isabella for the worst.

But he'd left it so late that he could barely speak coherently. In short gasps between the pulsing spasms he tried to explain. He lifted his shirt and showed her the bruising. "Bleeding," he said. "Internal bleeding. Not good." He gave a weak smile. "Beautiful Isabella, I am not well, and I so wanted to ensure you would be safe."

"Don't talk." She patted his hand, her face like chalk. "Just rest."

Another wave of dizziness swept through him, and when he opened his eyes next she was watching him with concerned eyes. She leaned forward and whispered, "I'm just going to the entrance for a little fresh air. Only for a few minutes. Back soon."

Before she'd taken a step dizziness once again engulfed him.

# Fifty-Nine

Isabella edged into the blinding brightness of the afternoon sun. After hours half-underground her eyes watered with the intensity of the light, and she stood for a few moments adjusting to her new surroundings. The bridge was quiet. On any normal Sunday there would be regular traffic with townspeople going to town for supplies or entertainment on their day off, some even making their way to church. The thoroughfare was deserted, which confirmed for her that Quincey was still at large and the Sheriff had the route closed for the town's safety.

She edged gingerly forward, keeping

her back plastered to the vertical of the lodestone rock, and craned her neck to see up the cliff face Sebastian had fallen down. If she'd been hoping to see the Sheriff or Sir John Russell perched up there, looking to take potshots at their quarry, she would have been disappointed. The bridge approach was as empty of people as the bridge itself. So where, she asked herself, would the lawman's party have taken shelter?

She surveyed the canyon side and pondered. If Sebastian's speculation that Quincey was hidden under the bridge carriageway was correct, then perhaps the safest place to be would be directly underneath the bridge. It would also be the hardest angle for Quincey to get off any shots, unless she was unlucky enough to strike a section where there were big gaps in the boards. But it didn't seem likely that Kinghorn or any of his men were there, or she and Sebastian would have caught a glimpse of them during their long hours of watching.

A low moaning from inside the cavern jolted her to full awareness. She felt her insides quivering. She had to do something or Sebastian was going to die. She knew it. She'd glimpsed the dark mottling of extreme bruising like a band around his waist when he contorted in agony at one point. She knew he couldn't go on for much longer without water and medical attention, and she was the only one capable of bringing it.

With a sense of mounting urgency, she gazed around the steep bank that faced her. And then she saw a possibility. Something at the very farthest reaches of rationality, she recognized that. But if it was her only hope — well, it had to be, didn't it?

She turned her collar up, mussed her hair over her face to stop the sun picking up the planes of her cheeks and, hunching over, moved slowly along a horizontal ledge that ran away from the bridge.

The ground underfoot was dangerously unstable, slipping away into the canyon below in a dozen places, but it was overgrown with brush and seedling pines which held the rest firm. Slowly and carefully she picked her way under the spindly green cover, making her way to a much bigger pine further down, one that had not been affected by the bridge-building. If she could reach that tree, and then climb up it, she'd have a small hope of scrambling off one of its higher branches near the top of the gully, and hopefully too far away for

Edmund to notice if he was keeping any sort of watch.

Once she got to the top she could alert help, any help, and get a doctor in for Sebastian. She was so dry that her tongue was sticking to the roof of her mouth. Black spots danced before her eyes, and she was on the edge of dizziness. How she was going to manage climbing a tree in that state she had no idea, but she pushed on.

Doggedly she walked and crawled along the green tunnel to the base of the big pine. By the time she made it she was ready to collapse in a weeping mess, but she had to go on. She took off her shoes to grip the tough bark better and hauled herself up the trunk to the first branches. Her hands were already sticky with the resin which flowed freely in the heat. Gradually she worked her way up the trunk, pulling her body from branch to branch, gripping the trunk like a monkey when the stretch was too high. By the time she reached high enough to have a good view out, her palms and soles were scratched and stinging, but the discomfort was swept away in the exhilaration that washed over her.

One or two more branches, and she'd be high enough to be parallel with the bank at the top. Then would come the most treacherous part of the whole venture, moving out horizontally along the branch far enough to reach the ground without dipping too low or falling before she got there. She squeezed her eyes tight shut for a few seconds, steeling herself for the moment when she would start moving out from the safety of the solid trunk.

From here she had an excellent view

over the bridge and the surrounding area. The two towers that girded the suspension bridge at each end rose only a slight distance above her at this height, and on the other side of the gorge she could see a row of boatsheds jutting out at the water level. A few upturned dinghies rested on the shore. On this side she could see the Baptist church which stood hard up against the bridge approach. The parishioners would have missed not being able to sing their hymns there today, she guessed, and a small part of her hoped they'd said an extra prayer or two instead for the people caught up in this disaster like Sebastian and her.

She gazed down the bridge, watching for any sign of movement or activity that might give away the position of either Quincey or Black Pete, but everything seemed as sleepy as only a hot Sunday afternoon could be. She took a deep breath, said a little prayer for herself and another for Sebastian — "Please, God, don't let him die" — and set off on the outstretched bough, riding the branch like a black-bear cub.

The one thing she hadn't thought of, she realized to her dismay, was that her extra weight would make the branch dip and sway when there was not a breath of wind to explain the movement. Anyone looking out would very quickly ask themselves why that tree was moving on a still afternoon. She took it as slowly as she could, but there was little she could do to exercise control: the further she ventured out, the more the branch dipped and swayed. If she was going to be this obvious about it, she may as well dispense with trying to do it covertly and just go as fast as she could to get clear. She began scrambling along the branch, dispensing with any idea of staying under cover.

She was about six feet short of the clifftop, with a dizzying precipitous plunge below her, when she heard the crack of a rifle. The wood above her head splintered, and part of a branch fell directly on top of her. The swing of the branch became even more exaggerated. Crack! A second bullet. This one missed her hand by inches, exploding at the tip of the branch she was riding, reducing the length she had to move along by just enough to make it impossible for her to disembark on the clifftop.

She howled with shock and frustration. The third bullet plunged into the timber on her left, and she knew the fourth would more than likely split her brain. She let go of her grip and slid downwards, bracing herself to grab at the next branch down.

She hit it with a thump that momentarily knocked the breath out of her. Around her the air was laden with the clean smell of pine resin, and she could hear bees buzzing, oblivious to her panic, as they collected the pine sap they made into hive-healing propolis. She hung on, tears streaming down her cheeks, unable to even lift her head. In this position she was sheltered from further gunshots. A cliff jutted out at that point, and the branch was low enough that a line of sight from the bridge was obscured. The angle and direction of the shots meant that was the only place they could have been fired from. But the branch she was now lying along was not high enough or long enough to give her access to the top of the cliff. After all her effort, she had failed. And still no one realized that Sebastian needed urgent help.

The sound of gunshots jolted Sebastian out of his feverish torpor. He jerked up off the hard floor and was instantly hit with piercing pain around his ribs and abdomen. He gasped to breathe but hauled himself to his knees, calling in a raspy whisper, "Isabella! Izzy, where are you?"

An empty silence. He crawled for the cavern entrance on his hands and knees as more shots came from the direction of the bridge. From what he could tell they were being fired not to the bridge approach but further to the north, past the cavern and back towards town. He hauled himself up at the entry and winced, blinded by the bright sunshine.

He stared around him as his eyes adjusted, looking for any signs of life — Isabella sprawled shot, the Sheriff up above, even Quincey or Pete showing themselves on the bridge. Someone had broken cover enough to fire a weapon.

And then he glimpsed it, the splinter of light bouncing off a rifle barrel poking through a crack in the boards under the bridge. Someone, almost certainly Quincey, must be lying on their stomach in the narrow crawl space, lining up quarry like a sniper. As he stood slumped against the keel-like main rock for support, he heard another cracking report, and then the sound of wood splintering to his left. As he turned towards the noise he saw a figure falling through the pine canopy, clawing to arrest the fall. Fair hair. White jodhpurs and a blue jacket.

He screamed her name, but all that came out was a hoarse wheeze. His peripheral vision caught movement above him, at the top of the cliff. The shots had brought someone else out of cover. One man ran for protection behind the bridge-tower foundations, another darted along the cliff top towards the tree that was attracting the rifle fire.

Seb ripped his shirt off and stepped away from the cavern, out into full view of both the sniper and the men above. He waved the shirt like a flag of surrender, pointing to the bridge and crying out with his last ounce of strength "There! He's over there! See him?" See—" His legs buckled under him, but as the ground came rushing up to him he got a glimpse of a man stopping, turning, following the line of his pointed arm, and changing direction.

He pitched forward and knew nothing more.

Isabella clung to a pine spur, rocking wildly up and down, her weight threatening to peel the light branch away from its junction with the central trunk. The wild motion made it harder for the sniper to land a direct shot, but it wouldn't take much for him to cut through the limb if he hit it full on, especially if it stopped pitching like a boat in a storm.

Her heart banged in her ears so loudly she barely heard the cry "He's over there!" that floated up from somewhere far below. She was facing away from the cavern, and it was impossible to turn around on the fragile bough, but she could guess what was happening. Somehow Sebastian had rallied and seen she'd gone.

The swaying gradually eased and she began inching backwards, flat on her stomach, drawing ever closer to the staunch strength of the trunk. When she finally felt her toes tip the broad upright she gingerly pushed up from her prone position and eased her green-stained, resin-sticky buttocks back against the main bole.

She slumped there for a moment or two, the exhilaration that flooded her turning to tears as she gazed back and down. Sebastian's shirtless body lay spread-eagled in full sight outside the cavern, the ugly purple band around his middle showing more starkly against his pale flesh than before. It was plain that he'd collapsed unconscious again, and was in open firing line from the bridge. She began scrambling back down the tree she'd climbed so perilously fifteen minutes before, wondering with every step down whether he'd be alive when she reached him.

She'd just planted her feet at the needle-strewn base when another volley of shots rang out on the bridge, and she threw herself down panting, expecting every moment to feel the searing hot pain of a bullet in her body.

As she lay there she heard the tramp of running feet, then a stern voice shouting, "Edmund Quincey! Come out with your hands up or we'll shoot." It was Sheriff Kinghorn. She struggled up from her face-plant in the pine needles, scrambled to her feet and watched transfixed. Through the gaps in the bridge's side railing she could make out the silhouettes of at least three men advancing up the bridge, guns drawn and facing down into the planked surface. Clearly they'd worked out where Quincey was holed up, and were advancing on his final hiding place. She thought she made out Sir John Russell's powerful form and wanted to cover her eyes, so fearful was she that Quincey might fire up through the boards in a final vengeful flurry of death.

She hardly dared to breathe as the men on the bridge slowly advanced. Kinghorn called again. "Quincey, this is your final warning. Lay down your weapon and come out with your hands up." The lawman's group were halfway along the road deck; judging from the angle of fire, she thought Quincey could not have been much further along than this when he fired on her. Her heart was in her mouth. Any second now the Sheriff was going to shoot at Quincey, and unless he killed him with a first dead-on lucky shot, Quincey would return fire.

The hair stood up on the back of her neck. From the corner of her eye she caught movement at the very start of the bridge. A man had appeared from between the tower footings and was scrambling up the bank to the road. She wheeled around to follow his progress, thinking he must be one of the Sheriff's party. He took driving propulsive strides, covering the distance from the shelf under the bridge to the road surface in seconds. She could make out the barrel of a rifle, tucked against his far side.

When he reached the top, he pivoted to marksman's position, down on one knee, sighting along the barrel, and she realized with a roaring nausea that it was Edmund Quincey, and he was lining up on Sebastian, still spread-eagled at the cavern entry.

He was determined to destroy Sebastian — his nemesis, the architect of his public shaming, the antagonist who had once and for all destroyed any chance he might have had of getting his hands on Caroline Studebaker's fortune.

Isabella rushed forward, screaming and waving her arms in great arcs of distress, and saw Quincey hesitate, then swing the barrel towards her. She flung herself back into the pine leaf mold, burying her face in the musty dry odor, waiting for the end.

She waited for what seemed an eternity, but was probably less than a minute. She heard men's cries from the bridge — was it Sir John Russell's rich baritone and Kinghorn's slightly nasal answer? — and then another volley of shots shattered the mid-afternoon quiet. She stayed, her face pressed into the yeasty-smelling humus, too terrified to raise her head and regard Sebastian's bleeding body.

She heard her name: "Isabella! It's over. You're safe to come out." It was Sir John.

Edmund Quincey's body was lodged on rocks not far from where Sebastian lay, but it was clear from the bullet holes in his back that he would not be getting up and walking away. He was bleeding onto paper notes that fluttered around him — she guessed some of the greenbacks Sebastian had brought for her ransom that he'd been carrying when Quincey charged him off the cliff top.

She looked towards Sebastian. He wasn't moving. Even with the lingering warmth of late summer trapped within the canyon walls, he would get chilled lying on rocks shirtless. She shuffled back along the slippery ledge and knelt beside him, taking his wrist in her hands to feel his pulse. It was there, but slow and weak.

As she raised herself to her feet again she saw his brother already getting underway with a rescue effort. Two sturdy ropes had been hitched to the bridge railing and John and another man she recognized as Dr Tom Styles, the local medicine man, were already descending to meet them. They'd barely reached level ground when the ropes were hauled up again and a stretcher and blankets sent down after them.

She dropped to a rock still warm from the afternoon sun and watched dazed as the doctor checked Sebastian's vital signs and then gave the signal for John to gently load him onto the stretcher for the lift to the clifftop.

"He's fragile. Unmistakable signs of heavy-fall trauma and internal bleeding. The next twelve hours will be the decider." The doctor's quiet words floated in the air above her head like annoying flies she could not engage with or swat away.

*The next twelve hours . . .*

She was gazing away into nothingness. Now all the urgency was over, her feet were leaden. All her energy had drained out of her, and she was too exhausted to move. She squeezed her eyes tight to stop a sudden rush of tears, and felt a light nudge at her elbow. Sir John was standing beside her, a look of such kindness and concern on her face that she had to hold tight to not lose her control and break down.

"Isabella, I want you to come with us. You need to be checked out and given sustenance as well. You've been through a heck of an ordeal. I should be scolding you for being so reckless with your own safety, alerting us like you did, drawing the fire away from Sebastian. But truth is, if you hadn't made that crazy move he probably would already be dead. You gave him a second life, and if he pulls through it will all be thanks to you."

He seemed to sense she was so choked up she could not speak. He put his arm around her shoulders and turned her toward the dangling ropes. "Come on, Miss Rescuer. One last hurdle and you can let go. Sleep, eat, talk, do whatever you need to get it all out of your system."

She shook her head. "No, take Sebastian up first. He's urgent."

"He's in good hands now, don't worry. We need to make sure you're all right."

He shepherded her to the base where they looped the rope around her so she was semi-upright — it was just like sitting on a swing.

She was hauled up and back in Pine Street, wrapped in Lady Russell's consoling arms, before she knew it.

"Come on, girl, we're getting you back to the hotel for a hot bath and a good sleep." Pania ruffled Isabella's hair affectionately. "You look done in. No surprise there. But Dr Styles is in charge now, so you can rest."

She buried her head against Pania's comforting shoulder and allowed herself to let go. With Sebastian already on his way to Dr Tom's surgery — the closest thing the town had to a hospital — she was strangely bereft. Somehow these last few hours of drama had drawn them together in a way they'd never known before.

Then Sebastian's words to Quincey flooded back. *Beyond the simple decency of making sure she's alive and unharmed, I couldn't care less. I have nothing invested. She's just a decent young woman who does not deserve to be mixed up in this.*

She recalled the tough, penetrating edge his normally reasonable voice took as he spoke. He'd been more than convincing.

So what, she thought, that he'd stepped up to save her life, to distract Quincey and alert the rescuers when the outlaw had opened fire? That's what responsible, decent Sebastian Russell did. He would have done it for anyone. It didn't mean anything more than that.

# Sixty

"Amazing what twenty-four hours of good care can do."

Sebastian grinned from his central position on the Gold House sofa, wrapped in rugs, his red-gold hair and freckled face glowing in the late-afternoon sun slanting in. He had on one of Sir John's Chinese smoking jackets, a padded luxury in dark-green satin with sleeves that widened at the wrist and bestowed a benign authority on its wearer. But as Isabella paused in the doorway and looked across the room, her searching gaze easily spotted the paleness under the freckles, and the tight, tired lines around his eyes. *Typical*

*Sebastian, cracking hardy*. She wondered how he was really feeling.

"So good to see you looking so well!" she responded, though the hollow feeling inside didn't match her upbeat words. After all, what was this little get together but a kind of family war dance, a session of mutual reassurance that everything was just fine? Or was going to be, soon.

She perched in a chair a good distance away from the man of the moment. Pania and John and Huldah made up the party, and she felt a sudden pang of loss at the gaps. No Rosie, as her best friend was off on tour. No Alycia and Basil, and no Graysie and Nathan either. Funny that a year ago she didn't even know these people who had come to mean the world to her: Alycia, her grand-mère; Graysie, her precious half-sister. If only they could be here now. She had never felt so incomplete, so in need of the intimacy of close blood ties. She flashed a quick smile around the room and lapsed back into silence. She really just wanted to stay on the outer of this little circle; the way things were between her and Sebastian left her no other option. So she was startled when John leaned forward in his chair and looked directly at her, commanding her attention.

"Isabella, we have a confession to make." He glanced across to his brother. "Sebastian and I, that is. We've brought you here under slightly false pretenses." His pleasant baritone played on the work 'slightly' and Sebastian flashed him a grin.

Her stomach tensed. She hated surprises.

"We have a visitor due in half an hour or so, someone you have waited a long time to meet. Before he arrives, however, we have something to show you."

Her heart leapt.

*Someone you have waited a long time to meet. Was it ... could it be ... Surely it could only be Alejandro!*

She was locked so tightly inside she could barely breathe.

John reached down to his side and opened a leather case she hadn't noticed until now. From it he drew several fragile-looking glass plates — old photographs, she could see when she looked closer.

He stepped across and placed one on her knees. "Hold onto this carefully, and take a close look."

Barely able to contain her excitement, she bent her head to look at the image before her. A heartbreakingly lovely woman, her crown of curls lit from behind like a halo framing her face. A little girl of about four sitting cross-legged on the floor in front of the low sofa. And nestled in beside the woman, two younger children, a girl and a boy, one either side.

Her throat closed up, and when she tried to speak she could only cough. She cleared her throat and gasped out the question that at that moment was the most important she had ever asked or wanted answered: "Is this Elanora?"

*The mother I never knew, killed when I was just a little kid. And if this is Elanora, the children in the daguerreotype must be …*

She stared from John to Pania and finally to Sebastian, who said, "It is indeed Elanora. John and Pania have confirmed it. They both knew her well, as you know.

There's no doubt about it." His face was lit up with a joy she'd not seen in him before. "So we're pretty sure those children are you and your brother, and Graysie. It just makes sense, a photograph taken by a proud father. I think you can feel that in the way he's posed you."

Her hand went to her mouth. "I … I can hardly believe it. After all this time I get to see what she looked like."

"You do. And to top it all off, in another few minutes you'll be able to meet your brother. He's expected any minute."

She brought her hand to her head and massaged her temples. "I feel as if I'm going to faint." She hung her head down low and waited for the wave of light-headed ecstasy to pass over. "Oh, dear. I promise I won't pass out on you — but it's unbelievable!"

There was a light tap on the drawing-room door and Mrs Snively peered in, a tall young man hanging back in the hall behind her. "Your visitor, Sir John."

Isabella rose from her seat and turned to greet him, the brother she hadn't seen in seventeen years. He was tall and lean and dark, with high cheekbones and finely defined lips and eyebrows. He carried himself with a confident poise and returned her astonished gaze with one of sparkling serenity.

*I knew we'd meet, it was just a matter of when.*

He had the demeanor of privilege, but not entitlement. His gait as he stepped forward was courteous, self-aware, and she felt a rush of gratitude to the Senator. He hadn't become a farm-boy slave, starved and ill-treated. Whatever his sins, Senator de Vile had raised a fine son.

He walked towards her, his arms out stretched. "You must be Isabella." He gave a jubilant laugh and lightly embraced her before pulling back and holding her at arm's length, gazing delightedly into her face. "I am Alex. So good to finally meet."

He grinned and stepped away from her and crossed the room to greet the others, and suddenly the room reverberated with laughter and chattering. And love. Family love. She looked at Huldah, captivated by the handsome, endearing young man who stood before her. She glanced at Sebastian, enthroned in his invalid's blankets, his face pensive, watching her with an inquiring gaze, and for one moment her heart stabbed. Then he beamed, a broad, blissful smile, that lit up his whole face.

"You deserve this, Isabella." He spoke quietly, resolutely, as if they were the only two people in the room. "You've been faithful to the end. And I haven't yet had a chance to thank you for saving my life." He glanced away, as if embarrassed about how to continue.

"Nothing I've done can equal what you've done for me," she said fiercely, but with a smile. "Bringing my brother home." She reached out to gently grasp Alejandro's wrist. "Come and sit over here with me. We've got an awful lot of talking to do."

# Sixty-One

"Let's put it this way, Hector, man to man." John Russell took a sip of brandy and regarded the Senator coolly. "We have every reason to implicate you in the attack on Mrs Stockton." He raised his hand for silence as de Vile began to protest. "Come on, Hector. It's me and Sebastian you're talking to. We didn't come down in the last shower."

The three men sat in John's study, following a remarkably cordial evening where the Senator had been introduced to Isabella and acquainted with the feared daguerreotype. He'd had no option but to gracefully accept the family reunion as a fait accompli, and Huldah and he shared some private reminiscences about the woman who'd let them both down as sister and de facto wife.

He'd given them a brief account of his time with Bertha and confirmed it had suited his self-interest to introduce her to his father as his wife. But he'd been so credibly insistent about the joy the son who came to him as Alejandro had brought him they felt inclined to overlook the deception. They would have a lot of time to talk in coming days.

Now, though, the Russell men were intent on settling one final obligation, to Basil and Alycia. "Sebastian's spoken to both Burton Purdy and Hiram Williams. We *know* your hands are dirty, whoever pulled the trigger."

Sebastian took up the story. "We're not about to run off to your son and blacken your name by telling him of your nefarious activities — putting Hiram onto spying on him, engineering the attack on Charles Durant, the photographer who died." Hector paled at the mention of the name. "But I'm sure you understand how upset Alex would be to discover how little you trusted him."

There was a long silence as de Vile pulled on the cigar he'd lit as John was talking. Then: "So what's the quid pro quo?"

"Glad you're seeing sense," John said. "We thought perhaps you'd like to sponsor a charitable foundation for young boys with no families — fund their training in useful trades or professions to give them a start in life. The sort of thing your Alex might have needed if he hadn't been lucky enough to land in a home like yours."

De Vile halted on his cigar mid-draw and stared.

"To be known as the Alycia Stockton Educational Trust, or something similar. I'm sure in years to come Alex will be happy to continue on the legacy." John raked de Vile with a penetrating stare. "Seems like a fitting end to a very nasty chapter."

De Vile had the grace to look embarrassed. "Sounds like a very good idea. And thank you. For keeping it from Alex."

"We can't promise he won't find out some of this dirty laundry on his own in days to come. Isabella knows some of it — but we can undertake that it won't come from us."

The three men exchanged handshakes and sipped the last dregs of their brandy.

# Sixty-Two

"It's all my fault." Alex de Vile grinned up at Sebastian and flipped aside the lock of dark hair that had fallen over his face as he dismounted. His face was bright and flushed from the exertion of riding full-tilt up the winding forest road to Gold House. He held the reins of his shiny-coated black gelding in one hand, and the other was draped around the shoulder of his fair-haired twin sister.

He looked up to the veranda where Sebastian sat in an outdoor armchair, a blanket draped around his shoulders. "I asked Isabella how your convalescence was progressing and she said she had no idea, she hadn't seen you." He made a light stab at the lawn with the toe of his riding boot, lifting a wedge of turf, and drew Isabella a little closer to his side.

"Well, I thought that just wasn't good enough."

Sebastian relaxed his back into the bamboo basket where he'd spent many hours of the past week, resting on doctor's orders. He'd watched the purple-and-blue morning and evening shadows as they advanced and retreated over the distant mountains. He'd savored the mid-afternoon scents of roses and wallflowers that arose from the sun-warmed garden. And he'd ruminated. Plenty of time for that: returning again to the war and the unseen damage it had done to him, to Edmund and Alycia, and most of all, he'd spent hours reflecting on the charms of the spell-binding young woman who stood on the grass in front of him.

As Alex's twin, Isabella certainly presented a study in contrasts. He was tall, lean and all angles — a Renaissance Adonis with sculpted muscles on a spare frame, sharply defined cheekbones and narrow white teeth. Isabella's caramel complexion, broader cheek structure, rounded womanly curves and wide, mobile mouth announced her Spanish heritage as if with a rattle of castanets.

Her eyes, though, those sparkling blue pools that usually flashed with her unquenchable spirit — this morning they were muted, even a little wary, as she stood in Alex's protective shadow, an observer rather than a participant. Alex darted her a quick look but didn't seem to register her solemn demeanor. Either that, or he chose to ignore it. He gave a self-conscious laugh. "It's nearly a week since you brought Isabella and me together. We owe you so much, and we haven't had a chance to say thank you."

He gestured to his black mount and Isabella's chestnut, who were both contentedly cropping the lawn under their loosely held reins. "Could we tie these up for a few minutes and make a brief visit? We really would like to tell you how grateful we are. Apart from anything else you saved Isabella's life."

Sebastian snorted. "More like she saved mine — but yes, of course." He got up from his chair and pointed to the stables, beyond the orchard. "Drop them over there to Nelson and I'll call Mrs S and get some coffee brewing."

He smiled at Isabella, whose tense shoulders relaxed. "It's really good to see you, Isabella. Keeping Dr Tom happy is getting to be pretty boring. Pull up some chairs and I'll go tell the kitchen."

When he came back they were both settled in chairs beside his, and it was easy to chat on about the events of a week ago while they waited on coffee. "Because of all that carry-on with Edmund I never did get a chance to tell you what a fabulous show you put on at Hector's testimonial dinner," Sebastian enthused. "People certainly got their money's worth."

Isabella laughed. "Reverend Washington was just fabulous — he's a natural performer. I confess I had a lot of fun. Maybe I'll get to write shows sometime." Her voice faltered and a wistful expression came to her face. "Huldah and I are working out what's next. She's still keen to go back to Europe and see her family before the older generation disappears, but I don't want to be separated from Alex, having only just had the chance to get to know him." She smiled at Sebastian, and again he sensed a pensive underlying melancholy. "We've hardly been apart this last week, and it already feels like I've known him for ages. I don't want to go away now." Her voice gathered energy as she spoke, and by the end of the sentence she was almost back to her normal buoyant self. Almost.

"Isabella," said Seb, "remember that day we went riding in Sacramento, the day you were going crazy with cabin fever and then we met the gypsies? I'm getting strong enough to get out of this chair. I'm sure I am. I'd love to do a ride with you sometime, even if it's just a small one."

Her eyes widened. She wasn't expecting anything like the suggestion, he could see. She stammered as she responded. "That, that would be lovely. You, you know how I love to get out in the open air."

The coffee arrived and they moved on to other topics: how well Senator de Vile was getting on with Caroline Studebaker (was he even subtly courting her, Alex wondered), and Quincey's modest funeral, arranged and paid for by Sir John (Sebastian had been too ill to go, thankfully).

Then came the natural moment when the coffee was all drunk and the visitors would expect to depart. Sebastian watched from under hooded eyes, willing them to stay longer, to not leave him, but Alex made the move. "I've stayed long enough, and there is stuff I should be doing, so I'll say my goodbyes. It's been marvelous to see you."

They wandered across the lawn to the

stable. Sebastian turned to Isabella. "Why not stay a little longer and take a walk around the garden? I'm not quite up to riding yet, but I'd enjoy a walk."

Isabella's eyes danced. "Why not? I'll be fine to get back home without Alex. Maybe we could just do a round in the orchard and back? It's a glorious day."

They sauntered side by side among trees heavy with fruit, not feeling any pressure to speak, the sun warm on their backs, occasional bluebottles buzzing at their heads, the aroma of ripening apples mingling with familiar equine smells of sweat and dung from the stables. Better yet, when they got back to the house, Isabella agreed to stay for a second mid-morning coffee. When Sebastian returned to the veranda after a quick clean-up, he had retrieved the package he'd bought at Armin's Emporium, the emerald-green dress length and turquoise-and-gold earrings. An impulse purchase he'd never had the courage to present to their intended recipient, although there'd been many a night when, close to sleep, he would picture her wearing them, imagine how beautiful she would look in them.

Isabella's footstep was light and gay on the bare boards. "I've had such a lovely morning. Thank you."

He looked at her, suddenly serious. "Thank me for what? It's me that should be thanking you."

Her peal of laughter was spontaneous and musical. "We're not going to play the 'I owe you more than you owe me game', are we?" She looked at him teasingly. "Sebastian, relax. Occasionally let someone do something for you, instead of always being the one who's giving to others." She looked at him with shining eyes. "Attractive as that generosity to others may be."

For a long moment neither of them spoke. The electricity between them fizzed. Sebastian's skin tingled and his throat locked. He could not have said a word, even if he could think of something to say. He took a big calming breath and magically his blood started flowing again. "Edmund Quincey was right about one thing. I've got a hopeless record when it comes to women. Never seem to know when to press forward and when to retreat." He made a rueful grimace. "And I'm not even sure that military vocabulary is appropriate to the topic."

Her laughter bubbled forth again. "Understandable for a man who spent important years of his youth fighting for his country." Her gaze leveled and her expression darkened. "Don't let anything Edmund said stick. He was a liar from go to woe. Mainly woe. But let's not talk about him."

Seb lifted up the emporium parcel and set it before her. "This is for you. A little something I picked up when I was in Sacramento seeing Caroline Studebaker." He hesitated and looked into her mesmerizing eyes. "I just thought of you."

She glanced down at the package, blinking rapidly, and her hand went to her mouth. "Sebastian, you can't. You shouldn't." She gazed at him, still not taking the gift. "Why would you do this?" She faltered. "Aren't I just a silly chick-a-biddy?" A tear leaked out of the corner of her eye and trickled down her cheek. She dashed it away angrily with the back of her hand. "Sorry. I'm acting like a stupid girl, aren't I?" She gave him a bleak stare, and he could see she was fighting to stay bold.

He reached out and took her face in his hands, gently caressing her. "Oh, Isabella. If you only knew … I had to talk tough to him. If he'd had any idea of my true feelings for you — well, you wouldn't be sitting here." He bent down and gently began kissing her along her forehead, right on her hairline. "I didn't mean a word of it. Not by a long shot. But I had to convince him. I knew if I didn't it would be terrible for you."

She fell onto his shoulder and quietly sobbed. They stayed like that for a long time, until her sobbing quieted and then ceased, and she raised her head with a watery smile. "So I'm not just 'a decent young girl who doesn't deserve to be mixed up in this'?" The playful teasing light had returned to her eyes.

He leaned forward and kissed her gently on the lips. "Keep flirting like that, young lady, and you won't be decent for much longer." He put his index finger under her chin and raised her head so they could gaze at one another, eye to eye. "Now open the gift, why don't you? It's been waiting for you too long."


THE END

# THANK YOU SO MUCH - And What's Next?

**BOOK FOUR, TANGLED DESTINY is in the works . . . planned as a Christmas novella, coming November/December 2018. A FREE Download will be available at www.jennywheeler.biz so look for it there!**

**New York Christmas, 1847.** Elanora's life-long dream is realized when Eustace, her first and only love, asks her to marry him on her 21st birthday.

But her fantasies of a perfect life are shattered forever by a merchant father's squalid secret and grasping ambition. Forced to remain silent, Elanora is thrust into a tragic love triangle that will echo down the generations.

Building a relationship with my readers in one of the nicest things about writing. Of Gold & Blood is planned as a multi book series and in future volumes we'll trace the fortunes of characters we've already met like Alejandro and Rosie, and some new ones you haven't met yet – Nathan's half-sisters, and some of Pania's family, including her brother, Nikora. Not to mention some forgotten cousins from Elanora's side.

If you would like to keep in touch with the adventures of Gold Country and its people check out www.jennywheeler.biz

for news of the latest books, free giveaways, and 'old time' recipes just like the Russell men and their wives enjoy.

I'll promise I will never sell, rent, or misuse your information and of course you can unsubscribe at any time.

# Enjoy this book?
# You can make a big difference

Reviews are the most powerful tools in my kit when it comes to getting my books noticed. Much as I'd love it, I don't have the budget of a big publisher to buy bill board ads and other national advertising.

But I have the promise of something more powerful – something publishers envy.

**And that's a committed and loyal bunch of readers.**

Honest reviews of my books help them gain the attention of others who might appreciate them too.

If you've enjoyed this book, I would be grateful if you could spend a few minutes leaving a review (it can be as short as you like) on the book's page, or on Goodreads.

Thank you very much
Jenny Wheeler

# ACKNOWLEDGMENTS

I'd especially like to acknowledge the help I received from Sacramento Public Library archivist, James C. Scott, who responded to my emails in courteous detail and provided me with detailed information I had not been able to confirm anywhere else. It was a special treat to then discover he was also the author of a book I had acquired for reference years ago, with the delightful title *Sacramento's Gold Rush Saloons: El Dorado in a Shot Glass.*

Once again I want to reiterate my gratitude to librarians everywhere for the wonderful services they provide – not everything can be found online!

Thanks also to the friends and acquaintances who have read earlier work and given me feedback and encouragement.

Stephen Stratford as editor and Nikki Crutchley as proof reader have become my "go to" team for all editing. They have both done a remarkable job but, as is usual in these situations, any mistakes are entirely my responsibility!

And finally, thanks to Jason and Marina at Polgarus Studios for holding my hand through the painful process of formatting and production, and patiently answering my flurry of frazzled midnight emails. You have the patience of Job!

# ABOUT THE AUTHOR

Jenny Wheeler is the author of the Of Gold & Blood Old California mystery series:

Poisoned Legacy #1.
Brother Betrayed #2.
Double Jeopardy #3.
Tangled Destiny #4 (Christmas novella and Prequel.)
Unbridled Vengeance #5 due for publication  late 2019.
Boxed Set/Book Bundle Of Gold & Blood, Books 1 – 3.

Jenny's online home is at jennywheeler.biz or email Jenny@jennywheeler.biz

You can connect with Jenny on:

Facebook: @JennyWheeler.Biz

Twitter: @Jenny_Biz

Instagram: @jennysbingereading

Pinterest

www.pinterest.nz/Jennywheelerbooks